Beryl Kingston was bo[...] [...] taking her degree at L[...] [...] and Drama at various London schools as well as bringing up her three children. She and her husband now live in Sussex.

HEARTS AND FARTHINGS

Beryl Kingston

ARROW

Published by Arrow Books in 1997

1 3 5 7 9 10 8 6 4 2

Copyright © Beryl Kingston 1985

First published in Great Britain in 1985 by
Macdonald & Co (Publishers) Ltd

Arrow Books Limited
Random House UK Limited
20 Vauxhall Bridge Road, London SW1V 2SA

Random House Australia (Pty) Limited
20 Alfred Street, Milsons Point, Sydney,
New South Wales 2061, Australia

Random House New Zealand Limited
18 Poland Road, Glenfield,
Auckland 10, New Zealand

Random House South Africa (Pty) Limited
Endulini, 5a Jubilee Road, Parktown 2193, South Africa

Random House UK Limited Reg. No. 954009

A CIP catalogue record for this book
is available from the British Library

Papers used by Random House UK Limited
are natural, recyclable products made from wood grown in
sustainable forests. The manufacturing processes conform to
the environmental regulations of the country of origin

ISBN 0 09 978161 1

Printed and bound in the United Kingdom by
Cox & Wyman Ltd, Reading, Berkshire

To R.D.

 *Chapter 1*

The couple standing under the olive tree were kissing, he moving his mouth gently and languidly over hers, she holding his face tenderly between her hands, guiding and savouring. They were absorbed in each other, concentrating on their pleasure, and neither knew nor cared that they were being watched. They'd have been annoyed if they'd known but not very surprised, for the watcher was young Alberto Pelucci, the village nuisance, and everybody knew he was always to be found where he wasn't wanted. But Alberto was keeping very still, and they were in another world of pleasurable sensation, so the kiss went on. The setting sun mottled their ecstatic faces and their encircling arms with patches of gold, and as the slight breeze of evening stirred the grey-green branches all around them, the dappled shapes shifted and swam with the same luxurious rhythm as their kiss. To Alberto, sitting above them in the olive grove, they seemed to be sparkling with pleasure, their hair glinting as they moved, their flesh edged with fire. With the reasonable part of his mind, he knew that they were only Giulietta, who was really no better than the village whore, and her idle cousin Enrico, who'd never done an honest day's work in his life. But his senses were recognizing them in quite another way. To his senses they looked like gods, and he was profoundly and tearingly jealous of them.

He'd never been able to understand why the village girls had always rejected him. He knew he wasn't much to look at, with his big nose and embarrassing lack of height, but he could love them so perfectly, if only they'd let him. But they never would. 'Run away and grow up, little baby boy!' they mocked. And when his brow darkened at their taunts, 'Doesn't he like it then? Run home to Mummy, baby! Little baby!' Always this terrible insistence on his lack of size, lack of years, lack of experience.

One day, he promised himself, watching the kiss as it started again, one day some girl somewhere would arch her body against his just like Giulietta was doing, would hold his face between her hands or wind her arms around his neck in the

7

same beautiful abandoned way. Not here in Pontedecimo of course. In England. In his new life. Where he'd be a success, with a thriving shop full of happy satisfied customers and a grand new house full of the latest furniture, and a fine English woman to love him. Much better than Giulietta. A lady. With white skin and long fair hair. It would all be different in England. Nobody there would laugh at him behind their hands, or tell him to run away and grow up, or call him a pest, or beat him for the temper he couldn't control, or tell him that times were bad and that the youngest son would have to fend for himself. In England he wouldn't be a son, or the village nuisance, or stupid Alberto. In England he would be himself.

Now that the time for his departure was so very close, his emotions were in such a turmoil that he couldn't settle to anything. He couldn't eat and he couldn't sleep. He couldn't sit still for more than ten minutes and there was nowhere he wanted to walk. He couldn't even listen to the end of a conversation, particularly when he'd heard it all before. This evening he'd left the supper table before the meal was over, an unheard of crime in the Pelucci farm, and had wandered off into the olive grove without even being aware of what he was doing. Excitement, fear, regret, hope and impatience boiled in his brain and set his body into continuous alert. The occasional stab of anxiety only made matters worse and certainly didn't cool him or stop the mill race of sensation that seemed to be sweeping through him at every second of the day and night. Tomorrow he would be on board ship and bound for his new life. Tomorrow! Tomorrow!

He stood up carefully, dusting the seat of his trousers with the palm of his hands and looking down at the dry familiar earth under his feet. There was no sound in the village below him. It lay subdued under lethargy, almost without life. The donkeys in the low pasture were asleep standing up. The breeze had dropped, and even the leaves hung from the branches all around him, heavy and somnolent. It was all so dull, so crashingly dull. How could anybody live in such a boring place?

As he ducked under the low lintel of the farm door he sensed his father's brooding disapproval even before he saw it. A glance at the table showed him that his two sisters had already left the room, and he felt a flicker of relief that they wouldn't be there for the row that was bound to break the minute he opened his mouth. Vittorio and Claudio had stayed behind with their father. All three faces were dark and disagreeable. I'm for it, Alberto thought, and comforted himself that this would be the very last scolding he would ever have to endure. Tomorrow, tomorrow, his mind sang. Tomorrow was freedom.

But tonight certainly wasn't. 'Where the devil do you think you've been?' his father demanded, leaning back in his tall wooden chair to send a look like a knife straight at his son's face.

'I'm sorry, father,' Alberto tried. 'I just had to get out. I felt stifled in here. I needed air.'

'That's your trouble my son,' his father said. 'It's always what *you* want, isn't it. *You. You. You.* Never anybody else. You're so full of yourself you never give a minute's thought to anybody else. You don't care how you upset people just so long as you get your own way!' The complaint went on in its well-worn, familiar fashion. Alberto shut his ears to it and focused his attention on two flies crawling across the bread-board. One stopped halfway over, to clean its head, stroking itself with legs like black thread, delicately, first on one side of its head and then on the other. Alberto wondered if it could hear his father's voice droning on and on and on, and decided that it, too, had probably learnt the trick of not hearing sounds it didn't like or didn't need. The fly stretched out its back legs stiffly behind it, flicked open its wings and flew off. There was a pause in his father's peroration. Alberto looked up to see if a response was required, so he was paying attention when Vittorio weighed in to have his turn.

'You wouldn't have behaved like this when Mother was alive,' Vittorio said.

Alberto was stung and replied before he could stop himself. 'You leave Mother out of it,' he said, and now his voice was shrill. 'When she was alive we were a family. I was welcomed at the table. I enjoyed being here. Because she wanted me here. That was enough.' To his annoyance, he could feel tears rising in his throat.

'Your mother spoilt you,' his father said testily, drawing on his pipe again. He'd forgotten to smoke during his outburst so it had gone out. 'That's your trouble. You've been spoilt. I tell

9

you, you'll need to mend your ways if you're going to get on in England.'

'He won't last five minutes,' Vittorio said. 'You'll see! I give him three months, and then he'll be whining back here for us to give him a roof over his idle head and put food into his stupid mouth.'

'You needn't worry,' Alberto shouted, 'I wouldn't take your precious food. I wouldn't come back here if I was starving to death.'

'Then you'll have to work,' Claudio said. 'And mind how you behave. If you go sloping off in the middle of a meal in England, they'll give you the sack, I can tell you.'

'The whole things ridiculous,' Vittorio said. 'We're simply squandering money on his fare. How will he ever get a job? He's got nothing to offer. Nothing at all. No brains. No effort. He can't live on dreams.'

'He thinks he can,' his father said, getting his pipe to draw, at last, and covering the bowl with his thumb to encourage it.

Rage swelled in Alberto's chest. They were talking about him, as though he wasn't there, as though he'd gone already, making him feel insignificant.

'I'm here!' he yelled. 'I'm here! I haven't gone! I'm here! In front of you! You just talk to me.'

'Temper, temper!' Vittorio said, mocking him. 'You can't even control your temper. Look at you.'

'You treat me like dirt,' Alberto shouted. 'I'm your brother, damn you! Your brother! Treat me properly!'

'Behave yourself properly then,' Vittorio said, deliberately cold and very calm. 'If you act like a baby, you'll be treated like a baby.'

'Naughty! Naughty!' Claudio mocked. He got up from the table and advanced on his brother, grinning and enjoying the boy's discomfiture. 'Look at him, Father. He's crying. Cry-baby!'

'I'm not!' Alberto roared, furiously. But he was. He couldn't hold the tears back. He was shaking with fury and shame. 'Leave me alone, you lousy bullies.'

Vittorio joined his elder brother. 'And you think you're going to get a job in a foreign country. They won't even look at you, a snivelling little worm like you!'

'They don't like cry-babies in England,' Claudio said, tweaking Alberto's ear to emphasize his words.

The tweak was painful but the taunt and the mocking expression were worse. Alberto seized the bread-board in one hand and the bread knife in the other and lunged at his brother, beating him about the head with the board, weeping and shouting incoherently. Instantly, the kitchen was in uproar. Vittorio, trying to get out of the way of Alberto's attack, fell back against the great table, scattering the pile of used platters onto the stone flags. One rolled back under Claudio's foot and he lost his balance and fell backwards into the debris of the meal with Alberto on top of him, wielding the bread-board like a man possessed. Their father put his pipe carefully on its rack, took off his belt and waded in to restore order, beating the thick leather thong onto Alberto's back. At the first blow Alberto leapt from his brother and turned to face his father, knife aloft and snarling.

'Granny Bianchi!' Vittorio screamed. 'Granny Bianchi, come quickly! Alberto's murdering Papa!'

Granny Bianchi, Pina and little Maria were in the kitchen before he'd finished shouting, and Granny had taken the bread knife from Alberto's upheld hand almost before he knew she was there. 'Calm yourselves,' she said. 'Calm yourselves, you bad boys. When will you all learn to behave?'

'When this maniac has gone to England,' Claudio said, rubbing the side of his head. 'I should think he's given me a black eye.'

'And what have you done to me? Do you ever think of that?' Alberto said, still bristling. 'No, you never do.'

'Come away with me,' Granny Bianchi said quickly to Alberto, putting an arm around his shaking shoulders, just as she'd done so many times during his childhood. 'I've got a job that needs doing. Come along.' She turned to her son-in-law. 'Is the farm running itself now that you've got time to brawl?' she asked.

Alberto followed his grandmother out of the kitchen, thankful as usual for her authority and the speed with which she could calm them all down when their passions were running too high. She was the only person he would really miss when he left Pontedecimo, and he knew that he would miss her sorely, her strength and her good sense and her affection. Now the moment was approaching when he would have to say goodbye to her, and he didn't think he could bear it. They crossed the courtyard to the barn.

Alberto settled into the routine of milking, brushing the two goats, and putting feed in their stalls to occupy them while Granny Bianchi milked. He was calmed by the familiar work and the familiar sounds, the swish of milk into the pail and the steady chomp and rustle of feeding. Granny Bianchi rested her head against the warm flank of the senior goat and looked at her grandson.

'Off tomorrow then, my dear,' she said.

'Yes, Granny,' Alberto answered, suddenly overwhelmed by the misery of parting.

'I shan't see you again after tomorrow,' Granny Bianchi said, looking him steadily and lovingly in the eye.

It was too much. 'Oh don't say that,' Alberto pleaded. 'Please don't say that,' and he rushed towards her, arms outstretched.

Granny Bianchi turned on her stool to accommodate him, taking his head into her hands and down into her lap. 'Things must be said, my little Alberto,' she said sadly. 'I'm an old woman. I shan't last very much longer and I'm never likely to travel. Even if you come home to visit us when you're rich and famous, I shan't be here to see it. So we are really saying goodbye, you and I.'

Alberto was weeping now and quite unable to answer. Granny Bianchi let him cry for a little, then she wiped his eyes on her milky apron and brushed the thick damp hair out of his eyes. 'I've something to tell you Alberto,' she said seriously.

'Yes, Granny Bianchi,' he said, loving her more than he could bear.

'I don't know anything about London or England,' Granny Bianchi said. 'I don't really know anything about Italy, if the truth be told. Only Pontedecimo. But I know about human beings. And one thing I can tell you for sure is that nobody likes a foreigner. We don't trust somebody who's different. When your grandfather first brought me to this farm, *I* was a foreigner. *I* was different. I didn't fit in. I wore different clothes and I spoke a different dialect and people kept their distance. It was very upsetting and very lonely but I learnt what to do about it. After a very long time, it's true, but I learnt. Now when you get to England you will be a foreigner. Different. And they won't like it. You must make it your business to stop being foreign as quickly as you can. Find out how they behave and behave like them. Eat the same food. Wear the same clothes. Speak the same language. Worship in the same church. But be the same. Then they won't be afraid of you and gradually they will like you. Have you understood?'

'Yes,' Alberto said. 'I've understood.' He kissed her solemnly, feeling that it was almost as if they were in church, and he was making a vow. He didn't really understand her argument but he knew, with his instincts, that her advice was sound, and resolved to follow it. He had already thought himself halfway towards it anyway, because he was so determined that his life in England would be totally unlike his life in Pontedecimo.

At breakfast the next morning conversation was sparse, limited as it always was to the state of the livestock, the progress of the fruit, last night's milk yield and the morning's crop of eggs. Alberto drank his coffee slowly, savouring every sip, but he was too excited to eat.

Then the morning chores demanded all their attention and activity excluded speech, as it always did. Eggs and olives were packed for market, and the donkey was persuaded and coaxed until he finally allowed himself to be harnessed to the cart.

Granny Bianchi handed Alberto a bundle of food for the journey. 'Eke it out, my dear,' she said. 'Don't gobble it all up on the first day. You've got a long way to go.' Alberto was folded into her black serge embrace and kissed firmly. Her faded eyes were bright, but she didn't weep and neither, to Alberto's surprise, did he. After all the emotions of the past twelve hours, he felt numb, saying goodbye as if he were in a dream. His brothers kissed him on both cheeks and thumped his arms. 'You'll be all right! You'll see!' Claudio assured him and Vittorio said, 'Good luck! We'll be thinking of you.' Little Maria stood on tiptoe to kiss him, and said, 'Come back soon!' as though he were going on a holiday. Then only his father remained, standing apart, small and awkward in his earth-stained jacket, with his trousers tied at the knee ready for the day's work.

13

'You will write to us,' he instructed his son brusquely, as they embraced. His skin was rough and dry against Alberto's cheek, and as they drew apart the boy looked hard at the seamed, earth-brown face beside him. 'I will write to you,' he promised. Then he and Pina climbed into the cart and the family stood back ready to wave him goodbye. And the donkey wouldn't move.

Plainly the little animal was in one of his most cussed and intractable moods. They tried coaxing and scolding; they tried shoving and sudden whipping; they tried dangling hay a few inches in front of his nose. The battle rapidly became a combined effort by the entire family, and after fifteen minutes of useless heaving and shoving they were all hot and sticky and stupid with laughter. Then just as they'd almost given up hope, the donkey suddenly started to trot down the path, with the perfect sang-froid of his kind, exactly as though that was what he'd intended to do all along. Alberto, who'd been pushing from the rear, almost got left behind. He had to sprint after the cart and leap on board. His brothers gave him a cheer and that, finally, was how he left the house in which he'd spent the first eighteen years of his life.

He and Pina were laughing so much that he almost forgot to turn back for a last look. They'd reached the bend in the track before he remembered. A minute later and the farm would have been out of sight, hidden by the folded hills. It looked unreal, this house he would never see again, unreal and poor. Even at this distance, he could distinguish the broken stones of the door-step, and see how uneven the yard was. It was a higgledy-piggledy collection of stones, mud, wood, livestock and people. Yet distance had already given it charm. For a second, seeing it like that, he didn't want to leave it, but there was no stopping the donkey now. And anyway he'd made up his mind.

The trouble was he had made it up so quickly, on the spur of the moment, on impulse, and it ought to have happened after a lot of talk and thought and planning. They'd all been in the middle of a row and on the edge of violence. His father had been snarling at him, the buckle of that horrible belt already under his fingers, and Alberto had been yelling at them all. 'I hate it here! I hate every minute of every single day!'

It was Claudio's answer that had done it. 'Then why don't you leave?' he'd said.

'I will!' Alberto yelled. 'I will! I'll go to England! That's what I'll do. Then you'll all see!'

'Never on your life!' Vittorio had said. 'Don't make me laugh! *You* go to England. You're too lazy to walk to the village.'

He had walked down to Genova the very next day and booked a ticket at the shipping office, paying a holding fee with what little money he possessed and promising that his father would make up the rest the next time he came into town. Afterwards, toiling back home up the steep cobbled streets and the climbing hill tracks, he had been aghast at what he had done. He couldn't think why he should ever have said such a thing. It wasn't as if he'd been planning to emigrate, or even thinking about England. He hadn't. The idea had entered his mind at the same time as the words spilled out of his mouth. They were spoken and he was committed before he'd had a chance to think about it at all. And now his passage was booked. He climbed slowly, half hoping his father would forbid it, half dreading the row that he felt sure would follow.

To his relief, astonishment and dismay, he was wrong. Pelucci was thrilled by his son's initiative. He approved and he praised. He said it was the first fully adult action of Alberto's life. They even drank a toast to him at supper that evening. From then on the matter was settled and out of his hands. He was rushed along by the enthusiasm and excitement all around him, stunned, whenever he stopped to think about it, that the whole thing had only taken six weeks from start to finish.

It was mid-morning before they arrived in the Piazza de'Ferrari. Crowds thronged the square, and the pulse and bustle and noise of so many voices and so much movement triggered Alberto's excitement again. As he helped Pina to lower the side of the cart, his hands were shaking.

'You'd better go now,' she said, 'or you'll miss the sailing.' She was looking at him with her mother's dark eyes from under her mother's strong eyebrows. The similarity between them made things difficult. He was suddenly shy and ill at ease, embarrassed by this final parting.

'Yes,' he said, but didn't move.

'Go now,' Pina said, giving him a little push. 'Camillo will meet you, don't forget. He'll look after you.'

This time Alberto didn't look back. He kissed his sister once, twice, three times and walked quickly out of the square, his gait awkward and his shoulders hunched because he knew she was watching him. Once beyond the approval of her eyes, he began to run, dodging the crowds and stumbling over the uneven cobblestones, down and down, towards the Porto Vecchio, the bay and adventure. He raced through the narrow carugi heedless of the washing festooned above him that dripped water onto his head and shoulders. Ragged street urchins erupted at his pounding approach, squealing and cat-calling. Twice he cannoned into passers-by and couldn't even stop to apologize. By the time he reached the quay he was completely out of breath, charged with an excitement stronger than anything he'd ever known in his life, a sense of extraordinary elation.

The quayside was crowded with people, busy as ants and with as little apparent purpose. Behind him the fish sellers called their wares, raucous as gulls, and before him the quay was edged with gently bobbing vessels, great and small, tar-stained and tatty, or smart with new paint. Beyond the ships stretched the great free Mediterranean, not solid and stolid like those implacable mountains, but warm blue-green, perpetually moving and as alive as he was. It was the natural path to all the change he needed and desired, and he knew, in the crowded, clamorous moment, that good things were surely waiting for him, a few days away, just over the water.

Chapter 2

The *Belinda May* was a three-masted, top sail schooner, long and black and sleek as a seal, and she carried more canvas than any other ship in the bay. It was good, clean canvas too, neatly furled. Clean canvas on a clean ship. Her decks were scrubbed spotless, brass winked in the sunlight, her masts glowed as though they'd been polished, and her name shone in elaborate gold behind the profusion of yellow roses carved on her stem head. As Alberto arrived, cargo was still being taken aboard methodically, crate after crate of lemons, oranges and limes. The operation was being supervised by the Master himself, and one glance at the man explained the order and discipline of his ship.

This was plainly not a face to disobey. The set of the jaw under that thick, close-cropped beard was too determined and too stubborn, and the blue eyes wrinkled into that weathered face were direct and startling and hard, like rivets. He stood beside the forward hatch, black legs astride, shoulders broad and head held high on a straight solid spine, a powerful man, as strong as a mast. Alberto decided at once that it would be politic to wait on the quay until the loading was completed. He certainly didn't want to get in the way of such an obvious authority.

He picked his way through the litter on the quayside until he found a pile of barrels, a little above the dirt, and sat himself amongst them, glad to be able to put down his roll of bedding and Granny Bianchi's awkward bundle of food. There was nothing else for him to do, so he watched the loading, keeping a particular eye on the Master, since this was the man who would be controlling his life for the next fortnight.

Presently three young men came ambling towards the gang-plank. Two were tall and slim and very dark-skinned. They looked alike and moved with the same lolloping grace, as though they were walking barefoot. The third was small and fair with a tatty, incipient beard growing like blond cobwebs along the edges of his chin. Each of them carried a thick roll of bedding, and the brothers swung a bulging canvas hold-all between them. All three were smiling directly at the Master.

'Oreste!' Mr Hemmings said, holding out his hand to the taller of the brothers. 'How are you all?'

'Well,' Oreste said. 'Very well, as you see. Ready to sail.'

'Where is Domenico?' the Master asked.

'Married,' Oreste said grinning. 'Too busy for England this year!'

The Master looked at his papers. 'I have four bookings,' he said. 'As usual. Four berths. Four bookings.'

Alberto joined them quickly, clutching his ticket. 'It's me!' he said. 'I'm the fourth booking.' They all looked at him, but nobody spoke, and to his dismay, he felt himself blushing under their scrutiny. To cover his embarrassment, he introduced himself quickly, and Oreste shook his hand and introduced the others. 'My brother Pietro, and Ettore Fuscillo,' he said. 'And Signor 'Emmin, the Master.' It was a difficult name to pronounce, and trying it for the first time, Alberto wondered if all English words were going to be such a problem.

They were allowed aboard, Oreste leading the way. Once below deck, Alberto had second thoughts about the beauty of his chosen transport. There was an overpowering stink of fish down there. It filled his nostrils, and he wrinkled his face away from it. Pietro grinned at him. 'Salt cod,' he explained. 'They ship it in from Newfoundland, every year. It'll wear off after a while, you'll see.' Alberto hoped so. They arrived at a neat trio of doors, one directly in front of them and the other two leading right and left into what appeared to be two long wooden cupboards.

'Here we are,' Oreste said, opening the door to the left hand compartment. 'This one's yours. You share with Ettore.'

Alberto stepped gingerly inside. He found himself facing two lesser cupboards, fitted neatly between deck and bulkhead, one on top of the other, like coffins. Each had a small, rectangular porthole in its side. He put his head through the upper porthole, and realized that the coffin was his berth. This claustrophobic box would be his home for the next fortnight. It was uncomfortable knowledge, but he hardly had time to digest it, for Ettore had followed him into the cupboard and was growling him out of the way.

As he'd stumbled down the companionway for the first unsteady time, Alberto had made up his mind that he would watch the others and follow their example. Now he watched Ettore. And was confused. Ettore hadn't smiled once since they all stepped aboard. His sour expression had settled into a look of distaste. He threw his bedding into the lower bunk and unrolled it with one bad tempered flick of his left hand. Then he opened the locker beside the bunk and unpacked his carpet bag into it, grumbling all the time as much to himself or to the ship as to Alberto.

'It'll be another dreadful journey,' he said lugubriously. 'You'll see. It'll be awful from start to finish. I can feel it in my bones. There'll be storms from Gibraltar to the Scillies,' he told the inside of the locker. 'I shall be as sick as a dog.' The locker declined to comment and this cast him into an even deeper gloom. He was forced to address his misery to Alberto. 'I'm beginning to feel sick already,' he said.

Alberto didn't know how to answer this. Ettore seemed so determined to be ill, there seemed little point in arguing. 'Is it always bad weather at this time of year?' he asked.

'Always!' Ettore said. He was pulling handfuls of straw out of his mattress and stuffing them into his carpet bag. 'I am always ill. I've never had a good journey in my life.' And with that he tossed his newly made pillow into position, climbed into the bunk after it and lay inside his coffin with his eyes and mouth firmly shut and his hands folded across his chest like a corpse.

It was certainly going to be an interesting journey, Alberto thought. He climbed out of the cupboard to see if the brothers would be better company.

They were. 'Don't take any notice of Ettore,' Oreste said. 'He always does that. He's terrified of sailing, that's his trouble.'

'Then why does he do it?' Alberto asked.

'Money,' Pietro said succinctly. 'Do you smoke?' He offered Alberto a cigarette which he took, hoping he could smoke it like a veteran even though he'd never done such a thing before. The first mouthful was difficult but the brothers were careful not to notice. The smoke rasped the back of his throat, stung the inside of his nose, and after a few seconds made him feel dizzy at the top of his skull. He sat on the deck beside Pietro's legs and concentrated on smoking calmly, while the brothers unpacked and chatted. It was a new and pleasant sensation to be accepted so unquestioningly as a man among men, even if the price he had to pay for it was this acrid smoke burning the back of his throat.

'Are you going to England?' he asked.

'Yes, yes,' Pietro said. 'As usual. We are going to England.'

'We go every year,' Oreste said. 'Over in the spring and back in the autumn, ready for the grape harvest.'

This was impressive. 'All that way,' Alberto said, 'just for the summer?'

'We can make more money in one summer in London,' Oreste explained, 'than we could make in three years here. Even if we half killed ourselves.'

So London *was* a rich city, Alberto thought. He knew it. He'd always known it. His heart began to race again, and as if in answer to it, the ship juddered and his voyage began.

For the next six days the *Belinda May* made good speed, under full sail. As she threshed through the blue-green waters, she dipped and lurched with a motion as steady and unrelenting as a pendulum. True to his word, Ettore turned green while they were still in sight of Genova. From then on he lay in his bunk groaning, and complaining to anybody foolhardy enough to listen to him. Alberto was annoyed to discover that the movement of the ship was making him feel queasy too. He resented this sickness. It put him on a level with the cowardly Ettore, and that seemed irritatingly unfair because he was making such an effort to adapt to life aboard. Within a few hours he'd discarded his shoes and learned to keep his balance. He was pleased by his transformation into another rolling sailor. It gratified him that even old Tom, the mate, had noticed his competence. 'You found your sea-legs and no mistake!' he said, passing Alberto's careful walk on the very first afternoon and the words were undoubted praise, even if Alberto couldn't understand all of them. So it was discouraging when his stomach kept lurching away from him into nausea. He had to do something about it and quickly.

20

For a start he avoided his cabin. The combined smell of vomit and salted cod was too much even for the sternest constitution. At least on deck the air was clean. So he stayed on deck with the Chiapponcelli brothers, and watched and listened. The brothers were feeling sick too, but they were holding on, Oreste with a dogged quiet patience that Alberto found both irritating and sustaining, and Pietro by joking and clowning 'to keep his mind off it'. At midday all three of them rolled down to the saloon to eat what they could of young Tom's extraordinary cooking. 'You feel better on a full stomach,' Pietro said. 'If you're going to be sick you might as well have something to be sick with.'

Alberto liked Pietro. He had so many tales to tell. For a start he seemed to have sampled every single available female in his native village and was now compiling a catalogue of the feminine delights of Clerkenwell. 'That young Bessie Smith,' he sighed. 'Such flesh! More than enough for both hands, I can tell you. Wherever you care to put them! And Eliza of the beautiful blue eyes. Bad breath, but exquisite eyes!'

'Didn't it put you off, her breath?' Alberto wanted to know.

'Held my nose with one hand and fondled her with the other,' Pietro grinned. 'No. Didn't have time to notice. She came quicker than any other woman I've ever had. Very hot, young Eliza!' He licked his lips at the memory.

This was fascinating information. 'Is that usual, for English women?' Alberto asked, surprised by his new found presumption. He wouldn't have dared to have *thought* such a thing a week ago let alone put it into words. His presumption caught him in its own trap.

'Oh ho!' Pietro roared, delighted by his interest. 'So that's what you're going to England for. And I thought you were a good, clean-living Catholic boy. Like me.'

'No! No!' Alberto tried to deny. 'I only asked. That's all.' Then, as the conversation was getting embarrassingly out of hand. 'What work do you do in London? You said it was good work. You earned a lot of money.'

'We sell things,' Pietro said, allowing him to move on and away from any further teasing. 'On the streets. Okey-pokey ice cream, hot chestnuts, roast potatoes, music, fun. We're the most important part of the summer. The sun couldn't shine without us.'

'Do you really make money selling in the streets?' Alberto asked.

'You have to work at it,' Oreste said, 'and know where to get cheap milk, or ice, or bulk potatoes or whatever you need. Monkeys help, of course. Pietro's got a way with monkeys.'

'Among other things!' Pietro agreed. 'Nice little things, Capuchin monkeys. Nice little paws. Too small for a penny piece. They drop them you see. So then you say (dropping into badly pronounced English), "Poor monkey. You got little coin for him? He hold little coin good!" And they give him a little coin, a silver threepenny bit or a little sixpence, if you're lucky. Like these.' He fished two coins out of his trouser pocket and laid them in Alberto's palm. They felt solid and heavy and dependable, as he'd known English currency would be.

'Who is the lady?' he asked.

'The Queen,' Oreste said. 'Victoria.'

'She's very young,' Alberto said, admiring the slender neck and the girlish profile.

'Money can lie,' Pietro said. 'Didn't they teach you anything at Pontedecimo? Never trust money, my son. That lady is not young. They call her the grandmother of Europe. She's been ruling England for more than fifty years. She had her golden jubilee two years ago. Now that was really good for trade. Bunting out everywhere, and flowers, and the streets full of people, day and night. All celebrating. All drunk. All eager to part with their money. You could have sold them neat arsenic, never mind okey-pokey, and they'd have gobbled it down and never known the difference. We made a fortune. Never had such a good summer.'

'Except for Peppi,' Oreste said, opening his eyes to look sadly at his brother.

'Yes. Poor little Peppi,' Pietro said. They both wore sad expressions as they remembered Peppi, whoever he was, and the *Belinda May* rolled sickeningly on towards Gibraltar. Alberto felt obliged to shove the conversation along.

'What happened to Peppi?' he asked.

'Drowned!' Pietro said, beginning to giggle. 'In the ice cream. Before it set, of course. Well it was his own fault really. He shouldn't have been so greedy. We found him in the morning, set fast.'

'Poor thing!' Alberto said, and then, as another thought struck him, 'What a dreadful waste of ice cream.'

'No, it wasn't,' Pietro said. 'We didn't waste a mouthful Cut him out. Very neat job we made of it. Tidied up the hole, and sold the rest. New flavour! Capuchin monkey! Made a change from vanilla. We were sold out in an hour.'

'You're joking!' Alberto said. But sometimes it was difficult to tell.

Pietro had such a deft way with conversations. He seemed to be able to turn them in any direction he wished. Alberto admired and emulated. By the evening of the sixth day, he'd learned the trick of questioning that would provoke confidences, and so far he'd managed to avoid revealing anything much about himself. It was necessary at this stage of his life to stay hidden and protected, if he could. But on the evening of the sixth day he was caught out.

He and Oreste were squatting in the doorway of the Chiapponcelli berth smoking sleepily. Ettore was still entombed and still grumbling, even in his sleep, but at least he wasn't being sick. The rhythm of the ship was almost pleasant, and Alberto was drifting into a speechless languor when Pietro arrived.

'Gibraltar coming up!' he said to Alberto. 'Come and see it.'

Alberto said 'Um' without moving and without opening his eyes. What was Gibraltar to him in his present state of peaceful satisfaction?

'Come on, you lazy lump,' Pietro said, prodding him with the toe of his boot. 'It's a sight worth seeing. And you might miss it on your way back. The *Geogio* goes through at night.'

'I'm not coming back,' Alberto said. 'I'm staying in England.'

'Never!' Pietro said. 'Emigrating do you mean?' There was a note of interest and disbelief in his voice that made Alberto regret his quick answer. He felt exposed. He got to his feet quickly.

'What's it like, Gibraltar?' he tried.

The brothers followed his feet but ignored his words.

'You can't emigrate,' Oreste said. 'Nobody leaves Italy for ever.'

'I have,' Alberto said. 'For ever!'

'You'll come back,' Pietro said. 'You won't stay in England for long. I'd bet money on it.'

'Have you got a job in England?' Oreste asked. 'Or are you just chancing your luck? It's not a good place to be out of work, you know. The poor starve.'

'And you can't live off the land,' Pietro said darkly, 'because there isn't any. They've covered it with brick and plaster.'

They emerged on deck. It was already dusk and the light on the galley was like a little white eye. Under cover of half light it was possible to avoid telling the exact truth. 'I'm going to work with my cousin,' Alberto said. 'He has a shop. He sells food. In London.' It sounded good. He could almost believe it himself.

'Well, that's different, young Alberto,' Oreste said. 'Is it a big shop?'

'I don't know,' Alberto said, trying to be honest.

'What does he sell?' Pietro wanted to know.

Alberto tried to remember what his cousin had written. He had a vague recollection that apples and potatoes had been mentioned. 'Fruit,' he said, 'and vegetables.'

'And pasta?' Oreste suggested.

'I expect so,' Alberto said. 'And cheeses too, probably.' He was forming a vision of this shop, crammed to the ceiling with the good fresh Italian foods he was beginning to miss. 'Tomatoes,' he elaborated, 'and olives and grapes and eggs.' His mouth was watering.

'It sounds like a fine big store,' Oreste said. 'If you've got a job there your future is made. There's only one thing better than selling food in England, and that's selling drink. The English drink like fishes. Well, there's Gibraltar.'

The rock loomed to starboard, huge and grey-blue. To Alberto it looked very much like any other rock. He couldn't see why he should have been dragged up onto a cold deck to look at it, especially now that his mind was filled with the vision of Camillo's magnificent store.

'What's so special about Gibraltar?' he asked the brothers.

'My word, you are innocent,' Pietro said. 'It's the end of

the known world, that's all. From now on we're among foreigners. From now on everything changes.'

He was certainly right about the change. At two o'clock the next morning they hit bad weather. From that moment on, all conversation came to a halt, and so did sleeping, cooking, eating and even standing upright. For the next forty-eight hours everybody aboard was fully occupied fighting the storm. Alberto woke to find that his plunging, scudding world had been completely altered. The pulse of the water beneath them had become a deafening roar while above him the wind was screaming through the canvas like a demented spirit, and somebody was shrilling a whistle. The whole ship was juddering and vibrating with a violence he'd never felt before, shaking with effort, like a wild creature pitting its strength against a predator. He knew they were only going about, but he was shaken and excited by the extreme force in this now familiar sensation. There was an exhilaration and crackling sense of danger all round him. It drove him immediately from the bruising sides of his rolling cabin and up into the theatrical darkness on deck. Whatever it was, he wanted to be part of it, particularly if it was dangerous.

It was black as pitch up there and the deck was slippery and treacherous under his bare feet. He found a guideline quickly and clung to it, glad that he knew where it was. Lights appeared briefly out of the murk before him, swung, tipped sideways and disappeared as the *Belinda May* bucked and reared like a monstrous frantic horse. He could see very little of the ship and nothing at all of the sea and sky, but the power of the storm was palpable. The unseen breakers of the Atlantic thundered down upon them from every side, hissing over the bows in a swirling torrent of white-needled spray, while all around him heavy air roared and beat like an engine, knocking him off his feet, pushing the breath back down his throat and obscuring what little vision he had with sudden flurries of stinging salt water. After a few seconds his eyes adjusted to the darkness. Now he could make out the ghost-white flicker of the shrouds, and catch a glimpse of the masts as they rolled across his line of vision.

Pietro was a warm shape at his elbow, shouting words he

couldn't hear into the howling air. Stumbling in and out of the enveloping blackness were the shadows of the crew, toiling and gleaming in the flickering lights. All four of them were on deck, the taciturn Ben and Young Tom in the bows, and the Master and Old Tom fighting the wheel. After several glances at the shifting darkness above his head, Alberto realized that most of the sails were already reefed. Only the jibs and the two mainsails remained and it was their canvas that was screaming alarm.

He turned his head towards Pietro's black outline and had just opened his mouth to shout at him, when they were both engulfed in a mass of sea water that fell down upon them with such force that Alberto felt as if his bones were giving way. The next few seconds were a confusion of fear and action and terrifying sound, rending, grinding and screaming. He fought the pressure of the black water with all his strength but it forced him down, flailing and battered until he was pinioned on the deck. He couldn't draw breath, and he couldn't open his eyes. He tried to twist his body away from the weight of the wave to relieve the pain in his lungs. Then the water was dragging away, pulling him with it down the slope of the deck with a roaring hiss that filled his ears with pressure. He grasped wildly as he fell and his hands found a rope and clung to it, burning and desperate, while the rest of his body went on fighting, almost automatically as though it no longer belonged to him, struggling up towards the lifeline until he was entirely curled around it, clinging with arms and legs like a monkey, breathing fast and with his eyes still tightly shut.

Somewhere to his right he could hear Pietro calling, 'Are you there, Alberto? Alberto?' and he answered quickly, 'yes, yes. Where are you?' Then the sea roared again, the words were lost and the deck swung beneath his feet like a bell. Above his head a sail was flagging like a great broken bird, and somewhere below him Young Tom was shrieking. A rope trailed down towards his hands out of the wetness, and he caught at it instinctively as it passed and held on. Ben was beside him, legs wrapped around the guidelines, tugging on the same rope, then Pietro, then Young Tom. Without words they found a common rhythm and pulled together, flexing themselves against intolerable weight. The rope was like a live thing and as powerful as the storm. It lifted all four of them with ease, rising and flailing above their arms; then without warning it slackened and seemed to relax for a second, so they were able to hand it in, just a little, before it rose in full power again.

Alberto worked without being fully aware of what he was doing. He knew the sail above them was ripped. Now and then, in a clear second after a blink, he saw the torn length of canvas kicking into the black sky above them, and he knew from the fear and excitement around him how vital it was to bring it down, but things were happening too quickly. It was only after the sail had finally been hauled out of the tumult and reefed at last that he realized the danger they had all been in, and even then the next breaker was already crashing down upon them.

The *Belinda May* rode the storm all night and Pietro and Alberto fought it out alongside the crew. There was no dawn for any of them. The peaceful division between night and day had been obliterated by the tempest; pitch black sky gradually became a low, shifting mass of bruised cloud, grey, black and purple: pitch black sea was terrifyingly revealed as a solid wall of slate grey water towering and toppling inexorably towards them. The horizon no longer existed. Time had no meaning. There was nothing but the menace of that close-pressing sea and the terror in the trough of the wave.

Alberto did as he was told, stayed on his feet and worked so far beyond fatigue that by the time the first lull in the storm gave them a chance to catch their breath, he was almost incapable of thought. Miraculously Young Tom managed to make coffee and to pass half a mug of it to everyone on deck. Alberto gulped his gratefully but without being aware of hunger or thirst. He was functioning on instinct and observation alone. He reacted and he watched. And the man he watched most closely was the Master. All the other men on deck showed strain or fear, however much they were trying to hide their emotions. Young Tom was the worst, with bolting eyes and a face strained under taut grey skin; Old Tom kept calm, but the occasional quick squint he gave towards a sudden shift or a particularly ugly wave was more revealing than he knew; Ben's lips were chapped and bitten; Pietro seemed darker than ever and had developed a new habit of tucking his head down towards his chest to keep his fear out of sight. Only the Master was unchanged. He moved about the ship like a soft-footed shadow, partly obscured by driving rain and a haze of flung spray, but always there, controlled and contained. Any change of wind direction, any new danger produced immediate activity, but no sign of fear. He seemed to be digesting the storm and making sense of it, and his calm gave Alberto an ineffable sense of security. No matter what happened he knew they would all survive. As the heavy walls of water crashed down towards the *Belinda May* his heart was racing with excitement and exaltation. 'Do your worst!' he yelled at the riot all around him. 'You can't beat me! I won't drown and I won't give in! I've got you beaten! I've got you all beaten! I am Alberto Pelucci. You can't kill me!' And the waters rolled away under the ship, leaving the growling sky, purple and engorged in its place, and neither had harmed him.

The third lull in the storm brought sufficient light to see by and allowed speech to be heard for the first time in hours.

'What a night!' Pietro shouted to Alberto.

'I think it's day,' Alberto shouted back.

'It's been going on a long time, whatever it is,' Pietro yelled, grabbing at a line for support. 'Time slips at sea like the rest of us!'

Young Tom cooked a stew and two by two they staggered down to the saloon to eat it as best they could on a table rocking violently and unpredictably. Then the storm increased, and they were all fully engaged on deck.

Soon it was growing dark again but whether this was because night was approaching or because they were in for even worse weather, Alberto neither knew nor cared. He felt he'd been working the bilge pumps for most of his life now and would have gone on until he dropped, if Old Tom hadn't stopped him.

'You're all in!' the old sailor said, putting a hand on Alberto's wet arm. 'You cut off an' get some shut-eye, me dear.'

The sense of what he was saying was obvious even though the words themselves were foreign. Their effect was immediate. They released Alberto's fatigue from the confines of his excitement. He felt like a balloon that had suddenly been

28

deflated. He was too tired even to answer. He crawled down the companionway, hanging onto the rail like a man weakened by long illness, and fell into his berth. Hardly aware of what he was doing, he stripped off his soaking clothes, wrapped himself in a blanket and was asleep the moment his bones touched the mattress.

When he woke it was daylight and the storm was over. The *Belinda May* was humming through the water, and he could smell coffee brewing. He crawled stiffly through his porthole and picked up his shirt and trousers. They were both running with water. His palms felt sore against the rough, wet material, and when he examined them, he saw to his surprise that they were criss-crossed with deep grazes, and thick red weals. Just looking at them made him aware that they were really quite painful and yet he hadn't noticed them at all until that moment. He was still considering the mystery when Pietro arrived with an old pair of canvas trousers and a very holey jersey.

'Put these on,' he said, tossing the clothes at Alberto. 'Domenico left them behind last year. They're not exactly beautiful but they're better than nothing and you won't be wearing any of that lot today,' and he kicked the pile of streaming clothes at their feet.

In fact they took three days to dry out. Alberto didn't mind a bit. He rather fancied himself in his borrowed outfit. Even the fact that it was torn and dishevelled only gave it an extra touch of romance. It suited the new life he was living. For the first time since his mother died, he was proud of himself and the way he'd behaved. He'd come through the storm without being sick and without making a single mistake. It was a triumph. He'd made new friends and he'd found a man to admire and emulate. The calm and strength of the Master had impressed him on the very first day, but now that he'd watched his stoical handling of a tempest, he had come to a decision. He wanted to be like the Master. And it was possible. He felt sure it was possible. The change in him had already begun. Now all he had to do was to let it develop, to calm his excitable nature, quell his temper and keep his emotions under control. By the time they reached London, he would be a new man.

The rest of the journey was steady and almost uneventful. They sailed through two more storms, but after the massive impact of the first one they hardly noticed them. Young Tom's cooking improved, the torn sails were stitched together, cuts gradually healed and bruises faded. Alberto learned a lot more English, Pietro remembered another song and on the twelfth day Ettore stopped being seasick, had his first wash and joined them on deck. The voyage was nearly over.

Then the empty waters of the Atlantic were left behind and they were in the busy English Channel, enlivened by a plethora of trade and traffic. They passed battered fishing fleets and lone trawlers heading out towards the fishing banks, and were passed in their turn by steamboats and merchant men and once by a tall clipper resplendent under full sail. And at last came their first sight of land, a row of needle sharp cliffs and the frothing shore-line of a green island. Behind it, low hills lay blue in the distance, under banks of complicated cloud, that billowed one over the other, dove grey on lilac, cream tinged with apricot, blue edged with white, merging, enlarging and shredding, now trailing an abrupt grey fringe of rain, now puffing into the upper reaches of the sky like smoke from an engine. Alberto was intrigued by such a manifestation of natural power, a display of force no puny human could match or tame. It had the same inexorability as the sea and excited him in the same way.

By the time they reached the mouth of the Thames he was trembling with anticipation again, despite his vow to model himself on the Master. When they dropped anchor and settled down to wait for the pilot, he prowled the decks with impatience. Ships from every part of the world lay at anchor waiting to approach, or were edged gently into the new docks ahead of them. Thames barges, heavy with hay, bellied their brick red sails towards the city. The skyline fluttered with sails: the mud-brown river frothed with moving hulls. He couldn't control his excitement.

'Come on! Come on!' he said, his mouth working with impatience. 'What are we waiting for?'

'We're nearly there,' Oreste comforted. 'We should be docked before evening.'

Before evening! Alberto thought. It couldn't be true. It couldn't possibly take all that time to get from the estuary to the city.

It was a beautiful river, Alberto thought, but they were travelling it much too slowly. If he'd had his way, they'd have charged into London under full sail, knocking all the other craft aside like skittles. But at last, at last they were in the Pool of London among a winter forest of masts, and the *Belinda May* was turning very, very slowly, ready to be inched into the London Dock. Alberto stood at the rail taking in as much of his new city as he possibly could.

It was a very smokey place, what he could see of it. Grey-brown fumes drifted up from every chimney to collect above the grey roofs in a slow-moving cloud. How rich Londoners must be, Alberto thought, to run so many fires. The warehouses that lined the riverbank were fine, prosperous buildings, and although their yellow brickwork was already blackening in the smokey atmosphere they were plainly the storehouses of a very rich city. And on the north bank, directly in front of them, was a building that looked like a castle from a fairy tale. It was a walled citadel of tessellated towers and grey stone battlements, and rising from its midst was a square castle, panelled grey and white like a wedding cake, every panel set with black curved windows and every corner embellished with a fine grey and white tower capped by a glossy black dome.

'What is it?' Alberto asked, impressed.

'The Tower of London,' Pietro said.

'Where the Queen Victoria lives,' Alberto said, thinking how appropriate it was.

'Nobody lives long in the Tower,' Pietro said sardonically. 'It's a prison. That's where the Queen Victoria sends all the people she doesn't like. If she doesn't like them much their legs are broken on a machine called the rack and they're locked up in dark little cells where they can't breathe. And if she doesn't like them at all, they chop their heads off.'

'You're making it up,' Alberto laughed. 'England is a free country.'

'England,' Pietro said sternly, 'is a rich man's country.

Never forget that. The rich have enormous power and endless supplies of money, so they're almost entirely corrupt. If it wasn't for us coming here year after year to relieve them of some of it, I don't know what would become of them. You may laugh, Alberto, but never underestimate the rich. Take as much money from them as you can but treat them with caution. They may do as they please.'

'I'm going to be a rich man myself,' Alberto promised. 'I'm going to own a store of my own and buy a fine big house and marry a fine rich English lady. You'll see!'

'Well, good luck!' Pietro said. And he grinned.

Chapter 3

The quay was rolling from side to side like a ship, shifting and jerking under his feet. It seemed ridiculous to be staggering about when he knew he was on dry land again. His reason told him that the wall six feet in front of him was as solid as the corrugated iron that covered it, yet nevertheless it lurched before his eyes just as though it were made of water.

It was a narrow quay, little more than twelve feet wide, hemmed in on one side by the black flank of the *Belinda May* and on the other by the corrugated iron shed, and enclosed even further by three small wooden cabins that were cantilevered out from the first floor of the shed to house the crane drivers who were now busily and noisily employed unloading the schooner. After fourteen days watching a boundless horizon, Alberto felt as though he'd suddenly been packed inside a box.

The space was crowded with people, all of them men and half of them working. It didn't take Alberto long to recognize that there were two distinct types of individuals in this corner of working London, the dockers and the watchers, and that they were worlds away from one another, however physically close they might be. The watchers were as dapper as blackbirds and had the same sharp eyes and the same alert rigidity of spine. They stood in front of the shed, warm in their well-cut worsted and their well-polished leather, bowlers glossy, gloves spotless and white shirts miraculous in that grimy setting. And they watched fiercely and with concentration, as though their livelihoods depended upon it, which for all Alberto knew, they very well might.

The dockers on the other side of the quay were begrimed and stained and dishevelled. Everything about them revealed the back-breaking nature of the work they had to do. They all wore the same work-soiled uniform, flat filthy cap, dirty choker, heavy, stained shirt, clumsy boots grey with dust, and a waistcoat and heavy trousers so misshapen, ripped and patched that it would have been hard to find more than six inches of cloth with its original shape and colour. They worked

33

in teams, from time to time calling to one another in their clipped, incomprehensible language. Alberto, used to the careful tuition of young Tom, found this dock-side English ugly and harsh and bewildering.

As he listened, he was scanning the crowds for the first sight of his cousin's face. He was beginning to think that he ought to look for an exit, just in case Camillo was waiting for him there, when a hand grabbed his shoulder, so suddenly that it made him jump. It was Camillo, certainly, but not the Camillo he remembered.

He was a great deal paler than he'd been in Pontedecimo and he seemed to have shrunk. His clothes were ungainly. Even to Alberto's inexperienced eye, they looked second-hand. The shoulder seam of his battered jacket was halfway down his upper arm, his trousers were hoisted a good six inches above his ankles, and both were grimy and torn. He still wore his soft, high-crowned Italian hat, but the crumpled choker knotted round his neck was an English addition and an extremely dirty one. It had obviously started with a red and white pattern of swirling flowers and leaves, but now it was red and grease-brown. He looked uncared for. He was smiling to see Alberto again, and thumping his arms with affection, talking quickly and gesticulating with pleasure and excitement. But the set of his mouth had altered too, and when he was in repose, listening to Alberto's reply, there were new lines on his face that gave him a discontented look, an air at once disillusioned and weary. Whatever else, it certainly wasn't the face of a successful business man.

'Shall we go straight to Clerkenwell?' he asked Alberto. 'Or would you like to see the city first?'

Alberto was ravenously hungry, his stomach contracting at the very thought of food, but he didn't want to do the wrong thing, especially now that he was trying so hard to be like the Master. After all, Camillo was his host. So he said he didn't mind, and Camillo led him away for an incomprehensible tour.

They left the dock through a wide gate angled across the corner between two busy roads. One was a broad highway, lined by blackened warehouses and full of vehicles, vans and huge carts and little rocking cabs. It was spitting with rain again but as Camillo didn't seem to notice it, Alberto ignored it too. They walked towards the grey towers of the fairytale palace and were soon following a path that circled its high stone walls, where a row of hansom cabs stood despondent and empty in the dampness. Alberto decided to put Pietro's latest tale to the test.

'What is this place?' he asked.

Camillo didn't even bother to look at it. 'The Tower,' he said.

'Is it a palace?' Alberto insisted. 'Who lives there?' At close quarters the stained battlements were chill and forbidding.

'Nobody much,' Camillo said. 'Guards, I think. They keep people locked up.'

'What for?' Alberto asked.

'Treason,' Camillo said. 'It's a capital offence. Like poverty!'

So Pietro wasn't joking after all. Alberto was horrified that the English Queen should have so much power. 'Do they execute traitors here?' he asked.

'Yes,' Camillo said. 'They do. They chop their heads off.' He didn't seem perturbed or even interested. 'Come on! I've got much better things to show you.'

They wandered through a blur of grey cobbled streets, past row after row of black brick walls, grey columns and brown shop fronts, accompanied throughout by the non-stop, mind-battering noise of grinding wheels and iron hooves. Travel and loss of time had numbed Alberto's senses. Camillo's information about the Tower had been the very last thing his mind could digest. Very little of what he now saw was actually getting past his eyes and ears to his brain. Camillo's non-stop commentary was just a dirge, droning on and on like a wasp at a window. He had a vague impression that London was a grey-brown place full of people all dressed in black and all far too busy to look at one another, and that, for some reason that he couldn't appreciate in his present befuddled state, the English treated their shops and houses like school slates, covering every available surface with words. Even the buses were loud with slogans. 'Sturdy Strength All Day on Grape Nuts', they shouted. 'Lipton's Tea.' 'Nestle's Milk.' 'Disinfect with Sanitas.' Everywhere bright colours and bold print proclaimed the power of the written word, a babel of individual and discordant voices.

There didn't seem to be any plan or cohesion about the city

either. Roads ran where their fancy took them, winding or curving or simply stopping abruptly, and the houses had been built in the most haphazard way, one jammed up against the next and all different shapes and styles and heights. The roadways were full of traffic, carts and wagons, buses and cabs, all going in different directions in alarming and uncontrolled confusion. He was astounded by the patient way the horses withstood all this rush and unpredictability, and appalled by the skinny boys who scuttled between their flying hooves to collect their droppings in huge, smeared shovels. They were inches away from the most terrible injuries and yet they were grinning like monkeys, almost as if they enjoyed it. He grew more confused, fatigued and hungry by the minute, until finally need got the better of good manners, and he ventured a direct question.

'Are we anywhere near your shop, Camillo?' he asked.

'Shop?' Camillo asked. 'What shop?'

'Your shop,' Alberto said. 'Where you sell food. You told Granny Bianchi about it.'

'I never said it was a shop,' Camillo said and he laughed an ugly, bitter bark of a laugh that made Alberto's hopes sink. 'Well, use your eyes! Do I look like a shopkeeper?'

Alberto had to admit that he didn't, and the admission made him feel disappointment like a small hand crushing his chest. He'd come all this way to help Camillo in his shop, and now the fool was calmly telling him it didn't exist. Anger began to growl up in him. He made an effort and controlled it, as the Master would have done. 'You said you sold food,' he urged his cousin. 'You said Londoners were good customers.'

'Oh, that!' Camillo said airily, as though it didn't matter. 'Yes. Well, I *did* sell food. Of a sort. But not in a shop. I sold potatoes in the street, if you must know. And roast chestnuts too, when I could get them. But potatoes mostly.'

A street seller, Alberto thought furiously. Just a street seller! The liar! And he'd made it sound like a fine big store. They'd all been taken in. His anger was bubbling in his belly, but he calmed himself again, deliberately remembering his vow, willing himself to concentrate on something else. He was very, very hungry, so he turned his attention back to the problem of food. 'I haven't eaten since this morning,' he said.

36

Mrs Dobbs said she'd get something for us,' Camillo said. 'When we got in. How would that be?'

Alberto said it would suit him and tried to sound as though he meant it, but he needn't have bothered because Camillo wasn't listening.

'Come on!' he said. 'You must see St Paul's.' And he darted across a road full of formidable horses, dragging Alberto with him.

Even though he was jaundiced with hunger, Alberto had to admit that the cathedral was impressive. He would rather have been impressed on some other occasion, but impressed he undoubtedly was. They stood beside Queen Anne's bell-shaped plinth and gazed up at the weight of the building above them.

'What do you think of it?' Camillo asked proudly, as though he'd built the place himself.

Alberto thought it was tremendous. Almost as tremendous as his hunger.

'Oh, come on!' Camillo said grumpily. 'I'll take you home.'

They set off again through the confusing streets, this time heading north. It was spitting with rain and soon umbrellas sprouted all around them like a field of black mushrooms.

'It rains a lot in England,' Alberto observed.

'In England,' Camillo said slowly, 'it rains all the time. It's a terrible country. I can't think why I ever wanted to come here.'

This was ominous but Alberto tried not to be discouraged by it. Camillo was tired and rain like this was enough to make anyone disgruntled. He turned up his coat collar, tucked his rock-hard bedding more firmly under his arm and followed his cousin through the drizzle. But the farther north they went the smaller and dirtier and meaner the houses became. Soon they'd left all the fine new three-storey mansions behind and were in a world of small, square, blackened boxes with dusty windows and broken doors. Camillo left the main road, dodged across a crowded side street and turned down a flight of steep, broken steps into a narrow alley. Now Alberto could see the necessity for all those street cleaners whose perilous activities had alarmed him earlier. The alley was ankle deep in straw, horse dung, bits of old rag, torn paper and shavings, and it smelt worse than any farmyard. It was full of warehouses and

37

stores, jerry-built and wooden and bulging with goods. Mud-spattered horses toiled up the steep incline hauling over-laden carts, or stood bowed and patient beneath the open upper doors of their particular shed while the merchandise they carried was swung away and dragged into the shadows by teams of stained and sweating men. As the cousins picked their way downhill through the debris, avoiding boots and hooves and wheels as best they could, they moved from one pocket of highly flavoured air to another, from the ammonia of horse dung to the piquancy of spice, from the crisp scent of cinnamon to the oily languor of leather, past pepper and hemp, and musty rags and meaty hides, as the alley narrowed and the smells concentrated and intensified in the diminishing space between the sheds.

'Where are we now?' Alberto asked.

'Saffron Hill,' Camillo said. 'Nearly home.'

Saffron, Alberto thought, remembering the delicate crocuses and the golden rice they'd eaten at cousin Augusta's wedding. What a name for a dirty little alley like this! As they continued downhill, the cobbled path became so narrow that they could barely walk it side by side. They'd left the warehouses and were passing a row of sagging houses, filthy, squat, chipped and run down. Some of the dusty windows were festooned with grey rags, others with cobwebs. Most of the doors were warped and hanging off their hinges and grey grass struggled up between the broken stone of the doorsteps. The bare-footed children who sat against the grimy walls were uglier than any Alberto had ever seen, even in Genova, their limbs bony, their teeth decayed and their faces grey and pinched like old men.

'Here we are!' Camillo said. He had stopped in front of the filthiest house in that filthy alley and was leading Alberto into a dark passageway. He couldn't mean it, Alberto thought. Please God, let it be a mistake. But it wasn't. And if the outside of the house was bad, the inside was worse.

The front door was set in the side of the house so it had to be approached through the passage, and the passage was a black, evil-smelling pit. It had once been painted dark brown but now it was encrusted with a thick layer of oily grime that lay in beads and bubbles along every surface and heaped the skirting between wall and earth floor with a black oozing excrescence. It looked like tar and smelt like a cesspit. Camillo plunged into it. Alberto edged through it with great caution. The front door was ajar, so they entered the house. That smelt like a cesspit too, but it was a cesspit where someone had been boiling cabbage.

'We are 'ome, Mrs Dobbs,' Camillo called in English. 'Mrs Dobbs!'

A raucous voice answered from behind a brown door. 'You bin a long time intcha!' it said. 'I'll bring it up direct.'

Camillo nodded and led the way up the rickety staircase that faced them. 'Mind the stairs!' he warned Alberto. 'The fourth one's a bit rocky.'

And the sixth, and the tenth, and the eleventh *and* the twelfth, Alberto thought, negotiating them with difficulty.

At the top of the stairs was an enclosed landing where the foul smells accumulated. Four more oily brown doors stood askew in what was left of the broken plaster. They went through the nearest into a room like a grey tomb. Dust lay heaped on the floorboards and piled in the corners like a thick grey shroud and the broken plaster was as grey as a skull. So much of it had fallen that the laths were revealed, and they too were grey and crumbling. The window was dark with dust and had two broken panes stuffed with pieces of torn rag. Even the soot mounded in the little chipped fireplace had a dust grey coating and was dotted with piles of fluff. The only furniture in the room was a three-legged washstand and a sagging bedstead covered by a very stained mattress and two matted blankets. Under the bed, almost out of sight but stinkingly obvious, was a chipped chamber-pot, encrusted with dark brown sediment.

'For God's sake, open a window,' Alberto said, 'and let's have some fresh air.'

'You do that,' Camillo said, 'and we shall be crawling with flies.'

'Never mind,' Alberto said with his hands on the lower frame. 'At least we'll be able to breathe.'

'We won't,' Camillo said. 'There's an earth closet out there. You open the window and the smell will knock us out. I warn you.'

'We can't stay here!' Alberto was beginning. He got no further because the door was flung open and their landlady arrived. Mrs Dobbs was such an assault on the eyes that after the first glance Alberto had to look away. She wore a blood-red Garibaldi blouse, a plaid skirt and a shawl that beggared belief. A quieter garment would have been called a Paisley, but this was a shattering blend of crude artificial colour, bright pink, butter yellow, peacock blue, purple and emerald green. But worse than any of the garish colours of her clothing was the lady's hard and incredible head. Her hair was a uniform and unlikely gold, rising from black roots above a face that looked as though it had been drawn in charcoal, so deep and dirty were the lines etched into it. Such a sour, white, ill-tempered face it was to be set above such an hysterical assembly of colours. The life she led was plainly not the life she desired, and this gave her a truculence that turned her into a walking irritation.

'Where 'ave you bin, Cammy, you varmint?' she said. 'I been up them stairs twicest already. It don't do me no good, I'll have you know.' She put the saucepan she was holding down on the washstand with a thump. 'That'll be thruppence,' she said.

Camillo made a pretence of searching through his pockets, and then turned to Alberto. 'You haven't got any English money on you, have you, Alberto?' he asked.

'I haven't got any money,' Alberto confessed, and pride made him add, 'I shall earn some tomorrow.'

Camillo shrugged his shoulders and, with an obvious effort, addressed his landlady in a tortured version of her native tongue.

'Tonight,' he said, gesticulating with both hands to aid her understanding, 'no money. Tomorrow we earn. Both. We earn. Then we pay.'

The colourful lady folded her arms across her bolstered bosom with the air of one about to give battle. 'No pay, no grub!' she said. 'I told you before, Cammy. And you ain't give me no rent for nigh on two months neither. What about that?'

'Tomorrow we work,' Camillo explained. He didn't seem at all ruffled by her attack. 'Two work. Both. Make money. Then we pay.'

'That's six and thruppence you owe me,' Mrs Dobbs said, arms still folded and still glaring. 'I've got it all writ down. I hope you know that.'

'Tomorrow, Mrs Dobbs. I promise,' Camillo said. He

managed an ingratiating smile, which to the watching Alberto was even more awful than his discontented scowl.

The landlady relented. 'All right,' she said. 'Tomorrow. But it had better be!' She gave Alberto half a smile and made an exit, slamming the door and descending the stairs with a great deal of noise, as though she intended to crush every step to sawdust by way of compensation.

As soon as she'd left the room, Camillo produced two tin plates and two buckled spoons from the drawer in the washstand and lifted the lid of the saucepan with a sigh. Inside was a steaming mess of boiled mutton and potatoes, oily and glutinous and, to Alberto, totally foreign.

'What is it?' he asked nervously.

'Edible,' Camillo said and dished it up.

To his surprise Alberto found the stew quite tasty, although it lay heavily on his empty stomach. At least there was plenty of it. Even after they'd both eaten a good plateful there was still some left in the bottom of the saucepan.

'Do you want to finish it?' Camillo asked.

Manners versus hunger again. This time manners won. 'I don't mind,' Alberto said, although he could have eaten the lot with ease.

'We'll leave it then,' his cousin decided. 'Come on.'

Alberto wasn't sure he entirely approved of all this rushing about. It was a new habit for Camillo, who'd been rather shy and quiet in Pontedecimo. As he followed his cousin down the clumping staircase he gave the matter what thought he could gather, and decided it was probably a good thing that London could change people so much. It would help him with his own planned transformation.

They went to a little pub just round the corner, an ornate edifice called the Hat and Tun, which to Alberto's relief was warm and clean. The landlord was a hefty man with a rubicund face and fat moustaches and although he was in his shirt sleeves to serve he was plainly prosperous, as Alberto could see at a glance from the good leather on his feet and the fine gold watch chain suspended across a comfortable paunch.

'What'll it be, sir?' he said to Camillo. Alberto made a mental note of the phrase 'Wottle it be?' It was certainly going to be very difficult to learn this language. Everybody spoke so quickly. He hadn't understood a word that awful women had said, and he had a suspicion that Camillo hadn't grasped much of it either.

Camillo fished a handful of copper coins out of his pocket and sorted them through on his palm. 'Two pints please, Mr Mannheim,' he said.

'I thought you said you hadn't any money,' Alberto said.

'Quite right,' Camillo agreed, grinning. 'This is money for drinking, not for rent. Take my advice, Alberto. If you want to stay sane in London, always keep enough money for drinking. The rent will always wait, you can get along without eating much, if you have to, but you neglect drink at your peril. Isn't that right, boys?'

The boys who had gathered round them at the bar all agreed wholeheartedly, and as if to demonstrate how sound their opinion was, they immediately got down to the serious drinking that was to occupy them for the rest of the evening. They were a motley crew, as dishevelled as Camillo, all very friendly and all Italian.

'Is this a special Italian inn?' Alberto asked when they were all settled on the brown leather benches under the gas lights.

'No,' Camillo said. 'It's English. This is English beer. There are Englishmen here, too, I expect. All sorts. You listen.'

Alberto listened but he could only hear Italian. There were now so many people crushed into the little pub that it was quite impossible to distinguish one speaker from another.

'You just come over?' one of the young men asked, and when Alberto nodded, he said, 'Thought so.' He explained, 'You're in Little Italy here. Little Italy, that's what they call Clerkenwell. Just across the road there is a nice Italian church. And down behind that are all the nice Italian homes, with nice Italian mammas, and very nice Italian daughters.'

'Who keep you at nice Italian arm's length,' another thin face said dourly, and they all laughed at him.

Alberto gave this some thought. He couldn't stay in Little Italy. He'd come to England to be English. He sipped his English beer, and decided he didn't like it very much. It was too bitter to blend well with all that oily stew and after a while it made him belch. But as everybody else was belching and farting with abandon, he didn't let it worry him, although he

42

wondered at odd moments during the noisy evening what Granny Bianchi would have thought of his new London behaviour.

The pub was a cheerful place, and the more they drank the more cheerful it became. Camillo and his friends, now warm and settled, moved on from beer to gin and grew steadily happier and more incoherent. Alberto, eking out his beer, wondered how he would ever persuade Camillo to come home.

He needn't have worried. Mr Mannheim had a way with closing time. For at least thirty minutes before midnight the pub and its occupants had been skilfully and surreptitiously prepared. Empty glasses and tankards gradually disappeared, and soon even partially full ones were being spirited away. By ten to twelve the pot boys had left and were out in the back, swishing glasses in the sink, glad that their long day was nearly over. By two minutes to midnight the gaslights were lowered to a flicker and half the shutters were up. By midnight there was nothing for it but to go obediently through the door that Mr Mannheim was so kindly holding open for you, even though you had a sozzled suspicion that it wasn't really what you wanted to do.

Outside the road was dark and the pavements were running with rain. Camillo and Alberto walked as fast as their cotton-wool legs would allow, back to Mrs Dobbs' dark, disgusting box. There were no lights anywhere in the house and the passageway seemed to be full of old sacks and piles of newspaper.

'Stand still!' Camillo said, swaying gently. 'Got a candle somewhere.' After considerable fumbling and swearing, he produced the stub of a candle from the pocket of his waistcoat and by dint of enormous effort he and Alberto managed to hold it steady for long enough to strike several lucifers and finally get one of them close enough to the wick to light it. The bundles of rags stirred in the faint yellow light, and gave off fumes of alcohol and decay. An unshaven, scarred face rose briefly from one pile and spoke thickly.

'No cause to go a-worritting wi' light,' it whined. 'I paid me penny. It ain't right to go dropping wax on a body. That it ain't.'

A second fearsome tangle of rope-dry hair and grizzled beard rose in sympathy to open a mouth full of rotting brown stumps. This one was more direct. 'Why don'tcha fuck off out of it?' it growled, and then fell back against the wall with a crack of its matted skull.

With stern-faced concentration Camillo managed to get his key into the front door, and together the two cousins fell up the stairs, dislodging plaster as they went. Their convivial, gin-soaked evening was over, and now there was nothing for them but the fuzzy-edged reality of their fusty room. It smelled worse than Alberto remembered, even though the windows were still tightly shut. This time there was a sour-sweet, penetrating odour added to all the rest. It made Alberto feel sick, and the sickness, oddly, reminded him that he was still hungry.

Camillo dropped the candle on the mantelpiece where, being well used to such ill treatment, it lay on its side and continued to burn. 'Gotta stand it up again,' he said. 'Set fire to the house! Burn old Mother Dobbs!' This was an irresistibly funny idea. It made him giggle for several minutes as he juggled with the candle.

'Was there any of that mutton left?' Alberto asked, because although he remembered not eating it, his reasoning was slow.

'In saucepan,' Camillo said. 'Help yourself.'

The saucepan was still on the washstand. Now he remembered. He picked it up and tilted it towards the candlelight to see how much was left. It didn't look the same. Surely it had changed colour. When they left it had been grey, with a coating of rapidly congealing yellow fat. Now the entire surface was dark brown, like paint, and it was moving, heaving and bubbling as though it was on the boil. But the saucepan was as cold as the room. Puzzled, he carried it across the room to the candle. Halfway there he suddenly realized with a frisson of horror just exactly what it was he was holding. It wasn't stew in the saucepan. It was a seething mass of cockroaches. He gave a low roar of revulsion and flung the saucepan into the corner of the room, as far away from him as he could get it. It fell on its side with a squelching thud. Within a second all the cockroaches had scuttled away from it in every direction, as quickly as a hundred slivers of black mercury. Alberto sat down heavily on the edge of the bed, feeling sick and angry and desperately lonely. What was he doing in this filthy room, in this cold, jabbering city, with a cousin who was a stranger?

Camillo turned with a slow, drunken fury. 'What are you playing at?' he asked.

'That bloody saucepan was full of bloody cockroaches,' Alberto said, and anger rose inside him like a fountain.

'So what!' Camillo said. 'They get everywhere. You'll have to get used to cockroaches if you're going to live in London.'

'Dear God,' Alberto said. 'How can you live in such filth? Cockroaches are filthy. They follow filth. Why don't you clean the room, for God's sake?'

'Not worth it,' Camillo said mildly, struggling to take his boots off. 'Only get dirty again. Don't fuss. Let's get to sleep.'

Now that his eyes were accustomed to the candlelight, Alberto could see that the soot in the fireplace was heaving with obscene brown bodies too. He wondered where else they were and shuddered. 'This bloody place is crawling alive,' he said.

Camillo's legs suddenly gave way under him and he slid to the floor grinning stupidly. 'That's right!' he said and began to giggle.

The giggle infuriated Alberto. 'Never mind, "That's right",' he shouted. 'What are you going to do about it?'

'Get a hedgehog tomorrow,' Camillo said.

'A hedgehog tomorrow is no good,' Alberto insisted. 'You must do something about it now. Tonight. Do you understand?'

'Be reasonable, Berto,' Camillo said, still giggling. 'What do you expect me to do? *I* can't eat the wretched things.' And still grinning he fell immediately into a profound sleep.

Alberto tried hitting him and shaking him and kicking him, but no blow, however violent, had any effect at all. Finally he resigned himself to a night of squalor, unrolled his bedding very, very carefully, gave his blanket a thorough shaking, enveloped himself in it and edged himself cautiously into the wreckage of the bed.

It was a most uncomfortable night, even worse than the ones on the *Belinda May* had been, and he'd thought them bad enough. Camillo woke several times to pee loudly, more or less into the chamber pot. On the second occasion he remembered where he was and finally got into the bed, which he occupied heavily and diagonally. Alberto, cramped into the remaining triangle, breathed ammonia fumes, dozed, fidgeted and fretted. He was glad of the morning, even though it was still raining and the room looked dirtier than ever in the early light. A chorus of city churches struck the hour. It was six o'clock.

Camillo was lying in a haze of sour sweat, still fast asleep with his mouth wide open. Alberto disliked him intensely.

'Wake up!' he said, jabbing his cousin in the ribs. 'Wake up! Time we were at work.'

'Go away!' Camillo said thickly. 'I'm tired.'

Alberto persisted. 'Wake up!' he said, shaking him. 'Wake up! Time for work!'

Camillo turned his face away from the annoyance of Alberto's voice and groaned. Alberto lost his temper. He seized his sleeping cousin under the shoulders, lugged him out of the bed and thudded him onto the floor, bouncing him up and down until he finally opened his eyes. Even then, Camillo was too weary to be more than aggrieved.

'What's the matter with you, you lunatic?' he said.

'Lunatic yourself,' Alberto shouted. 'Get up! Get moving. It's time for work. Work! Shift yourself.' And he accompanied every order with another vicious bounce.

Camillo tried to crawl out of range and back into bed. 'Leave off,' he said mildly. He was lugged back onto the floor for his pains. This time he sat up and looked at his cousin.

'If you want to work,' he said to the enraged face beside him, 'you work. I'm tired. I'm going back to sleep.'

'Look,' Alberto answered furiously, 'if you think I'm going to spend another night in this bug-ridden cesspit, you'd better think again. We're not going to live like this any more. Not another day! Not another minute. You're going to get up and we're going to work. We're going to earn a good wage and find a good lodging. Do you understand?'

'You work if you want to,' Camillo said, closing his eyes. 'I'm not stopping you.'

Good God, Alberto thought, what do I have to do to make this idiot understand? 'I shan't pay the rent for you,' he warned. 'If I work on my own, I spend on my own.'

'I don't pay the rent anyway,' Camillo said, finally climbing back into the smelly blankets.

'You're a disgrace to the family,' Alberto shouted. 'Idle, shiftless, dishonest! Aren't you ashamed of yourself?'

'No,' Camillo grunted, settling into the mattress.

'All right,' Alberto said with determination. 'If you won't work, I will. Where do I go?'

'What?' Camillo grunted.

'Where do I go to work?' Alberto said. 'You told Granny Bianchi you'd got a good job for me.'

'Well I haven't,' Camillo said. 'If you want work, you'll have to find it yourself. I'm not your nursemaid.'

I've come all this way, Alberto thought, and there's nothing for me, because you're just a rotten, idle liar. He stripped all Camillo's filthy blankets off the bed, opened the window wide to the appalling stench in the yard and threw them all out into the mire. Then while Camillo was still feebly protesting, he picked up his blanket and his bundle and banged out of the room.

The tramps were still sprawling all over the passageway. They were a damned nuisance and they made him feel angrier than ever. He trod all over them with the greatest satisfaction. It wasn't until he was right outside the house and standing on the cobbles of Saffron Hill that he remembered his vow to be calm.

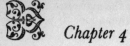 *Chapter 4*

At first Alberto had no idea where he was heading. Temper carried him on down Saffron Hill and past the sleeping shutters of the Hat and Tun, and after that he just kept going, following his private storm. It led him to a muddy road already busy with milk carts and delivery vans. And there, carefully picking his way through the churned up mess of mud and dung, with his long cream surplice raised to his knees, was a Catholic priest. Alberto's greeting was automatic. 'Good day, Father,' he said, speaking Italian without thinking about it.

'Good day, my son,' the Father said, answering in the same language, and flicking a little smile towards his new parishioner. Then he went on watching his feet as he proceeded across the road.

Little Italy, Alberto thought, and he remembered the words of the boys the night before. An Italian church and somewhere behind it Italian homes run by Italian women. Now he knew where he was going. He followed the priest across the road, anger fading.

The Italian church was embedded in a block of four-storey shops and flats. Only the entrance was visible from the street, but the entrance was familiar and reassuring, red brick against white stone, a flight of white steps behind a pair of high curved arches and above them a gilded panel of brightly coloured saints. It was a home from home, and just the sight of it lifted Alberto's spirits. The priest dropped his skirts and trotted up the white steps into his Neapolitan palace unaware that his presence had been a blessing. And Alberto went in search of an Italian home.

The little streets that led downhill behind the church were narrow and cobbled, but clean. Their sand-coloured brick was either muddied or blackened, but most of their windows were neatly curtained, their brown paint clean, and nearly every doorstep scrubbed into a neat white arc. In one window a caged canary sang to the early sun, in another a pot of basil grew luxuriantly. It was, Alberto decided, a proper, well-ordered place, as you would expect from an Italian community.

He had already forgotten the poverty of Pontedecimo and the slums of Genova, and was beginning to wallow in a sentimental nostalgia when a figure walking uphill towards him caught his attention. There was something about that particular jaunty strut, that cocky tilt of the head, that chirruping whistle! It was Pietro Chiapponcelli.

'Pietro!' he roared, running forward to greet his friend. Pietro set down the cart he was pushing and the two men embraced as though they hadn't seen one another for years.

'Where are you going?' Pietro asked when they'd taken the edge off their mutual surprise. 'Do you work down here?'

This was no time for posing or pretending. Alberto told his new friend the truth.

'Well, I call that a real piece of luck!' Pietro said when he'd finished.

'It's more than I do,' Alberto said disconsolately.

'Come with me,' Pietro suggested. 'I've got to get the ice. You can give me a hand and I'll tell you what I've got in mind.'

So Alberto followed him to the little dark shop in Summers Street, where they sold ice in huge lumps wrapped in sacking, and helped him to load the cart. Then as they pushed the ice carefully back through the quiet streets of Little Italy, Pietro explained. Without Domenico, he would be working alone this year, and that would cut down the amount of money he could make and impede him in his quest for local beauty. Alberto could take Domenico's place, if he wasn't afraid of hard work, rent Domenico's empty bed and go halves on the profits. It would give him a start. What did he think of the idea? Alberto was light-hearted with relief at the sudden change in his fortunes.

He was lucky in his new landlady too. Signora Bruno was a small, plump Italian. She was as brown as her name, with olive skin, shrewd, dark eyes and an abundance of thick, brown hair. Alberto liked her at once, she made such a refreshing contrast to the horrible Mrs Dobbs. She lived in a curved terrace of three-storey houses, and for many summers had let her front parlour and the two upper bedrooms to Ettore and the Chiapponcelli brothers. She was quite happy to accept Alberto as a substitute for the absent Domenico and showed him upstairs to the bedroom he would share with

Pietro. It was white and clean and well-ordered, with polished linoleum on the floor, white linen counterpanes on both the beds, a capacious wardrobe in one corner and even, to his delight, a jug and basin ready for use on a plain deal washstand.

'Would it trouble you very much, Signora, if I had a wash before I start work?' he asked.

'I will fetch warm water for you,' the Signora said, taking up the jug, and adding like the good business women she was, 'That will be tuppence extra though, you understand.'

Alberto worked hard that summer and learned a lot and enjoyed himself. Pietro had been good company on the *Belinda May*, but he was even better on the streets of London. And he was a good teacher. As soon as Alberto had washed away the grime of Saffron Hill, he was rushed down the stairs to the front parlour to begin his education. The room was full of carts and trolleys and cages. There were two ice cream wagons with bright red and white awnings, a charcoal brazier for chestnuts and a hurdy-gurdy so big that Alberto wondered how they would ever get it out of the front door. Oreste was patiently coaxing one of the little Capuchin monkeys into a red velvet coat. He looked up at Alberto's arrival and gave a slow smile. Ettore was sitting on the floor carefully re-touching the blue and gold flowers that enlivened the sides of their hurdy-gurdy. He was surprisingly cheerful and grinned at Alberto as though his appearance among them was just what he expected and wanted. 'It's going to be a very good day,' he said. 'We shall make a fortune.' Alberto was amazed at the change in his miserable travelling companion, but he wasn't allowed to discuss it because Pietro wanted to get down to business.

They carried a variety of beautifully written signs to suit almost any occasion. The one for this first morning was for rich children and their families. It read, 'Pure Ice Cream. Best Quality Ingredients. Health Giving Nourishment.'

Pietro provided an accurate translation. Alberto giggled.

'Don't laugh,' Pietro said. 'For the rich it has to be clean and nourishing. Those words earn money. You'll see.'

Alberto watched most attentively that first day and he soon saw how well Pietro understood his customers. Smart maids

in starched caps and snow-white frilly aprons came importantly up the area steps with their covered dishes to buy. Their
brisk no-nonsense appraisal of the cart and its contents was
quick but obvious. 'Better be clean!' one moppet said imperi-
ously. 'The missus don't hold with rubbish!' But another came
towards them all welcoming smiles. She called Pietro 'Antonio'
and asked how he was and had no eyes for anything but him.
Alberto thought it all most romantic, until after she'd gone,
bearing away a dish of economical scoopfuls. Then Pietro
ruined the vision by explaining that she was the renowned
Eliza, and that her breath smelt as bad as ever.

That afternoon in a park as wide as an estate where the rich
children walked sedately with their nurses or were pushed in
baby carriages like little over-dressed dolls, the scrutiny was
even more severe. Well-buttoned nurses put on stern faces and
descended upon the cart, more like insects than customers.
They noted the slightest smear left on the side of the canister,
they glared at aprons, they examined the scoops as though
they might contain poison, watching all the time to make quite
sure that the monkey was kept well away from the food and
their charges. Pietro smiled and bowed and stood back to
allow them the best possible view, and finally they were
satisfied and condescended to buy. They would have been
horrified at the old cotton rag he used when their backs were
turned, to polish the scoops and wipe away the offending
smears. But, as he said, hiding the grubby evidence under the
second lid. 'I just show them what they want to see. That's
good business.'

On hot days they were sold out by the middle of the afternoon
and then Alberto would be sent to Covent Garden to buy
chestnuts ready for the evening. They roasted them in the
streets outside whatever pub Pietro deemed likely and sold
briskly to incoming and outgoing patrons. If one pub brought
little trade there was always another on the next corner for, as
Alberto soon discovered, London was a city devoted to drink.

'We'd make even more money if we could sell beer and
spirits,' he observed to Pietro one evening after the last of their
chestnut-chomping customers had staggered away.

'You need a licence to sell drink,' Pietro said, 'otherwise I'd have sold it long ago. And premises of course.'

'There's money in it,' Alberto said. He'd seen so many prosperous landlords by now he was quite sure of that. In fact he was beginning to wonder whether it would be a good idea to work in a pub when the Chiapponcellis went home.

'You could do worse,' Pietro said. 'And then again, you could do better. Why don't you buy a shop of your own and run an off-licence?'

'With half a crown?' Alberto said.

'Save!' Pietro advised. 'Found an empire on hokey-pokey. Be the first chestnut millionaire!'

By the end of the first week the first chestnut millionaire had earned enough money to buy himself a stout pair of leather boots of the kind he'd coveted in Pontedecimo. By the end of the month he'd treated himself to a fine linen shirt and a fancy waistcoat. By the middle of June he was actually saving money. It was the first time in his life he'd ever had cash to spare.

When the weather was cool and the hokey-pokey didn't sell too well in the parks, they changed their pitch and sold in the back streets at half the price. This time their sign read, 'Cheap and Tasty', Peppi the monkey was allowed to play with the children who gathered round the cart and the scoopfuls were generous. Some were even handed across for nothing, particularly to a pretty face. 'You get little enough in this life if you're poor,' Pietro explained, 'and we can always edge it back from the rich tomorrow.' The rich were fair game, and a rich doting father with an infant in tow was the best of all.

'Double, eh? Two for the bambino!' Pietro would say, deliberately misunderstanding the order he'd just been given, and piling a second scoopful onto the cone before the loving father could demur.

'I don't know how you get away with it,' Alberto said as one bemused parent and his delighted offspring departed. 'One day one of these men is going to make you scoop the extra out again.'

'Never!' Pietro said confidently. 'They don't want to appear mean. Especially in front of two foreigners. It's a great advantage being foreign. Sometimes.'

It was certainly an advantage with the ladies. He flirted outrageously with any girl who gave him half a chance and when the blue eyes responded, he would wink at Alberto and escort his new beloved into the shade of the nearest clump of bushes. Alberto, left to mind the shop, was lost in admiration at the effrontery of it all. He wished he could work up enough courage and summon up enough energy to do the same. But for the first few weeks it was all he could do to keep up with the pace of Pietro's working day. A love affair was almost out of the question. Examining his face in the little looking glass in his new bedroom he decided that he would defer any attempt until his new moustache was fully grown and just concentrate on learning English. He couldn't risk failure in England too. Things had to be different here.

But he had reckoned without Pietro's driving urgency. The day came when stolen kisses in the midsummer bushes just weren't enough for the fiery Pietro. Alberto noticed that he was constantly on the move, all day long, prowling round the cart, fidgeting with notices, going off on unnecessary walks and, even when he did manage to sit down on the burnt grass for a while, springing up again after a few seconds to set off in hot pursuit of a pretty face he'd glimpsed on the other side of the park. Finally when all the hokey-pokey was sold, he packed the scoops and cloths away, settled Peppi firmly on his shoulder and announced that they were going to take a holiday.

'Are we?' Alberto said, surprised. 'But it's good trading weather.'

'I need a woman,' Pietro explained. 'I'm sick of all these flirting servants. I'm going to the West End to buy a whore.'

Just like that, Alberto thought, admiring him again.

'What will you do?' Pietro inquired. 'You can come with me if you like. I don't suppose you know where the whores are, do you?'

Alberto had to admit that he didn't, but he hid the depth of his ignorance.

'Well, what about it?' Pietro asked. He was so casual, he made the expedition possible.

'Yes,' Alberto said, his heart suddenly racing fit to choke him.

*

Despite Pietro's blend of casual unconcern and discreet tuition, it wasn't a success, being an unnatural mixture of tickling desire and fluctuating fear and anxiety. Alberto wasn't sure afterwards whether Pietro had helped or hindered him by his insistence that they both took the precaution of using Frenchies. The idea that there were diseases you could catch from women and that you had to be provided with a rubber coating to protect yourself against them was rather off-putting. So was the idea of haggling over the price. 'It shouldn't be more than sixpence,' Pietro said. 'If they ask any more say, "No", and look elsewhere.'

In a gaslit street full of obviously available women desire returned, strong and painful. There was so much flesh on display, breasts lifted for inspection by high boned corsets, white arms emerging plumply from lacy frills, bright-eyed faces and flushed cheeks under an extravagance of hair, red, blonde or black as jet, clustered in fat ringlets, heaped and plaited and twisted, or frizzed into a fashionable fringe, and not a bonnet or cap in sight. It was overpowering. Pietro chose his partner so quickly he was gone before Alberto had done more than look around, and that caused something of a panic. How did you approach these women? What did you say? He wasn't sure he would know the words he needed for such an exchange. A small, plump blonde solved his problem for him. 'D'yer want a bit a' fun, darlin'?' she said, slipping an ungloved hand through the crook of his arm. He said, 'Yes,' huskily, and couldn't find the words or the strength of purpose to ask the price, so she led him away.

The room she took him to was swathed in oyster pink satin and smelled of glue. Voluminous pink curtains obscured the window, folds of dusty pink turned the fireplace into a theatre, the coverlet on the high bed was frilled and flounced in oyster pink with brown stains, and even the cane chair had an oyster pink skirt. There were frills and ruffles everywhere, on cushions and pillows, round the legs of chairs, across the mantelpiece. It was like being enveloped in an enormous dirty crinoline. Alberto felt breathless and enclosed. He began to have wilting second thoughts. But it was too late. Business had begun.

'That'll be eightpence,' the lady said firmly, holding out a fat hand.

Alberto couldn't trust himself to speak, let alone argue.

Biting his lips with distress, he scrabbled miserably in his trouser pocket and produced a handful of coins. The lady helped herself from his palm, picking a silver sixpenny bit and three pennies which she locked in a wooden box that lay within its own pink frill on a table by the bed. Having completed the most important part of the transaction, she allowed him a smile.

' 'Ow d'yer like it, darlin'?' she said. 'Wiv or wivatit?'

He had no idea what she was talking about and his bewilderment was obvious. How hard her face was, he thought. Now that she was close to him he could see that her elaborate muslin dress was as stained as her bedspread, and that the ringlets he'd admired in the street were a different colour and texture from the rest of her hair. She had white powder on her forehead and a greasy paint on her mouth. He hadn't the slightest desire for her.

She took him in hand, and because he couldn't think how to stop her and half wanted her to continue anyway, he acquiesced. He was frantic now, in case he failed and was humiliated, but he found that by shutting his eyes and imagining his lovely English wife was in her place, he could just about reassert enough desire to manage. But it was a wretched climax, a tickle, over before it had begun. Not worth the effort and not worth the money. He could have done better by himself.

She pushed him away immediately and got up to adjust her skirts. Then she turned up the gas, which popped and spluttered under its dirty pink frill, and sat on the cane chair in front of the mirror to re-powder her face. He sat on the edge of her frowzy bed, trying to regain his composure, mouth working with distress, feeling ashamed and embarrassed and very, very lonely.

'You ain't stayin' 'ere all night!' she said to him sharply. 'Bleedin' foreigners, you're all the same. Push off out of it, will yer! You ain't paid the rent!' The face and tone were both so hard and so full of hatred, he ran from the room.

Stumbling down the stairs, sweating and ashamed, he made up his mind that the whole episode must be kept secret. Pietro was waiting for him under the street lamp at the corner. He decided to take the initiative in their first conversation and turn attention away from his own exploits at once.

'How was it?' he asked his friend as he approached.

'Satisfactory,' Pietro said casually. 'She served. Yours was no good, of course?'

'How did you know that?' Alberto asked, caught off-balance. Had he seen her?

'First time never is,' Pietro said. 'Never mind. It gets better. I can promise you that. Cheer up! One thing about whores, you get what you pay for and there are no strings attached.'

That was true, Alberto thought, but he vowed there wouldn't be a next time. It was too embarrassing.

But there was, of course, and it was marginally better, as Pietro had promised. But never loving, never entirely satisfactory and always leaving an inescapable residue of sadness and regret.

Life in the parks went on as usual and trade in that long hot summer was brisk. 'Beautiful sun!' Ettore enthused as they all set off together late in the morning. 'We will make a fortune.' It was his theme song all through the season.

Pietro and Alberto continued to enjoy one another's company. They developed a new game to wile away the tedium of long afternoons in hot streets and crowded commons, an anthropomorphic joke that allowed them to poke fun at anyone within eyesight. 'Get out the mackerel-flavoured ices,' Pietro would say. 'Here comes a man exactly like a walrus.' And sure enough the man waddling pompously towards them would be very much like a walrus, with the same drooping grey moustache, the same wrinkled jowls and the same small eyes set in heavy, fleshy pouches. Every peculiarity was noticed and enjoyed and giggled over. Nobody could escape because, as Pietro pointed out, nobody deserved to. So polar bears were seen plodding towards them and penguins were watched as they waddled from gate to gate; mice peeped from bonnets at the stoats and weasels that leered down upon them from under the respectability of top hats, while a whole menagerie of monkeys pretended to be children, squabbling and snatching, standing on their heads, crouching on their hands and scratching their fleas with abandon.

One afternoon Alberto found a splendid example. 'Just look at that woman by the pond,' he urged. 'She looks like a camel in a skirt. Just look at that long neck and that great jaw. I'll bet there's a hump under her shawl.'

'There's a circus tent over by the gate,' Pietro said, 'and it's waving at you.'

'Impossible!' Alberto said. 'I don't know any circus tents.'

'Know one or not, it's coming our way,' Pietro said and he seized a scoop so as to be prepared for anything.

Alberto turned to enjoy the circus tent and his heart sank. It was Mrs Dobbs. He'd know that lurid shawl anywhere. 'It's my awful landlady,' he explained to Pietro. 'The one I told you about. What shall I do?'

'Brain her with one well-aimed blow,' Pietro suggested, offering the scoop. But she was upon them.

'Oh Mr Ploochy!' she said. 'You ain't seen our Cammy, 'ave yer? I'm that worried I'm outa me wits.' Tears spilled down her pallid face, gathering grime as they went.

She was upset and it was something to do with Camillo, that much was plain. Alberto plunged into his first English conversation.

'Where Camillo?' he said.

'Gorn orf somewhere,' Mrs Dobbs answered, sniffing as the tears reached her nose and mouth. 'I don't know, Mr Ploochy. 'E owes me four months rent, and if I don't pay up soon, I shall have the baileys in.'

This was totally confusing. 'Camillo not pay rent?' he asked, struggling for clarification, and making a likely guess.

'No 'e ain't, the young bugger, saving your presence, Mr Ploochy, I'm sure,' the lady tried to explain. 'No 'e ain't. An' I got rent owin' to the landlord and no money, Mr Ploochy. I'm outa me wits!'

She sublets, Alberto thought, understanding part of the tangle of words.

'You need money,' he asked. She nodded. 'How much he owe you?'

'Two pounds,' the lady said, wiping her nose on her shawl. 'Two bleedin' pounds! It ain't right, Mr Ploochy, as you're my witness. I'm a decent Christian woman, I am, and your Cammy's took advantage somethink chronic.'

Two pounds, Alberto thought. That's a lot of money. He considered for a minute, chewing his upper lip and pleased by the sensation of his nice thick moustache. Then he made his

57

decision. 'Tonight,' he told Mrs Dobbs, 'I try find Camillo. I try. Tomorrow I come see you. I fix. Tomorrow.'

Mrs Dobbs' tears ceased immediately. She clasped him moistly by the hand and drowned him in a flow of incomprehensible English. He understood that she was pleased.

'A kind heart will be your downfall,' Pietro warned, as her over vivid figure scuttled through the park gates and out of his astonished sight. 'Are you really going to pay off Camillo's debts?'

'I don't know,' Alberto confessed. 'I'm going to find him first. Then we'll see.'

Camillo was sitting among his cronies in The Hat and Tun, still on beer, when Alberto arrived that night. He greeted his cousin with unfeigned delight.

'Berto! Where have you sprung from? Sit down! Have a drink!'

'No, thank you,' Alberto said firmly. 'Turn out your pockets, Camillo.'

'Here, hold on a minute!' Camillo said, puzzled by this abrupt attack. 'There's no call for that!' His friends gathered round him, looking anxious. Their anxiety increased Alberto's belligerence.

'Turn out your pockets!' he ordered. 'Or I will do it for you!'

Camillo obeyed amazingly quickly, and sat staring at the pile of debris he'd produced: coins, scraps of dirty paper, spent lucifers, stubs of candle and a considerable quantity of grey fluff. Alberto picked out all the silver coins from the pile and held them in his palm, clinking them together. 'You owe this to Mrs Dobbs,' he said. 'It's your rent. I will pay it for you tomorrow.'

The landlord was watching them suspiciously. Camillo noticed the look, gave him an ingratiating smile to show that all was well, and agreed with Alberto. It was an easy victory.

Back at his lodgings, Alberto discovered that he'd lifted seventeen shillings and ninepence from his cheating cousin. After some consideration he added twenty-two shillings and thruppence from his current store, put the whole lot in a stout brown envelope kindly provided by Signor Bruno and went to Saffron Hill early the next morning to settle the family account.

Mrs Dobbs, terrible in a black and purple wrapper, was so overwhelmed by his kindness he thought she was going to kiss him and escaped quickly before she could.

'Your cousin is a lazy good-for-nothing,' Pietro said. 'If that had been me, I'd have let him stew in his own juice.'

'I couldn't have done that,' Alberto said. 'After all, he *is* family.'

'Family,' Pietro said, 'is a liability! If you're going to be a rich man, you'll have to learn to put yourself first.'

It was a chill afternoon with quite an autumnal breeze blowing. Alberto was struck yet again by how quickly the weather could change in his new country.

'Pubs tonight,' Pietro said. 'Let's go to Whitechapel.'

It was a mistake, although neither of them thought so when they arrived. The streets were narrow and the houses black but there was a pub in rowdy action on every corner and the pavements were thronged with people. Many of them were already reeling a little with the drunken cheerfulness that was usually the prelude to good sales. Alberto was overjoyed at the sight of so many potential customers. As soon as the first batch of nuts were roasted he began to fill the blue paper cones, and for five minutes they sold fast.

Then trouble arrived. It bruised out of the dense crowd straight into their faces in the shape of two of the most formidable individuals Alberto had ever seen. Playing his new game almost instinctively, he recognized them at once as a couple of bulldogs, for both had faces like gargoyles, squashed and folded and battered, and both were growling. Bulldogs off the leash and spoiling for a fight. They wore flat caps so dirty and distorted that they were more like metal helmets than cloth, neckerchiefs that were twisted and knotted like chains, and an assortment of ancient coats and waistcoats, one piled on top of the other in various states of brown decomposition like old leather armour. Their legs were encased in solid corduroy, seamed with grey dust, and their feet were loud in iron-tipped boots. The flesh on their faces was multi-coloured with bruises and the few rusty teeth they still possessed were chipped and blackened. They were fighters, and they'd arrived for a fight.

It wasn't until the smaller of the two began to speak that Alberto realized with a shock that she was a woman.

'Clear orf aht of it!' she yelled, shaking a fist like a boxer's in Alberto's face. 'Bleedin' foreigners, queerin' our pitch! Shove orf, or it'll be the worst!'

Immediately, they were surrounded by a close-packed crowd, all eager and excited at the prospect of bloodshed. They were like an army, rank upon rank of hostile faces. The sight of them made Alberto quail.

The second bulldog joined forces with his mate. His attack was far more brutal. He brought up a huge mailed fist and pushed it into Pietro's face. The knuckles of all four fingers were encased in a set of ugly iron rings, each with a heavy spike sticking out of the centre like the top of a spear.

'If,' the gentleman growled, 'you don't want your physog all beat to a pulp, you jest scarper double quick. It ain't your pitch.' He paused for a second to observe the effect he was having and to allow time for his warning to sink in. Then he continued, accompanying every threat with the flint of a blow. 'I'm a reasonable man,' he said. 'I don't hold with violence so I give you fair warning. You scarper! Otherwise I might have to give you a bunch o'fives atween yer lousy eyes. Which wouldn't improve your physog none. Would it? Or on the other hand, I might jest belt you one round the lughole. Or push your nice little ivories straight down your ugly froat. Nah, that's fair warning. I've give you fair warning.'

The crowd was delighted and roared its approval at every threat.

'We don't like wops!' the lady said, pushing her face as close to Alberto's as she could get it. 'Nobody round here has no truck wiv wops. Savvy? Go back where you came from! Savvy?'

A third face from the crowd joined in. 'They want stringing up, the lot of 'em!' it shouted. 'Coming over 'ere. We oughter string 'em all up. That's what!'

' 'Oo arst you to stick your oar in?' the gentleman said, turning to attack his new ally. 'Shut yer trap, you! Nobody arst you!'

The diversion was unexpected but Pietro quickly took advantage of it. He turned immediately to Alberto and began to abuse him in passionate Italian. Alberto was very surprised and not a little hurt, and his expression showed it, but as the tirade continued, although the tone remained as abusive as ever, the words changed, and he recognized the game they were playing. 'You will go on looking upset!' Pietro said. 'You're doing very well. The idiots are quite tricked! Just look at their stupid faces. They don't know what to say now. Try to butt in and I'll shut you up and make it look worse.'

They played their pantomime violently for a few more seconds. Then Pietro shouted, 'Start packing up while I'm talking to the gorilla. Run as soon as you're ready. I'll join you.' He dropped into his most fractured English and addressed the pugilists softly and reasonably, with every placating gesture he knew. 'My friend 'ere,' he said, ' 'E tell me this Italian place. I sorry. We not understand. Foreign! Italiano! We leave now. Pronto! We leave!'

The female boxer growled as though she thought they ought to attack again, but her mate restrained her with his iron hand.

' 'Ang about, Mildred,' he said. 'They're going. 'In't yer?' he asked Pietro fiercely.

The two Italians answered with action. They seized the handles of their cart and trundled it through the crowd like a battering ram, running as fast as its weight would allow. The lady roared her triumph after them. 'Clear orf aht of it!' she yelled unnecessarily and the crowd applauded and jeered and whistled. It was an ignominious retreat.

It wasn't until they were out of danger and had stopped running that Alberto realized how upset he'd been. He was surprised by how quickly Pietro recovered. It didn't seem to take him any time at all to get his breath back, find a new safe pitch and start selling again. Although, as Alberto noted ruefully, they'd lost a lot of chestnuts during their sprint. It wasn't a good evening.

It was nearly September. Soon the Chiapponcelli brothers would be leaving London and he would have to make up his mind what he was going to do next.

'Come back to Italy,' Ettore urged, as they all sat round Signora Bruno's supper table late one evening. 'It's a fearsome journey, I'll grant you that, but once it's over you're home, among your own people and your own language and your own ways.'

'If Domenico means what he's said,' Pietro offered, 'if he's not coming with us any more, you could join us again next year. We work well together.'

Alberto was tempted. But how could he go back to Ponte-decimo? It would be admitting defeat. His father would never let him live it down.

'I can't go back, Pietro,' he said. 'I'm sorry. I'd love to work with you again. It's a most generous offer. But I must stay here.' The generosity of it was upsetting him. He chewed his new moustache first at one corner and then at the other, and the grimace revealed his distress. Pietro, quick to respond, became practical at once.

'If you're going to stay here,' he said, 'you'll have to find another job pretty soon.'

Signor Bruno, who usually sat quietly listening to the babble of his young lodgers, leaned forward to take a second cup of coffee from his wife and joined in. 'Would you like me to ask around and see if I can find something for you?' he asked. 'It would be shop work, of course, like I do.' His suggestion was greeted with delighted surprise, because it had never occurred to any of his lodgers that this quiet, unassuming man would ever involve himself with anyone outside the circle of his plump family. Signora Bruno gave him a hug at once and told him what a fine good man he was and what a splendid idea it was. And Alberto, sitting in the middle of his new family, felt honoured and loved.

The next day Signor Bruno came home with three addresses neatly written out for him. They were all shops said to be on the look out for shop boys and they were all in Clerkenwell. Alberto got up early the next morning and went job-hunting.

He'd have been prepared to work anywhere but he found, to his disappointment, that nobody would take him on. They didn't need any new staff, they said. Times were bad. They were cutting back for the winter. Or, most demoralizing of all, they'd just hired a boy. He was too late. The third shopkeeper, more outspoken than the others, explained his position with devastating clarity and directness. 'You look the part, my son,' he said, 'but your English is dreadful. You wouldn't understand the customers and they wouldn't like you. No offence meant, but you're foreign, you see. People don't like foreigners. I'd go back home if I were you.'

'Never mind!' Signor Bruno commiserated. 'There will be others. I'll ask around again.'

After the tenth refusal Alberto began to feel depressed.

'There must be a job for me somewhere,' he said to Pietro. 'Good God, it's a big enough city.'

'Courage!' Pietro said, giving Alberto's arm a little shake. 'You'll find something. I'm sure of it.'

'What if I end up like Camillo, scrounging and drinking my life away?' Alberto worried.

'Never!' Pietro said. 'You're not a bit like him. You're a worker, for a start. And ambitious. You came to London to be a rich man and marry a rich wife and own a rich store. Remember?'

Alberto hadn't forgotten, and his dream warmed him a little. 'You're right,' he said. 'I'll try again tomorrow. After all, there are plenty of rich men about. One of them must want a worker. What I can't understand is how times can be bad when so many people are so rich. If times are really bad, shouldn't they be bad for everybody?'

'Not in this world,' Pietro said. 'The rich are above bad times. They don't get affected by any of the things that knock us down. Except death, of course, and they can't buy death off. He will strike whoever and wherever he likes. But they can buy everything else. Good food, and the health that goes with it, marvellous houses, warmth, beautiful clothes, idleness. There's no doubt the world belongs to the rich. They're the ones with the power.'

'I don't think it's right,' Alberto said.

'It is if you're rich,' Pietro laughed. 'You just wait till you've married your rich wife and built your rich house. I'll bet you'll see everything differently then.'

'When *I'm* rich,' Alberto said, 'I shall use my money to help people.'

'Well,' Pietro said, 'you might.'

The days went all too quickly. Alberto still hadn't found a job when the moment came for Ettore and the brothers to squeeze their carts and that bulky hurdy-gurdy into the shed at the bottom of the Bruno's garden and feed the two monkeys for the last time that summer. Now that it was emptied of all their clobber the front parlour suddenly looked forlorn and Alberto felt deserted. Next day came emotional farewells and the rush and noise of departure.

'We'll be back next April,' Oreste promised. 'Come and see us.' But Alberto knew in his heart that he would probably never see any of them again.

'Good luck!' Pietro waved from the pavement.

And they were gone.

'You can stay on until Friday,' Signora Bruno told Alberto. 'But after that you'll have to find other accommodation because we will be closed. You do understand, don't you?' Her face was anxious but it was plain she meant what she said.

Signor Bruno put an arm round her shoulder. 'We never let our rooms in the winter,' he explained. 'It gives us time to be together as a family and give attention to our two little sons. You will find somewhere soon I'm sure. I heard about another job this afternoon. In Clapham. I think this will be the one for you.'

Alberto thanked him and hoped it would. He smiled as cheerfully as he could so as to reassure them, because they'd been very kind to him all through the summer. Secretly, he was near despair.

 *Chapter 5*

The chestnuts on Clapham Common were already shedding their leaves. Mounds of them lay under every tree and were blown across the pathways like discarded yellow gloves. The wind that set them scurrying was a chill north-easterly, so shoppers were well wrapped up that morning, the poor in bonnets and firmly tied shawls, the well-to-do in fitted coats and thick gloves and winter boots. Alberto, shivering, promised himself that if he got the job, he would use some of his savings to buy a winter coat.

The bus had set him down by a building that looked like a coaching inn. As he watched, four fresh horses were led out through the entrance to the stable yard by two ostlers in green waistcoats. The landlord, wearing a stout apron to his ankles, came forward to greet them. An inn, without a doubt, but what was it called? The sign that filled the entire space between the windows of the first and second storeys was enormous but incomprehensible. Plough Inn it said. Alberto wondered how these odd-looking words could possibly be pronounced and was more convinced than ever that he would never be able to read this extraordinary language. He was glad that Signor Bruno had written out the address of the shop he had to find, and even more relieved that he'd included a note on how to pronounce it. The ostlers were moving off across the High Street. Alberto approached the landlord diffidently, with his precious address clutched in his hand like a ticket to good fortune.

'Please, would you tell where is "de staw"?' he asked.

'The Store?' the landlord said, recognizing what Alberto meant immediately. 'Can't miss it, sir.' He took Alberto by the shoulder and turned him until he was facing up the High Street, looking back along the road he'd just travelled. 'On the third corner. Big place. See it? You can just make out the sign, look, up on the roof.'

Sure enough, the building he indicated had huge iron letters balanced on top of its roof to proclaim its name to the skies. It must be an important place, Alberto thought. Surely there'd be a job for him there. He thanked the landlord and walked rapidly towards his hope, his step bouncing with a growing excitement.

The shop was full of fish, spread out across a sloping slab of marble and artistically arranged with little grassy hedges of parsley set neatly between one type of fish and the next. It looked a prosperous store. Alberto's hopes lifted even further. The shop boy examined his note obligingly. 'You want Mr Grice,' he said. ' 'E ain't in fish this morning. Try down the road. Next door but one.'

This was puzzling, but Alberto did as he was told. Next door but one was a wide cool store with two marble-topped counters running the full length of it on either side of the entrance. Slabs of butter lay on the marble waiting to be weighed, with their butter pats stored coolly in buckets of iced water beside them; wicker work baskets were heaped with eggs, brown and white and as plentiful as coins; and fat cheeses lay wrapped in muslin awaiting the wire. It was a milky place, all gold and cream and pale brown. Behind the counter, a mural made of tiles depicted an ethereal milkmaid in white muslin and yellow ringlets pretending to milk an immaculate cow, and standing in front of this apparition was a living dairymaid with a red nose and chapped hands. 'Yerse,' she said when she'd read the note. 'You want Mr Grice, you do. That's 'im by the cash desk.'

Mr Grice was the sort of splendid gentleman Alberto would have expected to run The Store. He had a most impressive watch-chain, a very well cut suit and shoes as neat and soft as gloves. But he didn't want any more shop boys.

'I'm sorry,' he said. 'We don't need any further assistants. We are cutting back. Times are not what they were, I'm afraid. Do you speak English Mr, er, um, if I may ask?'

'Yes,' Alberto said, stung. 'I speak English good.'

'I see!' Mr Grice said, and the words were a sneer. 'Well there's no job here, I'm afraid.' Then money entered the shop, wearing a fur stole, and Alberto was instantly forgotten.

As he drifted away unnoticed, he felt depression sucking him down again. It was awful to feel so rejected and unwanted. What if he couldn't find a job at all? What if he ended up like Camillo? He gave himself a shake. This wouldn't do. What would Granny Bianchi say of a man who gave in so easily? He must simply ask anywhere and be prepared to take anything.

He tried every shop on both sides of the High Street, and was turned away; he approached the landlord of the Plough who remarked that he already had more help than it was worth; he crossed the wide road in front of the inn and began a long trek down all the big houses that lined the common, offering his services as groom or gardener or manservant. The uniformed maids who condescended to open the side doors for him looked down on him in every sense of the word and told him the missus wouldn't consider foreigners, so what was he thinking of? He found a street cleaner taking time off to chew tobacco and asked what he had to do to become a street cleaner. But the cleaner took exception to his inquiries and beat him about the legs with his broom. 'Fuck off!' he said. 'You ain't pinchin' my job and don't you go a-thinking it. Bleedin' Eyetie!'

A bit farther along the road two new tracks ran down towards a building site. The foundations of four long rows of terraced houses were already down and bricks and pipes were in position, but there was no sign of any activity and not a worker to be seen anywhere. Perhaps they need labourers, Alberto thought hopefully, picking his way across the rubble. There was a small wooden hut amongst the planks and scaffolding and crouched inside, boiling a kettle over a brazier, was an old man in earth-stained clothes. He was cheerful and friendly and no help at all. 'Shouldn't bovver wiv buildings,' he advised. 'We're all laid off, that's what. Times is bad they say. Run outa cash they 'ave, because o' the bad times, that's what. Can't see no work 'ere till long after Christmas. Come far, 'ave yer?'

'Clerkenwell,' Alberto said.

'Ah!' the old man said sagely. 'That'll be a fair step. Well, I'd go back if I was you,' and he sucked his gums in the manner of one who had just delivered excellent advice and turned his attention to the kettle.

Alberto walked miserably away, feeling cold and tired and undeniably depressed. The sky was full of rain clouds, swirling mauve and blue, and the wild common beneath them looked dark and unwelcoming. For the first time since his arrival he was feeling the impact of being alone in a foreign country.

There was nothing for him to do and nowhere for him to go and on top of everything else he was extremely thirsty.

Just ahead of him on the common stood a clump of luxuriant chestnut trees that seemed to be clustered around a collection of low buildings. He walked aimlessly towards them. The nearer he got, the more clearly he could hear voices, young, male English voices barking and guffawing from behind the foliage. Quite a crowd, Alberto thought, and pushed forward towards the sound to see what was going on. It led to a pub, and the pub led him, at last, to a job.

It was a beautifully kept pub, of yellow brick like the majority of the buildings in the town, but nowhere near so discoloured. The four windows on the first floor were painted white and below each one was a window box burgeoning with geraniums and lobelia, while between the windows on the ground floor ornamental trees grew from bright red tubs. The letters painted hugely across the upper storey said it was Ye Olde Windmill, and this time a brightly painted inn sign provided Alberto with a clear translation. The forecourt was crowded with men, leaning against the railings, lounging under the trees, sitting on benches as though there were no such thing as work, and bad times had never been invented. It was a most attractive place. Alberto felt welcomed just looking at it. A pint would be just the thing to quench his thirst and lift his spirits.

The public bar was a snug, low-ceilinged, panelled room, with a dazzling array of glass and bottles behind the bar. It was full of cheerful sounds and lively colour as many of the customers were soldiers in heavy red tunics and blue serge trousers. The wallpaper above the panelling was red too, heavy, flocked and as richly decorated as even the most ostentatious taste could have wished. Alberto felt entirely at home at once. He took his pint and squeezed himself into a corner by one of the two windows. What fine glass! It was like one of the great wedding cakes he'd seen on display in high class confectioners in the West End. He downed his beer and admired it contentedly. He would have gone on admiring it for much longer, had he not overheard a conversation that was going on at the other side of the window.

'Be a nice job for some lucky geyser, I'm telling you,' a rough voice was saying. 'A peach!'

68

'Don't look at me!' another answered. 'I can't see old Solly taking me on!'

'Nah. Course not!' the first voice agreed. 'Nor me neither. I never said nothink about *us*. I said a nice job for someone, didden I? A nice job for someone.'

It was heaven sent. Alberto put his head out of the window and spoke before good manners or reason or too much thought could stop him. 'Where is job?' he said.

'Allo! Oo are you?' a grubby face below him answered.

'Alberto Pelucci,' Alberto explained. 'I look for job.'

'Foreign, intcha?' the grubby face said.

'Yes,' Alberto admitted. 'I look for job.'

'What's it werf?' the second face said.

'I buy you a drink,' Alberto offered.

'Done!' said the first grubby face. ' 'Ere's a turn up for the books, Codger!'

'Wottle lit be?' Alberto asked, proud of his new command of the language.

They chose bitter and bitter it duly was. Then all three got down to business.

'Ta!' first grubby face said cheerfully and when he'd downed more than half the pint and rubbed the froth into his jaw with satisfaction, he said, 'Name of Dipps. And this 'ere's Codger. 'E's a fob worker, best in the business. I draws wipes. Pleased ter meetcha.'

'Wipes?' Alberto repeated. 'Is a job?'

'Ain't it just!' Dipps said. 'My eye, you wouldn't say so. 'Ave a butchers!' He produced three silk handkerchiefs from the capacious inner pocket of his vast jacket and spread them out for inspection. 'New drawed this morning. Not bad, eh?'

'Fobs is best,' Codger said. 'There's more money in fobs.'

'Made a pile outa fobs this morning aintchar. I don't think,' Dipps said mocking and laughing.

'Shut yer face,' Codger said, pleasantly. 'You know I ain't.'

Alberto couldn't follow any of this. 'The job is where?' he asked, trying to sound casual, but driven to urgency by need and lack of English.

'Solly Isaacs,' Codger said, after another draught. 'Keeps the pop shop off the Pavement. 'E trades wiv us, specially fobs. 'E can really 'andle fobs. Well Henery's 'opped it. So 'e's on 'is tod.'

Most of this was baffling but Alberto felt pretty sure that there *was* a shop, and that the shop had a vacancy. 'You show me where the shop?' he asked.

'If yer like,' Dipps said, looking hopefully at his empty glass. Alberto got the hint. 'Wottle lit be?' he said again.

Solly Isaacs kept the most crowded shop in Clapham. The window was crammed with every imaginable kind of bric-a-brac, rusty irons, chipped jugs and vases, shoes so old that their leather looked and felt like iron, bundles of gaudy tin trays, odd cups without saucers, stained mugs and battered teapots. In the middle of the muddle was a wooden drawer full of broken beads and cheap tie pins, several sets of false teeth and two glass eyes, one blue and one brown, looking at each other. Years ago Solly had had his name painted in ornate letters over the shop front, but the grime bouncing up from the pavement and oozing round the corner from the greasy alley next door had soon obliterated it in black dust. The three brass balls over the entrance seemed shining clean by comparison, and that was all that Solly worried about. After all, his name was known all over Clapham and trade was always brisk, particularly in bad times. It wasn't a shop you could take a pride in. It was simply a box for the disposal and retrieval of goods. But it did more trade on Saturday night than all the rest of the shops in old Clapham put together. On Saturday nights, Solly's customers jostled six deep at each counter, pushed and quarrelled in the doorway and queued beside the window. In fact Solly had organized the inside of his establishment especially to withstand the pressure. Two broad wooden counters set together in a V shape not only divided the space neatly in two but also allowed Solly considerable protection from the onslaught of his clients. Behind him every available spot was crammed with clothing. Coats hung like bats in close and smelly formation overhead, boots and shoes stood in martial rows on shelf after shelf, shawls lay in piles, pressed and folded and pinned and in the farthest corner, a grey *chaise longue* was heaped with bundles of washing.

The shop was always dark, even in high summer. Very little sunlight managed to push its way through the clobber in the windows and when it had given up the unequal struggle and retired behind cloud or succumbed to dusk, Solly's only concession to sight was a pair of beautiful but inadequate oil lamps which cast a pool of buttery illumination over each counter and left the rest of the room in shadow. Consequently the shop looked and smelled like an airless cave. Alberto, trying to get some idea of what sort of place it was by peering through the window, could hardly see anything. Codger and Dipps hovered on either side of him offering advice.

'Don't give 'im no lip,' Dipps said helpfully. ' 'E don't like it if you're lippy.'

'Lippy?' Alberto said. What an extraordinary language this English was.

'Yeh, you know,' Codger explained. 'Sauce! Cheek! 'E don't like it.'

Dipps tried again because he could see from Alberto's face that he hadn't understood a word they were saying. 'Mind yer Ps and Qs,' he said. 'Watch yer north and south. Savvy?'

Alberto didn't savvy, although he was trying very hard. 'I beg pardon,' he said, hoping politeness would rescue him from confusion.

' 'E means watch yer mouth,' Codger said. 'Don't give 'im no lip,' and then with some exasperation seeing Alberto was still baffled, 'Oh blin' me! Dontcha know *any* English?'

'I do what you say,' Alberto said smiling broadly to reduce their growing short temper. 'Now I see Mr Isaacs. Is right?'

'That's it, matey,' Codger said. 'In you go. You'll do all right,' he reassured Alberto. 'You look a treat.'

Alberto had taken great pains to look his best when he set out, but now after such a long disappointing morning he felt a wreck. He smoothed down his jacket, rearranged his hat, took a deep breath and stepped over the dark threshold.

The riot of bells he set off by opening the door rooted him to the doormat. Solly Isaacs blazed into the shop from his inner office like a torch into darkness, the shock of his ginger hair and his ginger beard quite startling in that musty interior. Everything about him was lighter, brighter and larger than life. He had the kind of physique that would have looked right behind a plough, or felling trees or digging ditches. His hair frizzed around his face like a lion's mane and his eyebrows stood up above the sockets of his brown eyes like two protective red wings. His nose was so fleshy it didn't seem to possess any cartilage at all, and his mouth was full and moist and as red as poppies, an incongruous expanse of naked-looking flesh in the tangle of his beard.

Looking at him, bold and dramatic in the middle of his dark store, Alberto quailed a little, convinced that when he opened that red mouth he would speak with tongues of fire. But despite his appearance, Solly was a quiet, gentle man, who said very little and then only after lengthy deliberation. Now, patting his beard gently with three stocky fingers, he was considering Alberto, summing him up, noticing, thinking. It was a little disquieting.

'Yes?' he said, at last, and his voice was soft.

Alberto had to gather courage to answer. When he found words they were bolder than he intended. 'I want a job,' he said.

Solly considered him again for several long seconds. 'Um!' he said. 'You think I should give you a job, eh?'

'Yes,' Alberto said hopefully. 'Please.'

'Um,' Solly said again, patting the red wire of his beard and thinking. 'Why?'

'I am good worker,' Alberto said carefully and earnestly. 'I work long hours. I am strong. I work *well* for you.'

'I need a boy,' Solly said.

'I know,' Alberto said. 'Henry has hopped it.'

'Who told you that?' Solly asked.

'Codger,' Alberto said truthfully.

'How d'yer get to know young Codger?' Solly wanted to know. 'You ain't a dip, are yer?'

'Dipps I meet also,' Alberto said, misunderstanding. 'He tell me the job.' Solly said nothing. For far too long. Alberto began to feel uncomfortable under this prolonged scrutiny. 'I work very hard,' he offered. 'I not afraid of hard work. I good.'

'It's a lot to learn,' Solly said. 'You ever worked in a pawn shop?'

'No,' Alberto had to admit. 'I work selling. I sell good.'

'I'm not selling, son,' Solly explained. 'I'm buying. You got to get value for money in this business.'

'I learn,' Alberto urged, mouth moving earnestly. 'I learn quick.'

'Um,' Solly said, considering again. 'How d'yer reckon to do that, if you don't know nothink about it? Tell me that.'

This was hard. Alberto wasn't sure he'd even understood the question, but he made a valiant effort to answer it. 'When I come here, England,' he said. 'I no speak English. Now I speak.'

'After a fashion,' Solly said and he smiled quietly, as though he were smiling to himself.

An English phrase Alberto had learned that summer jumped into his mind, ready and appropriate. He spoke it before he'd thought about it, 'Look who's talking!' he said. As he heard the words he realized, too late, that it could and did sound ill-mannered.

But Solly liked it. He thought it was funny. His red mouth spread sideways in a wry smile of acknowledgement. Then he resumed his quiet observation again. This time Alberto waited. A clock ticked woodenly, somewhere in the musty shadows.

'Leah!' Solly called, without turning his head and without taking his eyes off Alberto. 'Come down a minute, will yer!'

Leah Isaacs was a small, soft, fluttery woman, much given to frills and flounces, a brown moth to her husband's dramatic red candle. Her hair was straight and sleek and mouse brown under a thickly frilled brown cap, and her face was brown too, with small pale eyes and small pale mouth. Standing beside Solly in the dusk of the shop, she only seemed half his height and a lot less than half his bulk.

'We've a boy offered,' Solly said, still looking straight at Alberto with that disconcerting calculation. 'What d'yer think?'

'He looks likely,' Leah said. 'Strong I think. Are you strong?' she asked Alberto.

'Yes,' he assured her. 'Very strong,' and he offered her his hands so that she could see how strong he was. She examined them carefully: wide wrists, strong fingers, broken nails, palms calloused from pushing the carts.

'He's a worker, Solly,' she said.

'Shall we take him on, Leah?' Solly asked. 'That's the question, my dear.'

'There is always Hymie to consider,' Leah said, and although she spoke softly she gave the name an odd emphasis.

73

Hymie was obviously a most important person, whoever he was.

'Yes,' Solly said, smiling happily at his wife as though the whole matter had now been settled. 'Yes, my dear, there *is* Hymie.' He turned his attention back to Alberto. 'What's your name?' he asked. Alberto told him. 'Very well, Alberto,' he said. 'I will hire you. But on one condition, mind.' Alberto nodded to show that he didn't mind at all. 'We got a nephew, Hymie. I promised to keep this job open for him, you understand. He might not want it. He ain't said. But if he turned up, you'd have to go. D'you agree to that?'

'Yes, yes,' Alberto said. After all, anything might happen. Hymie might never turn up. What was important was that the job was being offered to *him*, now. 'How much you pay me?' he asked.

'Seven shillings a week,' Solly said, 'when trade's a hundred per cent. Less when it ain't, of course, in proportion. More when it merits.'

It was less than he'd been making with Pietro, but a lot better than he'd expected. 'I accept,' he said.

'It's hard work,' Solly warned. 'It ain't a rest cure.'

'I accept,' Alberto said and his face was determined.

'Be here five sharp tonight,' Solly said. 'Now skidaddle.'

Codger and Dipps were still lurking in the alley round the corner.

'How d'yer get on?' Codger asked.

'D'yer get the job?' Dipps said, and when Alberto nodded, he went on, 'Good for you, mate! Got lodgings, have yer?'

Alberto had to admit that he hadn't. In fact he hadn't even thought about lodgings until that minute.

'Soon settle that,' Dipps said. 'I got an aunt lets rooms. Just up the street. Suit you to a T, she would. Come on.'

'They clean, her rooms?' Alberto asked rather anxiously, remembering Mrs Dobbs and the cockroaches.

'Like a new pin!' Dipps said. 'Keeps everything tip-top, my aunt. Slap-up meals and everything. You get a right good blow-out wiv my aunt, I can tell you. You just wait till you taste her spotted dog!'

'Gor!' Codger said rapturously. 'Spotted dog and treacle!'

It must be one of their London jokes, Alberto thought, following them. She couldn't really serve dogs to her lodgers, could she?

They were walking towards The Store. It gave Alberto a peculiar sense of triumph that he'd managed to get a job for himself despite that snooty manager. It pleased him to see how tired and dirty the fish shop boy looked, his face and apron stained with blood and slime, and to notice that the morning's impressive display was now broken and dishevelled. The cod had gone, leaving a blood-smeared gap behind it, the mackerel wheel had lost all its spokes bar two and three solitary flat fish had been beheaded and tossed on a pile of wilting parsley. The goods were being sold off cheap.

'There she is!' Dipps said suddenly, darting into the shop. The ample lady who turned from the sprats to hug him into her shawl couldn't be anybody else but his aunt. She had the same wide, smudged features, the same pug nose and the same bold blue eyes. And she was plainly very fond of her nephew. Dipps was patted and kissed and hugged and bounced for a good noisy minute before he could introduce Alberto.

'Well now, aren't you the lucky one, Mr Ploochy!' the lady said. 'And me just on the very point of puttin' out me card, so I was. Was it board you were wantin'? I was just on the point of buying meself a few sprats for me tea. Now would that suit yer? We can discuss terms while they're a-cookin', so we can.'

But Alberto had been caught once and he didn't intend to be caught again, no matter how beamingly friendly the lady might appear. So they discussed terms across the marble slab, while bargain hunters jostled all around them. It was finally agreed that, if the room was acceptable, Alberto would board with Mrs Molly Molloy for two shillings a week, and that she would undertake to provide breakfast and supper for the princely sum of half-a-crown, making four and sixpence all told.

'I suppose you'll want feeding now, the pair of yer,' Molly said, smiling happily at her two ruffians now that business was completed.

'Is it sprats?' Codger said, licking his lips.

The sprats were very palatable, and Mrs Molloy's kitchen was as warm and untidy and friendly as she was herself. The room she offered Alberto was untidy too and really rather

75

dowdy with its faded patchwork counterpane, and its chipped jug and basin, and a dusty rag rug on the grey linoleum, but it looked clean enough and the bed was comfortable. Alberto said he'd take it, and Mrs Molloy said she was 'that obliged' and at last his affairs were settled.

Work began in earnest that evening and Alberto soon discovered that Solly wasn't joking when he'd warned that it wasn't a rest cure.

'You're punctual,' he said approvingly when Alberto arrived. 'Come out the back and I'll show you what you've got to do. Friday night and Saturday morning we bring out the goods for Saturday night. There won't be much trade tonight, only casuals.'

'Out the back' meant a back room behind the shop that looked like a huge wardrobe, it was so crammed with clothes, coats and jackets, suits and skirts, clean sheets and table-cloths, bundles and bundles of washing, the Sunday best of an entire neighbourhood. Every article was labelled and num-bered by a pawn ticket pinned neatly in a prominent position and every article had to be carried into the shop and arranged in neat ranks and perfect order. Solly was most particular about the need for order. It was like a military operation.

After his first shattering week-end in the shop, Alberto could see why precision was so important. His first Saturday night was a nightmare. He was overwhelmed by it, so many hands waving tickets, so many demands for goods to be redeemed 'double quick', so many men aggressive with a week's pay and the first drink of the day. The women were almost as bad, although for a slightly different reason and in a slightly different style. The men bullied; they cajoled and pleaded. They had to get the house ready for the week-end, so couldn't he look sharp about it; they needed the sheets for Sunday, there wasn't a minute to spare. Solly shut the doors on the stroke of half-past nine, and by then Alberto was fit for nothing. He felt bruised and exhausted, and was glad that Solly had sent him down to the off-licence for a beer before the onslaught began.

They quenched their thirst at a table no longer covered with washing, and actually sitting down on two chairs that had been revealed by the clearance. Then work began again. The price tags on all the unredeemed articles had to be rewritten. They were in for another week and, at tuppence in the shilling, they were already earning money. Still, Alberto thought, as he wrote out the last ticket, at least the place isn't so crowded. A lot of stuff's been redeemed. If we could get rid of a bit more, the place would look quite tidy.

'Good eh?' he said to Solly. 'More room!'

'You wait till Monday!' Solly said drily.

On Monday all the goods returned. This time there was no urgency. They arrived calmly, were handed across slowly, and patted farewell before the official transactions were made. On Monday Solly's dark little shop became a club, where lurid tales were told to a general acclamation of negative delight. 'Well I never!' they cried 'I'd never have believed it!' ' 'E never did!' Alberto heard how Seamus fell down the stairs 'from the top to the bottom and never even broke so much as a finger nail'; how the Bowyer Arms couldn't close on time and how they all sang all the way back to Bromells Buildings, and Mrs Radmop fell in the gutter and lay there till next morning, too drunk to move; and how the coppers arrived and threatened to lock Jimmy Murphy in the cooler, until Mrs Murphy offered to crack somebody's head if they didn't leave her lad alone. 'Ah well,' the women said to one another as they finally left the shop, after an hour's happy gossip, 'must get on! The work won't wait!'

By the end of the day the back room was as crowded as it had ever been, and on Tuesday morning the bundles of washing came back too.

'Mind you open every bundle,' Solly warned. 'You never know. Had a woman in once with a fine heavy bundle and paid her accordingly and didn't check. Two days later her bundle was stinking the place out. She'd put a cabbage in to make weight.'

So Alberto inspected every bundle, weighed, paid and was told the latest gossip; how young Peg had a black eye and wasn't telling how she got it; how the twins had left home, which was good riddance to bad rubbish; and how the travellers were back in Bromell's Yard, and a right, dirty, slovenly, thieving lot they were. 'Steal the shirt off yer back,' one amiable lady explained, 'if it wasn't safe in here with old Solly!'

By Thursday trade had slackened off a bit, but before they had time to catch their breath it was Friday and they were shifting goods again. Solly was right. It was very hard work. But at least it paid, and at least it wasn't dull.

During the second week Solly took himself off to his inner sanctum and listened while Alberto struck his first solo bargain. 'Neat!' he said when the client had left the shop, and Alberto felt pleased with his success.

In the third week Codger arrived when the shop was empty and he and Solly disappeared out the back and were ensconsed together for several minutes. Fobs, Alberto thought, now he knew what they were, but he didn't ask, because by then he'd learned not to.

At the end of the fourth week Solly announced that he would be out of the shop for the day because he was going to Whitechapel to see an uncle. Alberto's heart sank. It must be because Hymie wanted the job. What bad luck! Just as he was getting on so well.

'Is it about . . .?' he began to ask, and then saw the thunderous expression that had gathered across Solly's broad face.

'Asking is impertinence,' Solly said. 'Impertinence is ugly. Curb it! Much better you don't know nothink.'

Alberto blushed at his clumsiness and dropped the subject immediately. But Solly was gone all day, and all day it worried him. Finally he couldn't bear the suspense any longer and asked Leah.

'Is Hymie coming for the job, Mrs Isaacs?' he said.

'Hymie?' Leah said and for a second she looked mystified. Then she smiled. 'Ah yes. Hymie,' she said. 'No. No. He ain't coming. He don't want the job. Why you ask?'

'Well,' Alberto said, 'Mr Isaacs went to Whitechapel. I thought . . .'

'Don't you worry your head,' Leah said. 'Solly's out for business. Nothink to do with Hymie. Hymie ain't coming.' And she went off upstairs, chuckling as though the whole thing was a grand joke.

Alberto was relieved to know that the job really was his after all. He liked working with Solly, even if the job was hard, and he quite liked Mrs Isaacs too, even though she was so often quiet and miserable and seemed convinced that the world was a bad place.

And Solly himself, although he seemed detached and withdrawn, was really remarkably observant. From time to time he would pay Alberto what he called 'a bonus in kind'. It was always something he needed, a thick winter coat as the weather got worse, a pair of woollen blankets, new boots, and once, after he'd arrived late three mornings in a row, a clock to keep in his bedroom. 'A good timekeeper!' Solly said, handing it across. 'Worth imitating.' Alberto resolved to take his advice, but getting up in the morning was hard, and it got harder as the weather grew steadily colder and colder.

He woke in the mornings to see his breath streaming in front of him like steam, and to discover that his window had been transformed overnight. It had become as ornately carved as any glass in the Windmill, covered from the sill upwards with a complicated pattern of white frost leaves, swirling and spreading one into the other with a crisp-edged beauty like some mysterious engraving. Alberto thought them extremely pretty, despite the fact that the air in the room was so cold it hurt to inhale it. But to find ice covering the water in his jug was not so pleasant and neither was the absence of hot tea in the morning when the pipes had frozen, which they did on several thirsty occasions during that first hard winter.

Molly Molloy took the winter stoically. When there was water, she brewed hot tea to start the day, when there wasn't, she fried up a bit of bacon and washed it down with beer. The climate was a natural enemy and one she felt competent to tackle. Alberto found it a great deal more difficult. The first fogs of autumn, curling up from the pavement in sulphur yellow swathes, reduced his ability to breathe so suddenly and dramatically he thought he was going to choke, and although Molly showed him how to fix a scarf across his mouth whenever he went out in 'the nasty stuff', he hated the taste and he hated the smell, and ended up coughing for over a week after it had finally cleared.

The snow brought worse trials but at least the snow was beautiful. On the morning of the first snowfall he lay in a bed now considerably warmer by the addition of those two blankets from Solly's store and watched the fat flakes meandering in and out of the top frame of the window, delighted by their delicacy and waywardness. When he rose at last and wrapped himself in a blanket and shuffled across to the window, the sight that met his eyes quite charmed him. All the roofs across the tumble of tenements behind Mrs Molloy's little back garden were coated with a thick white unblemished layer, and the garden itself was hidden under snow. There was no sign of the untidy flower bed, the broken flower pots, the ragged lawn. Only the path remained, as a lower trough, in a pleasing expanse of pure white. As he watched, a cat jumped over the fence at the bottom of the garden and picked its way across the white field, leaving little black pits as it went and lifting its paws delicately one after the other to give them a little flick of a shake before putting them delicately down again into the unfamiliar cold.

The charm soon faded. It snowed every day for a fortnight and although for the first few days the snow had melted or been trodden into slush by the evening, after a week it had begun to lie, and after a fortnight it was piled in solid drifts against every wall and blocked some of the narrow alleys with sharp-edged mounds like icebergs. Alberto, climbing painfully over them to get to Solly's shop, wondered how long they would remain, and found he could hardly remember what the alley looked like without them.

Christmas came and Clapham was still half hidden under the stained mounds of a now filthy accumulation. All the pristine beauty of that first fall had long since disappeared. Snow fell on brown pitted slush and soon became brown and pitted in its turn; dogs left yellow trails against every iceberg; and the horses soon turned the white roadway into a brown smeared track.

'I'm off to me sister's fer Christmas,' Mrs Molloy said. 'You can stay on here all right till I get back, can ye not?' She was cheerfully confident that Alberto could manage without her, and as he didn't want to disappoint her, he said that, of course, he would be quite all right and not to worry. But it left him with a problem.

'Do we work Christmas?' he asked Solly.

'You can work if you like,' Solly said. 'I shall stop at nine sharp on Christmas Eve, no matter what. You just wait till you see the trade we'll do on Christmas Eve. They'll all want their Sunday best for Christmas. Best trade of the year

Christmas. Tiding over so's they can lay in more food and then all redeeming at the last minute, so's they can wear their best for midnight mass. Oh it's a good time, Christmas!'

It was the longest speech Alberto had heard Solly deliver since he arrived. Christmas must be very special indeed.

It was, and as Solly predicted it exhausted them both. But it introduced Alberto to Luigi and Luigi's mouth-watering cuisine.

After the bustle of Christmas Eve, he stayed in his warm bed in Molly's empty house until long past midday. There was nothing to get up for, and in any case he was aching with fatigue. But by twelve o'clock there was no denying his hunger. He got up and dressed, in his thick trousers, his thickest shirt and a heavy jersey he'd bought from Solly for tuppence. Then he squeezed into his coat and went off in search of food.

There was a half-completed rag rug slung across Molly's chair. The table had been scrubbed and the stove lead polished to perfection but the only food Alberto could find were two rashers of bacon, curled and yellowing, and a very dubious egg. He tried to light the stove, but it defeated him, so even tea was impossible. Hungry, thirsty and disgruntled, he put on his overcoat, wound a muffler round his neck, pulled his hat down over his ears and set off into the snow. There was a strong wind blowing against him, and the snow was deeper than it had been the day before. He trudged disconsolately along the High Street, searching in vain for a shop or a café where he could buy some food. There must be one open somewhere. But every shop was closed and shuttered and the street was as quiet as death. Even his own footsteps were muffled to a soft thud. It was eerie, walking so silently on this dark morning in an empty town. So empty. Almost as though the rest of the world had vanished overnight.

He reached the Plough, but that was shut too. There wasn't a sign of life anywhere except for the smoke rising whitely into an iron sky. All the great houses were still and self-contained. Lights might be blooming in the tall windows and here and there he could see a Christmas tree starred with candles, but nobody was out in the street. The High Street was closed down and it was pointless walking over the common, so he set off in the only direction available, down Clapham Park Road. And two hundred yards down the road he found a café called

Luigi's, which was not only open, wonder of wonders, but from the delectable aroma drifting out of its door, actually cooking food. Alberto ran in at once.

Luigi was the Englishman's dream of an Italian. He was short, dark and stout. His hair was slicked to his skull with a heavy coating of Macassar oil and he had a fine pair of waxed moustaches.

'Good day,' Alberto said to him in Italian. 'Are you serving a midday meal?'

Luigi gave him a huge grin. 'No good talking to me in that lingo,' he said in English. 'Can't understand a word.'

'You are Signor Luigi?' Alberto asked, feeling foolish at his mistake.

'That's me,' the gentleman agreed, 'but I ain't Eyetalian. It's a trade name, Luigi. Thought it 'ud be good for trade, you see. My real name's Len.'

But Len or Luigi, he cooked a capital roast and Alberto dined like a lord in his little shop. As he left late that afternoon, he promised his new, non-Italian friend that he would come back as often as he could.

'And bring your friends!' Luigi said. 'Happy Christmas!'

The winter went remorselessly on. Alberto got chilblains, on his toes, on his fingers, and finally and most painfully on the lobes of his ears. From time to time he was aware that he was lonely, that he needed a woman, that he still hadn't started his search for a wife. But he was too cold, too tired, and too skinny to make the effort yet. He would wait till the weather was better,

One day, he promised himself, he would have his own shop and his own house, and his beautiful English girl to love him. Not right at the moment, it was true, because things weren't exactly perfect just at the moment. But things could change. He would work hard and make money and be a success. It was only a matter of time.

 *Chapter 6*

'Day off today,' Solly Isaacs said. 'Holiday.' He was wearing a brown suit and looked impressively business-like.

Alberto had only just arrived. 'Is a special day?' he asked, wondering what had brought this on.

'Got company,' Solly said. 'The shop's shut.'

A deal of some sort, Alberto thought, and he wants me out of the way. He knew better now than to ask questions about it. 'When you want me back?' he said.

'Tomorrow morning,' Solly answered, and resumed his brooding, patting his beard as though the rhythmic beat assisted thought.

It was a lovely day for a holiday, but at first Alberto didn't know what to do with it. He left Solly's shop and wandered down towards the common, aware that the air was warm on his face, warmer than he'd felt it for a very long time, and that blackbirds were singing in the neat front gardens of the great houses he admired. He'd worked so hard during that long cold winter, he'd hardly had time to notice anything, but now he saw that new grass was springing on the common and that the chestnuts had put out new leaf. He realized with a sense of release that spring had begun.

There was a horse bus waiting at the Plough. The sign on the front of it said 'Tooting', and although he had no idea where or what it was, he decided immediately that Tooting was where he would spend his holiday.

The bus took him past the common, past the building sites, where work still wasn't under way, and on downhill between hedgerows, newly green. They passed the occasional isolated home standing by its own neat lawn, while the tangled fields around it fed cows and allowed chickens to wander untidily in and out of the hedges. Then they were at the bottom of the hill and in the countryside. Alberto could smell the old damp familiar scent of ploughed earth. He'd been so long in London now, he'd almost forgotten what it was like. The sensation excited him. Perhaps this Tooting was a village with farms and farming people. He felt he would like to be among farmers again. Perhaps he would find his beautiful English girl out here in the country.

It was a town, a bustling, thriving place, full of people and with more carts and carriages and delivery vans in its narrow High Street than he could count. The shops on either side of the cobbled street were the latest style. Their blinds were sensibly down to protect the goods, which showed a good sense of trade. In two side streets new houses were actually being built, with a great deal of noise and energy. It was definitely a lively town, every bit as big as Clapham but not nearly so upper crust. He set off happily to explore.

There was a variety of shops, a dairy, three butchers, and a fishmongers, for a start, to say nothing of milliners, hatters and boot and shoe shops. On the opposite side of the street, a dusty pub called the Castle spilled imbibers onto the pavement. Inside, somebody was thumping a tinny piano into an almost recognizable tune, urged on by a medley of mockery, cheers and raucous laughter.

As he stood listening, a boot came flying out of the open upper frame of one of the windows. It rose in a neat arc and fell straight into his hands. The cheering and cat-calling inside the pub, roared out of the window after it and a boy with a mop of fair hair ran out of the door, trailing the other boot of the pair by its laces and laughing aloud. He saw the first boot in Alberto's hands and tossed the second one to him too. ' 'Ide 'em, quick!' he said.

Alberto just had time to put the boots behind his back when the shock-headed boy was followed by a second who was shorter, darker, red in the face with laughter and in his stockinged feet. 'You bloomin' idiot, Harry Jones,' he said. 'Give us me boots back!'

'What boots?' Harry Jones said. 'Never seen no boots. What you on about?'

The dark-haired boy began to hunt for his lost footwear and was soon joined in the search by six or seven earth-stained assistants who had come trundling out of the door after him.

'Ain't yer found 'em yet, Dickie?' one asked.

'I don't reckon you never 'ad no boots on when you come in,' another offered.

'Oh yes!' Dickie said. 'Course I always walk round Tooting in me socks. Come on Harry. What yer done wiv 'em?'

Harry was speechless with laughter, falling into the wall of the pub, holding his sides and gasping. 'Oh gawd, Dickie!' he gulped. 'Oh gawd!'

'You look a caution in them socks,' another boy said.

' 'Is feet don't half pong though,' yet another suggested winking at Harry.

Harry left the wall and knelt at his friend's feet to sniff his socks. The smell was apparently so overpowering it caused him to fall backwards in a faint, which was rapturously applauded by the company, and from which he recovered immediately. 'My life Dickie!' he said. 'You got some prime Cheddar in there. 'E ain't washed them feet in weeks.'

'Shame! Scandal!' the others called, enraptured by the shock and horror of such a discovery. ' 'Ow unhygienic, Dickie Chanter! 'E oughter wash 'is feet! Dirty boy!'

'Stow it!' Dickie said. '*My* plates don't smell. You won't find a sweeter pair of feet this side of London Bridge, I'm telling you.' This provoked screams of laughter, and total disbelief.

Harry sat on the pavement, holding his friend firmly by the ankles. 'We can't let this go on, Dickie,' he said. 'If he don't wash 'em, what say we do it for him?'

The others agreed. 'Yes! That's it! Be an act of charity, that would,' they said, and it was clear from their expressions that although this was going to be a harrowing experience for all of them, they were prepared to make even extreme sacrifices for the good of their friend. Dickie didn't share their opinion but that didn't make a scrap of difference. Four of his friends seized him by the limbs and, whooping and cheering, they manhandled him down the High Street towards the nearest wash. Alberto followed happily, clutching the boots.

A hundred yards farther on, the High Street was joined by two lesser streets, a narrow lane from the west and another from the east that was important enough to be considered a roadway. At their junction they widened into a fair-sized square, or to be more accurate, a sizeable triangle. Here buses waited for custom, people met to talk or do business, and in the centre of the bustle was a drinking fountain kindly donated to the people of Tooting by the London Temperance Society. It was an imposing structure made of pink and grey stone with a fine brass tap above a stone scallop shell, on each of its four sides, and surmounted by a statue of a plump winged boy riding a dolphin. The hapless Dickie was spread-eagled like a ritual sacrifice at the foot of the fountain and denuded of his socks. This caused screams of outrage from every member of the party; from Dickie because he would have preferred them to remain on his feet, and from everybody else because of the supposed effluvia that rose from the uncovered extremities.

'Oh dear me!' Harry rebuked his friend. 'It's worse than the sewers!'

The struggle was prolonged and noisy and much enjoyed by all the participants, although it provoked considerable adverse comment from several elderly passers-by and one wealthy lady in a pony chaise removed herself from the scene at speed, immediately it began. They soon collected an admiring crowd of street arabs and excited mongrels, who pressed as close to the action as they could get, and barked and jumped and squealed with the most satisfactory sense that they were assisting. The elderly and more respectable gentlemen of the town stood on all three surrounding pavements and enjoyed the rumpus from a distance. Finally Dickie's feet had been soused in sufficient water to satisfy even the most hysterical of the mongrels who had become soaked and dishevelled in the process. The company began the drift back toward the Castle, still laughing. Dickie sat by the fountain, wringing out his socks and shaking the water from his hair like a dog on a river bank.

'Nice way to treat a friend!' he said affectionately to Harry Jones, who was almost as wet as he was. 'Where's me boots?'

'I got them,' Alberto said, handing them over. He too was very wet. Water drops lay like crystal beads among the hairs of his moustache, and his face glowed with exertion and happiness.

'Well, ta!' Dickie said, smiling broadly at him. 'That's very civil of you. Come and have a drink.'

Alberto followed his two new friends into the Castle and

was treated to a beer. They exchanged names and Dickie said Alberto's was a name and half and Harry, pushing his fingers into his matted hair said he'd never remember it in a thousand years.

'Yes you will,' Dickie said. 'Ploochy. There you are! I've remembered it.'

'Gaw dearie me!' Harry said. 'Ploochy! Where d'yer get a name like that?'

'In Italy,' Alberto said, but he wasn't paying attention to the conversation any more because he'd suddenly noticed Harry's boots. They were caked with dried earth and mud, and were so exactly like the boots he'd worn himself in Pontedecimo that for a fleeting moment he felt quite homesick. Fortunately a negative emotion like nostalgia couldn't survive long in such animated company. Nobody in the bar, except the landlord, was any older than twenty-five, and even the landlord had long since succumbed to the volatile pace of his young clientele. Now he was trying to get them all back to work on time.

'Come on, young Harry!' he said. 'All the others 'ave gone. You'd better buck your ideas up.'

' 'Nother five minutes yet,' Harry said.

'You'll 'ave Mr Pennyman after you, if you don't look sharp,' the landlord persisted.

'You work on farm?' Alberto asked, excited that, quite by chance, he'd found the farmer he was looking for.

'Can't yer tell?' Dickie said. 'Looks a proper yokel our Harry does. Straw in his ears and everything!'

'Least I've got a job-a-work,' Harry said, grinning at his friend. 'Not an idle obble-de-hoy, like someone I know.'

'Obble-de-hoy, maybe,' Dickie agreed. 'Idle, never!'

'What work you do?' Alberto asked.

'Brickie, in' I?' Dickie said. 'When I can get work. Only most of us is laid off. Times are bad. Most of the building round 'ere stopped dead last autumn.'

The news made Alberto feel uncomfortable. If this young man was out of work he surely couldn't afford to buy beer for a stranger. Dickie caught his look and understood it as quickly as Pietro would have done.

'Good job I got a second string to me bow, eh?' he said, and when he saw Alberto didn't understand, he went on,

'Got a second job in here playing the pianner. 'E don't reckon ter pay me nothink, spite a' me brilliant virtuosity, do yer Toby? But we get freeman's now and then, free drink, you understand. No pay.'

How quickly he can put things right, Alberto thought. Just like Pietro, and with the same quick gesture, the same trick of turning his head to one side to listen or provoke agreement. 'You play good,' he said, trying to show his appreciation.

'Hear that, Toby?' Dickie said. 'I play good. You oughter take me on full time. I keep tellin' yer. People 'ud come fer miles to hear me play. Just think of the trade you could pull in. You'd be doing yourself a real favour.'

'How do I know they'd come fer miles?' the landlord asked, half grumbling, half entertained. 'You might put 'em all off. Then what?'

'Ask him,' Dickie said, turning to Alberto. 'You'd come to hear me play. Wouldn't you?'

'Yes,' Alberto said. 'I come to hear you. You play good.'

'It's no good asking him,' the landlord said. 'He's foreign.'

'Oh dearie me,' Dickie said with humour and impatience. 'What a load of old guff and gubbins you do talk sometimes. Course he's foreign! Half the population of London's foreign. That's the whole point. You ain't runnin' an English pub no more. Can't yer see? London's changing. Tooting's changing. You gotta move with the times, ain't yer? You have entertainment in pubs now. That's what draws crowds. Music and singing.'

' 'E's too quick for me,' the landlord said. 'I can't foller 'im, half the time.'

'Well, I'm off,' Harry said, pushing his empty glass aside. 'Old Toby's right about me, at any rate. I shall get the sack if I don't get back to old Pennyman. See you tonight, Dickie. Ta-ta, Ploochy,' he said to Alberto. 'Nice ter meetcha,' and he ambled out of the pub.

Dickie finished his beer too. 'You come to live 'ere, 'ave yer?' he asked Alberto.

'No,' Alberto said. 'Is a day's holiday. I no work today.'

'What d'yer do?' Dickie asked.

Alberto told him, adding, because he'd known it since he first arrived, and it had just occurred to him again. 'I not stay there for ever. I work Clapham little time. Then I find other place.'

'You wanna come here,' Dickie suggested. 'It's a nice town. Plenty going on. Definitely on the up!'

'I like live here,' Alberto said. 'Is good.'

'Drink up,' Dickie said, 'and I'll show you round. There ain't no bricks want laying today, funny enough. I'll show you some I laid last year.' He gave Alberto his wide smile, and Alberto drank up happily, and took up his hat ready to leave. As they went through the pub door he said goodbye to the landlord, 'Good day, Mr Toby,' and was puzzled by the roar of laughter he caused.

' 'Is name ain't Toby really,' Dickie explained, when he'd finished enjoying the joke. 'We only call 'im that cause 'e looks like a Toby Jug.'

'What is?' Alberto asked, pleased that he'd made Dickie laugh, however inadvertently he'd done it.

'Well, there ain't one in the Castle,' Dickie said, or I'd show yer. You have to go to a Charrington's house to see a Toby Jug. It's a little jug made like a little old man with a 'orrible squashed-up face. Like this. See?' and he squashed his own face between his hands as though it were made of India rubber, spreading his nose and lips into a distorted grimace. Alberto saw at once what he meant. He was playing Pietro's game. He decided to go on playing it, just to see what would happen.

'The lady by the fountain,' he tried, 'she look like . . .' but he didn't know the English word for *pappagallo*. 'Big bird, green, big nose!' He demonstrated by drawing a parrot's beak in front of his own nose and squawking,

'Don't she just, though!' Dickie said, delighted, and roared with laughter again. 'A parrot! Oh, that's rich!' Alberto liked him more and more every minute.

The triangular square was quiet now in the new spring sunshine. It was the lunch hour and even the horses were feeding, noses buried deep in dusty nose bags, and oblivious to the pigeons that cooed and strutted between their hooves looking for titbits. Most of the mongrels were pretending it was high summer and were lying in the newly acquired shadow of the drinking fountain as though they were overcome by heat. Only two of their company were still on their feet, and they were very busy, concentrating hard on the endeavours of a quartet of sparrows who were noisily picking over a pile of horse dung.

The lady by the fountain had crossed the square and was now stomping along the pavement to their right, passing a building that despite its age, or perhaps because of it, was obviously important. It was built of rough stone in the shape of a church, with one aisle chopped away. The tall triangular gable-ends between the grey tiled roofs were smothered in a forest of ivy, where birds rustled and chirruped and quarrelled as loudly as any congregation. Even the chimney was important. Its solid grey stone pile was topped by a decorated crown, as if to imply that the building could have been a castle had it wished.

'That's the Vestry,' Dickie explained, 'where they rule the world.'

Alberto could well believe it.

'Your parrot lady's old Ma Perkins.' Dickie went on. 'She's going to get it all ready for the meeting tonight. Come on!'

They set off together down the narrow lane that ran in a south-westerly direction out of the square, between the walled and wooded grounds of a very large house, which Dickie said belonged to the local brewer, and the high windowed power of a new Board school, all disciplined red brick and rectitude. 'Me an' Harry went there,' Dickie said.

'What it was like?' Alberto asked, impressed by the size of it.

'Bloomin' awful!' Dickie said.

Next door to the school was a row of sagging, weather-boarded cottages with five small dormer windows sticking haphazardly out of their broken tiles. Dickie pointed to the middle one. 'That's where we live, me an' Harry,' he said. 'That's our room. Up there. Where the little winder is.'

'What is like?' Alberto asked again, feeling the English words awkward in his mouth, and wishing he could speak freely and easily like his companion.

'Worst a' both worlds,' Dickie said cryptically, 'freezing cold in the winter, baking hot in the summer. Still, it's better than nothing. Got to say that.'

'You live there long time?' Alberto said.

'Three, four years,' Dickie said. 'Since my old woman was

took.' He saw Alberto's lack of understanding and explained with more painful clarity, 'My old mum died of the pneumonia. Harry's mum and dad took me in. Said I could live with them. Good old pair, Mr and Mrs Jones. Tooting people. Been here generations, working on the Pennyman estates. You'll like them, Ploochy.'

For a moment Alberto thought he was going to be taken into the cottage and introduced to Harry's parents, but they continued their walk instead, past a row of plain, three-storeyed houses, almost as overgrown with ivy as the Vestry. 'Doctor lives in the end one,' Dickie said. 'That's 'andy!' The lane curved ahead of them, and they followed it into the shadow of trees. To their left several of the fields had been partially given over to house building. Half a street was already up and occupied. In other places foundations had been laid, walls begun and materials gathered, and then work had stopped.

'I built some a' that,' Dickie said, stopping to look over a fence at a series of half-finished walls. 'It ain't much to look at, and that's a fact.'

'No,' Alberto agreed. 'When you finish it?'

'When trade picks up, I expect,' Dickie said. 'Hope it's soon. It's no fun kicking yer heels all day, I can tell yer. Nor owing money neither. Old man Jones never says nothink, mind. 'E don't push. It's bad though.' He shrugged the unpleasant thought away. 'Come on,' he said. 'I'll take you down Love Lane. There's some finished houses down there. Very a la! Detached. You'll like them.'

From where they stood their narrow lane ran straight down a slight decline towards an apple orchard and the distant roofs of a large house, where it humped across the hidden chasm of a railway cutting. As they walked they could hear a train chuffing and rattling somewhere out of sight, and presently the tell-tale puff balls of white smoke rose first on one side of the bridge and then on the other and were quickly lost among billows of white cloud. They passed a side street full of decaying cottages that were shrouded and crowded by a thicket of dark trees, yews and hollies and poplars. Smoke from their tottering chimneys trailed grey-white against the mass of dark green foilage. It looked forbidding. 'That's the Grove,' Dickie said. 'Big fever hospital down there. Behind all them trees. Smallpox and scarlet fever. Things like that. Good job they've hid it, eh?' He gave Alberto a shuddering grimace and looked downhill at the orchard and the bridge to change the subject.

It was a very large orchard and very well kept, extending for some distance down the north side of a wide earth road that ran left out of their narrow lane just before it crossed the bridge. On the south side of the road and just below the level of the bridge stood an old-fashioned plain house in an old-fashioned formal garden, with a waterfall, an arbour and a pattern of herb beds set out in geometrical shapes. Beyond the herb beds the narrow strip of land between the road and the railway cutting had been staked out into sizeable building plots. Before the railway had cut its huge swathe through the middle of it, the field had been bordered by hawthorn and elder and may. Some of the trees still stood, but a lot more had been uprooted to make way for the builders. It looked a busy site, Alberto thought, as though the work gangs had just left and would be back to start again within the hour. The wood of the huts had hardly begun to weather and the ruts in the road looked new, as though carts had been driven into the site no more than a day or two ago.

'They work here now?' he asked.

'I reckon they will soon,' Dickie said. 'Now the weather's picked up. Chippies was in yesterday. Shouldn't be long. After all, they're good houses these, though I says it who shouldn't. Stand a hundred years they will, you mark my words. Built for the nobs, see. Quality'll live 'ere, carriage folk, gentry almost. Be "yes sir, no sir" up 'ere. Skivvies to wait on 'em hand and foot. Cooks to feed 'em. Trains up the end a' the road to take 'em off wherever they want. What a life, eh, Ploochy?'

'One day,' Alberto said seriously, 'I will be rich man. Just like that.'

'Me an' all,' Dickie agreed. 'Be a bit of all right that would.' He gazed longingly at the wealthy width of Love Lane, where the dust was smooth and tidy, and even the horse dung lay in neat brown cannon-balls, entire and undisturbed. A peaceful place. 'Some lucky geezer's just bought our fourth one,' he said. 'Lawyer or somethink, so they say. Come and see.'

They walked down the dust of Love Lane, between gnarled may and ancient elderberry, beside nettles and brambles, cow parsley and coltsfoot, while sparrows quarrelled in the hedges and skylarks sang above the fields beyond the railway. It felt and smelt like the depth of the country. At the end of the orchard they came upon four new houses, square, solid and double-fronted, their new tiles blue in the spring sun, their gardens spreading behind them like parks. Dickie saw at once how impressed Alberto was, but he asked his unnecessary question anyway, just for the pleasure of hearing the answer.

'Grand, ain't they?' he said.

'They the best houses I see in London,' Alberto said, beaming first on the brickwork and then on the brickie. It wasn't flattery. He meant every word. They were everything fine houses ought to be, imposing, graceful, ornate, impressive, beautiful. And the second one was the best of the lot. He stood in front of it, his mouth working with speechless admiration. It was a dazzling house. Unlike the others, its upper storey had been faced with white stucco, so that it shone as surprising as a chalk cliff among the yellow brick and brown trees that surrounded it. The slick grey tiles on the high roof gleamed under rolling cloud, and the clean glass of its wide white windows caught the colour of the sky in their black depths and glowed like sapphires. The ground floor was dominated by two wide bay windows and a fine carved porch, gabled like the prow of the *Belinda May*. Within its shelter the stained glass of an imposing front door dropped pools of coloured light onto the white step, amethyst, topaz, emerald and ruby red. It was a jewel of a house.

'That's a beauty, that one,' Dickie said, admiring his handiwork. 'They've got a marble fireplace in the drawing room, just think a' that. And the ceiling's a sight for sore eyes.'

'When I live in Tooting,' Alberto promised, 'I buy this house.'

'You won't 'alf 'ave a job,' Dickie said. 'Cost the earth, a place like this.'

'I work,' Alberto said. 'I earn.'

'Stone me!' Dickie said, almost to himself. 'I think 'e means it.'

A blue and green gig clopped towards them along the lane, bearing two fashionable young ladies, well fed and well corseted. 'Better walk on,' Dickie warned. 'That's the young Miss Plunkett. She won't like us gawping at her house. She can be a rare old Tartar when she likes.'

They walked on up the lane, pretending to be deep in conversation. But the house hadn't finished with them yet. As they passed the side gate, a delicious smell of fried steak and onions wafted out upon them. It made them both aware of how hungry they were, far too hungry to be able to hide the fact even from one another.

'Is shop to buy food in Tooting?' Alberto asked.

'Good pie and mash in Mitcham Road,' Dickie said, but even as he spoke he began to look worried.

Alberto spoke quickly before he could embarrass his new friend any further. 'I buy food for us, yes?' he said. 'You buy beer. Now I buy food.'

Dickie grinned. 'Fair exchange!' he said.

'Fair exchange,' Alberto grinned.

They took a short cut over a stile and along a footpath that cut through what was left of the fields between Love Lane and Mitcham Road. Now, had they wished, they could have explored all ten of the building sites they'd glimpsed on their way downhill. But neither of them had eyes for bricks and mortar. Their minds were intent on food.

The pie and mash was hot, cheap and filling and they both enjoyed it very much for all three reasons.

'Ta very much, Ploochy,' Dickie said as he finished his last mouthful. 'Glad I met yer.'

'I am glad, too,' Alberto said, beaming across the table at his new friend. Dickie Chanter, he decided, was very much like Pietro, dark and impish, with the same sleek hair, the same black moustaches, the same crooked white teeth, even the same sort of grin, as though he enjoyed life in the same sort of way, mocking its follies, aware of its pleasures and temptations. What luck to have met him like this! It was as good as being back with the Chiapponcellis.

'Let's go down and see if we can cadge another drink out a Toby,' Dickie said. So off they went, and soon they'd completed a round tour and were approaching the triangular square again.

Alberto had been so absorbed all through the day digesting one new experience after another that he hadn't had time to analyse what it was about this town that attracted him so much. Now, approaching the square with Dickie pointing out landmarks again, he knew what it was.

'There's the Manor,' Dickie said, 'and old man Gulliver's shop, with the saddles and harness outside, and the new Bank. D'you recognize where you are?'

'Yes,' Alberto said. He was in the centre of a town where the rich lived next door to the poor, where posh rubbed shoulders with impossible, where the new was built boldly alongside the sagging and elderly, and it was all acceptable. Clapham, he now realized, was two towns that didn't mix, the rich expanding in their splendid Crescent, and their great houses overlooking the common, and the poor huddled in the dirty alleys of the Old Town. And that was what he didn't like about Clapham. This place was different. 'We are in the square,' he said.

'It's called the Broadway,' Dickie said. 'Tooting Broadway, because it's broad, see, wide.'

The Broadway, Alberto thought. Like everything else about the town it was appropriate but jokey. There was such an atmosphere of irreverence in the place, a cockiness, a sense of daring and bravado. The poor hadn't been put in their place, once and for all. Here they could hope to move out of their hovels and inhabit the better world that was being built all around them. There was an unmistakable feeling in this bustling cosmopolitan little town that if you worked hard you could and would get on.

It was very late by the time Alberto got back to Prescott Terrace and by then he was bristling with the news of his discovery.

'I find a place called Tooting,' he said to Mrs Molloy, flinging his arms wide to emphasize the importance of the event.

'Fancy!' Molly said, and she made the word sound like an acid rebuke. 'There's this chump chop been on and off the stove for over an hour. I should think it's done to a cinder be now. There won't be a mouthful of nourishment in it. Not a mouthful. Well you can't blame me. I warned yer the very first day not to be late for your meals, so I did.'

She was very annoyed, banging about the kitchen with displeasure, and too cross even to look at him. She banged his dinner down in front of him with such force that the chop nearly jumped off the plate. 'Don't blame me for the state of it!' she said. He ate it like a penance, and gave up trying to tell her anything.

Solly wasn't interested either.

'I had good day, yesterday,' Alberto said, by way of introduction the next morning.

'More than I did,' Solly growled. 'Get that stuff shifted. We ain't got time for chitchat.'

The deal hadn't gone well, Alberto thought. He got on with his work quietly, swallowing his excitement for the second time in twenty-four hours. But the vision of that house and the voices of his new friends filled his mind to the exclusion of everything else. Solly lost patience with him several times that day because he was so slow. 'Buck up, boy,' he said in rebuke. 'It ain't like you.' But Alberto was lost in his dream. He had found the place where he wanted to settle and seen the house where he wanted to live and he was charged with the need to share his good fortune and tell his good news.

That night, on the way home, he bought pen, ink and the best notepaper in the shop, and after he'd done full justice to Mrs Molloy's stew, and told her how splendid it was, and been given a grudging forgiveness, he retired to his grey room to compose a letter to the one person he knew would listen to him, to Granny Bianchi.

'My dearest Grandmother,' he wrote. 'I have found the place where I am going to live. It is a town called Tooting. It has everything anybody could want, modern shops, clean water, plenty of good food and some fine new houses. I have seen the one I am going to buy one day. It is a white house, and the man who built it says it will stand for ever. I am working hard, and now I will work even harder. You are always in my prayers. Give my loving greetings to all the family and especially Pina and little Maria. When I have bought the house, I will send you the fare and you will come to England, and live here with me and I will look after you.'

He addressed the envelope with the feeling of exquisite happiness, an overpowering sense of fulfilled ambition, and went to bed, too excited to sleep. From time to time during that restless night, he propped himself up on one elbow to look at the white ghost of his letter balanced against the clock on the mantelpiece. How pleased she would be to get his news! Dear Granny Bianchi!

Chapter 7

Six days later the letters arrived, two of them, thudding onto Mrs Molloy's doormat just as she and Alberto were settling down to savour their bacon and mushrooms. 'That'll be me sister, I shouldn't wonder,' Molly said, shuffling off to collect them, but they were both for Alberto. One was from Clerkenwell, addressed in Camillo's untidy scrawl, the other was postmarked Genova.

For the first and only time in his life Alberto decided to defer pleasure and deal with difficulties first. Feeling rather smug, he put the Italian letter beside his plate and opened Camillo's grubby missive. Predictably, his cousin was in debt again, Mrs Dobbs was harassing him for back rent and he seemed to have run out of ready cash. Could Alberto help him? Just this once. Alberto grinned ruefully at his cousin's protestations, accepting that he would probably help the wretch, even though he didn't deserve it. Then he turned his attention happily to news from home, warmed by the thought of Granny Bianchi and his two sisters even before he slit the envelope roughly with his thumb.

The letter knocked an empty hole through the centre of his body and stopped all feeling for the rest of the day. It was from his father and informed him, brusquely, that Granny Bianchi was dead. She'd taken a fever during the winter, because the weather had been far too cold for far too long, and though she'd put up a good fight, all things considered, she simply couldn't hold on till the spring.

Details about the funeral swam away from Alberto's vision, too trivial to be comprehended. His body yearned and ached around the void at its centre.

'Is it bad news, Mr Ploochy dear?' Molly asked, concerned by his stricken expression.

'My grandmother is dead,' he said, and then the tears rolled into his eyes and filled his throat, and he had to bolt from the kitchen for fear of disgracing himself before his landlady. His tears were hot and hard and brought no comfort. Why did she have to die? Just when everything was going so well, when he'd found the place where he was going to live, when he was making plans to send her the fare? What was the point of making plans when they could be changed so quickly? The grey room closed in upon him like a tomb. He had to get out into the air.

But out in the air the sense of pointlessness was more terrible than ever. He was alone in a city full of uncaring foreigners. He didn't even belong here. Nobody knew how he felt, and even worse, nobody cared. He walked stiffly to Solly's shop, like an automaton. For most of the day he really didn't notice what was happening either to him or around him. Solly did though. 'What's got into the boy?' he asked his wife, watching as Alberto blundered through the shop, clumsy and stony faced.

Leah narrowed her shrewd pale eyes and watched too. 'That,' she said eventually, 'is a boy wid grief. That boy is eating sorrow. Don't I know that look!'

''E ain't hisself, and that's for certain,' Solly agreed. 'We ought to send him home, maybe?'

'Home for him,' Leah said 'is Italy yet. Leave him be, Solly my dear. Grief takes time. When the time come, then we help him. Now it ain't.'

So they left Alberto empty, clumsy and alone, and waited for the moment. It came at the end of the third day, when the sorrow that, so far, had only numbed him, suddenly overwhelmed him in tears he couldn't control. Solly, pulling his beard with distress, made unaccustomed speed upstairs to fetch Leah. Alberto, engulfed in grief, didn't see him go, so he was startled to feel an arm being laid gently around his shoulders, and to hear a voice soothing him in a completely foreign language. Leah, was it? Astringent, bitter Leah speaking such compassion and gentleness in her strange language. Still weeping, he followed her up the back stairs to her spicy kitchen, where she sat him in Solly's dishevelled chair and gave him a large piece of sheeting to cry into. Then she set about making tea, from time to time patting his bowed head gently as she passed beside him. By the time the tea had been brewed, and served in a glass with a slice of lemon, and placed gently in his hands as though he were a baby or an invalid, his tears were beginning to dry, and he had collected himself sufficiently to feel that he ought to apologize.

'Tch!' Leah brushed his apology away before it could begin. 'A death you say sorry! What next?'

'My grandmother,' Alberto said and wept again.

'Of course,' Leah said, sipping her tea. 'In Italy.'

'A good woman,' Alberto said, when he could.

'Of course,' Leah said again. 'To be so loved. This you expect. A good woman, of course.'

'I can't bear it,' Alberto said.

'For a month,' Leah explained, 'maybe more, you will feel this. You will cry. To cry is good. You eat your sorrow, it eat you, I know. After a month, maybe a little better. After a year, you bear it. Five years, you grow a scar. Still there, sometimes pain, sometimes just there, almost you don't notice. I know. Who better?' There was sadness and bitterness in her voice, but her face and her hands were still gentle. In her own way, as Alberto recognized with his tender senses, she was comforting him.

He drank his tea slowly, savouring it even though the unfamiliar taste dried his tongue. 'You too?' he said to Leah.

'Oh yes,' Leah said sighing, 'many, many years ago. In Polish revolt in Warsaw. Eight years old I was. Ai, how I remember. Sixty-three. In Warsaw. Terrible it was. Your grandmother, she die of old age? Illness? Eh?'

'Both,' Alberto said, listening intently, because the expression in Leah's pale eyes was so compelling.

'Old age, illness,' Leah said, 'the will of God. God you can forgive. In time. Men is different. Men don't take natural like God. Men kill. Men you don't forgive. Never in a thousand years.' She stopped speaking. Her face was very still, remembering, her eyes looking back into her past. Alberto waited for her to go on, watching her tight pale mouth for the words that were gathering.

'My whole family they kill,' she said calmly. 'My father they cut down. Such gashes! Such gashes! You never would believe the blood. Everywhere. I sit under the table, all in among the trousers and the sleeves and I watch. Everything. He was tailor, you see, my father. A very gentle man. Never raise his voice to no one. Just sitting, stitching, all day, all night stitching. They cut him down, he still had the thread in his hand. And my mother she fight them. Like wild, she fight. So her they cut, too. All in her long hair. Fighting. I hide in the cloth under the table. A rabbit, afraid to move, afraid to breathe and the blood rolls into the cloth. That you don't forgive! Never in a thousand years! The next day, home they bring my brother and my sister, clubbed to death, both, and I come out from under the table and my uncle Moishe he say, "On to the cart quick, for the love of God." I get on the cart, in the darkness. Nothing I have. No mother, no father, no brother, no sister. Just my uncle Moishe, and he ain't no uncle, just a good man. Running from the killers. We go to Paris, travel at night, hide by day, me and Uncle Moishe and four rolls of cloth, and all the neighbours they ain't kill.'

In the face of such a story, Alberto's grief acquired a new proportion. Now it was his turn to offer comfort. 'I so sorry for . . .' he said, awkwardly.

'No need,' Leah said, still calm. 'It a long time ago. Man is born to sorrow. It will always be so, eh? You grieve, little Alberto. Grief will heal you. You see.'

'Why did they do it?' Alberto said.

Leah raised her eyebrows at his naivety. 'We were Jews,' she said.

It's no reason, Alberto thought, not for cruelty like that. Here he was, raging against a natural death, and she could accept a massacre as though it was to be expected. It's all wrong, he thought. It shouldn't be. But he hadn't sufficient words to tell her how he felt, and anyway her expression had brought the conversation to a halt. He turned their attention to more mundane matters. 'I been working at the Windmill,' he said. 'In the evening. Behind the bar.'

'Have you?' Leah said, narrowing her eyes. 'Why?'

Alberto explained about the house and how he wanted to rent a shop of his own in Tooting, and how he was trying to save money. A week ago it had all seemed desirable and possible. Now . . .

'Good,' Leah said briskly. 'Good to work. You work. Work cure the pain. You see. Little bit by little bit.'

So Alberto worked and saved, as though there were something to work for. And Leah comforted him in her own strange way. And the first bad days passed slowly by. And it was Sunday again. At first he wasn't sure whether it was still a good idea to go to Tooting and meet his new friends as they'd arranged. He thought about it as he walked across the common early on Sunday morning. He'd be such bad company. Perhaps he shouldn't burden them with his misery like this. The trouble was, he couldn't think of anything else to do instead. His mind seemed quite incapable of coping with new ideas or making new plans. Anyway the bus was waiting. So he went.

Afterwards he realized that it was the best thing he could have done. Harry and Dickie were waiting for him at the Broadway, both in their Sunday best and both grinning happily. Harry was wearing a clean shirt and a spotless muffler, and his springy fair hair was almost neatly combed. Dickie was bristling with good humour, his dark curls standing up around his face, his crooked teeth much in evidence. He dragged Alberto off the bus.

'Whatcher think, Ploochy,' he said, 'I got took on. Been working since Wednesday. How's that fer luck?'

'We got a picnic,' Harry said, turning his shoulders so that Alberto could see the haversack he was carrying. 'We're going up the Watermeads. 'E reckons we oughter celebrate.'

'What you build?' Alberto asked, swept along by Dickie's delight.

'I'll show yer,' Dickie promised. 'It's down Amen Corner. We're going past it. Come on.' And the three of them set off towards Mitcham.

Despite Alberto's misgivings, it was a happy day.

The Wandle at the Watermeads was a shallow gravel bedded stream bordered by ancient willows and a thick fringe of rushes. It was the ideal spot for a picnic.

'Is good here,' Alberto said an hour or so later. He lay propped against a tree, his hat tipped over his eyes because the sun was so strong it was dazzling him. He was replete and almost contented. 'Next time,' he said 'I buy a ham from The Store. How you like that?'

'That'ud be 'andsome,' Dickie said.

Harry grunted. The flies buzzed about their bread and jam. The river licked the reeds. Two coots plopped their white heads into the blue water. The unexpected peace and friendliness of it all was beginning to effect a cure.

'I'm dry,' Dickie said presently. 'I got cobwebs in me froat. We got any a' that ginger beer left?'

'In the river,' Harry said, waving a lazy hand to where the two stone bottles were cooling among the reeds.

'Get 'em for me, will yer?' Dickie said.

'What disease your last servant die of?' Harry said. 'Get it yourself.'

'No, you,' Dickie persuaded. 'You're nearest. Go on Harry. I'm dying a' thirst.'

'You're a bloomin' nuisance,' Harry complained pleasantly. He was too relaxed to make the effort to stand up and walk the two paces to the river. Instead, he simply rolled down the bank. It was a mistake. Although he didn't know it, the food they'd discarded lay between him and the reeds, so by the time he reached the river he'd squashed the remains of the meat pie into his left trouser leg. 'Oh gawd, Dickie,' he groaned, kneeling among the reeds. 'Look at that!'

Dickie was instantly wide awake and chirruping with delight. 'You mucky pup!' he said. 'You been rolling in the pie.'

'That's nice,' Harry said, picking bits of pastry off his thigh, 'I done it for your bloomin' ginger pop.'

'Your old woman'll kill you,' Dickie said happily. 'Look at the state a' them bumbags!'

'Rub it wid grass,' Alberto said, gathering a handful. But that only made matters worse, spreading grease and gravy further and deeper into the cloth.

'You won't 'alf get what for,' Dickie gloated.

'I'll 'ave ter wash 'em,' Harry said, casting his handful of greasy grass into the river. 'You're dead right. The old girl'll go crackers if I go home like this.' He peeled off his jacket and dropped his braces.

'You'll get run in, you go on like that,' Dickie warned.

'Who's ter see?' Harry said. 'I can 'ave it done in a jiffy.' He was unlacing his boots. Dickie and Alberto were delighted. Things were getting better and better. Despite their shrieks of enraptured protest Harry stepped out of his trousers and knelt at the water's edge to start his laundry.

' 'E's got no shame!' Dickie said to Alberto.

'Next time,' Alberto said, 'we bring a screen.'

'Or a nappie,' Dickie agreed. 'Gaw, will yer jest look at that bum!'

' 'Orrible!' Alberto said.

The bridge behind them creaked under an approaching foot. Alberto and Dickie turned as one. 'We got company,' Alberto said grinning from ear to ear. What timing! It was too good to be true. The most delectable company was giggling its way across the bridge in the shape of two plumply pretty girls.

'What a lark!' Dickie said. 'We'll 'ave to 'ead 'em off.'

'What?' Harry said, finally aware that something was going on.

'Get in the river quick,' Dickie hissed. 'There's women on the bridge.'

Harry jumped into the reeds like a flea into a fleece. One second the white moon of his backside was bold at the water's edge, the next it was decently under the water. 'Get rid of 'em quick!' he said, his pale face peering anxiously through the bars of the reeds. 'It's like ice in 'ere!'

Dickie and Alberto thoroughly enjoyed their encounter on the bridge. It was spring, the girls were pretty and Harry was half naked and freezing. What situation could have been better? Dickie's imagination soared in an inspired flight of fancy. 'Mad swan,' he explained to the two deliciously wide-eyed faces in front of him. 'Warden left us 'ere to warn the public.'

'Just fancy, Mildred,' the bolder of the two girls said. 'I never seen no swan 'ere before. 'Ave you?'

'We guard,' Alberto explained. 'Because of the bite.'

'Last girl 'e bit turned septic,' Dickie said, aware of the scowling face in the reeds.

'Fancy that!' Mildred said. 'Good job you was around today then. I wouldn't like to be bit, would you Ethel?'

'No fear,' Ethel said, making eyes at Alberto. 'Least, not by a swan.'

'It's the mating season,' Dickie explained rather unnecessarily, 'sends 'im frantic.'

' 'E get worse,' Alberto said as the swan made growling noises in the reeds, 'we lock 'im up.'

'Couldn't yer get a mate for 'im?' Ethel said, greatly daring.

'Oh 'e's much too fierce fer that,' Dickie said.

' 'E's 'issing,' Mildred said, craning to get a better look.

The conversation proceeded most agreeably while the discomfited swan shivered and shifted in the chilly water. Finally the girls decided that they ought to be going. Ethel took a last look at the white mass behind the reeds. 'I'll say this for your swan,' she said, ' 'E's got a big bum.' And she and Mildred went giggling back the way they'd come.

Dickie and Alberto couldn't contain themselves a second longer. They fell about with laughter and were soon weeping and choking and beating one another on the back. Even the goose-pimpled Harry began to giggle, once he'd been dried on the tail of his shirt and bundled into his clothes again. They laughed all the way to the Fair Green, where they got another attack of the giggles and had to lean against the Nag's Head sign to recover. And even inside the Nag's Head itself, with beer frothing before them, they did more cackling than drinking. It wasn't until they were on the top of the bus and rattling back to Tooting that they finally simmered down and the conversations took a serious turn.

'We've 'ad a laugh today,' Harry said, 'and no mistake.'

'Done yer good, ain't it, Ploochy,' Dickie said. 'You was a bit down this morning.'

'Yes,' Alberto said, remembering. 'I had a letter from home. Italy. Bad news.'

'Thought as much,' Dickie said 'Very bad, was it?'

'My grandmother is dead,' Alberto said, wishing he knew enough words to wrap it up a bit. It sounded so blunt blurted out like that. Harry and Dickie were embarrassed.

'Bad,' Dickie said, looking at his boots and Harry mumbled into the fist he'd put in front of his mouth to hide his feelings. The sight of their faces made Alberto wish they'd never brought the subject up. He changed direction at once. 'I had another letter,' he said. 'Same post. From my cousin Camillo. The one I tell you. In Clerkenwell. He want I should pay 'is rent for 'im.'

'Ain't 'e got a job?' Dickie asked, cheering and practical again.

' 'E no work,' Alberto said. ' 'E too lazy. 'E stay in bed.'

'Let 'im get on with it then,' Dickie said. ' 'E's a dead liability, you ask me.'

' 'E's 'is cousin, Dickie,' Harry pointed out. 'Family. Makes a difference, that does. Being family.'

'You take my advice, Ploochy,' Dickie said. 'Don't you give 'im a brass farthing. 'E's taking you fer a ride.'

' 'Ark who's talking,' Harry laughed. ' 'E'd give the shirt off 'is back if it was 'is cousin. 'E don't mean a word.'

'What you think?' Alberto asked. 'You think I send the money?'

'You got ter do what's right, ain't yer,' Harry said.

So Alberto made up his mind.

The next morning on his way to work he called in at the Post Office and bought a money order to send to Camillo. And that was how he came to have such a very good view of the two soldiers.

They were standing in front of Solly's shop window, peering into the muddled gloom. Both were young, red-faced and ill at ease. The taller of the two was talking urgently to his companion, spitting the words out and down towards the pavement. 'They never ask questions. Not that lot,' he was saying. 'He's a Jewboy. Look at the name. If he can make a quick bob and no questions asked . . . Whatcha say?'

'It's a risk,' the companion said. 'I don' say it ain't worth it, but it's a risk. You gotta admit.'

Alberto stepped quietly into the side alley and gently opened the back door into the passage. Something about this furtive conversation made him feel he ought to be as careful as he could. Solly was in his office, busy with his book-keeping, his face wrinkled with concentration, his broad fingers drumming with effort.

'Good morning,' Alberto said. 'I think we got two early customers.' The shop bell rang as he was speaking, as if to prove him right.

'Take it, will yer?' Solly said vaguely, without looking up.

The soldiers were even more ill at ease amongst the crowded muddle of the shop. The blond pulled nervously at his jacket and gave a little deprecating cough before he spoke.

'You buy things, dontcha?' he said.

'Sometimes,' Alberto said, 'Sometimes we buy, sometimes we pawn.'

'Well,' the soldier said, 'I got a few things here to sell. I want a good price, mind. It ain't rubbish.' He took a small cloth bag from the pocket of his jacket and emptied its contents onto the counter. It was a collection of gold jewellery, five rings and mourning brooch set with seed pearls and neatly plaited hair. Even to Alberto's inexperienced eye they looked expensive and extremely unlikely to be legally in the possession of an ordinary private.

'Belonged to my aunt,' the soldier explained, rather too quickly. 'She left 'em to me. Sort of heirloom, you might say. Well, what'll you offer?'

Alberto picked up the pieces and examined them slowly and closely as though he were Solly at his most deliberate. 'They are very pretty,' he said. 'Not worth much money. What sort of sum did you have in mind?'

' 'Undred pounds?' the soldier said.

' 'Undred pounds?' Alberto said, feigning incredulity and rather pleased with the way he was doing it. 'For this? It not gold!'

'Not . . .' the soldier said, surprised and aggrieved. 'Course it's gold.'

'How you know?' Alberto asked, pressing his advantage.

'Because my aunt told me,' the soldier said, but his cockiness was evaporating. He was beginning to look worried, and his companion was even worse. He looked frightened.

'I told you so, Mitchell,' he said. 'She'd have locked it up somewhere if it 'ud been worth money.'

'I bet you it's gold,' Mitchell said, trying aggression again, but still not at all sure of himself.

'Well,' Alberto allowed, 'maybe I wrong. I call Mr Isaacs for you.' Which he did.

Solly shuffled out of his back parlour like an amiable brown bear and took up the rings in his vast paw. Each one was raised in turn to his professional eye-glass. After four had been examined his verdict was unequivocal. 'Nice pieces,' he said. 'Fancy-ware, a' course, gilt and paste but very good quality. French I shouldn't wonder. Give you five pounds for 'em. Throw in the little brooch and I'll make it guineas. How's that?'

'Not good enough,' Mitchell said. 'I'll take 'em somewhere else. That's gold, that is.'

Solly picked up the fifth ring and examined it slowly as though there were no argument ensuring. 'Ah!' he said, stressing the word with satisfaction. 'Now I'm telling you wrong. You got a good piece here. You're right about this one.

This is the real McCoy. Nice hallmark. Yes. And that's a real shiner. Bit on the small side, but it's a good stone. Yes. This one's worth money.'

'How much?' Mitchell asked, too eagerly.

'This little ring,' Solly said, smiling at the ring as though it had gone out of its way to please him, 'is worth more than all the rest put together. A tenner.'

'Well . . .' Mitchell said, fingering his moustache.

'Fifteen pounds, the lot.' Solly said.

'Make it guineas,' Mitchell said, satisfied to be bargaining. 'Make it guineas and you're on.'

'Done!' Solly said, looking straight at his two customers without a flicker of expression.

'Done!' said Mitchell, and done he certainly was.

Solly and Alberto stood still behind the counter until the door clicked safely behind the greedy red backs of their military customers. Then Solly rolled into action. All the jewellery except the ten pound ring was scooped into the shovel of his hand and hidden away inside his capacious jacket. The ten pound ring was slotted neatly into one of the black velvet trays in the office. 'Mind the shop,' he said to Alberto. 'If the rozzers come, I'm at Abbie Goldberg's up the road. Which I ain't.' He gave his beard a tug and was off.

The morning was disappointingly quiet after that. Solly returned quietly too, just in time for Leah's dumplings. The law didn't arrive until two days later.

Sergeant Pinner was a self-important, ignorant man who prided himself on his ability to handle foreigners. He was built like a barrel, and that plainly had led him to believe that the best way to tackle any obstacle was to roll straight through it. His method of questioning was brusque, uncompromising and very loud.

He came straight to the point without greeting or preliminary. 'You had any rings in recently?' he said to Solly.

'One or two,' Solly said blandly. 'What sort a ring was you after?'

'Never you mind!' the Sergeant said, slapping his notebook down onto the counter. 'Got 'em 'andy, 'ave yer?'

Alberto was sent for the velvet trays and the Sergeant examined the jewellery with much sucking and popping of his lips. It didn't take him long to find what he was looking for.

'Who brought this in?' he said, hooking out the ten pound ring on his little finger.

'Couldn't say,' Solly answered laconically. 'Young feller, I think.'

'D'yer remember when?'

'Coupla days ago,' Solly offered. 'Maybe a bit more. We do a good trade in rings. Raise money you see, rings.'

'Quite,' the Sergeant said. 'Got any more, 'ave yer?'

'That's the lot,' Solly said.

'What about brooches?' the Sergeant said. 'Got any a' them, 'ave yer?'

'Brooches ain't my line,' Solly said.

'Um,' the Sergeant said, and he sucked his lips in and out for a few minutes to assist his thought processes. ' 'Ave to take this along,' he said eventually.

'Hot, is it?' Solly asked.

'Nicked Friday,' the Sergeant said. 'Out the Crescent. Though I ain't supposed to tell yer, so you don't know nothink about it, understand?'

'Just my luck,' Solly said, gathering up the trays. 'Honesty don't pay, do it?'

'Might get a reward,' the Sergeant said. 'You never know.'

'I should be so lucky!' Solly said, returning to the back parlour.

'That's it then,' the Sergeant said, folding up his notebook and turning abruptly to Alberto. 'You wouldn't remember nothink about that young chap, would yer?' he asked.

Alberto had relaxed, thinking the matter was dealt with. Now, his guard down, he said the wrong thing, knowing it was wrong from the moment the words were out of his mouth. 'Not much,' he said.

'But somethink eh?' the Sergeant said, onto Alberto's ambiguity in a flash. 'Colour of hair, maybe? Height? Well what? Come on! I ain't got all day. Hair?'

'Fair,' Alberto said, bullied into it, and resenting the pressure he was under.

'What sort of clothes?' the Sergeant went on. 'Come on. Start with the 'at.'

'Well . . .' Alberto floundered.

'Wore 'at, did 'e?' the Sergeant said, rolling on, hard and heavy and determined.

'Well . . .' Alberto said again.

'Well,' the Sergeant insisted, leaning across the counter, to bully Alberto with his face.

'Uniform,' Albert said miserably.

'Now that's better,' the Sergeant said. 'What sort a uniform? Soldier, was it?'

'Yes,' Alberto had to admit. This was dangerously wrong and he knew it. Where was Solly? He couldn't cope with the pressure of this man, all on his own.

'What regiment?'

'I don't know.'

'Don't give me none of that,' the Sergeant said. 'What colour jacket?'

'Red, I think,' Alberto said.

'What is red?' Solly said, emerging from the office.

'Colour of your soldier's coat,' the Sergeant said, winking craftily. 'You know, Solly, the soldier what sold yer the ring.'

'Don't remember that,' Solly said smoothly. 'And yer don't want ter take no notice of 'im. 'E gets everything muddled up, dontcha, Ploochy? We get all sorts in here. Soldiers, skivvies, costers, road sweepers. Even policemen. Could a' been anyone. You got all you want, 'ave yer?'

'I have now,' the Sergeant said, and he rolled cheerfully out into the sunshine.

'Never tell that lot nothink!' Solly said, when the Sergeant was safely out of earshot. 'Rich men's lackeys, they are. The rich got enough already without us helping them to more. Next time, play dumb. You made a mistake there.'

'I know,' Alberto said. But he didn't realize just how serious a mistake it had been till more than a week later.

It was a very black night. Most of the stars were obscured by low rain cloud, and the moon was new and inadequate. They'd done a brisk trade in the Windmill that evening. It had taken much longer than usual to deal with last orders, wash up and clear the bars, so it was way past midnight before Alberto finally emerged from the acrid warmth of the saloon to the muddy blackness of the common. A strong wind creaked the branches of the chestnut trees, and pushed his coat tight against his shoulder blades. After such a long heated evening, the chill air made him shiver. I shall be glad to get home, he thought, peering through the darkness ahead of him. It was almost impossible to see where he was going, and he had to concentrate hard to avoid walking into the trees, so it was some time before he realized that someone was following him. His senses sprang into prickling activity at once. Now he could hear the scuffle of boots on leaves, and muffled instructions growled under the sound of the wind, but he still couldn't see a thing, and the sense of being surrounded and outflanked made fear close his throat.

The attack was sudden and ferocious. He was surrounded by pummelling fists and flailing boots. Six, seven faces, maybe more, teeth and eyes flashing like knives. He could smell horses and violet pomade and the strong male musk of arousal and rage. One of them had lit a little lantern and swung it towards his face. All instinct now, he kicked it out and made a bolt for it in the confusion that followed the smash. But they were after him at once. He was caught before he'd gone five paces. He fought frantically, twisting his body to get away from the worst of their blows, protecting his face with his arms, hitting out violently at the nearest hostile flesh, but nothing helped him, and finally they had him pinioned between them, spreadeagled for the blows he could feel, in his fear, even before they landed.

' 'E's all yours, Mitchell,' a harsh voice said, close to his ear. 'Lay into 'im all yer like.'

'That,' Private Mitchell said viciously, punching Alberto's face with abandon, 'is fer being a bloody copper's nark. And *that* is fer being a bleedin' Eyetie an' all.'

The blows thudded and grazed and tore, each one making him feel sicker than the last. Pride kept him going. He wouldn't cry or call out or even groan. He struggled and he endured, as he'd endured his father's beatings in Pontedecimo. And at last they'd had enough. The hard fists let him fall and he could hear their heavy boots thudding away across the common.

For a long time he lay where he was, panting and groaning and bleeding into the damp cold mud under his face. Then his bones began to ache and his cuts began to sting and he knew he ought to make an effort to get home. It took a long time because his bruised legs would only move slowly, and his nose was swelling up so fast he found it difficult to breathe. But at last he blundered into the kitchen at Prescott Terrace and collapsed with his head in Molly's rocking chair, where he lay half unconscious until Molly herself came down early in the morning to light the stove.

'Holy Mary Mother O' God!' she said. 'Will you look at the state you're in, Mr Ploochy dear.' But by now Alberto's eyes were so puffed up and swollen he wasn't in a fit state to look at anything.

Molly cleaned his cuts and bandaged them as well as she could with bits of lint and an assortment of odd rags. Then she propped his heavy arm across her shoulders and lugged him up the stairs to bed. The day disappeared between discomfort and sleep. It wasn't until a bright sunset stained the pale wallpaper behind his head that he finally climbed out of bed to pee. His shirt and trouser were spattered with mud and blood and his face was unrecognizable. Both eyes were sunk in swollen flesh, black and blue and mauve, and his nose was twice its normal size. He stooped painfully before his little looking glass and tried to get his mouth open so that he could see whether any of his teeth were missing. Molly found him pulling up his swollen lips and peering into the reflected wreckage of his face.

'Now don't you go a-worritting with that old looking glass Mr Ploochy dear,' she advised. 'You're bound to look bad for a day or two. It stands to reason. You'll mend quicker if you don't look. Now I've a wee spoonful of broth here. Would you be feeling up to it?'

She was itching to know what had happened to him, but to her credit she contained her curiosity until the swellings on his face had subsided, and speech was possible if not exactly comfortable. She was horrified by his story.

'Soldiers, of course!' she said. 'Never did trust the military. They're worse than the police, so they are. Great hulking brutes! What a thing to be doing to you, Mr Ploochy, dear!'

On Sunday, Dickie Chanter and Harry Jones arrived on the doorstep, self conscious but determined to visit their new friend. His postcard, 'Can't make Sunday. Been in fight.' was much too intriguing to ignore. They were deeply impressed by his bruises.

'You been in the wars, aintcha,' Dickie said with admiration, 'You got a right pair of shiners there and no mistake.'

'Shiners is diamonds,' Alberto said, finding speech and understanding equally difficult. 'What shiners I got?' How hard this English language was!

'A shiner's a black eye,' Harry explained. 'And you got two beauties. D'yer feel well enough fer a pint?'

'No he does not,' Molly said firmly. 'I got a nice little egg custard for him later.'

'Pint a porter wouldn't hurt a fly,' Harry urged, seeing Alberto's grimace. 'There's an off-licence on the corner. I could be there and back in a jiffy.'

'Well,' Molly relented. 'It might perk him up a bit. What do you think Mr Ploochy dear?'

It did perk him up, considerably, and the milk stout they bought for Molly gave her a fillip too. Soon they were all sitting round the stove joking and swapping tall stories and the visit had become almost a party. It would have been a totally enjoyable occasion if Molly hadn't suddenly remembered the letter.

'Came for you yesterday, Mr Ploochy dear,' she said. 'I've a head like a sieve so I have. Now where could I have put the dratted thing?'

If it's anything like the other two, Alberto thought, I'm glad you've lost it. He'd had enough bad news to last him a very long time. But the letter was found under the tea caddy, and handed solemnly across to him. It came from Clerkenwell and was from Mrs Dobbs. It was barely legible. The lady wrote in a large scrawling hand, the letters so badly formed that they made no sense to Alberto at all. 'What she say?' he asked Dickie handing the letter over for his friend to decipher.

'Gaw! What awful writing!' Dickie said. 'It's worse than yours, Harry and that's saying something.'

'Can you read it?' Alberto asked.

'I'll 'ave a go,' Dickie said, squinting at the scrawl. 'Not wishing to be a burden to you,' he read, 'and seeing as how you was so kind to help me the last time well not to put too fine a point on it well I ain't had no rent from your cousin Mr Cammy Bianchi not since before Christmas it was and the bum baileys is in again and I'm at me wits end and so I would be much obliged to you to settle it being your cousin.'

'Oh,' Alberto said, enraged. 'What he done with the money?

I send 'im the money like you say Harry. He no give the money to 'er.'

'Spent it, I'll bet,' Dickie said. 'Sticks out a mile. Well you can't say I didn't warn yer.'

'I don't like the sound of it at all,' Molly Molloy said, putting down her empty glass. 'If I were you, Mr Ploochy dear, I'd be off to that there Clerky-well to see fer meself, so I would. Not with your poor old face the way it is. When you're well again.'

It sounded like excellent advice to Alberto, so at the first available opportunity, he took it.

It was easy enough to find Camillo. He was with his usual set of cronies snug in a corner of the Hat and Tun, huddled over a table laden with empties. He didn't seem surprised or worried by Alberto's sudden appearance. He didn't even have the grace to look guilty.

'Hello, Berto,' he said cheerfully. 'What's brought you to Clerkenwell?'

His effrontery astounded Alberto. 'You have,' he said fiercely and if his face hadn't been so bruised and scarred he would have scowled.

The tone of his cousin's voice made Camillo look up. 'What's happened to your face, Berto?' he asked.

'Never mind about my face,' Alberto said. 'What's happened to my money?'

Now Camillo looked shifty. But only for a second. He soon recovered. 'I had other debts, more pressing, I expect,' he said. 'I'll pay the old lady one day. Don't worry about it.'

'I send you my good money,' Alberto said furiously. 'I worked hard for that money, and you've just poured it down your throat, haven't you?'

'Well, it's gone now,' Camillo said, 'so what's the point of complaining?'

The old family rage rose in Alberto. He seized his cousin by the throat and threw him against the flock wallpaper. Mr Mannheim, using his stomach like a battering ram, was between them in an instant. 'You got any little arguments gentlemen,' he said, 'you settle 'em outside, if you please. There ain't room fer fisticuffs in the 'at.'

'No argument,' Camillo said, placatingly, looking first at Mr Mannheim and then at Alberto.

'Yes,' Alberto insisted. 'Big argument. Very big. Fight.'

'Out then, the pair of you,' Mr Mannheim said, and he frog-marched the protesting Camillo straight through the crowd and out onto the pavement, with Alberto following behind them.

Just for the moment Alberto was only scolding, holding his rage in check by the force of words. 'You're a disgrace to the family,' he shouted, using all the same phrases that had been hurled at him for so long in Pontedecimo. 'A useless, idle, good-for-nothing! You stay in bed all hours. You don't work. You waste your money in drink. Well, don't think you can waste mine too. I value my money. I work hard for it.' He was shouting so loudly and speaking so fast he had to pause for breath.

'Finished, have you?' Camillo asked insolently, the old cheeky expression reappearing on his face.

'No, I have not!' Alberto roared.

'Well hurry then,' Camillo said. 'we've wasted enough drinking time as it is.'

This time there was no table in the way. The blow Alberto aimed landed fair and square on Camillo's nose, drawing blood and bringing tears to his eyes.

'Enough!' he said, jumping back out of range into the astonished arms of a passer-by. 'Stop! You've drawn blood, you fool! What are you thinking of? I'm your cousin!'

'You've wasted my money!' Alberto shouted. 'That's what I'm thinking of. I sent you money for the rent and you've drunk it and you're not even sorry. I'll kill you!' The rage had risen in him like a furnace, and nothing could stop it now. His face was dark with it, and even despite his scars he was scowling in a way that made Camillo take to his heels. He fled like a thing demented, dodging through the throng on the pavement down into Hatton Garden where the crowds were even thicker and would give him more cover. Alberto pounded after him, his temper giving him speed.

Camillo's lungs felt as though they were bursting, but he charged on, heading for the old St John's Gate. If he could just slip through those narrow arches he could hide from Alberto in the tangle of cobbled alleys on the other side. But his luck was out that day. A carter's van had got stuck in the central arch and the crowd that had gathered completely blocked the roadway and both the narrow arches on either side of it. Push as he might, he couldn't force his way through the mass of bodies. Alberto caught him easily and now he had neither the breath nor the energy left to fight. Fortunately, neither had Alberto, but rage was still strong in him and he had to express it in action of some sort. Camillo sank down on his knees beside the sooty stones of the gate and begged for mercy. But Alberto was beyond mercy. He hit Camillo for all the things he'd had to endure since he came to England, for cockroaches and chilblains, for long hours of work and the ice of winter, for the humiliation of his own terrible beating and the numbing misery of Granny Bianchi's death. He went on, punching his cousin's hands, thumping his arms, pounding his huddled back until his anger was used and spent. By then Camillo was in tears and they'd gathered a jeering crowd of their own, but he didn't care. When it was over he simply walked away, as though it was nothing to do with him at all. It was over. He'd beaten Camillo out of his system and out of his family. From now on he was on his own.

Chapter 8

'Bonus!' Solly Isaacs said to Alberto, handing over a bundle of banknotes. 'Made a good price on that jewellery. Reckon you've earned that, the pasting you took!'

'Thirty quid!' Alberto said to Dickie later that day. 'What I do with all that money?' He was still stunned by the size of his windfall.

'Put it in the London Joint Stock at Tooting Corner,' Dickie advised. 'You keep it in the 'ouse. It'll only be frittered away or nicked.'

Solly thought this was an excellent suggestion and was quick to offer practical help and advice. 'You deal with money, you gotta look money,' he said. 'Treat yerself to a good suit fer a start, new collar, new boots. I can lend you a good solid signet an' a fob. You gotta look the part.'

So suitably attired and embellished, Alberto Pelucci brought his savings to the London Joint Stock Bank and, rather to his surprise, was welcomed like royalty. Money was plainly more important than nationality.

Mr Chalmers, the bank manager, was an impressive figure in his high starched collar and neat grey cravat. To Alberto he looked like a creature from another world, he was so pink and clean and scrubbed. The baby pink skin showed clearly through the thin cap of pale ginger hair combed neatly across his skull, and his eyelashes and eyebrows were so sparse they looked as though they'd been washed away. His hands were unmarked by age or labour, as clean and white as a lady's, the nails shell-pink and perfectly formed. Now he fitted their well-manicured tips neatly together and looked benignly at Alberto over the pink arch they made. An account would be opened at once, of course. Had Mr Pelucci thought of any investments? Mr Pelucci hadn't, but half an hour in Mr Chalmer's company convinced him that investments were a sound and sensible step on the way to the rich life he intended to lead. He emerged from the interview with a sense of considerable achievement.

*

'You gone up one rung a' the ladder, aintcha,' Dickie said. 'You're one a' the swells now!'

One of the working swells, Alberto thought, as he put away his good suit, and replaced the signet ring and the watch and chain in Solly's office, and went back to altering pawn tickets. But at least work was bringing rewards now. Trade was picking up everywhere and there was money to be made. If he was ever going to realize his dreams, work was the only way. And hadn't he come to England to work and make good?

Dickie was busy, too. The recession was over and now houses were being built very rapidly on more than a dozen sites round the village. Tooting was changing so fast, Harry said it made him feel dizzy to look at it.

'Won't be no farms left come the finish,' he complained, 'and then where shall we be?'

'Rich!' Dickie said happily.

'All right fer some,' Harry said and his expression was doleful. 'I shall be out a' work.'

'Never on yer life!' Dickie said. 'We gotta eat, ain't we? Stands ter reason.'

'That's all good farmland you're building on,' Harry said. 'All goin' ter waste.'

'Makin' a big fat profit fer the farmers,' Dickie said, 'an' rich pickings fer the builders. That ain't waste. That's progress.'

'Um,' Harry said, but there wasn't time to argue, because there were cows to milk, and Alberto was due at the Windmill in half an hour.

That summer work dominated their time and drained their energies. There was so much to do, that Alberto never got a chance to go wife hunting. But he was saving steadily and perhaps it was more sensible to wait until he was really established. He could hardly expect his English beauty to marry a poor man, after all. And in the meantime, there were always whores to relieve his desire, and Harry and Dickie to provide company and entertainment.

In August, they bought three secondhand bicycles and spent a bruising afternoon in the Broadway, trying to master the entirely new art of keeping iron upright and mobile. Harry said he'd rather have a horse any day. At least they didn't keel over on their sides when you let go of them. Alberto, his mouth working even harder than his feet, could soon ride quite well, providing he didn't get the giggles. But Dickie surpassed them all. He rode like a prince from the moment his bottom touched the saddle. By their next Sunday together, they were proficient enough to set off on their first exploration of the Surrey countryside.

One afternoon, on their way home from a trip to the Serpentine, they stopped for a rest on Westminster Bridge. It had been a muggy day, the trees in Hyde Park sweating in the heat, ice-cream melting in the cone, and all three of them were hot, sticky and sore-footed. There wasn't the slightest hint of a breeze, even from the river, but Dickie said it made him feel cooler to look at the water, so that's what they did. The Thames was calm and mud brown and too lazy to do more than inch its skirting of squashy black slime just a little closer to the new embankment. Three Thames barges, their red sails furled, lay still and empty just below them. For once it was an idle river, a Sunday river played out by the heat, just like them.

The arrival of the first brougham was no more than a noisy nuisance behind their backs, the second was an echo of the first, but the third and fourth, which arrived together with a prodigious clatter of hooves, convinced them that they were standing alongside an event. They turned to see what was going on.

The fourth brougham contained what could only be described as an apparition, for 'woman' was too tame a word for such an imposing personage, and she was decidedly no lady. She was dressed in the most outrageously flamboyant style, nestling inside a cloak of ostrich feathers, dyed purple, green and gold, and displaying a green silk dress so flounced and fulled and beribboned it looked like a Christmas tree. Her face was boldly painted, and her hair a complicated confection of fat curls and thick waves, topped by a frond of green feathers. Harry and Alberto stared at her open-mouthed, but then wonder became astonishment when she swayed forward out of her feathered nest and greeted their friend Dickie Chanter by name.

'How's me old cock sparrer?' she said. 'You comin' up the Canters are yer? I'm number seven!'

Dickie, blushing darkly, leapt to the side of the brougham and misaimed a kiss at her departing hand. 'We'll be there!'

he promised devoutly, as the fat hand flashed its rings at them and the brougham picked up speed.

'*Who* was that?' Alberto said dumbfounded.

'Florence Entwhistle,' Dickie said, still gazing after the brougham. 'Ain't she a bobby-dazzler?'

'How d'yer come to know a woman like that, me old cock sparrer?' Harry asked, mocking happily.

'She was up the Empress, Monday,' Dickie explained. 'They give old Tilley a turn, first house. I played the joanna. She was top a' the bill. Never thought she'd remember me though. Ain't she a bobby-dazzler?'

'We go to the show?' Alberto asked. 'Yes?'

After such an introduction to the delights of the London music hall, how could they do anything else?

Alberto was instantly and totally bewitched by the place. It was so cheerful, so vulgar, so noisy, full of smoke and steam, strange scents and crackling heat. Everybody and everything in it seemed to be charged with energy, perpetually on the move. The auditorium was crowded with hats and caps and bonnets, and every one of them was bobbing and trembling with anticipation. Crowds besieged the bar, their faces already damp and reddened by alcohol, their glasses rocking foam like miniature tempests; while from the six wide ovens under the galleries, clouds of steam and the appetizing smell of jacket potatoes rose like incense. It was a carnival, Alberto thought, a carnival without the stricture of religion.

'No good Pietro come here,' he said biting carefully into his hot potato. 'No trade outside a' this theatre.'

'Good, innit!' Dickie said, shifting his potato from hand to hand to cool it. 'Good beer! Good grub! And you wait till you see old Florrie!'

'It's a bit of all right,' Harry said, and, for him, that was real praise.

Then the first card was put up on the proscenium arch and the first turn took the stage to a cacophony of welcoming cheers and catcalls. Song followed raucous song, and although Alberto couldn't always understand the words, the tunes were catchy and the innuendo unmistakable. Soon all three of them were singing the choruses like everybody else in the hall, members of the huge boozey family all around them. Florrie Entwhistle, her garish paint softened by strong stage light, looked bright and cheerful and very nearly natural, and the song she sang, 'Who wants ter come out an' play wiv me?' was as innocent as her smile was suggestive. She was followed by a line of chorus girls wearing short frilly skirts and wide stiff smiles, their bare necks and arms like marshmallow, soft, pink and powdered. They flashed eyes and teeth and heels as they tripped across the stage, displaying a daring length of plumply filled stocking above their fine laced boots. A male impersonator followed the chorus, and was followed in turn by a man with a performing dog, a sprightly terrier who wore his ham bone frill with disdain, and, by way of encore, cocked his leg against one of the plaster columns on the stage, an activity that delighted his ribald audience and provoked the longest and most fulsome applause of the evening.

All three of them agreed later on, it was the best night out ever. They had discovered a taste that none of them ever discarded. From then on, they went to the music hall at least once a week, and sometimes, when they were flush, twice or three times, and they were rarely disappointed.

So their lives continued, in a comfortable pattern that suited all of them very well.

Change, when it came, was sudden and unexpected. In the autumn of '94, when the harvest was safely gathered, old man Jones was given a week's notice and told he had to leave his cottage within the month. Mr Pennyman had sold more land to the developers and this time the parcel included his five tied cottages at the Broadway.

Mr Jones put a brave face on it, and swore he wasn't the least bit surprised; he'd seen it coming; wasn't that just the way they always went on. But Harry and Dickie were flattened by the news. Their long, light-hearted summer was suddenly over and neither of them knew, nor, for that matter, cared to face what would happen to them next. The rest of the Jones family rallied round at once. Within two days Harry's sister had arrived from Norfolk with the news that Ma and Pa could come and live with her and Jem, and that Jem was off after a job that very minute as ever was, which was some comfort although it didn't solve Harry's immediate problems or Dickie's.

'We'll get lodgings somewhere. You'll see,' Dickie urged. It was getting more and more difficult to cheer poor old Harry and the strain was beginning to make his voice sharp.

'Oh yes!' Harry mocked. 'Down Amen Corner with some drunk old harridan, in with all the rats and the bedbugs and all them rubbishy street arabs.'

'They oughter pull all that lot down, too, while they're about it,' Dickie said. 'Make a lot a difference that would. I know it's bad they're pulling down the cottages but at least the Salvador's going too, and that can't be bad. You gotta look on the bright side.'

'It's all very well fer you, Dickie Chanter,' Harry said. 'You don't stand ter lose nothink.'

'Not much!' Dickie said. 'Course, I don't live in the cottage no more!'

'They'll build on our land,' Harry said, and he spoke with more bitterness than Alberto had ever heard in his voice before. 'You'll get work out of it.'

'Oh come on!' Dickie protested. 'That ain't *my* fault. *I* didn't sell the bloomin' land! You can't blame me!'

'You'll get work out of it,' Harry growled.

The tone of their voices alerted Alberto in the old familiar way. They were going to have a row. The notes of real anger and grievance were unmistakable, and the fact that it was the first time in the five cheerful years of their friendship that such a thing had happened made it all the more alarming. He had to do something about it, and as quickly as possible. He cast around frantically for a solution. The answer was literally staring him in the face.

They were sitting on the bench outside the Mitre gazing idly across the width of the Mitcham road towards Tooting Church, lying at anchor among swirling seas of holly and yew like a great stone man o' war. Lilac clouds shifted behind the four stone spears that tipped its castle towers, and beside it Church Lane meandered uphill between thick chestnuts that crowded against the palings of the churchyard and obscured the horizon with their close-set foliage, massed dark green clouds that mirrored the grey and purple mounds mushrooming in the sky above them. The pump at the foot of the hill was idle, the spilt water at its foot a stain as dark as wine in the deepening light of evening. Everywhere colour glowed and grew richer in the rays of the setting sun, yellow brickwork creaming and even the flat grey stones of the church touched with a warm brown patina. There was only one patch of white in the entire view, and it caught Alberto's eye immediately. It was a billboard stuck outside the corner shop directly opposite them. 'For Sale,' it said. 'Off-licence for sale. Draught Beer. Wines and Spirits. Groceries and Provisions. Apply C. W. Fisher. The Broadway.'

'That it!' Alberto said. 'I buy that shop. That the answer.'

It took a little while for Harry and Dickie to comprehend. ' 'E's gone off 'is rocker,' Harry said. 'You can't go buying shops.'

'Why not?' Alberto asked. He was on his feet, finishing his beer in rapid urgent gulps.

'Why not?' Harry echoed. 'Why not? People like us don't buy shops, that's why not.'

'I do!' Alberto said. 'Come on.' He set off towards the Broadway, walking briskly as his excitement gathered.

Twenty minutes later they were standing inside the corner shop with young Mr Fisher, the estate agent.

'Needs a lot of work,' Mr Fisher explained. 'The previous owner didn't really make a go of it. Well, you can see that for yourself.'

They could. The shop was dark and dusty and smelled sour. What little food there was on the shelves looked stale and neglected, and the floorboards were littered with dirty sawdust and stained by beer. A pile of blue paper bags on the counter had obviously lain there unused for a very long time. They had faded in the sunlight and the top one was coated with dust. Beside them a sack of lentils had split open to spill a mound of dry orange husks onto the counter.

'None a' this stock's no good,' Dickie observed, beginning to recover his spirits. He took up a handful of the elderly lentils to prove his point. 'You'll have to chuck all this, Ploochy. You couldn't sell stuff like this.'

'That's all been taken into consideration, of course,' Mr Fisher hastened to soothe. 'You'll find allowance has been made for any – um – deterioration of stock.'

Behind the shop was a little office with a patterned glass window encrusted with black grime and a roll-top desk erupting with bills. The clock on the wall said twenty past three; the office said, 'Give up hope.'

'Need a lot a' work, this will,' Harry said unnecessarily as they all trouped back into the shop.

'It's a good site,' Mr Fisher urged. 'Corner site's always good for trade.'

'Let see upstairs,' Alberto said. His face was rounded and beaming with exhilaration and excitement. The thought of all the extra effort that would be needed to 'make a go' of this shop was simply filling him with energy. As they climbed the first flight of narrow stairs behind the shop, he began to hum to himself.

They inspected 'the living accommodation': a kitchen, looking out over the back yard towards the church, and a parlour across the front of the shop with a wide window overlooking the Mitcham road.

Up another steep flight of stairs were two completely empty bedrooms, one over the kitchen and one over the parlour. They stood in the main bedroom and looked down at the distant pavement and the Mitre confronting them darkly.

Alberto had made up his mind.

'I will buy this shop,' he said.

 *Chapter 9*

Mr Chalmers couldn't help liking Alberto Pelucci, although he had to admit that there were times when he found the young Italian rather alarming. Ordinarily he would have refused a loan to such a young man. This time, however, all his caution had been swept aside by Alberto's urgency. When the interview was over, and the loan had been arranged, and young Ploochy had clattered down the stairs to buy the shop he'd so obviously set his heart on, doubt and common sense returned, too late, to Mr Chalmers. Sitting in his fine new office, he fingered the tooled green leather of his fine new desk and wondered what on earth Head Office would say. How dreadful it would be if he'd made a mistake.

Harry Jones was thinking much the same thing. 'What if it don't come off?' he said anxiously to Dickie. 'It's a lot of money. Life savings, you might say.'

'It'll come off!' Dickie reassured him, assuming a confidence he didn't feel. 'It'll be a little goldmine. You'll see. And we'll help him. He's got us. I'll tell all the boys on the site. That'll be a start.'

It wasn't anything of the sort. The boys on the site were totally unimpressed by the news. If some idiot wanted to run an off-licence a quarter of a mile away, let him. They weren't traipsing all the way down that hill for their beer. Not when they had the Castle just as near. What a waste!

The idiot moved into his off-licence, nevertheless. Within three weeks of his purchase, he and Dickie were struggling up the narrow stairs with their bedsteads and three flock mattresses rolled into a bulk that they could only manoeuvre round corners with considerable swearing and the removal of a great deal of skin from Dickie's left hand. For two days after their arrival, water ran rust red from the kitchen tap, and made the most evil-tasting tea. Harry's socks turned up in the saucepan and the stove smoked abominably and spat black specks at them whenever they opened or closed the kitchen door. But by the third day they had grown accustomed to their new surroundings and their new life style, and Alberto had taken delivery of his very first order.

The minute Charrington's dray had gone creaking off towards Mitcham, he put on his stout linen apron and stood behind the counter ready to welcome the custom he felt sure would flock to buy. Not a soul entered the shop.

He waited impatiently for a quarter of an hour, and then strode to the door to find out where his customers had gone. There were four men loitering beside the entrance to the Mitre opposite, but otherwise the street was as deserted as the shop. It could have been a ghost town.

The day passed emptily. Occasionally a slatternly woman or two would clatter down to the pump to squelch out fresh water and pass the time of day. They paid scant attention to Alberto and less to his shop. The second time he heard the pump squeaking, he went to the door and called out, 'Good morning ma'am!' to the woman working the handle. She didn't even smile at him. He was beginning to feel invisible.

Midday came and went. He didn't think it would be sensible to shut shop and go off to get something to eat. What if somebody came and he missed his very first sale? So he stayed where he was and nibbled a few raisins from his stock and waited. Still nobody arrived.

Towards teatime a gang of girls came giggling down Church Lane with their buckets, chaperoned by a filthy mongrel with a thick set of mud-caked whiskers. This time his greeting earned one or two smiles from the girls, and immediate interest from the dog who trotted across the road to investigate. Alberto stood aside hopefully to let him enter, but although he was in the shop for the best part of twenty minutes, and put his forepaws on both counters, and sniffed at everything he came into contact with, including Alberto's legs, nobody called him or came to collect him and eventually he galloped out of the door as abruptly as he'd arrived, and all action for the day was over.

Supper that evening was a morose affair, even though it had been provided by Ma Jones and was one of her most savoury hotpots. Harry had spent most of the evening helping his parents to pack up their bits and pieces. The cart was ordered for seven o'clock the next morning and already his old home looked chill and deserted. Dickie had had a terrible day too, worked off his feet because the builder was on site and wanted everything speeded up while the weather held. They ate their hotpot in silence, and drank beer as though it were hemlock. The fact that they were sitting over a shop crammed with the stuff and hadn't been able to sell any of it made drinking it an ironic necessity, that none of them really enjoyed. They went to bed more dispirited than they'd ever been.

The next day was worse. Even the dog didn't turn up. Alberto decided he would have to do something about it.

He found an old tin pail in the shed, boiled up their biggest kettle of water, unearthed bar soap and scouring powder from his store and set about scrubbing all the shelves, surprised by how grimy and dusty they were. Then he tackled the windows and by late afternoon he'd started on the floorboards. He was on his knees, cheered by activity and now whistling tunelessly, when his first two customers finally arrived. Skirts delicately raised, they picked their way across the wet patches to buy a pound of tuppenny rice and two pounds of best white flour.

' 'Aving a good clear out, aintcha,' the first said approvingly, searching in her purse for pennies. 'We seen yer doin' the winders, didn't we Maudie?'

' 'E was a dirty old thing, that old Mr Renshaw,' Maudie said. 'Never cleaned nothink the whole time 'e was 'ere.'

'Dirty shop, no good,' Alberto agreed and found to his delight that his accent caused a stir. It was plainly attractive to both his customers, who grinned and bridled and became quite girlish.

'Oh-er!' the first lady said. ' 'E's foreign! You're foreign, aintcha Mr – Um?'

'Pelucci,' Alberto supplied.

'Ploochy!' the lady echoed. 'Well I never! Think a' that! Well nice ter meetcha Mr Ploochy.'

'Come again!' Alberto said, putting the pennies into his empty till and giving both ladies the benefit of his widest smile. 'Tell your friends is clean shop now!'

That evening he left the shop for ten minutes and rushed down to the Broadway to buy white card and a thick wax crayon, and on the way back, three tempting portions of pie and mash for their supper.

By the next morning both shop windows were full of goods and eye-catching cards. 'Rice 2d a pound, clean and cheap.'

'Today's bargain. Cheap food in clean shop. Beer and ale. Spirits cheap.'

'That should do the trick,' Dickie said, admiring it.

Before he opened the shop Alberto marched up the hill to Dickie's building site. It was a busy place and full of labourers, Alberto noted with satisfaction as he clambered over a pile of planks towards Dickie and his mate. When the foreman wasn't looking, Dickie obliged his friend by pointing out the odd job boy, an undersized urchin who seemed to be wearing at least three coats, all of them too big for him, and who was dreamily mixing mortar in one corner of the site. 'Yessir?' he said, when Alberto approached him. 'Was there somefink?'

'How you like to make a bit a' bounce?' Alberto said. 'On the side.'

'Chance 'ud be a fine fing,' the urchin said, wiping mortar across his forehead with the flat of his hand.

'When they send you for beer midday,' Alberto said, 'you come to me. I pay you. On the side.'

' 'Ow much?' the urchin said with a sideways glance over his shoulder in case the foreman was around.

'Threepence,' Alberto said.

'Fruppence?' the urchin said. 'Was that fruppence a day, or fruppence a trip? I gets sent out twicest most days. Free times if there's a rush on an' they gets 'ot.'

'Threepence a trip,' Alberto promised. 'That the address on this card. Off-licence, corner a' Church Lane.'

The urchin took the card and examined it on both sides as though he could actually read it. He sensed that somehow he had the upper hand in this situation. He'd certainly got the best of the first bargain. 'Take too long, all down there,' he said, re-opening negotiations, 'Sides, I don't fancy lugging a load up that there 'ill.'

'No need ter lug,' Alberto said at once. 'I lend cart to you. And I give you free beer. Free beer to you and threepence. How you say?'

'I'll fink about it,' the urchin said regally. Then his tone changed abruptly as he caught sight of an approaching figure. ' 'Op it, quick!' he warned. 'I'm s'posed ter be working.'

Although he wasn't really sure whether his triple coated sprat had actually taken the bait, Albert dragged the handcart out of the shed and dusted it down ready for use. To his great relief, he wasn't disappointed. The urchin arrived at midday with a very big order. Dickie must have been encouraging thirst. In the afternoon Maudie reappeared with two of her neighbours. It was an improvement. Only a small improvement, if he was honest about it, but better than nothing. That night they dined on chops bought out of the takings, and there was still a little cash in hand to replenish stocks the next morning. It was certainly going to take a lot of hard work to bring his first dream to reality, but at least he'd made a start. He retired to Solly's lumpy mattress feeling like a general who'd just won a victory.

Gradually word got round. The locals told their neighbours that the corner shop was lovely and clean now, and that young Ploochy was a one, always larking about and ever so obliging. Alberto sold as cheaply as he could and custom grew. By mid-September the three of them felt confident enough to shut the shop at ten o'clock one evening and catch the last house at the Alhambra. By November Alberto had started to pay off his loan and Mr Chalmers was beginning to relax at last.

November was an unpleasant month, dark, dismal and water-logged. When it wasn't raining, a mustard yellow fog hung in the air, clogging lungs, obscuring light and coating every surface with a clammy black dew; when sufficient wind gathered to clear the fog, it brought torrents of sharp-edged rain to sting the skin and penetrate even the stoutest clothing. Harry came home in the evenings with so much mud on his moleskin trousers it took two of them to drag them from his legs, and then they were so stiff and sodden they stood upright on their own accord, and even though they were left in front of the fire all night, they were rarely dry by morning. Dickie wasn't much better off, but at least he could spend part of his day huddled round the brazier in the doorway of the site hut. All three of them began the mornings cold, bad-tempered and complaining about the weather, but at least it brought in plenty of trade. So many people had coughs and colds. The sale of whisky went up most agreeably.

'That young Ploochy knows a thing or two,' Maudie told her cronies. 'Foreign you see. I had this cold on me chest sommink chronic. Fair wheezin' wiv it I was. Well 'e told me I could cure it in a jiffy wiv a tot a whisky took in 'ot milk last thing a night. Worked a treat! 'E's got 'is 'ead screwed on right enough, that one!'

Unfortunately, any head, no matter how well screwed on, is vulnerable to a head cold. Alberto, having been sneezed on by a week's worth of customers, began to cough and splutter himself. He struggled through the next twenty-four hours puzzled and annoyed because he felt so ill, lifting crates although his arms ached ridiculously, smiling at his customers despite a red nose and a throat like a raw wound. By two o'clock the next morning he was delirious, raving incomprehensively in Italian. Harry and Dickie were alarmed. Neither of them knew very much about nursing the sick. They'd always left that to old Ma Jones. As soon as it was light Harry went down to the Broadway to call Dr Power.

It was a quick visit and an even quicker diagnosis. 'You've got the influenza,' the doctor said, 'like everyone else in Tooting. Stay where you are. Keep warm. Sweat it out. Light nourishing meals. Rest. Don't go out of doors or you'll end up with pneumonia.' He'd taken up his hat and gloves and was at the door before Alberto had digested half of what he said, but he paused on the threshold long enough to deliver his parting blow. 'I'll send my bill round later,' he said, smiled his professional smile and was gone.

'Bill!' Alberto groaned. 'I got no money. I got debts up to my ears. How I pay a doctor's bill? Why you call 'im?'

'You was ill, mate,' Dickie said. 'We thought you was gonna snuff it.'

'How I pay a bill?' Alberto wailed. Then a burst of coughing made speech or complaint impossible. And of course he knew that, somehow, he would find the money. He wasn't going to end up like Camilo!

Dickie pinned a notice on the door of the shop, 'Shop shut. Regret Mr Pelucci ill.' and then he and Harry set off to work through the dark air, feeling rather sorry for themselves.

By the evening they were feeling even sorrier. Both of them had the fever, so now there were three patients in the shop and no sick nurse at all, however incompetent. They were extremely uncomfortable, coughing and sneezing and groaning, as they tossed in their crumpled sweaty beds. The fire went out and none of them had the energy to relight it. Soon the room was so cold they could see the plumes of their breath flowing before their mouths every time they spoke, just as though they were out in the road. Their limbs ached, their noses ran, their throats were sore, they craved for something to drink. From time to time one or the other would wrap himself in a blanket like a dishevelled Indian, and shuffle downstairs to the kitchen for another jug of water. The remains of their last evening meal littered the table and the room was beginning to smell, but cleaning up was beyond any of them. Harry had left his boots on the stairs and Dickie fell over them, which didn't improve the 'flu or his temper. They used up all their handkerchiefs and couldn't find any rags except for an old polishing cloth in the broom-cupboard that Harry said made him feel sick. It was a bad time.

On the afternoon of their third fevered day together, help arrived. They were all sleeping fitfully and it took a little time before Dickie realized that someone was knocking at the door. 'Now who's that?' he grumbled. 'I put a notice. Why don't they leave off and go away?' But the knocking continued and presently there was a lull in the rattle of traffic under the window and they could hear a girl's voice calling 'Harry! Harry Jones! You all right?'

'It's Em!' Harry said, and he got up at once and trailed his blanket to the window, which he opened far too wide. A gust of damp air blew in upon the other two invalids.

'Fer cryin' out loud!' Dickie growled. 'Shut that bloomin' winder! D'you wanna give us all the new monia?'

'Oh give over, Dickie,' Harry said. 'It's Em. We got the influenza,' he called down to the figure below.

'Thought as much,' the girl's voice answered. 'Our ma knew you was ill. Chuck us down the key.'

Harry left the window and shuffled out of the room, sniffing.

' 'E is mad!' Alberto said, beginning to understand what was going on. He tried to sit up and finally managed it, even though his skull was pounding. 'You not to let no one in 'ere!' he shouted.

Harry was downstairs and didn't answer. They could hear him shuffling round the kitchen and thudding about from room to room. Presently they heard another sash cord raised.

' 'E's opening all the winders!' Dickie said. 'Hell fire! We shall all catch our death. Harry, will you come up 'ere directly or 'ave I got ter come down there an' get yer?'

'You not to let no one in!' Alberto yelled. 'You mad? She a woman!' He was chewing the end of his moustache with distress.

'No she ain't,' Harry said, returning swathed in the doorway. 'I told yer. It's Em. She ain't a woman. She used ter live next door.'

'Shut that bloody winder, will yer!' Dickie snarled.

'Language, Dickie Chanter, if you don't mind!' Em said, following the blanketed Harry into the room.

The effect of her arrival was electric. Dickie and Alberto covered themselves with the tangle of their blankets and cowered before her like naughty children. Harry climbed into the wreckage of his bed, lay flat and closed his eyes with relief.

Em was a self-possessed young woman and a competent sick nurse. Within two hours she had her little hospital warm and clean and obedient. There was an air of such healthy determination about her, her buxom arms flushed and busy, her red cheeks puffed out with energy, her round blue eyes bland with the expectation of compliance. She took her coat off and got down to work at once. The invalids watched with mixed feelings as she cleaned the grate, thumped up the stairs with a scuttle full of coal and lit a huge fire in their bedroom.

'No wonder you're ill,' she grumbled. 'A room wiv no 'eat, and you wiv the influenza. What was you thinking of, Harry?'

Harry protested that he felt like death but she wasn't at all moved by that. 'You stay where you are like good boys,' she said, 'and I'll be back.'

'I wasn't thinkin' a' going nowhere,' Dickie tried to joke.

'Daft happorth!' she said and was gone. In half an hour she returned with two baskets, one full of clean rags, the other full of saucepans. In her wake was a tousle-headed urchin, clutching three orange boxes. He stood in the doorway looking foolish until Em told him to put a box by each bed and be off out of it. Soon there was a pile of clean rags and a tin mug of water on each improvised bedside table and a chamber pot full of disinfectant in the corner of the room. Order had arrived.

'Now when that kettle's on the boil,' Em said firmly, 'you're ter come down ter that bathroom and get yourselves cleaned up. I dunno how you can bear to be in such a muck. I'll bang on the banisters when it's ready.' There was no possibility of argument or disobedience. One by one they staggered to the bathroom according to her orders, and crept back meekly into beds so tightly made there was barely space for them beneath the covers. 'Good boys!' she said, and gave Harry a broomstick as a reward. 'Anythink yer want, bang on the floor,' she said. 'I'm off ter take a mop to that kitchen or you'll get mice!'

They lay in their clean, neat beds and listened to the fire licking the coals and the ash falling softly into the tray. As sleep drifted him away, Alberto was searching for the words to tell her how grateful he was. He woke to the plop of the gas as she lit it. It was late afternoon and dark. The fire was casting a rosy, reassuring pattern on the ceiling above his head, the blinds were drawn and the room was full of the appetizing smell of broth.

'You are very good,' he said and felt the words were totally inadequate.

She gave him her rounded smile. 'What are neighbours for?' she said.

For over a week Em kept an eye on her patients, coming in early in the morning on her way to work at the Manor and checking in again to see all was well on her way home in the evening. She fed them and teased them and kept them warm, and gradually they recovered. On Sunday she brought a little cake to tempt them and they ate it like manna from heaven even though the crumbs made them cough. By the time her afternoon off came round again, they were almost cured.

'You ain't 'ad a fever fer twenty-four hours,' she said to Dickie as he sucked up his second bowl of stew. 'You can get up termorrer if you're good.'

She made up the fire again that night and left them with her usual warning. 'Be good boys, stay in the warm and keep that fire in. I'll see you in the morning.' They settled for the night intending to obey her, but the night had other ideas.

At two in the morning Dickie was woken by the sound of clinking bottles. He sat up at once to listen. There was someone in the yard.

'Wake up, Ploochy!' he said, shaking Alberto by the rump. 'There's yobs in our yard.'

They crept into the empty back bedroom and looked out of the window. Sure enough, small shadowy figures were creeping about between the crates. Four, five, six at least.

'They're nickin' the bottled beer,' Dickie hissed. 'What sauce!'

Harry was breathing chestily behind them. 'What's the game?' he asked.

'Thieves!' Alberto said, anger rising in him and bringing strength with it. 'They steal our beer! Come on!'

They threw on trousers, jackets and socks, thought better of boots and crept down the stairs, careful to make as little sound as possible. As they tiptoed along the passage towards the door to the yard, Dickie was beginning to enjoy himself. 'Keep yer 'ead down,' he whispered, 'or they'll see yer shadder through the glass.'

They knelt beside the door and peered into the darkness. 'When I say, "Go," ' Alberto instructed, 'we run out and we grab them. I grab middle, you grab left, Harry, you grab right!'

It was a successful ambush. They managed to get the door ajar before their visitors were alerted, but their eruption into the yard caused a panic. 'Scarper!' a hoarse voice yelled. Bodies fell in every direction, and for several enjoyable minutes the three thumped at moving limbs and punched retreating heads with an exhilarating sense of righteous indignation. The thieves hurled themselves at the fence where they'd built a ladder of crates to aid their get-away. The first two got across without any trouble, but Harry caught the third by his trousers, and Dickie and Alberto pulled the fourth to the ground before he could put a foot on the crates. Two prisoners! What success!

'What'll we do wiv 'em?' Harry said, sitting astride his particular victim.

'Bring inside a' the shop,' Alberto said. He was still raging with anger at the thought that these two struggling bodies had been trying to steal his hard-earned cash. 'I think I kill them!'

'We ain't done nothink,' one of the bodies said, as well as he could with Harry sitting on him.

'You shut yer face, you!' Harry said, yanking the miscreant to his feet, and the procession marched indoors.

Once inside the comparative warmth of the shop, Alberto's anger began to evaporate. For a start the thieves looked a sorry pair in the low gaslight. Both were dirty, ragged and bare-footed; both had running noses and scabs around their mouths; and both were surprisingly small.

'How old are you?' Alberto asked.

'Nine,' the bigger one said. 'I fink. Look 'ere, we ain't nicked nothink mister. Honest! We was only look-outs.'

'I only come wiv Charlie,' the little one said, trying a few tears to see if they would soften the three dark faces around him.

'Stop snivelling,' Dickie said fiercely, 'unless you wanna thick ear.'

'I ain't nicked nothink,' the bigger boy insisted.

'They're out the rookery, I'll bet,' Harry said. 'Right little nest a' tea leaves, that is. Live up the rookery, dontcha?' he asked the nearest dirty face.

'Joe,' the face said. ' 'E does. Me and Jamie, we live in the Grove now. We used ter live in the Salvador only there ain't much a' that left now.'

'Gaw! That's worse!' Dickie said. 'We caught a right pair a' villains here, Ploochy. By rights we oughter take 'em straight down the cop shop.'

But Alberto was looking at his prisoners' feet.

'Where your boots?' he said suddenly to the smaller boy.

'Ain't got none,' the boy answered.

'Boots cost money, mister.' Jamie offered. He was encouraged by the kinder tone in Alberto's voice. If he boxed clever they might just get away with it. 'We ain't got a penny piece,' he said, pulling his pockets inside out to prove it.

'No boots,' Alberto said. 'In this weather, no boots!' It upset him.

'None of 'em got boots in the Salvador,' Dickie said. 'They're a right lot down there. Got money fer booze though aintcha?'

'Not tonight we ain't,' Jamie said. 'That's why we was nickin' it.'

'Bloody sauce!' Dickie said, enraged. 'They want their 'eads kicked in.'

Alberto was thinking. His rage was completely over. 'What you say,' he asked the two boys seriously, 'if I give you job?'

'You're joking!' Harry protested. 'They're yobbos! They'll rook yer!'

'Straight up?' the bigger boy asked. 'You ain't 'aving us on, are yer?'

'I buy you pair a boots,' Alberto said. 'Pair a boots each. You wear 'em working fer me. How about it?'

'You're on!' the big boy said. 'Whatcha want us ter do?'

'Be here eight o'clock sharp termorrer,' Alberto said. 'Then I tell you. Eight o'clock sharp. Now 'op it.' He was feeling very tired and wanted to get back to bed.

The urchins hopped through the shop door with alacrity.

'You want your head examined,' Dickie said in disbelief as they climbed back to bed. 'You should've took them lot straight down the cop shop. Buy 'em boots! Whatever next? You don't seriously think they'll turn up termorrer, do yer?'

'Yes,' Alberto said. 'They will.'

' 'E's barmy,' Harry said. 'What you want, Ploochy, is a good yard dog. I'll get yer one. High time we was all back at work anyway. You openin' the shop?'

' 'Course,' Alberto said drowsily.

To everybody's surprise, including Alberto's although he would never have admitted it, the two street arabs turned up next morning on the stroke of eight. Em was not impressed by their arrival or their appearance but she let them in the yard and allowed Alberto to come down and attend to them. He took them off to the Broadway at once and treated them both to a pair of boots, cheap but stout. Then they all stomped back to the shop and he hung a placard round both their necks and gave them their instructions. They were to walk round Tooting until it got dark and then they were to bring boots and placards back to the shop. Despite Dickie's forbodings, they kept their word and for the next five days they paraded the streets like miniature sandwich men to earn their boots, collecting a crowd wherever they went and telling the story of the night's escapade and Ploochy's unexpected generosity over and over again. It did them all a power of good. Trade picked up,

Alberto's reputation spread and the urchins had good boots to pawn the next time they needed a drink.

Harry kept his promise too. Three days later he came home from the farm leading a miserable looking mongrel on a short rope. 'Put 'im in the yard,' he advised. 'I guarantee you won't 'ave no more trouble wiv yobs.' The dog looked up apologetically at Alberto, showing the whites of his eyes out of a matted coat the colour and texture of an old mop. They put him in the yard, where he stood beside the door and shivered.

'What'll you call 'im?' Harry said.

'Dog,' Alberto said.

Alberto quite enjoyed having an animal around the shop, even though he wasn't at all convinced about his usefulness as a guardian, and Dog loved Alberto with an undivided passion, although he was quick to get out of his way at the first sound of temper in his voice. To be spoken to kindly was joy enough. He could live for days on a single sentence. Which was just as well, because Alberto had neither the time nor the inclination to give him more than glancing attention, now that his mind was full of dreams.

Ever since Em's arrival in their sick room, Alberto had been nurturing a fantasy. Sometimes it involved the most passionate love-making, sometimes a summer wedding, but whatever form it took, it originated with the plumply luscious Em saying yes to whatever form of ardent activity he was proposing. It occupied a large proportion of his waking time and provoked the most devastatingly erotic dreams.

Spring came early that year, and with the spring the dream intensified. Now Em's face was all he ever seemed to see, waking or dreaming. From time to time when the shop was empty and he felt it was safe enough to leave it for a few minutes, with Dog in charge, he rushed off to the footpath behind the Manor and waited, lurking beside the dusty elderberry bushes, breathing the acrid mixture of tom cat and stale earth, in the hope that he might be in time to meet her and escort her home. When his plan worked, she was always pleased to see him, and allowed him to carry her basket, and chattered happily to him all the way back to Vant Road. The trouble was she chattered too much and he couldn't stop her long enough to steer the conversation the way he wanted it. So he had to put up with it while she told him what a bad lad young Harry had been at school, and how Ma Jones had whopped him, and what mad games they'd all played when they were neighbours. It was pleasant to walk beside her in the evening, but frustrating to make so little progress. So he invited her to the music hall.

That didn't turn out the way he intended either, for Dickie and Harry came too and as he couldn't find a way to hint that he would have been happier without them, trips to the halls became a regular outing for all four of them. He had to share her company and make the best of it. The weeks went by and still he hadn't managed to talk to her. He comforted himself that the summer was coming and then he could take her to the Mitcham Fair. They would go on the swings, and round the sideshows, and in the twilight, he would walk her home, and kiss her, and she would put her arms round his neck and kiss him back and agree to marry him. It was just a matter of time and patience, that was all. It wouldn't be proper to rush things. Not in England. Not as an Englishman. He'd waited such a long time to find the girl he wanted to marry, he could afford to wait a little bit longer.

Mitcham Fair was a terrible disappointment. For a start she said she didn't like the swings. She'd rather go to the freak show with Harry. So Alberto and Dickie spent most of their afternoon mooching about beside the coconut shies, trying to pretend they were having a good time, and studiously avoiding any mention of their two absent friends. Then Tilley joined them, saying she had a 'predigus' thirst, and she and Dickie went off arm in arm to assuage it. Dusk descended, to suspend the stalls in oily cradles of darkness between the naptha flares, and Alberto was caught in a grey net of sudden loneliness. There was no sign of Harry or Dickie anywhere, and the fair seemed tawdry and tasteless. He went home to the shop on his own, glad that at least he had Dog to confide in.

They consumed two chops between them and Alberto drank half a bottle of claret. Then they sat beside the stove, in doleful and companionable silence, watching the coals glow behind the black bars of the grate, and listening to the ash shift and scatter. Midnight sounded, and as Harry and Dickie still hadn't returned, Alberto and Dog went their separate ways, Dog to his kennel, warm and satisfied that, for once, he hadn't been relegated to the yard all evening, Alberto to a chill bed, still puzzling over the unexpected failure of his plans.

The very next morning Harry provided the explanation. The shop was shut and he, Alberto and Dickie were down in the cellar manhandling fresh barrels of beer into position beneath the pumps.

'Got a bit a news,' Harry said.

Alberto waited, but the news wasn't forthcoming. Harry's expression was so puzzled he didn't like to question. They stood for a while in the murky cellar, leaning against the barrels to get their breath back.

'Pennyman wants me ter run the piggery up Totterdown,' Harry said finally.

'That good!' Alberto said, beaming with pleasure at his friend's promotion. But the beam faded, because Harry didn't share it. He still seemed perplexed.

'Offered me a cottage. That's the trouble,' he said.

'Tied?' Dickie asked.

'A course,' Harry said. 'That's the trouble.'

'You don't have to take it,' Alberto said. 'You can stay here, long as you like.'

'Em wants ter take it,' Harry said. 'That's the trouble.'

Em? Alberto thought. What had Em got to do with it? But even as his mind was framing the question he knew the answer and was inwardly cursing himself for his folly in not understanding something that must have been obvious to anyone in his right mind, anyone, that is, who wasn't besotted with dreams. Em and Harry! Of course. Em and Harry. Hadn't she always sat next to Harry at the halls; hadn't she talked about him, non-stop; hadn't they always been together?

'Well it's about time,' Dickie was saying, thumping his friend between the shoulder blades. 'Never thought she'd catch yer, though, ter tell yer the truth. What she do? Tie yer feet together?'

'Give over,' Harry said, blushing.

'When you marry?' Alberto asked, pleased by the speed of his recovery and thinking fast.

'Well that's it, innit,' Harry explained. 'She wants fer me ter

take the cottage. She's got the weddin' planned fer the end a'
September.'

'Good fer her!' Dickie said. 'Whatcher waitin' for?'

'Well,' Harry said, 'a tied cottage! I ain't sa keen on the
idea, now. Not after . . .'

'Then you rent a place,' Alberto said firmly. 'I see Mr
Fisher for you tomorrow.' Warmth and balance were returning. He was beginning to thaw with the pleasurable sense that
he was helping his friend. His silly dream had already receded
and reshaped, beaten back by his embarrassment.

Later that day, standing behind the beer pumps as the
afternoon sun columned in through the shop window, he tried
to make sense of his stupidity. It seemed ridiculous now that
he'd ever imagined that Em could be interested in him. The
signs had all been there, as clear as sunlight. How could he
have missed them?

No, he decided, he wasn't ready for marriage yet. He was
still making too many mistakes. He would defer these frivolous
thoughts for the time being and concentrate on the more
immediate business of making money.

For several weeks now, Mr Chalmers had been hinting that
he should buy a parcel of land from Mr Pennyman and put up
the money to build a pair of houses. He knew he could easily
raise the capital and although there were risks attached, he
felt sure he could make a success of a venture like that. After
all, business was predictable, unlike love.

He chose a good plot, close to the Broadway that seemed
right for development and built two houses designed to the
taste of his regular customers. By the time Harry's wedding
had been arranged, building was well under way, Fishers had
offered to buy, and Alberto was set to make a considerable
profit out of the transaction.

Chapter 10

'Be some changes now,' Harry said happily. 'New king an' all.'

' 'Bout time too,' Dickie said, gulping his beer with great satisfaction. 'We been stuck in the mud quite long enough.'

'I ain't so sure I want to change,' Alberto said. 'Things are all right the way they are.'

The three friends were in their favourite corner in Jack Beard's, the new pub in the Mitcham Road. They'd been reading the evening papers and admiring pictures of their new King.

'Be funny to 'ave a king after all this time,' Harry remarked.

'Do us all good,' Dickie said. 'I told yer. Time fer a change!'

'Started all-a-ready,' Alberto said. 'I 'ad old Solly Isaacs in the shop this morning. 'E reckon 'e move to Tooting. 'Is place is coming down. For the new road.'

'Could do worse,' Harry said. 'Lots a' trade fer 'im in this place.'

'I think 'e take the shop opposite,' Alberto told them. 'I fixed it for 'im.' It had been a lovely moment, finding a shop in Tooting for his old master. And a shop so close to his own.

'Change, yer see,' Dickie said approvingly. 'It's a good thing!' And he went off to get them another round.

'What's 'e up to?' Harry asked. ' 'E's up ter something, sure as God made little apples. Keepin' all on about change. We don't want ter change. Not us. We never change.'

But he was wrong. Their lives had actually altered quite a lot during the last six years, although as most of the changes had been natural and gradual, they'd been assimilated in the same way and barely noticed.

Harry had married his Em, and within two years had fathered two fine sons, amiable boys with hair as thick and fair as his own and Em's bland face and blue eyes. He'd changed jobs twice too, as Pennyman sold off more and more of his farmland to the builders. But as each change had meant a rise in pay, he'd accepted them happily and with little comment.

Ploochy was now a naturalized British citizen and had changed his name from Alberto to Albert, but as everyone he knew called him Ploochy, it hardly made any difference to him at all. He was still buying up parcels of land, and building houses on spec., still making money, still working energetically and for ridiculously long hours, but that all seemed part of his character now.

It was Dickie's life that had changed really dramatically, but that was all so long ago they'd forgotten what a break it had been. Soon after Harry's wedding, he'd handed in his notice as a brickie and set up on his own as the manager of a troupe of music-hall artists, arranging their bookings, playing their accompaniments and eventually setting up house in Clapham to provide them with lodgings. Now he had a healthy bank balance, an entertaining life style and an interesting piece of news that he was trying to find the right moment to drop into his friends' ears.

'Whatcha doin' Sunday?' he asked casually as he returned with their drink.

' 'Nother one a' your parties, is it?' Albert asked. Dickie was renowned for his parties.

'In a way,' Dickie said, and now his cautious tone alerted both his friends. 'It's a sort a celebration. Me an' Tilley are settin' up tergether.'

'Gettin' wed, d'yer mean?' Harry said, beaming at him.

'Not exactly,' Dickie admitted, and now he looked rather sheepish. 'Tell the truth, we ain't thinking a' marriage. On account of Tilley's got an 'usband al-a-ready.'

It was astounding, but they swallowed their surprise with their beer and promised to be at the party, come what may.

'After all,' as Harry said to Albert on their way home along Charlmont Road, 'you gotta give yer mate a good send off, when all's said and done.'

It was a riotous party, with plenty of food and drink, and singing bubbling on into the small hours. After a long week at work, Albert found it quite hard to keep awake after midnight, even with Tilley hanging on to one arm, and Martha Goodyear, the soprano, squashed against the other.

'You're done in, aintcha sunshine,' Martha said, patting his cheek with a plump hand. 'Our Ploochy's worn out,' she said to Dickie. 'Whatcha been doing to 'im?'

'Been working too 'ard, aintcha Ploochy,' Dickie said. He was full of Albert's three star brandy and very happy, for after all, it was a sort of wedding day. He took out his handkerchief and polished the top of his head. The action seemed to stimulate his brain. 'Got an idea!' he said. 'An idea!' He stood before them holding the idea into his skull by the pressure of his handkerchief.

'Go on then, you soppy old thing,' Tilley said, laughing at him. 'Spit it out!'

'Take a day off,' he said. 'That's my advice. Shut the shop, and take a day off. Get up late, come over here, meet us in the Plough fer a quick one, and then we'll 'ave lunch at Luigi's. How about that?'

It was so obvious, Albert thought, once it had been said. A day off. Of course. It was just what he needed. He could afford a day off.

When he got back to the shop he sat in the warmth of his kitchen and composed a notice to hang on the front door. 'Mr Pelucci regrets that the shop will be closed today,' he wrote, 'for . . .' The explanation presented a considerable problem. He dragged his mind back from the dizziness and euphoria of drink to focus upon it. For what? He could hardly say 'for a day's holiday' or 'for a rest'. It took a long time and some painful concentration before the answer arrived in a mindburst of inspiration. 'Closed today,' he concluded, 'for the morning.' Then as a helpful afterthought, he added 'Open again this afternoon.' and signed his name with a flourish.

What bliss it was to lie abed until he was really ready to get up. To look at the clock on his bedside table saying half-past nine, and still be luxuriating under warm bedclothes. For once in his life he took the time to have a really good breakfast. Then he boiled two kettles and had a thorough wash in warm water, drying himself on a fresh towel warmed in front of the fire. By the time he emerged to the world, he felt like a lord.

It seemed appropriate and proper that the horse bus waiting

beside the Vestry should be brand new. The green paint gleamed, the brasses shone and the horses breathed warmth and well-being, holding up their heads and frisking their tails.

'You got a smart turn-out this morning,' Albert told the driver as he climbed up to sit beside him.

'Got six new in the yard this week, Mr Ploochy,' the driver said. 'Spanking, innit!' The horses set off at a trot and he clicked his teeth at them. 'Full of oats this morning,' he explained. 'Had a holiday you see. It's put new life into 'em.'

Albert knew how they felt. They bowled past the Broadway shops, past a row of hedges, past the corn already standing waist high, towards Upper Tooting. Larks sang in the air above the fields and a haywain creaked past them on its way down to the Mitre. The warm scent of its cargo drifted back and over them. Albert sat in the sunshine swaying towards Clapham in a well-fed dream. There was something easy and soothing about a bus ride in summer. The horses clopped steadily over the cobbles, the coach creaked, the passengers buzzed and murmured, and Albert's head began to nod towards a doze. He had no idea that the next few minutes were going to alter the course of his life.

They were heading towards the Plough and the bus had just stopped beside the Long Pond to pick up more passengers. Somewhere behind them, a dog fight began with two high-pitched yaps and a snarling like a sawmill. Albert was instantly alert and interested. He loved a dog fight. But he never got to see this one, for as he turned his head, he caught sight of the girl in the garden.

She was hanging out the washing, a small slender girl with a heart-shaped face and long, straight, fair hair. Her arms were stretched above her head to peg the heavy linen, and the strong sunlight gave her a golden outline, highlighting her forehead, her cheeks and her bare forearms. She seemed to be standing in a spotlight. There was something about the movement of her arms, something in the glint of sunlight on flesh and glowing hair that stirred a long-submerged memory. Albert became all instinct in that second. An overpowering excitement rose in him like a tidal wave, obliterating reason and drowning control. This was his girl! The one he'd been waiting for all his life. He knew it as surely as he knew he was breathing. His girl! And just a few feet away from him, behind that ordinary garden wall. The bus began to move and the movement jolted him to action.

'Stop the bus!' he said to the astonished driver. 'I gotta get off!'

'We just started, Mr Ploochy,' the driver complained. But Albert insisted, the bus ground to a second halt, and he leapt to the ground. Stairs were too commonplace for such excitement. He crossed the road in three bounds and ran to the garden wall, searching his way back along it to find its front door.

'What's up with 'im?' one of the passengers asked.

'Gone off 'is chump!' the driver said.

Afterwards, Albert could never remember finding the front door or ringing the bell. He must have done both, for presently the door was opened by a flustered maid, her arms still damp and red from washing and her cap askew. 'Yerse?' she asked.

'I come to see the lady of the 'ouse,' Albert said. 'My card!' and he produced one of his splendid cards with a flourish.

'About a young lady was it?' the skivvy said.

'That about the size of it,' Albert said happily. He was so excited, it didn't even occur to him to wonder how she knew.

The maid ushered him into a dark front parlour, and went off to fetch the missus, wiping her hands on her grimy apron. The room was crowded with fat upholstery and heavy curtains. Everything in it, from the windows to the legs of a little upright piano, was swathed in heavy dark brown material. Even the aspidistra rose from a swirl of folded cloth, and the sepia prints that crowded every inch of wall space were embellished with a trailing convolution of brown ribbons. Albert waited impatiently, breathing in cotton fibres and wondering how his lovely girl and the flowing lilt of those white arms could possibly exist in such a claustrophobic room.

The door clicked and stiff skirts swished through the felt curtain into the room. The lady of the house was a formidable personage, and obviously someone to reckon with, as Albert realized even from the heights of his excitement. She wore a purple gown over corsets so long and so rigid that she looked like an ornate purple chimney. A thick starched jabot seized her throat in sharp-edged claws and lay as heavy as carved wood on her steep bosom. From under the solid bell of her skirt protruded black buttoned boots, brilliantly polished, and to Albert's eyes, far too big for a woman. But it was the face above the jabot that really made him quail. The lady had a jaw like a boxer and embedded in it, a tight lilac-coloured mouth. Her nose was long and surprisingly sharp, a knife of a nose in that heavy fleshy face, and above it, two pebble grey eyes, shrewd and wary, watched him from beneath bushy eyebrows. A wart, sprouting hairs, decorated the corner of her chin and above the creases of her forehead, thick grey hair was disciplined into a row of tight sausage curls. The whole edifice was surmounted by a high lace cap of such complications that Albert, in his present state of combined shock and excitement, thought she had a deformed skull. Confronted by such an apparition, he began to wonder what he had let himself in for.

'Do sit down Mr Pelucci,' the lady said. She had a musical voice, deep and gentle, and to Albert's surprise, she pronounced his name properly. He sat on the edge of one of the upholstered chairs and turned his bowler round in his hands.

'You wished to see me about a place. Is that right?' the lady went on. She sat higher than Albert and seemed even more formidable in the chair than she had been on her feet.

'A place?' Albert echoed stupidly. What was she talking about?

'Is it for a daughter?' the lady pressed on. 'Or the child of a friend perhaps. We *do* have one or two places available.' She paused and then as Albert still sat bemused in front of her and she obviously felt she should say something else, she went on, 'I'm sure you won't mind me asking, Mr Pelucci. How did you come to hear of us? Were we recommended by one of our parents?'

A school, Albert thought. Of course, she runs a school. He put his hat on the cluttered table beside him and plunged into an explanation. 'There is a young lady hanging out the washing in your back garden,' he said. His words were rushed and badly pronounced but he was too far gone to care. 'I see her from the bus. I wish to be introduce' to her.' The expression on the lady's face urged him on. He *had* to explain himself, somehow, and quickly. But even to him the whole situation was beginning to seem inexplicable. He looked straight into the pebble grey eyes and smiled his most charming smile. 'With view to matrimony,' he said.

'Good heavens!' the lady exclaimed. She didn't smile back but rose with a rustle of skirts and swept out of the room.

Albert, left among the claustrophobic curtains, felt deflated. He needed to smoke, but the room deterred him, so he sat where he was and fidgeted. Presently he could hear feet and voices outside the door, followed by an eruption of swishing skirts. Good God! There were two of them. Purple Satin was shadowed into the room by a mound of grey frills and flounces. If one was a decorated chimney, the other was a frilled tea cosy, plump and cushiony with a fat round face and at least three chins.

'This is my sister Amelia,' Purple Satin said. Grey Frills tucked her head to one side and made a faint murmuring sound. 'This is Mr Pelucci,' Purple Satin explained. 'He wishes to be introduced to Alice. He says he wants to marry her.'

'How very romantic!' Grey Frills sighed. She held out a little fat white hand from the froth of grey lace that engulfed her wrist. 'So pleased to make your acquaintance.'

'That is all very well, Amelia,' Purple Satin said sternly, 'But it won't do. After all young man, we don't know anything about you, except your name.'

Albert relaxed. It was all right. They were on familiar ground. 'I am the proprietor of a thriving business,' he said grandly. 'It has a turnover of three thousands pounds a year. My card.' He produced a second card and handed it across to Purple Satin, wondering what had happened to the first one.

The ladies were impressed, Grey Frills tremulous, Purple Satin stately. So far, so good. 'That sounds satisfactory,' Purple Satin said. 'Tell us about your future prospects.'

By the end of twenty minutes close questioning both sisters were almost entirely satisfied by the qualifications of their niece's extraordinary suitor. And at last, at last, the bell was rung and Alice was sent for. Albert, who had calmed during his catechism, now crawled with excitement again. His heart was beating in such an alarming way that it was making his coat jump, and his throat was so full he wondered how he would be able to speak. Purple Satin and Grey Frills sat and watched him as the clock on the draped mantelpiece ticked on far too many minutes.

She had opened the door and was inside the room before Albert had heard a sound. How quietly she moves, he thought. She brought a scent of soap and starch into the crowded room. To Albert it seemed like a breath of fresh air. The lovely straight hair had been knotted into the nape of her neck, and now that he was close to her, Albert could see that his first impression had been right. She had a calm, unruffled, wide-browed face and her eyes were pansy brown. She looked straight at Albert without smiling as Purple Satin made the formal introductions: Alice Towers; Albert Pelucci. Albert cleared his throat with difficulty, made an appropriate sound and clutched her hand. It was small, rough and damp and when he looked down at it, he could see it was reddened with work. He had a fleeting vision of himself as a knight in armour rescuing his lady from the life of a slave. Then his excitement plummeted away and he found himself wondering what on earth he was doing in this strange cluttered room with three woman he didn't know. He began to feel he was making a fool of himself.

Purple Satin seemed equal to any occasion. 'Mr Pelucci,' she said to her niece, 'Wishes to know if you would like to accompany him to . . .' She paused delicately and half smiled at Albert. 'Where was it you said, Mr Pelucci?' she asked.

'To lunch at Luigi's,' Albert stammered.

'That's very kind of you, Mr Pelucci,' Alice said. She spoke with the same husky voice as her aunt, only a tone or two higher. She was still perfectly calm, as though situations like this were an everyday affair. 'When were you thinking of?'

She was going to accept. Joy roared inside Albert's head. 'Today!' he said. 'Now!' He didn't stop to think how unlikely it was.

Alice looked at her aunts. 'What about the wash, Aunt Phoebe?' she said.

Purple Satin smiled again. Her face was almost sunny. 'Would you like to go, my dear?' she said.

Alice considered for a second. She was still entirely calm. 'Yes,' she said, slowly, still looking at her aunt, 'if it wouldn't put you out.'

*

So half-an-hour later, after poor quality sherry and *petit beurre* biscuits, Alice and Albert set off together to lunch at Luigi's. Albert couldn't believe his luck. Alice, although outwardly calm, was walking in her sleep.

Chapter 11

When she was four years old, Alice's father left her in the British Museum. It wasn't an act of cruelty, he'd simply forgotten her. He and one of his cronies had been deep in conversation and the child was lagging behind. Her feet were sore and she was finding it really quite hard to walk, especially as the four black legs in front of her were moving faster and faster with every word. Finally her father had grown tired of her dawdling. He had lifted her onto a chair beside one of the tall glass-fronted cabinets that grew all around them like a forbidding forest. 'Sit there like a good child,' he instructed. 'We'll be back for you bye and bye.' The black legs and the droning conversation continued on down the echoing passage, and Alice, like the good child she'd learned to be, sat where she was and waited. The hours passed gently. Sometimes she dozed for a few minutes, and woke with anxiety in case they'd come back and she'd missed them. And once she fell into a deep sleep, and woke to find that the great room was filling with black shadows, and the black shadows were creaking.

She was very frightened, but she knew she wasn't to make a fuss. 'Papa!' she called in a small frantic voice. 'Papa!' But her father was in a hansom cab, halfway home to Clapham and she was a long way from his thoughts.

Aunt Phoebe was furious with her absent-minded younger brother. 'God save us, Ernest,' she said, her formidable eyebrows meeting with anger, 'What were you thinking of? Leaving the little mite like that! And in that fearful place! You must go back directly. Amelia, re-call the cab!'

The museum was locked by the time Mr Towers had finished the round trip and was at its door again. The porter had to be knocked up, keys found, a lantern lit, and several miles of dark corridor negotiated before the frightened child was found, still quiet and still enduring, and still sitting on the chair where he'd left her.

Aunt Phoebe was boiling with anger when they finally got home. She sat the exhausted child in the armchair next to the kitchen range and carefully removed her little boots. Her socks were blood-stained to the ankle. 'Have you no sense at all?' she rebuked her brother. 'You've walked her little feet red raw. Poor soul! And never a word of complaint, little lamb! You don't deserve such a good child, God knows.'

Aunt Amelia sat at Alice's feet and washed away the blood and wrapped the sore patches in lint and soft bandages. 'There's my good girl,' she crooned, as the child submitted quietly to her ministrations. 'Phoebe's quite right,' she said, addressing her brother without looking at him. 'You don't deserve such a good little girl. No fuss, you see.' She smiled at her niece with pride.

Alice had learned all about not making a fuss at a very early age. Aunt Phoebe had taught her. 'Little girls who cry get no supper,' that lady had said sternly to a weeping two-year-old. 'Tears won't get you anywhere. Nobody wants a naughty child.' But quiet children who didn't complain were given sugar sticks for a reward, and allowed a kitten and, wonder of wonders, given a picture book all of their own. In a school full of enormous girls presided over by the two unrelenting aunts, the small Alice soon understood that no matter what her distress or her grief might be, expressing it would only bring punishment and make her feel worse. So she grew up quietly, absorbing sorrow and accepting pain, her silence and fortitude rewarded from time to time when one of the aunts chanced to notice it.

As she grew older she learned that she wasn't pretty and that her father didn't want her. One chill April day not long after her tenth birthday, she'd been sitting in the window seat in the back parlour, quietly reading, out of everyone's way, when her father and his friends came into the room to smoke and talk. She took too long to decide whether to let them know she was there. While she was still dithering they'd begun to talk about her. Blushing with embarrassment, she shrank into the curtains.

'What you going to do about the kid, Ernest old man?'

'Don't ask me,' her father replied carelessly. 'Marry her off to some nabob.'

'You'd have a job,' a second voice said. 'She's deucedly plain.'

'Isn't she just, though,' her father agreed. 'Don't take after me.'

'She travellin' with you?' the first voice insisted.

'No fear!' her father said. 'I'd sooner have a millstone round my neck. Have some brandy, William?'

So she was a millstone, Alice thought. She didn't know what a millstone was, but it sounded horrid. It didn't surprise her that she was being compared with something horrid. She'd half expected he would say something nasty about her. And in a way she was rather glad she would never be going to India with him. She preferred it in Clapham with her aunts.

Perhaps it was because she was plain that he didn't like her. How she wished she could have been pretty like Mama. Poor dead pretty Mama, whose picture smiled at her from her bedroom wall.

It worried her to be plain. It was so important to be pretty. It wasn't just that fathers preferred pretty daughters. Being pretty was the way to catch a husband, and that, she knew, was the most important thing a girl had to do. Both her aunts never stopped reminding her. 'Don't sit like that, child! It isn't pretty!' 'You'll never catch a husband if you look like that.' 'Eat prettily please!' 'Keep your hair neat.' 'Don't dirty your clean pinafore.' 'Turn your toes in when you walk, child.' 'Be pretty!' 'Look pretty! You want to catch a husband don't you?' And she did. Of course she did. It was what all the girls in the school wanted, except Polly and you couldn't count Polly because she was a Blue Stocking.

Once she plucked up enough courage to broach the subject with Aunt Amelia. They were baking bread in the warm brown kitchen, and Aunt Amelia was powdered with flour like a pink cottage loaf.

'Am I very plain, Aunt Amelia?' she said, looking down at her fists embedded in the dough.

Aunt Amelia wouldn't be drawn. 'Handsome is as handsome does, my dear,' she said cryptically. 'You're a nice, quiet, obedient girl. Just you be satisfied with that. Nobody could ask for more.'

Alice *could* have asked for a great deal more, but she didn't dare.

When she was fourteen, her father wrote from India to say that he had married again, and wouldn't be taking any more home leave. He hoped she was being a good girl, and giving her aunts no trouble, and he signed himself 'Your affectionate Papa.' Six months later another letter arrived written in the most extraordinary English, in barely legible handwriting, on pale brown, strangely scented notepaper. It said 'It had the honourable to inform you that Ernest Towers was died.' Then, as far as Alice and her aunts could make out, it went on to describe the death which was 'sadly borne out' and 'in accordance.' It was signed, 'Yr obedient servant.' The signature was completely illegible.

'I suppose I'm an orphan,' Alice said calmly, when they'd finally deciphered all that they could of the letter. She didn't feel sad, or upset. In fact she didn't really feel anything at all. The news hadn't touched her.

'In many ways you always were,' Aunt Phoebe said grimly. 'Poor motherless child! Ernest was a feckless individual. It's just like him to die in India.'

And that was the last that was ever said about him, at least in Alice's hearing. Life went on in Crescent Road as it had before the letter arrived, and on the whole it was a good life. There was certainly plenty to do, and Alice was a worker. She recognized that her aunts had been very good to her. They'd given her a home and good food, they'd taught her to read and write, and embroider, how to paint flowers and how to play the piano. In every way they'd treated her like a daughter. It only seemed right that she should help them with the chores. And, of course, there were always plenty of girls of her own age to play with.

By the time she was sixteen, Alice had decided that her own sex was infinitely preferable to that other misshapen, clumsy and alarming one. She liked the softness of women, their smell and their predictability. She liked quiet voices, soft colours, gentle movements. She was satisfied with her dreams. And just when she'd got all that sorted out in her head, she fell in love.

In the spring of her sixteenth year, when Albert was rounding the Bay of Biscay in his ship full of green and heaving sickness, two uniformed strangers arrived on the doorstep at Crescent Road. One was a colour sergeant in the East Surreys, an alarming six-footer who smelt of bad cheese and Brasso, and said he had brought a present from India for Miss Alice Towers from her father. Sure enough, his companion, a frail young private in a brand new uniform, was carrying an enormous hat box. The aunts invited them in immediately, all agog to know what it contained.

The colour sergeant seemed to expand as he entered their little front parlour. He was too big for everything in it. He perched awkwardly on the edge of Aunt Phoebe's delicate *chaise longue*. His long legs in their heavy trousers threatened the occasional table and he held one of the best bone-china tea cups in scarred hands so enormous that he couldn't get his fingers through the handle. The private subdued himself on a hard-backed chair in the corner and drank his tea neatly, like a mouse sipping water. From time to time he glanced shyly at Alice, and Alice, catching him at it, smiled back, flattered and sympathetic. But the colour sergeant terrified her. He personified all the worst things she knew about men. The back of his neck was red and pitted. Exactly the colour and texture of rump steak, she thought. The bristles of black hair that protruded through the red skin filled her with loathing. He was ugly, coarse and loud, and the longer he sat in their warm parlour, the more vile he smelt. But at last the tea had been drunk and the present could be opened.

Alice was given the honour of lifting the lid. Inside was a quantity of brown paper, crumpled and stained, and under it what appeared to be the ebony top of a footstool. She lifted it out, feeling no more than a vague curiosity, but when she set it on the carpet and saw it properly in the cool spring light, her gorge rose in her throat and the colour left her face. It was an elephant's foot, the nails enormous, cracked and yellow, and the long-dried skin grey-brown and hard as the bark of an oak. A horrible image occupied her mind. She could see the live elephant sinking down on its knees to die, heavy choppers cutting the feet from their poor powerless legs, and blood pouring in great streams from every cut. She tried to shake the picture from her mind by focusing on Aunt Amelia, but Aunt Amelia was twittering and seemed to be pleased with her disgusting present. It was Aunt Phoebe, dear sensible Aunt Phoebe, who came to her rescue, thanked the colour sergeant for his kindness, rescued her chattering bone china from his huge fists, and finally smiled both military gentlemen out of the house.

'If you don't like it,' she said to her niece, even before Alice could think how to explain her aborrence, 'we'll give it away. The Colonel has a house full of . . . things from India. He'd love it!' She looked at Alice and waited for a decision. As Alice was slow to respond, she went on, rather sharply. 'Well make up your mind, child, d'you want it, or don't you?'

So the foot went to embellish the Colonel's hall, where it stood between the aspidistra and the hat stand and was much admired by all his guests. And Alice thought that was the end of an extraordinary episode. But it wasn't.

On the following Monday Private Mitchell returned. He didn't see Alice because she was busy in the school room re-filling the ink wells and polishing the desks. Aunt Amelia entertained him and told him how kind he was and made small talk for half-an-hour. As he left he looked so down in the mouth that she felt obliged to comfort him. 'It's been very nice talking to you Private Mitchell,' she said. 'You must call on us again.'

It had been a polite noise, really no more, as Amelia explained to her sister afterwards. 'I was only saying it. You know how you do.' But Private Mitchell accepted her offer at once with a peal of smiles. He had leave on Thursday. Would Thursday be in order? So of course, it had to be. Aunt Amelia asked him to tea.

Alice didn't look forward to the tea party, but she needn't have worried. She found that the private had been as appalled by the slaughter of elephants as she'd been. Within ten minutes of his first awkward sandwich, they were talking of the need to care for animals and not make stools of their feet. By the end of the afternoon, the aunts came to the firm conclusion that this was a sensible young man. When he asked, hesitantly, whether it would be agreeable for Alice to walk out with him, on the common, after church on Sunday, they all felt that it was a very good idea.

So that was how Alice found herself the blushing possessor of a real live beau, and realized that she was actually walking out. It was an agreeable state of affairs. Aunt Phoebe's young ladies were very impressed and wanted to know every detail of this fairy-tale suitor. How tall was he? What colour were his eyes? Did he smoke? What regiment was he in? Many happy hours were spent after school work was over, walking slowly home to the imposing houses in the Crescent, comparing notes on their various beaux amid delighted giggles and love-lorn sighs. At first Private Mitchell was an entirely suitable suitor. He looked the part, with his soft fair hair and his bold blue eyes, standing tall and straight in his impressive uniform, and, at least in that first sun-drenched summer, his behaviour was impeccable.

On Sundays he would wait for Alice beside the wooden fence that circled Holy Trinity Church, and they would take a turn on the common before Sunday dinner. On that first Sunday, as she walked beside him among the chestnut trees, Alice was happily aware that other strollers were smiling and nodding in their direction. We make a handsome couple, she thought, perhaps I'm getting pretty after all. They exchanged Christian names and she was delighted to discover that his was Lionel. Such a nice name. A name with style. How awful it would have been if he'd been called Johnnie or Tommy or something common like that. They discussed the bad habits of the regiment and both felt very superior and moral and proper. At the end of their stroll, Lionel dutifully delivered her to her front door and shook her hand politely, bowing slightly, just like the private in the fairy tale. They agreed to walk again, but this time in the evening, in the dusk.

Alice decided that a romance was an enjoyable experience after all. She took to day-dreaming in church, imagining herself in bridal white at the altar rail with her handsome suitor beside her, whispering her vows, shyly, of course, to a church full of friends and well-wishers. She woke in the mornings to the bright light of another summer day, and the knowledge that she was sixteen and Private Mitchell loved her. Sometimes as they walked home across the common in the scented evening, they would stop under the swooshing branches of the chestnuts and he would bend slowly towards her and brush his mouth gently across hers. She would stand still to receive his kiss, feeling romantic and thinking how she would contrive to tell the other girls all about it next day.

Late the next autumn though, the Surreys were sent on manoeuvres. He came back a different creature, and it was a creature she didn't like at all. For a start, he now walked with a decided swagger. Very cocky, she thought, not at all nice. He'd put on weight, taken up smoking and grown a sizeable moustache. Being kissed by him was really quite unpleasant because the bristly hairs either tickled or irritated her. She could have put up with that, and probably endured the swagger and the smell of tobacco, if it hadn't been for his new style of talking, and that was really too much. As they went for their first walk after his return, she listened with growing revulsion to the things he told her, stories of torture and decapitation, and what sounded to her like the massacre of entire local populations.

' 'Course the square's your great strength. If you can hold your square they can't do a thing to you,' he explained grandly to Alice, as though she, too, was a soldier of the line. 'But by God, you've got to keep on the qui vive with savages. Not like Christians, they're not. Don't care what they do. Well take this battle of Hasin, for instance, they hacked all the camels to pieces. Nine hundred camels. The place was awash with blood. Couldn't hack the British Army. That's a different story when they're up against trained men. The East Surreys was there, you know. At Hasin. Killed thousands of them Arabs, they did. Thousands.'

He's bragging, Alice thought. He's showing off. She didn't like it at all. It reminded her of the way her father used to talk when he and his friends had been drinking brandy.

The regiment left for India in the following spring. Alice gave her soldier a lucky St Christopher charm as a keepsake and he kissed her goodbye, unnecessarily roughly, she thought, and was gone. A letter arrived nearly three months later saying that they'd landed in Bombay, which was a smelly hole, and that he couldn't wait to get stuck into the savages. She never heard from him again.

For over a year Crescent Road waited for another letter, which Alice knew wouldn't come. The aunts kept up a polite pretence that mail from India was bound to be delayed, and that anyway, the army was bound to be keeping Lionel very busy. But when the summer season came round for the second time since his departure, even romantic Aunt Amelia was beginning to wonder. 'Something must have happened to him,' she said. 'A nice young boy like that. He'd never have left his sweetheart in the lurch, so something must have happened.'

They followed the news avidly, scanning the columns to see if the East Surreys had been mentioned, especially if there was news of a skirmish. Finally their patience was rewarded. In April came the news of a splendid battle at a place called Chitral Fort, and the East Surreys had been there. The aunts read every detail, praising the courage of our gallant boys who had marched on through the mountains even when they were all snow blind and suffering what the papers called 'incredible hardships'. 'Fighting the frontier tribesmen, you see,' Aunt Phoebe said, nodding knowledgeably, 'and everybody knows they're the worst fiends in India.'

No letter arrived from Private Mitchell after the battle. Now Aunt Amelia had no doubt at all about what had happened to him. 'He must have been killed,' she reasoned. 'If he'd been wounded, he'd have written by now. Or got somebody to write for him. Or been sent home. It's terribly sad, but I think we'll have to face it. Those terrible tribesmen have killed him.' Soon his gallant death on a foreign field had become entirely real to her and she was passing it on to the day girls in a suitably hushed whisper. The day girls were shocked. Several of them wept with sympathy, and pressed Alice's hand to show how sorry they were. Alice had her own views about what had happened to Lionel Mitchell, but she kept them to herself and merely looked pale and interesting.

And so her life continued, quietly and uneventfully. She settled down and became steadily more useful about the house, accepting household chores willingly and without complaint because she didn't want to be a burden. From time to time she would try to help in the classroom, teaching the little ones their letters, or their scales, or providing a dancing partner for the older girls, but she really preferred the housework, especially the sort that could be done quietly and alone. The weeks came and went, the seasons changed, the ex-pupils grew fat and motherly, but Alice didn't alter. She was still as slim at twenty-eight as she'd been at sixteen. Her youthfulness pleased her, whenever she took time to notice it, but it didn't occur to her, after a lifetime of thinking she was plain, that her looks would ever catch her a husband.

Albert Pelucci's arrival was the biggest surprise in her life.

Chapter 12

When they arrived at Luigi's, the place was crowded with customers and savoury with the smell of served food.

'Table by the winder, Mr Ploochy,' Luigi said, manoeuvring past them with a loaded tray held deftly above his head. 'Mr Chanter's give your order.'

Dickie rose beaming towards them as they threaded their way between the cane chairs and black knees that crammed the room. Albert was delighted by the splendid surprise that registered on his good friend's rosy face when he caught sight of Alice. He introduced them, swelling with pride and the most satisfactory sense of his great achievement.

'Well, well, well!' Dickie said, dumbfounded. 'Stop the cab! If this don't beat all! Ploochy, you old dog. You kept that very quiet, diddencha?'

'*We* are discreet,' Albert said, chortling with delight. 'Aren't we, Miss Towers?'

'Of course,' Alice said, agreeing with him in almost total bewilderment. Was he going to pretend they'd known one another for a long time? What an extraordinary man!

Dickie was looking worried. 'I've give the order for two,' he said apologetically. 'You never said you was bringing company.'

'Soon put that right,' Albert said, expansive and happy. 'What are we having?'

'Cut off the beef,' Dickie said. 'Luigi said it was good. Scotch.'

'Would you like the beef, Miss Towers?' Albert asked, and when Alice nodded, he roared at Luigi's departing back, 'Make it three, Luigi! And we will have a bottle of claret.' Then he turned his attention to his new girl and his old friend, gratified to notice that they were already happy in one another's company. They talked about food and music and music halls, and Alice was impressed to learn that Dickie was a theatre agent.

'Come up the Duchess tonight and see us,' Dickie suggested

as he left them. 'We've got Little Tich to top the bill. You'd enjoy him.'

'Would you like that, Miss Towers?' Albert asked. So it was agreed.

'Now,' he said, 'where would you like to go this afternoon?'

Alice was confused. 'I don't know,' she said. She couldn't think of anywhere she wanted to go. Not later in the afternoon anyway. After her aunts' sherry and all that wine all she really wanted was 'to go and see Aunt Jane', but she could hardly tell him that.

She didn't need to, for Albert was nothing if not practical. 'We will go to the river,' he said. 'To Hampton Court. It just the day for it.' He caught a passing waitress by the string of her apron, 'Whoa back, Angelina!' he said. 'My young lady would like to freshen up. Show her where it is, will you.'

So Alice 'freshened up' and Albert settled up, and the two of them set off to Hampton Court, sitting side by side on the top of one of Tilling's splendid buses. Alice took care to tuck her skirts neatly down behind the modesty board and was glad she'd used two pins in her hat because it was quite breezy up aloft. Albert watched her every movement with approval, both satisfied and aroused that her body could now be so close to his, and delighted to be breathing in her particularly scented blend of warm flesh, clean cotton and starch. They talked all the way to Hampton Court, changing from one bus to another at the end of each line without really being aware of it, happily cocooned inside an enchanted web of sensation and communication.

They exchanged Christian names and discussed the relative merits of Clapham Common and old Clapham town. Alice told Albert about the aunts and the school and the wealthy pupils who lived in the Crescent. He told her what a terrible reception he'd had on the one occasion he'd ventured into that august square. They agreed that wealthy people were snobs, and confessed that they both thought going to church was boring.

'It might be better if we had another Vicar,' Alice said. 'The Reverend Jenkins is so cantankerous. He's always on about hell-fire. He never says a word about heaven or anything nice.'

Albert thought it was heaven just to be sitting, jammed up against her side on that crowded bus. He wondered what she would say if he put an arm round her shoulder but he decided against it, in case he shocked her.

Hampton Court was magical too that day, its lawns incredibly green and trim, its red brick glowing against a cobalt sky. The sun had brought out the crowds, but here even the crowds had a theatrical style as far away from the working world of Clapham and Tooting as it was possible to be. Here were elegant young men in rakish straw boaters and blazers like humbugs; here were the most decorative ladies, frilled, flounced, sashed and beribboned in gowns like Parisian fashion plates; here too was a troop of flamboyant cavalry, clanking, rattling and snorting their way into the Barrack Yard, for all the world as if they were at Balaclava. Resplendent in red and blue, astride plump and shining horses, they brought with them an exhilarating sense of excitement and occasion. Alice, glancing up at her holiday escort, had to admit that he'd certainly been right about Hampton Court. It was just the place to be.

Suitably stylish, Albert bowed towards her and offered his arm, grinning at her with an expression that was half delight and half daring. As they'd come to Hampton Court to see the Palace, they duly did the rounds, echoing through the vast spaces of the Great Hall, looking in at Wolsey's little oak-panelled parlour, and dawdling through the interminable miles of corridor and stateroom, past stale, rock-hard beds, and wall-sized portraits, and long dead furniture. They weren't really paying attention to any of it. They were simply and happily discovering each other.

Alice was intrigued by the variety of the expressions she saw on his face that afternoon and impressed by his open acceptance of them. Each one gave his face a different shape, and seemed to turn him into a different person. He had the most mobile mouth she'd ever seen. It was never still. Even when he was listening he stretched it from side to side, or smoothed his bottom lip over the top one, or made a sudden chewing movement that tipped his moustaches first to one side and then to the other. Anxiety drew in his eyebrows and made him tuck his chin towards his chest and suck in his lips to a triangular point. Delight made his eyes snap, his moustache bristle and his mouth spread wide and red. Determination hardened the flesh all over his face and set his mouth within a well-defined and shapely edge. Watching him, she wondered how she would ever be able to describe him to the aunts, he changed so often and so quickly.

Albert, in his turn, thought she was marvellously ladylike, gentle and neat in all her movements. She listened to him with her entire attention, her brown eyes watchful, and her face almost too still and placid. It took time for a smile to begin and longer for it to grow. He watched the whole process and found it both charming and touching.

When they'd finished their long trek through the staterooms and finally emerged to sunlight again, Albert headed straight for the river.

The Thames was as blue as the sky and extremely busy. Every available punt and skiff was on the water, each one in the charge of a young blood in a blazer and driven to the squealing delight of his silly frilly ladies. Alice and Albert settled down under a full-skirted willow to talk and watch the nobs at play.

They discovered, to their mutual delight, that they were both orphans. Albert hadn't talked about his mother for years. Now he found himself remembering her again and describing her to the attentive face beside him.

'She was only a little woman,' he said. 'Short. A lot shorter than you. And a bit fat. Well, very fat really. Stout. Her wedding ring sank right into her finger. And she had two, three chins, and a lot of flesh here,' patting the lower half of his cheeks. 'Wobbly.' No, he thought, that's not a good description. He paused for a little and tried again. 'I thought she was beautiful when I was a boy. I was young, you see. But she wasn't beautiful. Not to be truthful. She had a big nose. Like me.'

Privately Alice agreed with him. He did have a big nose, fleshy and heavy. But she didn't say anything. It wouldn't have been proper, and anyway she could tell by the movement of his mouth that his thoughts were upsetting him.

'She was very strict,' Albert went on, 'but she never raised a finger to me. Never. She didn't need to. One word from her and I was good. She never raised a finger.' He remembered those blunt, brown fingers and how he had wept to see them lying useless and dead across her chest on that awful day when they'd nailed her into her coffin. He could hear the sound of those hammers still, that ugly, cold sound, and for a few seconds he felt again the old bleak sense of loss and emptiness, even here sitting beside his lovely girl in the warm sun of an English summer. 'She was a good woman,' he said, his eyes and mouth troubled by the memory. 'A good mother. She lived for her children.'

His distress was so obvious, that Alice brimmed with sympathy. 'You must miss her terribly,' she said. 'I'm *so* sorry.'

'It was all a long time ago,' Albert said.

Alice tried again. 'I can't remember anything about my mother,' she confessed. 'She died when I was born. I can remember my father, though.'

'What was he like?' Albert asked, glad of a chance to turn his attention to something else.

Caught with her emotions off-balance, Alice answered quickly and without thinking about the propriety of what she was about to say. 'He was horrid,' she admitted. 'He didn't like me and I didn't like him. He lived in India most of the time. I only saw him once a year.' Then she blushed. She was being indelicate. Fancy saying a thing like that about your father!

Albert was charmed by her confusion. 'Tell the truth and shame the devil,' he said. 'If he was horrid, he was horrid. You were lucky you only saw him once a year. I saw my father every day and it was much too much.'

'You didn't like him either?' Alice said, surprised at her boldness but carried away by the pace of these confessions.

'No, I didn't,' Albert agreed. 'He wasn't the sort of man you could like. He was too brutal.' His mind was filled with the image of his father's rough, stained hands wielding that heavy belt. 'Now I come to think about him. He was a bully. He bullied the earth and the animals and the farmhouse and my mother. He even tried to bully me.'

'Was he a farmer?' Alice asked.

'I think you would call him a peasant,' Albert said, replying carefully because he was using vocabulary he wasn't quite sure about. Was a man like his father a peasant in England? He gave Alice a grin.

'Don't sound right,' he said. 'A peasant.'

'I don't know what my father was,' Alice said. 'I don't think he ever really existed outside India.'

This was more than Albert could cope with. 'Let's have some tea,' he said.

They had strawberries and cream in a little white weatherboarded tea house down by the water's edge. Then they set off on their involved bus trip to the Duchess Theatre.

They caught the first house and Little Tich was on form. By now Albert felt as though he'd grown a foot taller in the last twelve hours. Every experience was bound to be a good one he decided. He only wished the day could go on for a week. He felt he had the energy for anything. Alice, following him into the dazzling auditorium, was beginning to wonder how she could persuade him to take her home. Most of the acts that Albert was applauding so rapturously were simply a blurred impression. It took the artistry of Little Tich to rouse her from her fatigue. He made her gasp and laugh almost despite herself, as he flung himself from the point of one grossly elongated shoe to the other.

'He looks like a stork,' she said to Albert as they applauded his last extraordinary somersault. 'How on earth does he do it?'

'Practice, he says,' Albert told her.

'Do you know him?' Alice asked, impressed.

'We are acquainted,' Albert said proudly.

Alice would have liked to ask what the little man was like off stage but the heavy red and gold curtains were looping open again for the final chorus, 'You are my honeysuckle!' led by a short girl with ringlets, who sang raucously and very flat. Albert sang with the rest, 'I am the bee,' beaming at Alice, his dark eyes glowing in the soft light of the theatre. He can't sing at all, she thought, but she was warmed by his pleasure and enthusiam.

It was growing dark as they emerged from the naphtha flares and limelight into the early evening air. The pavements were crowded with evening shoppers. For the first time that day, Albert remembered his off-licence and hoped he wasn't losing too much trade. Then he turned to Alice again. Her hair was an even richer gold in the gaslight, and her eyes an even deeper brown. 'We will have supper?' he asked.

Being back on ordinary pavements again had reminded Alice of home, too. It made her feel guilty, as well as tired. 'Oh no, thank you all the same,' she said. 'I ought to be getting back really. Aunt Phoebe will be wondering.'

So he took her home and walked her to her doorstep, careful to play the gentleman. But as she turned her face towards him to say goodnight, she looked so very pretty and was so exactly the right height, that he couldn't resist temptation any longer. He took her face gently between his hands and gave her a resounding kiss, first on one cheek and then on the other. Her eyes rounded with surprise for an instant but she didn't seem displeased. Had he known it, she was secretly wondering whether her aunts could have heard what he was doing. His kisses had been so loud.

'I will see you tomorrow,' he said. It wasn't a request. It was a statement of intention.

The aunts were sitting up in the kitchen, eagerly waiting to hear how she'd got on. Phoebe was her usual well-corseted self, but Amelia was in her nightgown, with her hair in curl papers and her face already in its sleeping creases. She was obviously tired, and doing her best not to yawn, but she woke up quickly enough when Alice came in.

'Well?' she demanded, agog for gossip. 'What's he like?'

Alice considered for a moment. 'He's nice,' she said. 'He's like an express train.'

The express train was sitting in a kitchen that now seemed very empty, carefully composing a note to stick in the shop window the following morning. 'Wanted,' it said. 'Boy to help in shop. Must be strong and willing. Good wages.' Albert considered it. Now that he needed to leave the shop to go courting, it was important to get someone really reliable. Any old lad wouldn't do. He licked the end of his pencil and added a further enticement. 'Good prospects.' That should do it.

Four boys applied before breakfast. He didn't really like any of them. They were too wishy-washy. Wouldn't say boo to a goose. He wanted a lad with a sharp tongue and a quick wit, to sauce the customers and subdue the drunks. These were altogether too subservient.

He was standing behind the counter drinking a mug of coffee by way of breakfast when Harry arrived for his beer.

'Them old lettuces is coming along lovely,' he said, picking his teeth while Albert pulled his quart for him. 'D'you get the tomatoes?'

'What tomatoes?' Albert asked.

'Left you a note. Yesterday,' Harry said. 'Ain't yer found it?' And seeing from his friend's face that he hadn't, he wiped the toothpick on his trousers, put it carefully back into the pocket of his jacket, and went off to hunt for the note. It was still lying beside the doormat where it had fallen. Harry dusted it down on his useful moleskins and handed it across the counter. 'Come round twice,' it said. 'You was out. Hope you had a good day. Tomarters in shed. H. Jones.'

'That is very kind of you, Harry,' Albert said. 'I will have them for supper tonight.'

'Where was yer?' Harry asked.

Albert beamed with delight and devilment. 'I was courting,' he said.

'Well I never!' Harry said, impressed. 'That'll be why you're wanting a lad then.' He took his beer jug. 'How much I owe you?' he offered, as he always did.

'Fair exchange,' Albert said, as *he* always did in answer to one of Harry's gifts.

'You want young Nat,' Harry said fitting the jug into his work box. 'Just the chap for you. Sharp as a needle. I'll send him in.'

Nathaniel Hawthorne arrived that evening, clutching a bunch of red roses. He was a tall, lanky lad of thirteen with a shock of dark, tightly curling hair, bold green eyes and a grin like a slice of melon. Albert liked him at once.

'Come about the job, Guvnor,' he said. 'Name of Nat. Harry Jones sent me. Said ter give you these.' And he handed over the roses.

'Have you ever worked an off-licence before?' Albert asked.

'Pot boy I was, guv. On Sat-days and holidays and such,' Nat said cheerfully. 'When I could get off school.'

'Did you hop the wag?' Albert asked, putting on a stern face. He was alerted by this information. He didn't want a truant. A boy who could hop school would be just as likely to cut the job too if he felt like it.

But this boy was sharp. 'Not likely, guv,' he said grinning, 'that's a mug's game. All legal and above board it was. Old Miss Bullough let me go. She didn't reckon she could learn me no more, not once I could read and do me figures and such like. She said I was a good scholar. Quick an' 'andy. Worth half a dollar a week, any day, she reckoned.'

'Can you ride a bike?' Albert asked, keeping a straight face but admiring the cheek. It reminded him of the way he'd persuaded old Solly Isaacs to take *him* on.

'Like I was born to it,' Nat said.

Albert's mind was almost made up. 'When could you start?' he asked.

'Now if you like,' Nat said. 'Harry said you might want me straight away.' Again the grin and the cheerful sense of conspiracy. 'I told the old lady I might be late. Just in case.'

'I hire you,' Albert said. 'Start with half a crown a week. Five bob in September, if you satisfy.'

'That's dandy!' Nat said, smiling his wide warm smile again. 'You won't regret it, guv. I can promise yer.'

So late that evening, Albert got into his Sunday best for the second time that week and set off for Clapham, clutching his roses. So many extraordinary things had happened to him during the last twenty-four hours, he was beginning to feel that the gods loved him after all.

Alice hadn't had a good day. For a start, she'd woken up with a banging headache and no appetite for breakfast, which didn't please Aunt Phoebe. Then, as she sweated her way through a mound of ironing and her mind gradually cleared, she began to feel that she'd behaved extremely badly the day before. She'd been selfish and skittish and terribly indelicate. It made her feel ashamed.

The afternoon was very hot, so she took the mending out into the garden, and sat in the shade of the cherry tree, darning stockings and glad to be on her own with thoughts that were steadily growing more disquieting. By the time the last stocking was neat and entire again, she had decided that she really didn't want Albert Pelucci to call on her any more. He was a disturbing influence.

Aunt Amelia made matters worse by chattering romantic nonsense all through tea. She was thrilled by Albert. 'Just imagine,' she said, 'to be so taken with you, he'd come and knock on our door like that. And we perfect strangers. It's better than Marie Corelli.'

'Marie Corelli,' her sister said sternly, 'bears as little resemblance to real life as your spectacles do to a milk jug. Pass me another sandwich, if you please.'

Amelia passed the sandwiches, pouting. 'Sometimes Phoebe,' she said, 'I wonder if there's any romance in your soul at all.'

'Romance,' said Phoebe, 'doesn't pay the rent.'

But even she had to admit that Albert was a spectacular lover, when he arrived that evening with his arms full of red roses, and a cab waiting at the gate to take Alice off to supper. 'He may be a funny-looking little man,' she said to Amelia, after the cab had clopped away, 'but I'll say one thing for him. He's got style. And he doesn't let the grass grow under his feet.'

That was the trouble, his style and his speed. Alice set out that evening determined to put an end to her unexpected courtship. She never got the chance. This time Albert took her to a rather splendid restaurant where they dined by candlelight in a secluded alcove, all pink and gold and faintly perfumed. Alice felt terribly out of place in her cheap cotton skirt and home-made blouse, and at first she hardly dared to open her mouth. But Albert didn't seem to mind. He was bubbling with news and she was a good listener. He'd taken orders for twelve different parties during the day and they were invited to four of them. It was going to be a marvellous autumn.

And in many ways, it was. Alice had never been so petted nor felt so special. Everywhere she went with Albert, she was the focus of admiring attention as 'Ploochy's intended'. She was surprised by the number of people who liked him and claimed to be his friend, and by the way they thumped him on the back and poured him drinks and made him welcome. There was certainly something about him or he wouldn't be so popular. And his generosity was both touching and embarrassing. One evening she was foolish enough to complain that her hands were cold. The next day he arrived with an expensive pair of white kid gloves to keep her warm. She explained that her hair was in tangles because her hairbrush was getting old. Two days later he bought her a complete brush set. Even to admit to a weakness for Turkish delight proved to be risky. He bombarded her with the stuff. She began to realize that she would have to be very careful about what she said when she was with him, or he could turn her into a grasping woman. She tried to confide in her aunts but they were no help to her at all.

'I'm sure he shouldn't be buying me all these expensive things,' she said to Aunt Phoebe. 'It isn't proper, is it?'

'A girl's fiancé may buy what he likes for her,' Phoebe said. 'I wouldn't carp if I were you.'

'Your Albert's got a heart of gold,' Amelia sighed.

But Alice wasn't sure she wanted him to be her Albert. She was used to the pattern of life at Crescent Road, and she knew it suited her. Being a wife was a hazard, and no amount of pretty presents could alter her opinion of that. But she felt she was slipping inexorably towards this undesirable state. Soon, she knew, he would propose to her, and how could she possibly say no when they'd already come so far and she'd accepted all those presents.

Albert, unaware of her dilemma, lived in a rush of impatience, happiness, frustration and delight. Whores were useless now that he'd found his girl. But it was a torment to sit beside her and walk beside her and do nothing. After an evening in her company he went home aching with frustration, exactly as he remembered doing as a boy in Pontedecimo when the village girls had teased him so cruelly and led him on, laughing and mocking, and then said no. He remembered their bold eyes belittling him, and their strong arms pushing him away and his sense of inadequacy and impotence, his tears and his puny anger. This girl, his lovely Alice was different, thank God. She didn't mock or tease. She listened quietly, her brown eyes fixed on his face. She was cool and proper and gentle, just like a wife ought to be. But at night he dreamed of making love to her, naked and glowing and passionate, her mouth hot for kisses and her pale arms wound about his body. It made day time control very difficult. He wished there was some way he could speed up his courtship, but he was afraid to rush her in case he lost her. Surely soon it would be the right moment to mention the wedding. The affair was progressing very well. They shared the same taste in so many things, and they were the things that mattered, food and wine, music-hall songs, and even, as he discovered one warm October evening, homes.

They had walked on Clapham Common so many times that they were both bored with it. The paths between the ponds and under the chestnuts, up to Holy Trinity or down to the Windmill, were too familiar, too well worn. So that night they headed north towards old Clapham village, between the Gothic splendour of the red brick Alexandra with its balcony and its fine green dome, and the little antique Plough. The pavements were crowded with evening shoppers, pressing against the brightly lit windows, chattering and examining, while the High Street was full of traffic, cabs and carriages and late delivery vans, jostling for right of way. Alice had never liked crowds and noise, and that night she found them even more difficult to endure. Albert's solid body beside her was at least protection and she slid her hand, in its new kid glove, gratefully into the crook of his arm and was glad when he put his free hand across to hold it.

'Too many people, eh?' he said. Sometimes he seemed to understand her feelings so well. 'Come on. We will go away.'

They went away, turning out of the High Street into Manor Street, a long, cool lane full of squat, grey, old-fashioned houses. There were only a few people in this street and most of them were strolling down towards the shops.

'These old houses don't wear very well,' Alice observed.

'They should be pulled down,' Albert said. 'They are old-fashioned. Too plain. Too small.'

'They look like boxes with windows,' Alice agreed. 'Fancy building houses with flat roofs in this climate. It's ridiculous. Now those nice new houses on the common . . .'

'Quite different,' Albert said. 'They have got style. Windows that look like windows and a door that looks like a door. That one,' waving at a plain brown Georgian entrance they were passing, 'looks like a stable.'

It was a delightful topic. They criticized every house the length of Manor Street and at the end of the road, as if to prove all the points they were making, they came upon six brand-new brick built homes grouped prettily round the old parish church of St Paul's which lay below them on the path down to the Wandsworth Road, the very new beside the very old.

The churchyard was cool and quiet after the bustle of the High Street, and dark too, shadowed by tall yews and thick holly bushes, their lower branches grey with London dust. Alice and Albert walked into the shadow of the old building still arm in arm.

They came out on the cold north side to a panoramic view of their city. Below them the ground dropped steeply away to the Wandsworth Road, and beyond that, even more steeply to the Battersea marshes and the river. The sky was already lilac with dusk. Between the ranks of dark grey slates below them, they could see an occasional glimpse of shining olive water. Across the river, the tall white houses of Chelsea were wreathed with smoke. Grey gauze ribbons of it trailed from every chimney and drifted westward, massing into cloud as it went. In the west, above the gentle grey tiles and sand yellow bricks of Fulham, the sky blazed with sumptuous colour, orange, deep lilac and *eau-de-Nil*. A train crossing the viaduct headed towards Clapham Junction, puffing out gobbets of white steam. It looked no bigger than a toy. Below them in the Wandsworth Road miniature horses toiled before palm-sized carts and buses. Albert and Alice stood side by side leaning against the railings just looking at it all. It was a new experience for both of them and they were moved by it, although neither of them could have explained why.

'When you stand here like this,' Alice said, trying to put her feelings into words, 'you can see what a big place London is.' She looked at the vast reaches of the city spreading as far as the horizon and her words seemed inadequate.

'The capital of the world,' Albert said, trying too. But that wasn't right. He'd heard it too often before and it sounded trivial in the sight of a thousand homes and the thought of a million people.

Alice tried another tack. 'Are you glad you came here, Albert?' she asked.

'Now I am,' Albert said with ineffable contentment. 'Now I meet you, now I am happy.'

A breeze blew across the churchyard and Alice shivered, feeling chilly for the first time that day.

'You are cold?' he asked.

'No,' she said rapidly. He was wearing his determined expression, so she thought she'd better reassure him quickly before he rushed off to buy her warm clothing. 'I've got a thick coat for the autumn. It's just I didn't think it would be cold enough to wear it this evening.'

'You would like a new coat,' he said with satisfaction. 'Next Wednesday we go to town and buy a nice warm coat for you.'

This easy, out-going generosity, she thought. He'd give me the shirt off his back if I wanted it. He really is very dear. 'Albert,' she began as she turned towards him. The scent of her movement and the affection in her voice was too much for Albert. The Alice of his dreams stood beside him in the twilight, looking at him with love, just like he'd always known she would. With one movement he swung her into his arms. It was so quick and so deft he even surprised himself. It caught Alice completely off-balance. Before she had time to protest or even to think of protesting, her face was being covered with whiskery kisses

'Carina, carissima,' Albert said into the salty skin of her cheek. 'Bella, bella, bella,' with his mouth a fraction of an inch above hers. To be kissing her at last and holding that warm soft flesh so close! He encircled her face with both hands and his fingers caught her hair. It was silky soft, fine and smooth, just as he'd known it would be. 'Bellissima!' he crooned to her, kissing her mouth with all the tenderness and passion he'd been subduing since the summer. But she was drawing away from him, turning her head to avoid his kiss.

'Albert,' she said frantically. 'Shush! Please! Someone's coming.'

He straightened and drew apart from her just in time, as an elderly couple and a black and white mongrel ambled along the path beside the church. The language that had deserted him in his passion returned to help him. 'Good evening!' he said to the two passers-by and tipped his hat to the lady, surprised that it was still on his head.

Alice was shivering in earnest now and there was no doubt that the evening was drawing in fast. Her cheeks were flushed but there was no way of knowing whether the flush was love or embarrassment. He'd gone too far now. He would have to speak. And now, before he lost his confidence.

'Alice,' he said. 'When shall we get married?'

It was said. How could she reply? She couldn't say no when he'd been kissing her like that and she'd allowed it. She'd have to marry him now. Things were happening too fast again. 'I'll have to ask Aunt Phoebe about it,' she said.

He took her left hand and raising it to his lips, kissed it so gently she could only just feel the warmth of his mouth through her white kid glove.

'My lovely Alice,' he said, 'we will be so happy. I promise you.'

Alice looked at the dark brow bent over her hand and thought how romantic this was. She wished love could always be soft and gentle and undemanding like this. The urgency and hunger of those other kisses had alarmed her. And her alarm had been intensified by the odd excitement that had stirred and risen in her belly. No lady, she knew, should ever have felt like that. She couldn't marry him. She simply couldn't. Aunt Phoebe would have to find some excuse for her.

But Aunt Phoebe wasn't prepared to find excuses for her. And Amelia was worse than useless.

'A proposal!' she sighed. 'What did you say, child? You accepted him, of course. What did you say?' She was avid for details, her old cheeks pink and her faded eyes gleaming.

'I don't want to marry him,' Alice confessed. 'I said I'd ask you.'

'Why don't you want to marry him?' Phoebe asked, stern above the tea cups.

Alice faltered and thought for quite a long time. How could she answer that? 'I like it here with you and Aunt Amelia,' she said at last. 'I'd like to go on living with you and helping in the school.'

Aunt Phoebe put down the tea pot, folded her big blunt

hands in her lap and considered her niece for some time from under her formidable eyebrows. It's almost, thought Alice, quailing before her, as if she knows what I'm thinking. How awful! But the pronouncement, when it came, was worse.

'You can't stay here for ever child,' Phoebe said, 'because we can't run the school for ever. We're getting on, you know, and it won't be long now before we have to close. If it came to that we couldn't afford to keep you.'

'We wouldn't throw you out, of course my dear,' the tender-hearted Amelia was quick to intercede, seeing how her niece's face had fallen. 'But we'll all be a great deal poorer, you must see that.'

Alice did see it, and she also saw how opportune her love affair must have seemed to the two dear old ladies now watching her face with such anxiety, Phoebe stern and tightly controlled, Amelia quivering and slightly crumpled.

'He wants me to fix a date,' she said, closing her face and abandoning her hopes.

'No need to rush things,' Aunt Phoebe said, roughly, because she had upset herself with the need to be so harsh to her niece. 'You'll want at least six months' engagement, you tell him that, if you're to have time to get ready properly.'

I don't want to get ready at all, Alice thought despairingly. She tried one last gambit. 'You used to say what a nuisance men were, Aunt Phoebe,' she said. 'You told me I was better off without a husband.'

'That,' said Phoebe, 'was before you had the offer of one. Of course men are a nuisance. We all know that. But you can only exist without them if you can earn your own living. And how many women can do that? If I thought you could take over the school, and run it, and enjoy it, I'd hand it over to you straight away and be happy for you to stay a spinster. But you couldn't do it, could you?'

Alice had to admit unhappily that she couldn't.

'There you are then,' said Phoebe. 'You'll find it's all turned out for the best, my dear. Albert's a good man. He won't keep you short, he won't beat you and you'll never want, you mark my words. Why, he's got success written all over him.'

'And he's so romantic,' Amelia said, cheered by the turn the conversation was taking. 'He'll shower you with presents! What sort of engagement ring will you have? A little ruby would be nice, wouldn't it Phoebe? Do you think he would run to a ruby?'

But Alice was remembering the heat of his mouth on hers and the strength of his arms, and wondering, not for the first time in her life, just exactly what married people did in bed, and whether she would be able to endure it, whatever it was.

Albert did rather better than a little ruby. Having enlisted the aid of Solly Isaacs, he bought her a half loop of diamonds. Once again she was pleased, embarrassed and excited all at once. He never does anything on a small scale, she thought. It's always the grand gesture with him. Now she was beginning to notice how much he talked with his hands, and how extravagant he was. He's very Italian, she thought. And then, I shall be marrying a foreigner.

Albert rushed her through the winter, happy and busy. They decided that May would be a suitable month for their wedding, and chose the third Wednesday so that they could have four days honeymoon and be back in time to open shop again on Monday. Albert scanned the advertisements in the *News and Mercury* until he found a seaside boarding house that sounded suitable, and wrote off happily to book a double room. Then he turned his attention to the bed in which they would sleep for the rest of their married lives. He went to Whiteley's and bought the most impressive brass bedstead he could find, with a thick feather mattress to match. Then he moved his uncomfortable wooden cot into the empty back bedroom and had the decorators in.

Soon the bleak brown shell in which he had slept alone for far too long had become a bower. Pink rosebuds clustered on every wall and pink velvet curtains looped across every window in the most satisfyingly theatrical way. He was charmed by the transformation. It brought the wedding closer just to stand in the doorway and look at it. Soon, he thought, resting one hand on the downy softness of his new bed, he and Alice would be in that bed, and then . . .

He was disappointed that Alice was so shy. Modesty was all very well and he knew that he should value it, but sometimes he felt she was taking it too far. He had hoped that once they were engaged, she would have made opportunities for them to be alone together so that he could kiss her and fondle her. Surely she must see how much he wanted her and how difficult it was for him to keep his feelings under control. But she always seemed so calm, so quiet and so undemonstrative. She stood still to be kissed and never said no unless she thought somebody would see them, but she never kissed him back. If he lifted her arms and put them round his neck, she would keep them there, but she didn't seem to understand how much he wanted her to hold him of her own accord. Such thoughts made him sigh, with a little chill of apprehension, and that wouldn't do. Better to keep himself busy and not to think too much. Hard work was always a good remedy. May would arrive eventually, however slowly it seemed to be approaching, and once they were married everything would be all right.

If the calendar crept at a snail's pace for Albert, it rushed upon Alice like a coach and horses. Since she had accepted the inevitability of her marriage she had been numb to almost any emotion. She did the chores, amassed a sensible trousseau and accepted congratulations modestly, but nothing seemed real. She was sure that sooner or later she would wake up and none of these things would be happening to her after all.

But she didn't wake up, and the third Wednesday in May arrived and the Reverend Jenkins took his mind off hell-fire long enough to consecrate her marriage to Albert Pelucci. Still in a dream, she drank champagne in her aunts' flower-packed front parlour, smiled mistily at the guests, and forced down a slice of wedding cake that would make her feel sick all the way to Eastbourne. Then she said goodbye to a weeping Amelia and a stoical Phoebe and set off to start her married life, with Albert triumphant at her side.

Chapter 13

'Where's old Ploochy, then?' Harry asked Nat that Wednesday
evening.

'Gorn off a-honeymooning,' Nat said, pulling beer for Mr
Chamberlain, who was leaning artistically against the counter,
like a dandy against a mantelpiece.

'Never!' that worthy exclaimed. 'Well if that don't beat all!'

'That accounts for this morning, then,' Harry said. 'I seen
him go off. All done up like a fourpenny 'am-bone. Thought
'e was up to something. Good old Ploochy!'

'You in charge then, Nat?' Mr Summers asked. 'Pint a'
black and tan.'

'That's about the size of it,' Nat said happily, flicking the
counter dry with the napkin he now wore expertly across his
left shoulder.

'Where's 'e gone then,' Harry asked, as Nat pulled the black
and tan.

'Seaside, he said,' Nat answered. 'Got the weather for it
ain't he?'

'Well good luck to him,' Mr Summer said. ' 'E's a hard
worker, when all's said and done. Deserves a 'oliday, he do!'

'If I know Ploochy,' Charlie Chamberlain said, winking at
the others 'He's having a rare old time. Lucky dog! Wouldn't
mind being in his shoes myself. She's a pretty little thing they
do say. Be a rare thing to pot the red there.' And he winked
again.

At that very moment the lucky dog was trying to eat a rock
hard chump chop that his new landlady, 'Mrs Montgomery.
Bed and Breakfast a speciality. Supper Optional,' had specially
burnt for him. Alice, still pale and nauseous from the combination of wedding cake and steam train, had picked at her
meal for two or three minutes and given up the struggle. Albert
was doing his best, because his new landlady was standing
beside the table watching him.

Mrs Montgomery looked like a fox-terrier and smelt like a

frying pan. She had a sharp, inquisitive, grey muzzle and small, sharp black eyes, always on the look-out for custom or complaint, for there was always too much of the latter, and too little of the former. She wore a tight-fitting, highly starched widow's cap and veil, tied under her chin with a broad ribbon that completely obscured her hair, if indeed she had any, and as her eyes were totally devoid of lashes and her eyebrows seemed to have fallen out years ago her face had a bald, uncompromising, quizzical look that Albert and Alice both found very disquieting. Her smile was hard, professional and uncaring, and she spoke in a cultivated whine, pronouncing each word with care, as though she'd just learned the language.

'Ai trust everything is to your satisfaction, sir and modom,' she snarled.

Albert made growling noises at his chop, and pushed it onto its third circuit of the plate.

'Eef there is anything else you maight require,' the fox-terrier said, snapping its jaws together, 'you hev only to ask.'

And probably feeling that she'd overpowered them enough for their first evening, she marched herself back into the kitchen, through whose doors a strong smell of rancid fat and sour vegetables wafted back towards them.

Alice looked at her plate. The chop was woefully overdone, as brown as mahogany and every bit as hard; the potatoes were grey and full of eyes, and the cabbage pale yellow and streaming water. It was the most unappetizing meal she'd ever seen, and it was served in the most unappetizing room. The paintwork was dark brown and looked oily, the carpet was the colour of brown Windsor soup and so well-worn that the threads were exposed wherever she looked, and the beige wallpaper was so patchy and stained that she wondered whether irate customers hadn't been throwing their meals at it in exasperation.

'I'm terribly sorry, Albert,' she whispered. 'I can't eat it.'

'Nor can I,' Albert agreed, 'It disgusting. Not fit for pigs.' His face was gathered with anger. What a way to begin a honeymoon, served pigswill in a filthy room by an old witch with no hair. It wasn't at all what he'd planned. Alice looked pale and upset, and that made him angrier than ever.

'We not stay here,' he promised. 'Tomorrow, first thing, I find another place.'

Alice smiled bleakly at him. Her effort was obvious. In the meantime, they had an evening to get through somehow or other. There was a play in the local theatre, but Alice didn't fancy it. Variety on the pier was booked out. So they settled for the fine fat bandstand on the front, where a military band was playing 'Medleys from Vienna'. It didn't go too well, for although the bandstand looked stylish, it was cold inside and neither of them had come prepared for the chill of an English evening by the sea. Alice tried not to shiver, in case she annoyed her new husband any further. She clapped as long and as loudly as she could in order to warm her hands. But Albert *was* annoyed; at her, because her face was pinched and her nose looked mauve with cold in the yellow gaslight; but also at himself for not organizing the holiday properly. I should have planned it like any other holiday, he thought. I've been too excited and too happy. And it wasn't as if he hadn't learnt to mistrust that terrible racing happiness. It had brought him trouble all through his life. And here he was at thirty-one, still making the same silly mistakes.

They walked back along the promenade trying to admire the moonlight shimmering a diamond-white pathway across the black sea. The water lapped against the shingle, lick, lick, lick, and blue stars sparkled above their heads in an immense black sky, but romantic as it all looked, it was simply too cold to be enjoyed. Finally they went back miserably to Mrs Montgomery's evil-smelling establishment, where at least, Albert thought, they could be warm.

They weren't. As they climbed the steep stairs they left behind what little warmth the ground floor still possessed, although the rank odours of the kitchen rose with them, cabbage and grease and another sickly sweet smell that Albert couldn't quite place. The fusty back bedroom that Mrs Montgomery had so grandly allocated to their use was bitterly cold.

'I am so very sorry,' he said humbly to Alice as they stood side by side on the chipped linoleum in their bridal suite.

'It doesn't matter,' Alice said, but her face was bleaker than ever.

'We will be warmer under the covers,' Albert suggested. But she made no effort to undress. She stood in the middle of the room still and pale. What was he to do? She didn't even look at him. He opened up his valise and took out his nightshirt, wishing now that he'd invested in a new one. There was altogether too much shabbiness about this moment.

'I find the bathroom for us,' he said.

When he came back she had changed into a voluminous cotton nightgown, and folded her clothes neatly onto the chair and was sitting bolt upright in the bed, her eyes round and staring. Now what was the matter?

'Alice?' he said, but she didn't answer. She was staring straight in front of her, but she didn't seem to be looking at anything. It was if she was listening, he thought, not looking. The room was very quiet. He could hear the clock ticking in the hallway below them. He sat down on the bed beside her.

'What is it?' he whispered.

'Can't you smell them?' she whispered back.

'Them?' Albert said. What could she smell? What was she talking about?

'Black beetles!' Alice said. 'Black beetles! You can smell them all over the house. The kitchen must be crawling with them. We can't stay here, Albert.'

Cockroaches! Of course. That was the smell he'd half recognized. For a fleeting second he remembered that soup in Clerkenwell heaving under those massed brown crawling backs. But the thought was in and out of his mind before he could think about it properly. Alice was talking again, a rush of words, high-pitched and growing steadily more hysterical. The impact of the new changed woman beside him drove all other thoughts from his head. Her eyes were staring and her hair wild, but she still didn't look at him, or move any part of her body but her mouth.

'They'll be in here next,' she said. 'Filthy, filthy things! Can't you smell them? We can't stay here. They'll crawl in under the door, you see if I'm not right. They'll crawl all over the bed. We shall be eaten alive. The place is swarming with them, I tell you. Swarming! They'll be in here before you can say knife. We shall catch some terrible disease. If we haven't caught it already, eating her dreadful dirty food. They'll have been all over that. Oh, we must get out Albert, before it's too late!'

'We will go. First thing in the morning. I promise you,' Albert said.

'No! No! Now! We've got to go now!' Alice insisted, and she began to cry, silently and almost as though she wasn't aware of it. Great fat tears rolled from the inner corners of her eyes and fell down her cheeks onto the pleats of her nightgown. This was dreadful, Albert thought. Worse than the journey, and the greasy supper and the freezing bandstand. Whatever was he going to do?

'Tomorrow! I promise,' he said. He tried to put his arm round her shoulder, thinking to coax her to lie down, but her body was as stiff as a board. 'Lie down and get warm, my poor little Alice,' he coaxed. 'I won't let them get into this room. I promise. I kill them all.' But it wasn't any good. She didn't move. 'In the morning, we go,' he promised. 'Lie down! Please!' He was beginning to feel desperate. And foolish.

There was no coaxing Alice. She was beyond reason now. 'I can't lie down!' she said, almost shrilly. 'Can't you understand? This place is crawling alive with black beetles. I couldn't *sleep!*'

'You can't sit up all night,' he said, and this time there was a harsher tone to his voice. 'You being ridiculous! Lie down!' He seized her shoulders and tried to force her down into the bed. It didn't have the slightest effect on her. Her spine seemed to be made of iron.

'I'm not having black beetles crawling all over me all night long,' she said. 'Either we leave or I sit up. That's all there is to it.' The tears continued to roll out of her eyes, but she didn't really seem upset, simply aggressively determined. Albert couldn't make any sense of it. He wanted to roar at her, but was fearful of the ears in the house.

'Lie down!' he hissed, suppressing real anger with difficulty.

She didn't say a word. Just sat there, white and determined and unyielding.

Albert was beginning to feel cold in the chill bedroom. His feet were numb, he realized. 'Well, *I* go to bed,' he said to his new wife, 'You do what you like. I go to bed.' And he got into his side of the bed, as well as he could, turned his back on his bride, and tried to get his feet warm again by rubbing them up and down on the undersheet. The movement made him more irritable and frustrated than ever, because it reminded him of what he would much rather have been doing. The bed was very uncomfortable, with lumps in all sorts of unexpected places and there was a dip in the middle like a crater. Albert's foot rubbing gradually shifted him down into the centre pit. He could feel the length of Alice's legs against his spine. For a second he was hopeful again. Perhaps she'd got into bed with him after all. He turned on his back to see. She was still sitting bolt upright, as stiff as ever, but the tilt of the mattress had pulled her into the centre too, and now she had a decided sideways list. Like a sinking ship, Albert thought and suddenly the situation struck him as funny and he began to giggle.

'You look so silly sitting there,' he tried to explain. 'Oh, come to bed Alice, for the sake of heaven. Is silly! We can't go on like this all night.'

She took no more notice of his giggles than she had of his anger. But now that she was off-balance, he thought, perhaps he could pull her down into the bed. He grabbed her round the waist and tugged. This time she did move, turning her head towards him so suddenly that it took him off-balance too. 'Don't touch me!' she said, more fiercely than he'd ever heard her say anything. Her face was blazing with such concentrated fury, it felt like hatred. Albert wilted away from her.

It was a most uncomfortable night. Alice sat and stared like a stone. Albert tossed and turned, sometimes falling into a fitful sleep, sometimes just lying among the lumps, feeling depressed and guilty at the turn the day had taken. Why, oh why hadn't he organized things? He should never have trusted to an advertisement. He might have known he wouldn't get the truth from an advertisement, even if it *was* in the *News and Mercury*. He should have come down for the day and found a comfortable guest house, tasted the food and tried the beds. *And* kept a sharp look-out for black beetles! He'd know better next time. How could he have been so stupid? He was racked by his terrible incompetence.

Towards dawn, a wind sprang up and rattled the blind at their one inadequate window, 'trill-tr-tr-trill-click,' over and over again. The sound irritated Albert. He got wearily out of bed, blundered across the dark, unfamiliar room, and shut the window as quietly as he could. The house was very still and he could hear the sea swooshing and thudding somewhere behind the building. That was better than the silly licking sound it was making last night, he thought. More like the rough sea he admired. It cheered him up. If it hadn't been for the cold, he'd have stood by the window and enjoyed it a bit longer, but his feet were going numb again, so he decided he'd better go back to Mrs Montgomery's lumpy mattress. I'd have had a better night's sleep on the beach, he thought, and wondered if the martinet had actually filled her mattress with pebbles to save money.

As he padded back across the chill linoleum, Alice gave a little shudder and slipped down the bed into the dip he'd left behind. She looked extremely uncomfortable with her head wedged down onto her chest, but she was undoubtedly asleep. He edged the blankets gradually back from underneath her and gently, very gently eased her down into the bed. Her hands and feet were icy, but she was actually lying down. At last! He piled the covers over her to warm her, and gathered her towards him so that her cold feet lay between his legs and her cold hands against his chest. To his delight, she half turned towards him, sighed again, and put her head on his shoulder. His heart began to race. This was better. This was real progress. Perhaps everything was going to be all right after all. As if to confirm his hopes, the birds chose that moment to begin their early morning chorus. Very softly, just in case she woke and was angry with him again, he began to kiss the top of her head. She didn't move away, or object, but shifted her face slightly so that her forehead was just under his mouth. He kissed her hairline, and her closed eyes and her cheeks, still salty with tears. Now, now his marriage could begin.

Alice woke in some confusion to find that her husband was on top of her, that she was lying in the most undignified position, and that what he was doing was giving her a sharp digging pain in that part of her body she couldn't even name, let alone think about. She lay still and hoped he would stop soon. He was muttering Italian again, and his voice was thick and frightening like it had been that night behind the old parish church. 'Alice, Alice,' he said into her neck.

She felt she ought at least to answer that. 'Yes,' she said.

'Oh my darling, darling, darling!' he said, hurting her more than ever. Then he was beyond speech or even thought, and into extreme sensation. The terrible day was gone, the greasy meal was gone, the dirty little room was gone, even Alice had gone. There was nothing but exploding pleasure filling the world.

When he finally lay still, Alice wondered what she was supposed to do. Nothing occurred to her, so she lay still too and waited, feeling sore but glad that the stabbing pain had stopped. He was very heavy and seemed to be getting heavier. 'Albert?' she said.

He didn't answer. It dawned on her that he was fast asleep. He's using me like a pillow, she thought. I wonder if I can wriggle out from underneath. She tried to shift her belly from his weight and was appalled to discover that something wet and warm was trickling out from 'there'. I can't be bleeding, surely, she thought. 'Her little friend' wasn't due for another two weeks. And then hard on that thought came another even more alarming. I shall stain the sheets! How perfectly dreadful! There was nothing for it. Even if it meant waking Albert she would have to get up and make some sort of pad for herself with her little hand towel. She began to wriggle again, and this time he lifted his body, still fast asleep, and she got away.

It *was* blood. How horrible! She would have to get dressed at once. At least then she'd only stain her petticoats. She found the hand towel. What a mercy she'd brought it with her. She dressed quickly and quietly so as not to disturb Albert. Then she hid her stained nightgown in her bag. By the time she'd finished the sun had risen and the room was light enough to inspect the undersheet. With her heart pounding, she lifted the counterpane, and a grubby matted blanket and searched the sheet for the tell-tale spots. There was only one. Perhaps that horrible woman wouldn't notice it.

She was still feeling very sore and uncomfortable. She wondered if she could sneak along the corridor and 'see Aunt Jane' without waking anybody up, but decided it was too risky. The room was full of daylight, so she drew the blinds, a careful inch at a time, and taking the chair to the window, sat with her head against the frame and looked out into the disorder of the back yard. It wasn't a desirable view but there wasn't anything else to look at, except the dirty room or Albert fast asleep, and somehow she didn't want to look at Albert. He made her feel embarrassed. So she sat quietly by the window and watched the debris and the bright sky, and waited patiently for the morning.

It arrived with a violent attack on a gong that woke Albert with a start. 'Whazzat?' he said, sitting up quickly.

'I think it's a signal for breakfast,' Alice offered. She couldn't bring herself to look at him. It was worse now he was awake.

Had she only known it, he was feeling as embarrassed as she was. And the sight of her dressed and sitting by the window made him feel guilty too. He scowled and took refuge in anger. 'It had better be worth eating,' he said.

It wasn't, of course. If anything it was even worse than the supper. The eggs had been fried so hard and so fiercely that there was nothing left of them but two solid yolks on a dark brown lace doily; the sausages were black on one side and pink on the other, the bacon was the cheapest streaky and the fried bread as thick as a thumb and oozing yellow fat.

'This,' Albert said, throwing down his napkin like a gauntlet, 'is the limit! I do not eat such rubbish!'

'Mr Per-lushy!' the fox-terrier said, scurrying to the table. 'Is everything not to your satisfaction?' The sharp eyes dared him to take issue with her. But there was no stopping Albert now, despite the upturned faces of the other guests, who had given up trying to devour their awful breakfast and were giving him their undivided and admiring attention.

'Your house is disgrace!' Albert said. 'Filthy, contaminate, disgrace. This is food for pigs. We eat the food we sick, ill, vomit.'

'Perhaps we could discuss this in the – ah – office,' the fox-terrier said, and her tone was all sugar, as false as her smile. 'That would be rather more appropriate, Ai think, don't you?'

'No,' Albert said 'I don't think it. You are dirty woman. Your table dirty. Your food burnt. Look! Your beds full of pebbles. Terrible. Your kitchen full of black beetles! You promise good food, sea view, comfortable beds. You don't tell the truth. You are a disgrace!'

'Ai'm sure you'd be much more comfortable in the – ah – office,' the fox-terrier tried again.

'I will be much more comfortable in my own house,' Albert said. 'I go to my own house.'

'Perhaps you would care to come to the – ah – office and we can settle up,' fox-terrier suggested, moving two paces towards the door to show him the way he ought to be going.

'I not pay a penny!' Albert said firmly. 'Not for filth! Not for cockroaches! Not a penny!'

Mrs Montgomery drew herself up to her full rigid height.

'Mr Per-lushy,' she said, 'Ai'm sure you would wish to honour your debt. Ai'm sure you wouldn't wish lawyers to be involved.'

'Involve what you like,' Albert said, really enjoying himself now, his chest swollen with delightful anger, his eyes snapping and his moustaches leaping for joy at every word. 'I tell them all about this place. This dirt. I tell them. I will not pay one penny! I only pay for satisfaction!' He looked round him at the upturned faces. Many of them were smiling approval and one or two were nodding.

'Very well Mr Per-lushy. There's no more to be said,' Mrs Montgomery said, as smoothly as she could. She began to walk out of the room and her going was a defeat. At the kitchen door, she turned to face him again 'Ai hope you realize Ai've got my living to make,' she said.

'Food like this,' Albert said scornfully, 'all you make is a killing. Come along, Mrs Pelucci.' And he and Alice swept out of the room, picked up their bags and hats and coats from the hall, and escaped.

'Oh dear,' Alice giggled, as she struggled into her coat and tried to pin on her hat in the brisk morning breeze, a few yards down the road. 'Wasn't she wild!'

'Serve her right,' Albert said. 'To cook food like that for *my* wife!' His eyes were pleading. Was it all right? Would she forgive him for such a terrible start?

She put her hand into the crook of his arm. Laughter had made it possible to look at him again. 'Are we really going home?' she said.

'We go wherever you like,' Albert answered, his spirits rising again.

'Let's go home,' Alice said.

They were back in the shop before midday and if Nat was surprised to see them so soon, he was much too cute to say so.

'Pie and mash for three, Nat. Quick as you can,' Albert said, sorting out the right change and putting the coins on the counter.

So Nat shot off to get the pies and Alice made her first pot of tea in the kitchen of her married life, and all three of them settled down at last to enjoy a meal.

'Tomorrow,' Alice promised 'I'll cook a good beef stew and a steam pudding. How would that be?'

'Handsome!' Nat said. And Albert, full and satisfied, beamed and nodded and glowed.

So they settled down to married life, and although neither of them spoke of it, they were both glad to be back at work in a familiar routine, putting ordered days and accepted nights between themselves and the nightmare of their honeymoon.

Chapter 14

It didn't take Albert long to come to the conclusion that it was much better to be married than single after all. A touch of luxury had entered his life and it was all the better for it. He slept soundly, swaddled in his new feather mattress, and woke to the delectable smell of bacon frying and the knowledge that presently Alice would bring up a kettle of hot water for him, and a fresh warm towel. He began to put on weight and the extra pounds suited him, rounding out his cheeks and bringing a glow to his skin. Whatever else, he thought, Alice was a mighty good cook. She kept the house spotless and she worked even harder than he did, coming down to serve in the shop of an evening after she'd washed the dishes.

'You got a pearl there, Ploochy,' Harry said and Albert agreed with him readily. She only needed one more talent and she'd be perfect. Given time, perhaps she'd stop being so shy and start to love him back the way he wanted. Meanwhile it was a well-fed comfortable existence, the shop was making money and the sun was shining. What more could anyone ask? If they went on this way, he'd give young Nat another raise.

Alice too, with one serious reservation, enjoyed being a wife. It was gratifying to have a kingdom of her own and to be treated with respect by all the shopkeepers. 'Of course, Mrs Ploochy!' they said, and the title gave her pleasure every time she heard it. It was a delight to her to put on her new grey suit with its smart jacket, and pin her hat firmly to her head and go off to the Broadway to do her shopping.

But the best day of all was Thursday, when she took a bus and rattled away to Clapham to visit her aunts. How pleasant it was to see Amelia and Phoebe again, and to sit in their cool front parlour among the draped sepia tints and the swathed chairs, to eat their familiar scones and drink tea from their familiar china and know that she had pleased them. Secretly, it also pleased her that now she was married, she knew something they didn't, although in her more honest and private moments she had to admit that she would really rather have done without the experience. However, as she now realized, it seemed to be something that wives had to endure for the sake of their very pleasant status, and seeing how little time it actually took, despite the fact that it was very sordid she felt it was probably quite a good bargain.

June was an extravagance of roses that year. They massed in every front garden, scenting the summer. 'Coronation roses,' Amelia called them, and Phoebe, although she deplored such sentimental talk, had to concede that the King had chosen a good time to be crowned. Albert had more orders than he could cope with and was thinking of buying another bicycle for deliveries, when the papers were suddenly full of the news that the King was gravely ill and the Coronation had been postponed. Some of the more pessimistic newspaper men even hinted that it might never take place at all.

Special services were arranged all over the country. The one in Tooting was going to be held at the Broadway in the open air. The citizens of Tooting were urged to attend it and 'offer their prayers together for the safe deliverance of their sovereign in his hour of trial.' It was very dramatic and rather exciting, and it gave Alice a chance to show off her wedding suit. 'Wear your best hat, of course,' Albert said, fondly and proudly when she had wondered about its suitability. 'I want everybody to see how well my wife can dress.'

So she ironed her very best blouse and assembled her grey outfit for the occasion, and as a last minute concession to style, she decided to wear her corsets. She was annoyed to find that they didn't fit. It was quite a struggle to tie the laces and she felt far more constricted than she'd expected to. She must have put on weight, she thought. That would never do. Nevertheless, surveying herself in the long wardrobe mirror, she felt it was worth the effort.

It was odd to be walking down Mitcham Road in the gathering dusk with so many other people all going the same way and all looking so serious and intense. So many cloth caps, so many bowlers, so many bonnets and shawls, all bobbing down towards the Broadway like corks on a tide. There was Harry coming down Charlmont Road with his nice plump wife on his arm, and behind him, the two pot boys from the Mitre, still in their aprons. Mrs Adams, driving her dog cart with careful delicacy, picked her way among the sober walkers, and there was Charlie Chamberlain charging down Franciscan Road waving cheerfully.

'Should we wait for him?' Alice asked.

'No fear!' Albert said. 'With those legs! He'll catch us up before we get to the timber yard.' And he did.

The road widened out at the Broadway and it was packed with people, dwarf shapes, shifting and darkening as the sun steadily descended. Mr Jung hadn't rolled up his blinds, and so many people were standing on the pavement beneath it that Albert couldn't see the shop front at all. The round dome that capped the corner tower of the shop gleamed *eau-de-Nil* in the half light, and as they watched the glint of luminous colour above them was answered by the gradual blooming of the gaslights, opening out one after the other, like yellow flowers above the dark pavements. As if the lighting of the lamps had been a signal, a band, somewhere out of sight, began to play 'Abide With Me'. The crowd at the Broadway turned like a wave towards the sound, and the people in front of Alice and Albert quickened their pace. The service was beginning.

Alice would have been content to stay on the edge of the assembly and just listen, but Albert and Charlie wanted to see it all. 'Come on!' Albert said, elbowing his way into the massed ranks in front of them. Alice followed in the wake of his determination, too hemmed in by shoulders and hats to see where she was, but secure as long as she could keep his broad back within an inch or two of her nose. They edged right round the Broadway, past the off-licence on one corner of the High Street and Jung's bakery on the other, until they were facing a roped-off enclosure for the band and could see the local preachers standing on a row of soap boxes that had been placed in front of it. One, resplendent in white and gold, was intoning prayers. Beside him stood the Reverend Simpson, wearing his most pious face. It all looked and sounded most impressive.

'Can you see?' Albert asked, as he and Alice finally came to a halt as near to the soap boxes as he could get. But he never heard her reply, for the band was off again, and all around them the crowd was singing.

Alice felt as though she'd been swallowed by a whale, she

was embedded so firmly in that dense moving mass of people. She clung on to Albert's arm, which delighted him, and concentrated on keeping her face up towards the air. The hymn was followed by another exhortation to prayer. It seemed so much darker now that the lamps were lit and the air that brushed her face struck chill, which was odd because she was feeling so hot all of a sudden. So hot and almost as if . . . She gave a low moan as the darkness rushed up towards her and Albert, turning quickly, was just in time to catch her as she toppled sideways. Concerned faces turned in their direction at once and several pairs of helpful hands reached out to assist. Between them they carried her back through the crowd to the low wall around the Vestry and propped her up against the railings. By the time they were finished, she was beginning to come round. Even in the gaslight Albert could see how pale she was.

'I seen Old Mother Kelly over by Jung's,' Charlie offered. 'Shall I nip across and get her?' When Albert nodded, he slid off through the crowd at once, like a long-legged shadow.

Mrs Adams and Molly Kelly, the local nurse, arrived almost simultaneously, one from each side, and both prepared to take over. Now that his Alice was conscious again, Albert could begin to enjoy the drama, but Alice herself was embarrassed by the commotion she was causing. 'I'm better now,' she insisted. 'I can't think what came over me.'

'She can ride home in my dog cart,' Mrs Adams said firmly to Albert. 'You don't want her dragging back through all that crush. I'm not surprised she fainted, poor girl. It's perfectly dreadful. Very badly organized, you see. I've said so from the start.'

'Very obliging of you, Mrs Adams,' Molly Kelly said. She'd taken a quick look at her patient, loosened the neck of her blouse and chafed her hands, and was well on the way to a diagnosis. She bent to whisper in Alice's ear, 'The sooner you can get home and loosen those stays, my dear, the better.'

Mrs Adams' little pony stood patiently waiting beside the Police Station. He'd had enough of crowds for one evening and was glad to be on the move again. He trotted happily and smoothly back along Mitcham Road with his heavy cargo. By the time he reached the shop Alice was feeling quite herself again. It had been very pleasant being driven home, but really this was a lot of fuss about nothing. All she wanted now was to get indoors and forget all about it.

She'd reckoned without Mrs Kelly. That ample lady was still firmly in command. She left Albert to thank Mrs Adams and swept Alice up the stairs to her bedroom before she could find the words to protest. Once there, the offending corsets were removed.

'I'd put them away if I was you,' Mrs Kelly said. 'You won't be needing them for a good long time if I'm any judge.'

Alice wanted to ask why not, but the conversation seemed to be taking a serious, almost medical turn, and she didn't quite dare.

'Well now,' Mrs Kelly said, settling herself down in the wicker chair. 'You ain't got a fever. You got a nice colour. Pink of health, I should say. So what's up?'

'I expect it was the crowds, don't you?' Alice said, beginning to feel flustered again at the doubt this question raised.

'Could be,' Mrs Kelly said laconically, 'and there again, could be something else. You been putting on weight, Mrs Ploochy, may I ask?' casting a professional eye on the burgeoning flesh now released from the corset.

'Well, yes. I have a bit,' Alice admitted. 'Could that be it, do you think?'

'Could be,' Mrs Kelly said again. 'Depends don' it. Depends on the reason. Now if you was just eating, which I doubt very much, knowing the sort of young lady you are, well that wouldn't have no effect at all. Leastways, not till you was a good deal older. On the other hand, if you was expecting . . .' She paused to let the information sink in. 'Well that would be a different kettle of fish altogether, wouldn't it?'

A baby, Alice thought. Yes, of course. That would account for lots of things, not just the fainting fit. A baby. Just like all the other girls she'd been watching out of school and into marriage. She wondered why she hadn't thought of it before.

The skilful questioning went on. It didn't take Molly Kelly long to establish that the baby would be born in late February and that so far the pregnancy was progressing in a perfectly normal fashion. The necessary note was made in her little book, Alice was advised to eat well and rest whenever she could, and left to digest the news.

After the two women had disappeared upstairs, Albert was

left to worry. He decided to open the shop so that trade would give him something to think about. There were bound to be lots of people who'd like a drink on their way back from the service. But although custom certainly arrived, his mind refused to be budged. When Molly finally came downstairs she found him serving two customers, but fidgeting and fussing and obviously very ill at ease.

'She is ill?' he questioned anxiously when the shop was empty again.

Mother Kelly put him out of his misery. His response was electrifying. He gave a whoop of delight and lifted her off her feet, to swing her round a full circle, legs dangling, before he set her down on the ground again. Then while she was still gasping and scolding and clutching at her hat, he kissed both her cheeks, two smacking kisses that quite made her ears ring.

'You are lovely lady, Mrs Kelly,' he said. 'Say what you like. You can have it,' waving his arms at his well-stocked shelves.

Molly Kelly settled her hat. 'Well, I wouldn't say no to a nice milk stout,' she said.

Three were put on the counter immediately, despite her protests, and she was kissed again, to the amazement of four customers who'd just come into the shop. 'This lovely lady,' Albert explained, 'is to give me a beautiful baby. In February.'

The newcomers started to make suitable congratulatory noises. Molly Kelly shrieked with laughter. 'Oh do give over, Mr P.,' she said, 'for heavens sake. It ain't me,' she explained to the customers. 'I'm a midwife. That's what he means. Oh Mr P. you *are* a soppy 'apporth!' she retreated, still giggling, clutching her milk stout.

'And what can I do for you?' Albert asked the newcomers, stretching his mouth to the full width of his smile.

'Well,' one of the gentlemen ventured. 'We'd really rather like some beer.'

'Tonight,' Albert said grandly, 'anything!'

The very next morning he sent for a sign-writer and gave him detailed and rapturous instructions that had to be carried out on the spot, to the entertainment of his regulars, who gathered in the street to watch. Soon the simple slogan, 'Albert Pelucci,' had been prettily embellished. Now the sign above the door read 'Albert Pelucci & Son.'

'Being a bit previous in he?' Harry Jones observed. 'Might be a girl. I bet 'e ain't thought of that.'

'He don't need to think of it,' Charlie Chamberlain said. 'Knowing old Ploochy's luck, be a boy as sure as God made little apples.'

'We'll have some sport wetting *that* baby's head,' Mrs Summers said happily. 'What d'yer bet 'e spoils it rotten.'

It was an exciting summer. Even without the prayers of the Pelucci household, the King managed to recover from his operation. So the Coronation went ahead as planned. The crowned heads of Europe turned back across the Channel again for another free banquet, and those of the indigenous population who could afford it, copied their monarch by throwing expensive parties. It was very good for business, as Albert had known it would be. He did so well that year, he took almost as much during the summer as he usually did over Christmas. Mr Chalmers advised him to buy more shares. The market was looking up, he said. Albert, his pockets full of bank notes, could well believe it.

The shop did an extraordinary trade at Christmas too. 'The baby brings good fortune!' Albert said happily to an Alice now beautifully rotund. He was rapturously happy that Christmas. For the first time in his life he was experiencing the joys of a family gathering in his own home, and he threw himself into it wholeheartedly, never one to do anything by halves.

The aunts were invited, of course, and Dickie Chanter too, although it took quite a bit of pressure to get him to agree, and that surprised Albert, for he'd never suspected that his friend could be shy. He and Alice decided that this was just the occasion to open up their empty front room. So for the second time that year the decorators were called in and Albert went to Whiteley's.

Soon their front parlour was warm with heavy flock paper, oak furniture, and swathes of red brocade. Secretly Alice would have preferred a nice refined brown velvet but there was no gainsaying Albert. They built a fire halfway up the chimney to drive away the chill from a room so long unused, and then they had their first meal in style. Albert, looking round happily at the second room he had created, was well satisfied. 'All we need now,' he said, 'is a Christmas tree.'

He bought one that was much too big and he and Nat had a terrible job heaving and shoving it up the stairs. Albert was not deterred. He rushed off to Mr Kay the next day and ordered a massive goose, much to that gentleman's amusement. 'He'll be eating it till May!' he said to his wife after the beaming Albert had left the shop.

Alice spent several happy days in the kitchen, steaming Christmas puddings, making mincemeat and baking and icing a cake. And unbeknown to Albert she also passed several secret hours in their newly decorated front parlour embroidering a splendid waistcoat for his Christmas present.

Christmas morning was dark, grey and objectionable, but neither of them cared. They woke at six o'clock too excited to sleep any more and lay in the dark whispering together like children. Finally Alice couldn't keep her secret any longer. 'Would you like your present now Albert?' she asked.

Albert had been so busy preparing this Christmas for everybody else that he hadn't stopped to consider that he might be given presents too. He was delighted with the idea and bounced from the bed at once to light the gas. Alice fished out her parcel from under the pillow where she'd hidden it the night before and handed it across, almost shyly. 'Happy Christmas, Albert,' she said, thinking, what if he doesn't like it?

He was thrilled with it and put it on at once over his night shirt to strut about the bedroom in it and admire himself in the long mirror. Alice was kissed and hugged until she could hardly breathe and told how marvellously clever she was. It was a great success. It was only after he'd thrown on the rest of his clothes and rushed downstairs to light the stove, that she realized that he hadn't given her a present. She felt a twinge of disappointment, but suppressed it at once and tried to reassure herself. Perhaps Italians didn't give Christmas presents. After all, there was still a lot she didn't know about him and his way of living.

Then Christmas Day began and there was no time left to think, with fires to light and the goose to roast and the pudding to boil and the vegetables to peel. They were both still hard at it when there was a loud knocking at the front door. Surely the aunts hadn't come so early. They weren't nearly ready!

'I will answer it,' Albert called from the front parlour, where he was still coaxing the fire, and was off down the stairs like a horse at full gallop.

Alice heard him draw back the bolts and listened for the voices of her aunts. But he was whispering down there and it was a man's voice that was whispering back. 'Cop 'old quick, Ploochy! Mind out!' It sounded like Harry Jones. The whispering went on. Then she heard the front door being opened again. It sounded as though they were giggling as they said goodbye to one another. What *were* they up to? She went on slicing apples for the sauce, wondering. Albert was coming back up the stairs now, suprisingly slowly, she thought. He took the last little flight one step at a time. Then he was inside the kitchen, blazing with excitement, and holding the lapels of his coat awkwardly together because he obviously had something hidden underneath them.

'Close your eyes and hold out your hands!' he ordered.

Alice did as she was told and was rewarded by a handful of warm fur. 'Happy Christmas!' Albert said. 'You can open your eyes now.'

It was a small tabby kitten. It sat where it had been put, in the curve of her cupped hands and looked up at her with round baffled blue eyes. It had a black stripe encircling its eyes like a pair of spectacles, a minute salmon pink nose, a biscuit coloured chin and a bristling crop of white whiskers. And it was shivering.

'Oh!' Alice said scooping it up into her neck to warm it. 'Oh Albert, it's lovely! It's a beautiful present. Just look at its dear little feet!' She stroked the small fragile bones under her chin and kissed the top of the kitten's soft head. For a second Albert was almost jealous of his present, but then it was his turn too, as she and the kitten and the bulky baby were all squashed together against him to hug their thanks.

It was a most successful Christmas. The goose was universally declared to be superb and the blazing pudding a joy to behold. They all ate too much, and both the aunts said they'd drunk too much, and Dickie Chanter, rosy with hock, said he couldn't believe it. When the meal was over and Alice and Amelia had cleared the dishes, they all sat round Albert's massive fire and toasted their toes and ate nuts and told one another how pleasant it all was. The kitten sat on what was left of Alice's lap on top of the bulge with its eyes closed and its small soft paws bent double under its chin. In a lull in the conversation it suddenly started to purr. It was a surprisingly loud purr for such a little creature and it sounded totally contented. It set the seal on the day for all of them. It was such an appropriate noise.

'What will you call it, Alice?' Phoebe inquired.

Alice had been thinking about it at odd moments during her crowded day. 'I think,' she said, 'I shall call him Jude.'

'That's a rum sort of name for a cat,' Dickie said. 'Why Jude?'

'I don't know,' Alice said. 'He looks like a Jude.'

The cold, damp, miserable weather continued into the New Year, and now that the excitement of Christmas was over Albert and Alice were both a little cast down. Trade was slack, of course, so there was very little to do and although Jude continued to entertain them when he was awake, there were still long stretches of the day when there was nothing to do but think, and both of them had things they really didn't want to think about.

The idea of actually having the baby terrified Alice. People died giving birth as she knew only too well. It made her shudder to consider that she might not even be here in a couple of months' time. And then there was the pain. She knew from the few snatched and whispered conversations she'd managed with the day girls that the pangs of childbirth were absolutely excruciating, even if they didn't actually kill you. Why, even the old Queen had had to have chloroform, so it must be bad. She was nervous about pain at the best of times and as the weeks went by and her girth steadily increased, so did her terror. Nature was very unfair, she thought. It was so obviously right that a woman should be a mother, so why was it necessary to make her pass through that terrible barrier first? The pain loomed before her as cruel and enormous as an iceberg and every twinge of discomfort reminded her of it.

The trouble was there was no one to confide in or to question. She wished she'd had an elder sister or a close cousin. She couldn't ask the aunts, it had been embarrassing enough breaking the news of her pregnancy to two such formidable maiden ladies, and Albert could hardly be expected to know. Perhaps when she'd been in Tooting a little longer and had got to know Mrs Kelly a bit better, she might be able to ask her. But by then, she thought sadly, it would probably be too late. It was perplexing, and very frightening. She envied Albert, safe on the outside of the drama.

Had she known it, Albert too had his secret fears, and he couldn't find anybody to confide in either.

He tried Harry Jones but that stolid gentleman didn't enlighten him at all, although he must have known something about it, with two growing sons.

'I suppose,' Albert began, one evening in the Castle, 'I suppose women are not the same.'

'No,' Harry agreed, supping his beer. 'Takes all sorts don' it? They come in all shapes and sizes.'

That wasn't at all what he'd meant. He tried again. 'I suppose they change when they're . . . um . . . when they're in the family way.'

'You can say that again,' Harry agreed, smoothing an imaginary belly in front of him and grinning at his friend.

That wasn't any good either. 'I mean,' Albert said, 'their affection might change.'

'Takes 'em all different ways don' it?' Harry said, setting down his beer and rasping the fair stubble on the side of his chin.

Albert decided to abandon this line of questioning altogether. He simply didn't have the words to pursue it. There were times when he wished old Harry wasn't quite so phlegmatic. He thought about his next question for quite a long time.

'How long does it take after the baby,' Albert asked, 'to get back to normal?'

'Don't reckon you ever get back to anything,' Harry said, most unhelpfully. 'Not once there's kids in the 'ouse. No such thing as normal then.'

Albert finished his beer sadly. His English just wasn't up to it. There was nothing for it, he'd just have to remain in ignorance. Perhaps having a baby would change Alice for the better after all. Once it was born perhaps she would love him the way he wanted. But the doubt was there, and very firmly too.

So the pregnancy continued and Alice and Albert grew just a little further apart from one another as the child grew between them.

Chapter 15

George Edward Pelucci chose a bitter day for his arrival. It had been blowing a gale all the previous night. Alice, wakeful as usual, had heard the rain squalling against the windows, and the yew trees in the churchyard creaking under the impact of a pile-driving wind. The child was unusually still so she should have been able to sleep. It annoyed her that something as natural and avoidable as rain should be keeping her awake. She lay uncomfortably beside Albert, resenting the ease of his uninterrupted slumber.

Rain was still streaming down the windows as a few dirty grey streaks appeared in the sky, and day arrived. It was very cold indeed and looked it. I'll get up in a minute, she thought, and light the stove. But the minute never came, for as she lay watching the scurries of grey water that kept filling the window frames, she felt a small twinging pain, low in her belly. It gripped her for a second or so, held and then faded away. She was instantly shaken with fear. This was the moment she'd been dreading all those months.

Albert woke slowly, turning before he opened his eyes, to cuddle into her side and stroke her hair and her cheek with a sleepy forefinger. She was cross because this day would be so easy for him and so uncomfortable and difficult for her. 'I shan't be able to light the stove this morning,' she said and her voice was tetchy.

He was awake at once, brown eyes alert with concern and mouth on the move. 'Has it started?' he asked and when she nodded, 'I will get Mrs Kelly.'

'Not yet,' she said. 'It takes a long time.' Even she knew that. 'Wait till after breakfast. Nat can go.' He seemed cast down by her decision, so she added. 'I'd rather you were here with me.'

That provoked kisses and more concern. Should she eat breakfast, he wondered. Neither of them knew. 'A cup of tea, perhaps,' Alice suggested. He crashed off downstairs to start the day. Alice could hear him charging about in the kitchen, singing to himself in his tuneless way. It seemed unfair, somehow, that he should be so happy when she was in pain. But at least he brought her tea, and she had to admit there wasn't much more he could do.

Mrs Kelly arrived at the end of the morning, swathed in her impressive white linen and briskly efficient.

'Coming along lovely,' she said, resting a light professional hand on Alice's contracting belly. It sounded reassuring, but Alice wasn't reassured. How could it be coming along lovely? It was torture. She had to brace herself against every pain now, and each one was more difficult to endure than the last. She wanted to groan or cry out and was growing more and more afraid that she wouldn't be able to control herself very much longer.

The day passed very, very slowly, punctured and fragmented by inexorable sensation. Albert ran up and down stairs every five minutes, partly to see how she was and partly to keep himself busy. Mrs Kelly aired the napkins and made up the cot and kept the fire stoked up. At four o'clock she made a pot of tea and a plate of bread and butter and coaxed Alice to take a little 'to keep her strength up'. But by that time Alice was really too far gone to eat.

By six o'clock she couldn't control herself any longer, and began to groan as the pains squeezed and drew her beyond endurance. From that moment things went from bad to worse. The groans became cries, and the cries became screams, and soon she had lost all contact with the world around her. There was nothing else in the day but pain. It filled the room, blotting out everything else. It no longer mattered to her that she might upset people if she made a fuss. She screamed and rolled about and clung to the bedclothes and begged to be put out of her misery.

Albert, torn by her screams, lurked outside the bedroom door in an equal agony of terror and remorse. Surely it shouldn't be like this. That terrible noise had been going on for hours. Surely the child must arrive soon. Mrs Kelly tried to reassure him, but even she was beginning to worry now. Eventually she decided to send for the doctor.

They were out of luck. Nat came back from Dr Power to report that he was out on a case and nobody knew when he'd be back. Dr Hutchinson was out too, delivering a baby at Streatham Park. 'Drat the man!' Mrs Kelly said. 'He's always off at Streatham Park when we need him in Tooting. Try Dr Fermanagh, and look slippy, Nat, there's a good lad!'

Dr Fermanagh was old and disagreeable. He took his time arriving and his time negotiating his fee, although by now Albert was so distressed he would have agreed to any sum the doctor cared to mention. He made a performance out of washing his hands, insisting that a fresh towel be brought for him from the airing cupboard, and warming his bottom by the fire while he waited for its arrival. 'It is an abominable day, Mrs Kelly,' he complained. 'I've not ventured out of doors for three days in this inclement weather. At my age, I need to husband my resources, as I am sure you appreciate. Let the younger fellas take the strain, eh? What's happened to young Hutchinson? Why couldn't you get him to turn out?'

Mrs Kelly explained but her explanation didn't satisfy. 'It's deuced inconvenient, this sort of thing, you know,' Dr Fermanagh complained. 'I shall catch pneumonia I shouldn't wonder, turning out in this downpour.' His backside now being warmed and his hands washed, he condescended to give his attention to his patient. He examined Alice in the same leisurely fashion, ignoring her screams, not looking at her face, but concentrating on the lower end of her anatomy.

'Too old for a first, that's the trouble,' he said to Mrs Kelly. 'Beats me why these silly women will have babies when their bodies aren't up to it. If they had a bit more sense I shouldn't be turning out in the rain.'

'I don't suppose she got much choice,' Mrs Kelly said, speaking quite sharply, because by now she was too tired and too anxious to agree with him and avoid trouble.

Dr Fermanagh ignored her. 'Well, we'd better help her out I suppose,' he sighed. 'This will be the third forceps this week, I hope you realize! Young Hutchinson had one only yesterday!' He made it sound as though it were all Molly's fault. This time she ignored him. He walked up to the head of the bed and addressed himself to Alice's tight shut eyes and screwed up face, talking down to her in every sense of the word. 'We are going to give you something to take away the pain,' he said. 'All right?'

Alice was long past speech and almost past caring, but after a few seconds the knowledge of what he'd said filtered through to her brain, and by the time he fitted the chloroform pad over her nose and mouth, she was nodding her head in some sort of agreement.

The baby was a surprise to both his parents.

Albert was disappointed in him. All through the pregnancy he'd nurtured an image of a strong, brown-skinned, lusty child, a little replica of himself, full of life and energy. Now, confronted with this pale, hairless, floppy bundle, he couldn't hide his disappointment. What sort of son was this? Molly Kelly was unaccountably pleased with him. 'Isn't he just a little duck?' she asked, holding the bundle up for Albert's inspection. But to Albert he looked more dead than duck-like, with his head flopping down sideways onto his chest, and two angry weals on either side of his skull where the forceps had held and bruised. For a few seconds he recognized that his instincts were denying this child. 'No son of mine!' Then he recovered himself and found a reply. 'I always said it would be a boy, didn't I, Mrs Kelly?'

Alice was still half unconscious, lying in a sticky sweet haze of chloroform and breathing noisily. He was almost glad she wasn't awake. At least it gave him time to think of the right thing to say. He didn't want to upset her. He felt she'd been upset enough already.

For a long time Alice was too exhausted and too bemused with chloroform to feel anything at all. She opened her eyes obediently when Molly called her, and after a considerable effort, managed to focus them on her new son, but he was less real than a dream and anyway seemed to be fading fast. She did notice the scars on his forehead and bestirred herself enough to ask about them. But she felt nothing, no love, no pity, not even relief.

It wasn't until the next day that her battered emotions began to reassert themselves and then she was surprised by the strength of them. As the baby sucked, he opened his eyes and gazed straight up at her, a dark-eyed stare, long and direct, as though he'd always known her. She was flooded, instantly, with a love so strong she felt she was melting. Her womb contracted with it and she felt her milk flowing downwards towards the soft little mouth. 'Oh, my dear little love!' she said. 'My dear little love!' and it seemed to her that she was giving her baby the most solemn promise. From that moment on, she was devoted to him, tied to him, absorbed in him. She had found her vocation.

The days passed in a milky euphoria. Now she had no need to ask Molly Kelly for advice. She knew instinctively what to do. If the baby gave his querulous cry, she fed him at once. If he whimpered, she picked him up. At every moment of the day and night she was aware of him, listening for him, whatever else she might be doing. It was just as though she'd grown an extra inner ear.

Albert watched her transformation with a mixture of admiration and misgiving. He'd always known his Alice would be a devoted mother, but it seemed uncanny that the baby had such a little voice and never gave more than a mew with it. He could remember how the village babies bawled and roared, kicking and threshing their arms, and dark in the face for attention, while his pale child merely fed and slept. Although he was plainly getting fatter, he only seemed half alive. Why, even Jude made more noise, particularly when a joint was roasting. It wouldn't have been so bad if only they'd all been able to sleep soundly at night. But after lying in his cradle all day like a limp rag-doll, the baby spent the small hours whimpering and snuffling and giving out bleak, bird-like cries that had Alice creeping from the bed every two or three hours to attend to him. Albert slept fitfully through the disturbance, waking from time to time to see his wife feeding the child in her wicker nursing chair by the fire, or walking him up and down the length of the room, her fair head curved down over the wailing bundle in her arms. In the mornings he was stiff-eyed and irritable with the need for sleep, and although she made light of it, Alice was in a worse state than he was. She grew thinner every day and developed hollow cheeks and purple smudges under her brown eyes, but she never complained and was always so apologetic when she woke him in the night that he felt shamed by her patience and didn't like to say anything.

It was Dickie who rescued him, by suggesting a mid-week trip to the Duchess. 'Got a new turn this week,' he said. 'Booked her at the Duchess Wednesday. You coming up?'

'Hope it's better than the last one,' Albert said. 'Brandy?'

'Ta,' Dickie said. The two of them were in their favourite

corner at Jack Beards and the evening was declining into exhaustion and desultory chat. The brandy was a long time coming.

'Oh, them acrobats!' Dickie said. 'They was chronic, I'll grant you. No, this one's got a lot more class. She ain't a marvel mind yer, but I think she'll do. Tilley's took 'er under 'er wing.'

'Song and dance is she?' Albert asked, more to please his friend than for anything else. He wasn't really interested. Most of Dickie's recent finds had been pretty terrible. He'd been quite down about it.

'Come and see her,' Dickie urged. 'First half, Wednesday.'

The brandy arrived. Albert savoured the first mouthful and then agreed. After all, he hadn't got anything better to do on Wednesday and at least it would get him out of the house, and away from the pressure of that wailing incomprehensible child he'd wished on himself.

It was a dreadful evening and a dreadful show. For a start, it was pouring with rain that night. The foyer of the Duchess was mud-stained and steaming with wet coats and umbrellas. The bar had run out of decent whisky and the new barman didn't have the faintest idea what anybody wanted. And the auditorium was only a quarter full.

The first act was a disaster, a nervous juggler who dropped more clubs than he caught and was given the bird before he was halfway through. Tilley did her best, at least giving as good as she got, but she had a rough ride too, and the applause that rippled her exit was only a grudging acknowledgement of the fight she'd put up. She was followed by Miss Queenie Dawson, Dickie's new find.

Albert's heart sank for her from the minute she made her entrance, walking shyly and quietly down towards the footlights as Dickie played her introduction as loudly as he could in a vain attempt to stop the barracking. She was a small, skinny girl with a mass of unruly red hair and very white skin. Poor little thing, Albert thought, looking at her bony arms, they'll take her to the cleaners. She was wearing a most unsuitable dress, one of Tilley's pale pink creations, cut down.

It didn't fit her and it didn't suit her, and for a second, as she reached the footlight, she looked as though she knew it.

'Get on wiv it!' someone roared at her from the front row.

'She ain't got it in 'er,' another joined in.

'Come on, darlin'. Show us what you're made of,' leered a third.

'I ain't singin' to a load a roughnecks,' she said. 'Bring us a chair, Dickie, will yer?'

It wasn't rehearsed, Albert thought, delighted by her daring. Dickie looked genuinely surprised but he did as he was told. Under the stagelights Albert could see that his friend's bald patch was shining with sweat, a sure sign that he was worried. Queenie settled herself comfortably on her chair, took off her shoes and rubbed her stockinged feet to the raucous delight of the front row. The audience was now in full cry, catcalling and booing and stamping their feet. Queenie ignored them all. When she'd finished rubbing her feet she turned her body towards the footlights and made signals to the barman at the back of the promenade, bending her elbow and raising an imaginary glass to her lips. 'Go on Charlie, give 'er one,' the audience yelled, looking back at the barman and enjoying the bawdy implication of what they were yelling.

The barman hesitated and glanced at Albert, who'd been leaning against the bar since the show began. 'Give her what she want,' Albert said. 'I pay you.' So a whisky was poured and set on a tray, and blushing and stumbling the embarrassed Charlie carried it up on stage. His troubles weren't over then.

Queenie took the glass with one hand and seized him firmly round the neck with the other. Her sudden embrace made him drop the tray, which provoked more laughter and ribald comment. This was getting better and better. It could be a good turn after all. Queenie drank her whisky with obvious pleasure, licking the last taste from her lips, but she still kept poor Charlie pinned to her side, and when the glass was empty she threw it at Dickie and called for her intro. Dickie missed the glass, which smashed to delighted applause. He plunged into the introduction, playing loudly and with a great many wrong notes.

Queenie began her number. Played straight it would have been an ordinary ballad about young love, and she wouldn't have got past the first eight bars, but she milked it for laughs at every possible moment, over-playing every emotion and using poor Charlie as the tailor's dummy recipient of her passion. All through the song she held him in the tightest grip, first around the neck, then by the shoulders, and then by both arms, working him like a puppet. At the climax of the song she suddenly let him go, and as he staggered forward with obvious relief, she stepped behind him and swinging his arms from the elbows, she made him dance the steps with her, almost in time with the music. She got the first real applause of the evening, and even then she held on to her puppet, making him bow and clapping his hands for him. She could easily have taken an encore, but didn't. Instead, she picked up her shoes and left the stage, blowing a last minute kiss at the retreating back of her victim.

'I oughter get extra wages. I must a' looked a right fool, dragging me up there like that,' the barman complained as he puffed back to the bar. Now that it was over, he was beginning to enjoy it. 'I never thought she'd do nothink like that, did you Mr Ploochy?'

Albert had to admit he hadn't expected it either. During the interval he went round to the stage door to congratulate Dickie on his new star. To his surprise the dressing room was in uproar. Dickie and Tilley and Martha were all shouting at the top of their voices and the newcomer was sitting pale and beleaguered among the debris of greasepaint, cotton wool and orange sticks. She looked small and pathetic without her make-up and had obviously been crying, but that didn't deter Dickie. 'What was you thinking of?' he roared. 'Drinks on stage! I ask you! Damn ridiculous thing ter do! We'll never get took here again, I hope you realize!'

'Leave off, for Christ's sake!' Tilley yelled at him. 'You're upsetting the kid. It ain't the end a' the world.'

'Ain't the end a' the world!' Martha shrieked. 'What if we ain't booked termorrer? What then? You ain't got the sense you was born wiv!'

As always, bad temper made Albert anxious and full of nervous energy. He had to get them out of this terrible steamy cell at once, before even worse things were said.

'What you say we all go down to Luigi's for a bite to eat?' he suggested hopefully. He got an immediate and mixed response Tilley said it would be a good idea and put her hat on at once.

Martha complained that she was that upset food would stick in her throat. Dickie, still angry, said they might as well, seeing it would probably be the last square meal they'd ever get. The girl said nothing, but as they all began to move towards the door, she jammed a decrepit hat on her unruly hair, wrapped herself in a matted grey shawl and followed them.

The restaurant was crowded but by dint of reorganizing several tables and rooting out two old chairs Luigi made room for them. Despite the adhesive condition of her throat, Martha managed to put away a steak and a considerable quantity of vegetables, and under the influence of warmth and wine and the savoury scents of Luigi's cooking, Tilley and Dickie relaxed and began to joke again. But the girl picked at her food saying nothing and growing steadily more ashen and distressed. Albert, watching her between mouthfuls, felt sorry for her and didn't know what to do about it. She was so ugly, he thought, like a bird straight out of the egg, all gawky limbs and protruding bones. Her nose was as sharp as any beak, and that red hair was spikey and fuzzy, like a young bird's floss of new feathers.

Suddenly she was on her feet, her table napkin to her mouth and she and Tilley were bolting from the room, more or less dodging the cane chairs and the rubber plants.

'She's more trouble than she's worth, that one,' Dickie said, watching her clumsy exit. 'I'm beginning to wish I'd never took 'er on, tell the truth.'

'We're due at the Tea Pot in 'alf an 'our,' Martha said, mopping her plate with a piece of bread. 'We shall 'ave to look sharp or we'll miss the bus.'

'What about Miss Dawson?' Albert said.

'She ain't got no more bookings ternight. Thank Gawd!' Dickie said. 'She can stay 'ere or go 'ome. It's up to her. Here's old Tilley back.'

In a few minutes, the three of them thanked Albert and left him, sitting among the dirty plates, to deal with Queenie Dawson. She returned, confused and embarrassed that all her friends had gone, but at least her blush brought a little colour to her cheeks.

'It was the whisky,' she explained. 'Made me sick. I'm ever so sorry, Mr – um.'

'Pelucci,' Albert said. 'I thought you liked it.'

'What?'

'The whisky.'

'Can't stand the stuff,' she said. 'But I 'ad ter do somefink, didn't I?' Then she burst into tears.

That was better. He could cope with weeping. Tears were easier than temper. He took the fancy handkerchief out of his breast pocket, handed it across and began to comfort. He told her how nobody noticed her rushing off in the middle of the meal, how Dickie's bark was worse than his bite, and how clever she'd been to handle a Wednesday night audience, while she sniffled and gasped and dried her eyes and rubbed her red nose and made a great effort to recover as quickly as she could.

'It all be forgotten in the morning,' he promised. 'You see.'

'You known 'im long?' Queenie asked. 'Mr Chanter, I mean.'

'Donkey's years,' Albert said.

' 'E ain't 'alf got a paddy on 'im,' the girl said. ' 'E frightens me out a' me skin. Still, I s'pose you get ter be tough in this business, dontcha?'

Albert thought about it and tried to find something diplomatic to say. He'd rarely seen Dickie in a temper. They'd come close to quarrelling when they all had the flu, but apart from that, all his impressions of Dickie Chanter were of a laughing, joking, light-hearted man. It was disconcerting to be seeing him through this child's eyes.

'You like some coffee?' he asked.

The coffee was ordered and the girl began to talk, quickly and nervously, the words tumbling over one another and twisting her mouth with their onrush. 'I never thought it'ud be like that, yer see, Mr – um –. All them fellers yellin' and booin' an' all. I come up 'ere ter make a name fer mesself. I can sing better'n I did then. I mean ter say, I was choked up on that stage, listenin' to 'em. Got me in a rare ol' state, all that yellin' an' all. 'E never said nothink about that, you know, when I was took on. 'Ere, you ain't paid fer this, 'ave yer?'

Albert confessed that he had, and his mouth flickered with amusement.

'It ain't funny!' she said sharply. 'I ain't supposed ter take gifts from strange men. My old woman was most perticler about that. I come from a respectable family.'

'It a gift to Dickie,' Albert said, hoping to placate her. 'To Mr Chanter.'

'All right,' she said ungraciously. 'But you ain't bought me and don' you think so.'

He was stung by her insolence. 'You are being a silly little girl,' he said sternly. 'I a married man. I old enough to be your father.'

'They're the worst!' she said, bolder and more insolent than ever.

'You have high opinion of yourself, Miss Dawson,' he said stiffly. 'Drink your coffee. I call a cab to take you home.' She made him angry, despite himself. What conceit! What presumption! The very idea that he could fancy any woman so bony and ugly and graceless.

He was still quite cross when he got home. Alice was in bed, and for once she was fast asleep, and the baby was as still as a white stone in his frilly crib. He stood in their calm, well-ordered bedroom looking at the full curves of her sleeping face and wished she would wake up. It had been such an extraordinary evening he wanted to share it. But she slept on peacefully and he hadn't the heart to disturb her.

It took him a very long time to get to sleep. He lay tossing and turning for more than an hour, reliving the highlights of the evening, and perplexed to realize that he was disturbed by his memories. And then, when sleep finally crept up on him, it brought him an even more disturbing dream.

He and Alice were travelling along a country lane in high summer, sometimes on bicycles, sometimes on foot. The sun above them grew hotter and hotter, and the barman from the Duchess came running on stage to offer them drinks. 'No!' Albert yelled, trying to refuse. 'She doesn't like whisky.' But Alice took the whisky and drank it. When she put the glass down, she was Queenie Dawson. She seized him by the arm and made him dance. He felt so happy dancing under the warm sun, he wanted the sensation to go on for ever. 'Don't stop!' he begged, but Dickie had taken both the bicycles and was riding away down the lane, performing a perfect balancing act, with a foot on each saddle, and waving his bowler hat. The audience roared and he was afraid they'd wake the baby.

'Please be quiet,' he begged them, but they didn't seem to hear him. Alice was dancing again. Or was it Queenie? He was struggling to make up his mind. Then he was falling down and down, still begging the audience to be quiet, and Queenie caught him in her strong bony arms and they began to make love. He was flooded with surprised delight, as she pressed herself closer and closer, kissing his face and fondling his body.

He woke bewildered and frustrated and in agony of desire. Alice had just finished feeding the baby and was climbing gently back into bed beside him. His need was so extreme he took her without a word, before his conscience could quell desire. She lay still and quiet and allowed him to do what he needed, without complaint or comment, as she always did, and when he'd finished she got up to wash herself. He watched her, spent and ashamed, feeling, as he always did, that he'd used her, and wishing he hadn't. And then to make matters worse, the dream came back into his mind, filling it with images stronger than the ones before his eyes, rousing and disturbing him all over again and making him feel more ashamed than ever. The day was off to a sour start.

Fortunately, the gloom at breakfast was lifted by the arrival of a letter from Aunt Phoebe. Alice read it quickly and with pleasure, making murmurs of agreement. 'Well, well, well,' she said as she finally put it down beside her plate.

Albert looked a question at her, glad that they were back on normal domestic ground.

'It seems I've got a cousin living in Tooting,' she said, smiling slowly as the thought took hold. 'Just fancy that! She's been here nearly a fortnight, Aunt Phoebe says. She's got rooms in Avarn Road.' The cat rubbed its back against her skirt, begging her for titbits. 'Yes, yes,' she said to him. 'Wait a bit, Jude. You shall have the rinds if you wait like a good cat.' Jude narrowed his eyes lovingly at her, and was rewarded by having his head stroked.

'Who is she?' Albert asked, annoyed because he felt jealous of the way she was fondling the animal.

'One of Aunt Eulalie's nieces,' she said, smiling at Jude. 'From Westward Ho. I shall write to her directly. I could go and see her Wednesday afternoon, couldn't I? Fancy having a cousin in Tooting! A relative, Albert!' The news had really pleased her. Her face was rounded with pleasure, her mouth and eyes lifted and lightened. Watching her, Albert felt another pang of jealousy, that a letter could move her so much, while his lovemaking had had no effect at all.

Then the dream filled his skull again, and he had to get downstairs to the shop immediately, to exorcize it with hard work.

Alice dressed carefully for her outing on Wednesday afternoon. She'd never seen this strange new cousin before and wanted to make a good impression. So she wore her corsets and her grey costume, and spent a long time pinning up her hair and anchoring her hat. Mercifully, Georgie was always placid in the afternoons, and dressed in his best long robe and the whitest cap he possessed he looked very presentable. She decided against the baby carriage If her cousin was poor, it might look ostentatious and it wouldn't hurt her to carry the baby in a shawl.

All the same, as she walked slowly down towards Amen Corner, she was anxious and unsure of herself. It was so easy to make mistakes and upset people. She seemed to upset Albert no matter what she did. He so rarely looked pleased with her these days, although she was making such an effort. If only Georgie would sleep at nights! Perhaps she wasn't feeding him properly. She had plenty of milk. That was no problem. But what if it didn't suit him? The trouble was there was no way she could find answers to questions as delicate and personal as these. Not for the first time in her adult life, she wished she had an older sister to guide her and reassure her.

Then a worse thought entered her mind. What if Georgie woke up and made a nuisance of himself while she was visiting her new cousin? That would be too embarrassing to be borne. She'd just reached the corner of Avarn Road when the thought stopped her feet. She stood where she was, considering the wisdom of what she was about to do. Perhaps she ought to go home and just not run the risk of failure. Her cousin might not like her. After all, there was no real reason why she should. She bit her lip in her indecision, looking down at Georgie, sleeping like a cherub in her arms.

A voice was calling her name. 'Alice!' again more tentatively, 'Alice?'

She looked up. A girl was walking down Avarn Road towards her, a short neat, stocky girl in an immaculate white blouse and a beautifully pressed skirt, her unseen petticoats rustling with starch. Everything about her revealed an anxiety as acute as anything Alice had been feeling, the placating attitude of her head, the round, snub-nosed face puckered and furrowed, even the carefully laundered clothes. With a sense of relief, Alice liked her at once. 'Yes,' she said, walking towards her cousin with outstretched hand. 'You must be Minnie.'

'I'm glad you've come, me dear, 'Minnie said, when they'd kissed a greeting. 'Once I got baby down, I been in and out and in and out on the look-out for you. Do'ee come in. The kettle's on the hob.'

'Have you got a baby too?' Alice said, delighted at the news.

'Little boy,' Minnie said, leading the way through her front door and up a narrow stairway into her kitchen. 'Didn't Aunty tell you?'

Her baby was asleep in a wooden crib in the corner of the room. He was a bold, rosy child with thick black hair. Alice was impressed. 'Isn't he big!' she said. 'How old is he?'

'Nine months next Thursday,' Minnie said proudly. 'Now let's settle your little lamb, shall we, and then we can have tea.'

One of the drawers from the dresser had been removed, and now, filled with a plump white pillow, it stood on the wide shelf in the chimney corner ready to do service as a cradle. As she lowered the sleeping Georgie gently on to the pillow and tucked his shawl warmly round him, Alice was wondering what on earth Albert would have said if he could have seen where his precious first born was being put. It gave her an odd sense of satisfaction and conspiracy to think how cross he would have been, and to realize that he need never know.

Tea was laid on a spotless white cloth and served in the best china. It was accompanied by a delicious cake. Alice was impressed again. There was no doubt her cousin kept a clean house and was an excellent cook. But wasn't that to be expected from a member of her own family.

The two young women spent an enjoyable afternoon together. After such an excellent start, it didn't take them long to discover that they had a lot in common. They discussed

Aunt Eulalie and her bad legs, and how very much worse they were getting as she got older. They compared babies and how to cope with the lack of sleep they caused, and Alice was reassured to learn that mother's milk was the best thing out and couldn't do Georgie any harm no matter how much of it he took. They swapped notes on where to find the best bargains in Tooting and were delighted to find that neither of them liked the new manager of Maypole Dairies.

By the time Georgie woke for his afternoon feed, they were getting on so well that after he'd been fed Alice took off his little lace cap and showed her cousin the nasty cradle cap that was growing like a flaky yellow skin just over his little soft spot where she couldn't rub it. Minnie knew exactly what to do about it. 'Just you drop a little bit of your milk on it, and spread it over with your little finger like that, and that'll all go, quick as a house afire!' she said. Then her boy woke up and ate a huge slice of cake and threw himself about and roared when she tried to wash his hands, and wouldn't be comforted until he was fed too. So the two women sat one on each side of the stove and suckled their young and were happy together.

It wasn't until she got home that evening that Alice realized that the one topic neither of them had mentioned was their husbands.

The middle of the week took on quite a different flavour for Albert and Alice now. They both had something to look forward to.

Chapter 16

'Met a funny geyser up the Duchess Wednesday,' Queenie told her sister.

'Did yer?' Ethel said, without very much interest. She was lifting the kettle from the hob so as to fill the enamel basin that stood on the scullery table, and that was a job that took all her concentration, because water was too precious to waste and the kettle was heavy and hot.

'Her little nightie's aired,' their mother said, taking the baby's flanelette nightshirt from the clothes horse and laying it across the edge of the table. Ethel's baby, little Maggie, was her very first grandchild so her bi-weekly bath was still a loving ritual that involved them all.

'Stinking rich!' Queenie said. ' 'E took us all ter supper after the show. You should a' seen the grub, Eth.' Her mouth was watering again at the memory of it.

Ethel tested the water with her elbow. 'Took a fancy to yer did 'e?' she asked slyly, and grinned when Queenie blushed.

'Do me a favour!' Queenie mocked, making a joke of her embarrassment. ' 'E's old enough ter be me father.'

'They're the worse,' her mother said sagely. 'You wanna watch him!'

'No,' Queenie insisted. ' 'E's all right. Not like yer average sort a' rich bloke.'

'An' what's yer average rich bloke like when 'e's at 'ome?' Ethel asked, still teasing as she tested a napkin against her cheek.

'Posh,' Queenie said, thinking it out. 'Distant. They don't look at yer, that's what it is. This bloke does. Right at yer. They sort a' look through yer. As if you wasn't there. 'E . . .' she thought again and then realized that her mother was looking at her quizzically. ' 'E's nice,' she finished lamely.

'Mind 'e don't take you fer a ride, that's all,' her mother warned.

'No fear a' that,' Queenie reassured 'You know me!'

It was a consolation to her mother and her sister that they did.

She'd always been a fierce, determined little thing, even as a child, quick and bright and entertaining, with a strong will and a terrible temper. Her mother still remembered the time when her father had taken her to Tower Hill to hear Ben Tillett speak to the Federation. She'd come back ready to change the world, single handed. But that was Queenie all over.

She'd been so determined to go with him. There'd been no stopping her, young though she was. 'Won't do her no 'arm, mother,' Jack had said. 'Make a Socialist of her. No 'arm in that.' And it had.

She'd stood beside her father's stocky protection and watched in wonder as the work gangs gathered all around her and the union banners cracked in the breeze above her head. The great space of Tower Hill was full of men, and they seemed to her, in their scarred, incoherent masses, like some great, dumb, strong-smelling beast. And then a little man had climbed up onto a platform somewhere ahead of them and the crowd had grown attentively silent and he had begun to speak. He was in his shirt sleeves and wore a white homberg hat and a dazzling waistcoat striped purple and cream. 'Comrades!' he said, opening his arms widely to them as though he wanted to embrace them all. And how they all roared to welcome him!

Much of what he said that afternoon was lost on the listening child, perched on her father's shoulders, watching with all her emotions, but one section of his speech settled itself into her mind even then, and remained with her for the rest of her life. 'Recognize your power,' he urged, and hadn't she felt it brooding all around her. 'Feel it! See it! Glory in it! It is the power of unity and co-operation. But never forget for a single second that the powers ranged against you are the most ruthless known to man. The class war is the most brutal of wars and the most pitiless. Capitalism is capitalism as a tiger is a tiger.' She had come home still transfixed by the power of it all, fiercely determined to fight that war with all the strength she had.

'You won't catch me bein' took up by a rich man,' she told her mother scornfully, lifting the baby from her makeshift cradle in the corner of the scullery. 'Not likely!' But this rich man *was* nice, she thought, there was no denying it.

*

Meanwhile the rich man, over in his corner of London, was busily making money. Tooting was changing again, and Harry was down in the dumps. The London County Council had started to lay their tramlines down towards the town, and Mr Pennyman had sold them more than a third of the Totterdown Farm, so that they could build a council estate at the end of the line. Now the farmhands were sure the rest of the land would go under the hammer as soon as the harvest was in. The line was nearly finished, and once the trams started to run, they were convinced the council would be on the hunt for more land. Local builders were already talking of a thousand council houses.

'A thousand council houses on good rich farmland,' Harry said morosely. 'I ask yer. Where's the sense? All that good land gone ter waste. And everyone out a' work?'

'You said that last time,' Dickie pointed out, trying to be reasonable. 'When your old man was laid off. Remember?'

'An 'e *was* laid off, wasn't 'e?' Harry said crossly.

'Well you expect that,' Dickie said. ' 'E was getting' on. Comes to all of us in the end. But *you* got another job didntcha? They never laid you off.'

'No,' Harry had to admit.

'There you are then,' Dickie said, but Harry wasn't convinced or cheered.

'It's all very well fer you two,' he grumbled. 'More trade fer you, all them buildings, but it's takin' away my livelihood.'

The rest of the land was sold that autumn, and by the end of the year the entire farm had been given over to council housing, all thirty-eight acres of it. Mr Pennyman offered Harry a job on the Furzedown farm, looking after the dairy herd, and although he complained that it wouldn't last five minutes, he was glad enough to take it.

But Albert made a killing, buying up as much land as he could grab. Now he was building houses ten at a time, particularly in the area between the new estate and the Broadway, and they were ridiculously easy to sell. People were quick to see that the new tramline gave them the opportunity to live in the country and work in town, and Albert was quick to see that expansion meant profit, providing you were ruthless.

But Alice was preoccupied with her baby and for all his

business success, he often felt lonely and neglected. It made him value his weekly escape into the welcoming hullabaloo of the music hall.

Sometimes he met up with Harry and Em and sometimes he saw the show on his own, because Alice couldn't bring herself to leave the baby, but alone or in company, the magic never failed to work. It soon became his lifeline, the one moment in the week that he could anticipate and remember with pleasure. In the warmth of the stalls, with the glow of good spirits inside him and around him, it was possible to ignore his sense of isolation and defeat. There was always a good chorus to rouse his deflated senses, and the laughter and bonhomie in the auditorium were infectious and healing.

After the show, Dickie and his players went on to the nearest restaurant and consumed the meal they'd all deferred until the performance was over and their digestive systems had started functioning again. It wasn't long before Albert had fallen into the habit of joining the party. It was pointless going home, to rooms sour with the smell of his sickly infant and a wife so absorbed in her maternal duties she hardly noticed anything else, even the cat. The meal was a logical and pleasurable extension of the evening. It amused him to notice how the players went on acting long after the curtain was down, playing their parts even as they ate.

The only member of the company who seemed to be simply and openly herself all the time and no matter what the circumstances was young Queenie Dawson. After a few months, Albert found that he was watching her more and more closely, refreshed and entertained by her reckless honesty. She was disastrously outspoken and her table manners were appalling. She spilt vegetables into her lap, trailed her sleeves in the gravy and spattered wine or coffee in all directions at nearly every meal. But the beauty of it was that it didn't seem to worry her. No matter how wildly her companions shrieked and protested, she wasn't the least put out by her clumsiness. 'Nobody told you ter sit next t'me,' she would say. 'You know I'm a muck-pot. Why didntcha sit somewhere else?' And even when the great impresario, Dickie Chanter himself, rose to his feet to roar that she'd ruined his best pair of trousers, she gave him the same saucy, careless answer, 'Oh do give over, Dickie.

It'll sponge off. Bit a dirt never did no 'arm. You don' 'alf make a palaver.'

In an odd way that he couldn't explain, Albert was comforted by her ability to row at the top of her voice and with corruscating venom and yet without taking any apparent harm from the experience. A row always left him feeling so bad afterwards, sick with guilt, shaken and ashamed. But she would be screaming abuse one minute and demolishing a vast helping of apple pie the next. It was extraordinary and impressive. Like her appetite. On many occasions he stayed behind after the others had left to buy her extra cups of coffee and a Finnan haddock, or a fruit cake, or whatever unlikely dish she fancied, just for the pleasure of watching her eat it. She might spill her food, but she never left a crumb, enjoying it to the last mangled mouthful, and then licking her lips, her fingers and even the plate, with a cheerful and engaging relish. 'You only live once, dontcha?' she would explain, polishing her spoon with her tongue. 'Might as well make the most of it!'

As the months passed and the spring blossomed, Albert enjoyed the hours he spent with the skinny Miss Dawson, with an ever-sharpening pleasure. Although he would never have admitted it, not even to himself, she had become a sort of pet, a sensuous, amusing, unpredictable, living doll. He could enjoy her company and be entertained by her daring without the need to accept the slightest responsibility for her. Her youthfulness made him feel mature and worldly wise, her vulnerability made him feel protective, her impertinence made him feel young and, although he didn't acknowledge it, amorous. Dangerous fantasies took shape in his sleeping mind, but he enjoyed them too much to be warned by them. Nevertheless the fact was it was Queenie's plain pale face and tangled red hair that appeared night after night above the passionate bodies he desired and embraced in the comfortable privacy of his dreams.

That summer a new song took the Halls by storm. It was called 'Sail Away', and Queenie and Tilley were very taken with it. Soon they were both singing it at every possible booking, and it wasn't long before their enthusiasm spilled over into open rivalry.

Matters came to a head at the sixth performance, when Tilley produced an elaborate new outfit, especially for her rendering of the disputed song. Queenie immediately demanded similar treatment.

'I done three matinees last week,' she pointed out, reasonably enough, 'and I ain't been paid a penny, as well you know. You ought ter see me right Mr Chanter.'

Dickie wasn't impressed. 'Do me a favour, Queenie,' he said. 'I ain't made a' money. You 'ad a new dress fer the Duchess.'

'Marie Lloyd 'as a new dress fer every song,' Queenie said.

'Marie Lloyd makes a hundred guineas a night,' Dickie said. 'You'd be lucky ter make ten in a week. Do give over!'

And that, as far as he was concerned, was the end of it. But Queenie persisted and her bad temper increased.

One evening when she came off stage at the Duchess, she was in a particularly ugly mood.

'That's done it,' she said, bristling with temper. 'Oo's the comedian left that bloody chair in the wings? All them spikes an' all. I might a' broke me leg.'

'Don't start, Queenie,' the juggler said, trying to placate, but signalling alarm. 'We wasn't ter know you'd come off left. You never done that before.'

'Left, right, what's it matter?' Queenie shouted. 'Wings oughter be clear. Oh, 'ello Ploochy. Never seen you in that corner. It's a wonder I ain't broke me leg. Look at that. I shall be black an' blue termorrer.' She put one foot on a skip and lifted the frills of her skirt to show him the damage. It was such an easy, thoughtless gesture, as though he were a dresser, or another female in the company, and of course, it gave him a chance to commiserate and admire in the same glance.

Unfortunately, the frill above the foot was one of Tilley's heavyweight adornments and just the sight of it provoked more bad temper. 'Just look at this daft skirt, will yer?' she said, addressing her remark to the theatre, but looking at Albert. 'I look an absolute frump. I ain't cut out fer all them frills.'

Albert was just about to say something soothing and complimentary when Tilley strode out of the dressing room, trailing a gown even more elaborately flounced and frilled than the one Queenie was objecting to. 'Ah, there you are,' she said. 'Dickie said ter bring this down. You was wanting somethink new, I understand. There you are. That'll do nicely.' There was such a deliberately patronizing note in her voice that even the juggler picked it up and was disconcerted by it. Queenie was roused to roaring temper in an instant.

'No, it bloody won't,' she yelled. 'This ain't a freak show, Tilley. I'd be laughed off the stage if I come on in a wreck like that.'

'And what's wrong with it, pray?' Tilley asked, acidly polite.

'It's a sight,' Queenie said, 'all them frills and that silly great flounce I'd look a right idiot. *And* it's second-'and an' all. I'm worth better'n slops.'

'I'll 'ave you know, Miss Dawson,' Tilley said, 'I've played ter packed 'ouses in this. Nobody never laughed at *me* when I wore it. Got style, that 'as.'

Queenie made a visible effort to be reasonable. 'It ain't *my* style though,' she said. 'That's just the point, innit. It might suit you. I don't doubt it. Might very well. It'ud make *me* look a freak.'

'Well that's your very 'ard luck,' Tilley sneered. 'I can't 'elp it if you're all bones. You'd look a freak in anything and that's a fact.'

'You shut yer bleedin' face,' Queenie roared. 'I ain't all bones. I got a damn sight more style'n you. Bloody cow.'

'Moderate your language, *Miss* Dawson,' Tilley said, delighted to have reduced her rival to such a state.

'I'll moderate your bleedin' face!' Queenie shrieked, leaping at Tilley, with claws at the ready.

There was a flurry of instant, preventative action. 'De Frece!' Martha hissed, and the fighters were bundled off in different directions and the argument came to an abrupt and undignified halt. A halt but not a conclusion. As the company gathered in Luigi's, later that evening, Queenie returned to the attack. This time she went straight to the top and tackled Dickie.

'I ain't beatin' about the bush, Mr Chanter,' she said. 'It ain't fair ter expect me to wear Tiley's cast-offs. I ain't a skivvy.'

'Never said yer was,' Dickie said, trying to deflect her. 'Whatcha want to eat?'

Queenie wasn't deterred. 'I want ter make it clear, Mr Chanter,' she said. 'I need a new dress fer that number. New. Not a reach-me-down.'

'I told yer before,' Dickie said, still affable 'I ain't got that kind a cash. Can't be done. Not now, anyway. We'll see about it in the autumn.'

'No,' Queenie said. 'We won't. We'll see about it now. If I don't get a new dress, I ain't goin' on.'

Dickie flicked the ash off his cigar and gave her a level, hard look of warning. 'Suit yourself,' he said, calmly. 'If you want ter cut yer nose off ter spite yer face, you go right ahead, but you ain't bullying me, and don't you think it. You cut a performance, you're out the company. So make yer mind up to it.'

Queenie stuck her bony chin in the air and left the restaurant without another word. Tilley was delighted. 'Good riddance to bad rubbish!' she said.

'Gone off 'ome, most likely,' Dickie said with relief. 'Now, what're we 'aving?'

Albert couldn't settle to the meal. He had to admit that he was feeling concerned for his skinny pet. There'd been something so ridiculous and vulnerable and touching about the deliberate defiance of that chin. He had to find her and comfort her. As Luigi darted from table to table and the little restaurant spun with busy legs and swirling skirts, he escaped into the indigo air of the London summer and began to search, strolling from street corner to street corner, from pub to pub.

He found her in the sixth, sitting alone in the furthest corner, with half a pint of ale and a grey pork pie. Her eyelashes were spiked with tears and her neck looked brittle, she was holding it so stiffly. He was overwhelmed with pity for her.

' 'Ello Ploochy,' she said. 'Fancy seeing you 'ere.' She was keeping her mouth steady with an effort of will and the strain of it pulled her cheekbones taut and made her eyes stare.

'That pork pie!' Albert said.

'Chronic, innit!' she said. 'I 'ad to 'ave somefink. That's all there was. Don't fancy it now I got it.'

'You would like a meal somewhere else?' he suggested.

'No,' she said, thinking what a kind-hearted man he was. 'Ta all the same. I've lost me appetite and that's a fact. 'Er an' 'er old dress. It ain't fair, Ploochy!'

'No,' he said sympathetically, because she was far too defeated for any other answer.

'I look a freak in that ol' pink thing,' she said. 'A right ol' sack a' potatoes that is. I'll be laughed off the stage Saturday.' Her eyes were awash with tears again despite herself. She turned her head away from him and tried to brush them away with the tips of her fingers before he could see them. He was touched by the subterfuge. 'I'd buy it meself if I 'ad the money,' she said, 'and sod the lot a' them.'

Such spirit she had, Albert thought, admiring her. Then an idea was through his mind and on his tongue before he could reconsider it.

'I tell you what,' he said. 'I will buy the dress for your birthday.'

'You're an old love,' she said, touched. 'My birthday's June.'

'A late birthday present then.'

'I couldn't,' she said. 'You know that, dontcha. I got ter be independent. I told yer.'

Albert's solution was immediate. 'I lend you the money,' he said, 'you buy the dress, you pay me back so much a week. Like a pawn shop.'

She thought about it for quite a while, assessing him and the situation with eyes made green by tears, her face as sharp as her mind.

'What sort of interest?' she said.

'I lend you without interest,' Albert said grandly. 'On one condition.'

She raised her red eyebrows in question, but didn't protest. Yet. After all it might not be *that* condition. You never knew with old Ploochy.

'You not argue. You just buy the dress.'

'Done!' she said, relaxing into the broadest smile and thinking how ridiculously generous he was. Then she stretched out a bony hand across the table to seal the bargain.

For a moment, holding her cold fingers in his warm palm, he thought how easy it would be to kiss them. But he resisted temptation.

*

She bought a dress with a decidedly nautical flavour, navy blue, with a white sailor collar and a pattern of white anchors all down the front panel. On stage, it was an instant success and made her rendering of 'Sail Away' as perky and resilient as Tilley's had been soulful and sentimental. But offstage, it caused a second outbreak of hostilities. Tilley saw it as an insult to her position and a threat to her performance. She took vociferous exception to a junior member of the troupe being capable of such extravagance. The house shuddered under the impact of her wounded pride.

'Women!' Dickie complained, in the snug at Jack Beard's. 'They're driving me up the wall. Whatcha want ter go and lend 'er the money for? You might a' know'd there'd be trouble.'

Albert was beginning to regret his offer now and did his best to apologize. 'I thought that would be end of it,' he said, moustaches drooping with distress.

'Never on your life!' Dickie sighed. 'Go on fer months this will. I can't talk sense to neither of 'em.'

'I truly am sorry,' Albert said, looking more miserable than ever.

'Bit late fer that now,' Dickie said. 'Bloody ridiculous thing ter do, you ask me. What's your ol' lady going ter say, when she finds out you bin buying clothes for other women?'

'She's not "other women",' Albert protested. Then he tried to justify his actions. 'I treat her like a daughter.'

'She ain't yer daughter though, is she?' Dickie said shrewdly. 'I'd watch out, if I was you. Tongues wag, yer know.'

'I don't need your advice, thank you,' Albert said stiffly, alarmed by the dangerous turn the conversation was taking.

'Suit yerself,' Dickie said, patting his moustaches into place. 'Just warn her off, that's all. She's made quite enough trouble for one season. Tilley's had a right bellyful, I can tell yer. It ain't right fer her to be put down by a bread-and-butter player like that. She's got a position, being who she is.'

'She not who she is though, is she?' Albert said, ungrammatically although accurately. 'She not your wife!'

Dickie's flush was angry and immediate. The two men bristled at one another across Jack Beard's polished mahogany, and Harry intervened quickly before they could come to blows. 'My round,' he said, gathering up the empties. 'Whatcha want, Ploochy? Dickie? Come on! Women ain't worth fighting over. Leastways, I never met one that was. Not even Em!'

Spirits might mollify Albert and Dickie, but nothing would appease the two women. Their quarrel dragged on and on and became a miserable carping affair.

Chapter 17

In April, the new tramline was finished, and the people of Tooting were informed that the Prince and Princess of Wales, no less, were to ride on the very first electric tram to their town. All shops and schools were to be closed for the day, so that the populace could come out on the streets and greet their royal family in the manner to which they were now accustomed. Em thought it was very exciting and determined to get a good position in the front of the crowd. Even Alice bought a new hat.

Now they were all standing on the pavement waiting for the royal tram to arrive. Em and Harry and their two little boys, Albert enjoying the crowd, Minnie carrying Percy and Alice with little Georgie on her shoulders.

Polite cheers announced the approach of the tram, which bore down upon them, swaying and bucking like a great white ship. It was hung about with customary evergreens, looped along its top deck like thick ropes, and its headboard announced, rather foolishly, that it was going to Clapham. It rocked to a halt immediately opposite Em's vantage point, so close that they could hear the metallic whirr and click of the steering handle as the driver wound it down.

There was a short pause, while the crowd fidgeted. Then cheers rippled a greeting, as the royal couple stepped gingerly out of their unaccustomed transport and inclined their royal heads towards their loyal subjects.

'Real pearls!' Em said, with overawed admiration. 'Look at that, Min! Six rows a' pearls. An' that's real silk, that coat. You can see. Ain't she lovely!'

The baby gave a curious little cough, a cross between a groan and a gurgle and Alice bent her head towards him, immediately and automatically, to rub his back and soothe him, as she always did. But this time her response turned to even quicker alarm. 'Albert! Albert!' she said, on a high and rising note of panic, 'Oh God, Albert, he's dying!' The child was limp in her arms and didn't seem to be breathing. His face was pale as paper and his open eyes had rolled upwards to reveal only the white. From one corner of his half-open mouth a trickle of frothy saliva oozed down onto the swans-down edging his jacket.

It was Minnie who took charge, simply and quietly and without saying a word. In one movement she handed her own infant to Em, in the next she had turned the unconscious baby onto his side in Alice's arms. She seemed to be fishing about inside his mouth with her little finger, but she was so deft and quick she'd finished what she was doing before Alice could worry or protest or even question. The child gave a shudder, his eyelids fluttered and he began to tremble.

'Oh thank God! Thank God!' said Alice, tears rolling freely from eyes red-rimmed and strained. 'He's alive! Oh my poor little lamb!'

Satisfied that the baby was breathing properly again, Minnie turned to Albert and spoke to him quietly and almost conspiratorially. 'He needs wrapping up warm,' she said, 'and keeping very quiet. We ought to go home Mr P. Directly.'

Now Albert could act. He took off his coat, enveloped the infant in its thick cloth and deposited the bundle in the perambulator. 'Come on,' he said, and they set off through the crowds together.

'Oh my poor little lamb,' Alice mourned, as the baby grizzled and shook. 'My poor little lamb!' I wish we hadn't come. I knew it was a silly idea. Everytime we have anything to do with royalty something awful happens. I might have known. I should never have brought him out in such a crowd. Oh, I wish I'd stayed at home. It's all my fault! Oh my poor little lamb.'

Minnie Holdsworthy, trotting to keep up with Albert's angry stride, glanced at his face and saw that his skin was dark and his mouth triangular with distress and bad temper. She tried to signal a mute warning to Alice, but her cousin's gaze was fixed on her baby, so her rambling monologue went on. Finally Albert couldn't stand it any more. He didn't look at Alice. He just shouted at her, suddenly and furiously. 'For Heaven sake, woman,' he said, 'if you can't talk sensible, don't talk at all.'

He sounded so implacably angry, Alice stopped at once. Now, and too late, she and Minnie exchanged glances, Minnie's commiserating and warning, hers the mute acknowledgement that she'd made a bad mistake but was under too much stress to avoid it. The procession continued, in anxious silence, and at the door of the shop, Minnie muttered goodbye and took herself off like a shadow. Albert didn't even notice her going. He was too busy ordering Nat to run and get Mrs Kelly.

The baby was still whimpering when they got back into the kitchen. 'Should I feed him, Albert?' Alice asked nervously. He'd upset her so much by shouting at her, she couldn't even trust her instincts now.

Albert was beginning to recover. 'Yes,' he said, still crossly. 'Of course feed him. Why not? There nothing the matter with him. It was a funny turn, that all. He perfectly all right.'

Mrs Kelly, however, didn't share his sanguine opinion. 'Sounds like fits ter me, Mrs Ploochy,' she said. 'Good job you had your cousin around, if you ask me. She knew what ter do right enough.'

Albert was furious, but this time he contained his temper until the midwife had gone. 'Fits!' he shouted. 'The idea! It was *not* a fit. Why a child of ours would have a fit? She no good. She don't know what she talking about. I will take him to hospital. To the best hospital. What a midwife know about fits?'

Alice looked down at her infant, lying still and pale in his crib. She could see blue veins clear and vulnerable beneath his translucent skin and a frail pulse quivering beneath the soft spot on his skull. Albert could roar and deny all he liked. She knew in her instincts that Mrs Kelly was right.

Nevertheless Albert had his way. Four days later, he and Alice took their fragile son to Great Ormond Street and paid ten guineas for a diagnosis by a child specialist. His opinion was exactly the same as the one Mrs Kelly had given them for ten shillings. Georgie was suffering from epileptic fits, only '*petit mal*' in all probability, but there was little doubt about it.

It took Albert a long time to recover. He resented the idea that his life was suddenly being shaped by events beyond his control. It was altogether too demoralizing, especially now, when he was working harder and making bigger profits than he'd ever done in his life. What unwitting sin had he committed to deserve such demeaning bad luck? There was no justice in it.

Alice, well schooled in humility and obedience, found it

much easier to adjust. Once she'd recovered from her initial terror, and knew what the trouble was, she felt she could cope. After all, Georgie had always been a delicate child. She'd already plenty of practice nursing him through croup and colic and sleepless nights. Handling fits would simply be an extention of their existing life style, that was all.

She took comfort from Minnie, who seemed to have a store of practical knowledge to draw on, despite her youth. Between them, they cosseted little Georgie day and night, taking it in turns to check him when he was asleep, and making sure that he was never out of their sight when he was awake. He grew slowly and timidly, and before three more months were out, he'd had over a dozen fits despite their care.

Alice was suffused with pity for him and torn by the urgency of her need to protect and resuscitate him. As the months passed, they were bound closer and closer to one another, and although it wasn't intentional, Albert was gradually left further and further behind.

Business was booming, just as he'd known it would be. For the last two months he and Nat had been run off their feet. There was plainly work and profit enough to hire another boy, and as soon as he knew about it, Nat provided one, his younger brother Frank, just thirteen and newly out of school. ' 'E's a bit slow on the uptake,' he said candidly, 'but honest as the day. An' willin'. You wouldn't believe how willin'. 'E'd jump orf the chimbley if you asked 'im to.'

The boy who arrived nervously, next morning, didn't look as though he had the energy to jump over the doorstep. He was certainly anxious to please, but he was desperately shy too, ducking his head to avoid meeting Albert's eyes. His wrists looked as though they would snap under the slightest strain. He might do for the shop, Albert thought, but he'd never lift a full crate.

'It's hard work,' he warned.

'I ain't afraid a' work, Mr Ploochy, sir,' Frank said, and for once, he dared to look up. He had the same widely spread brown eyes as his brother, and was smiling a subdued version of Nat's watermelon grin. So Albert hired him.

Despite his diffident manner, young Frank did well enough,

and turned out to be a good deal stronger than he appeared. For the first few days Nat treated him like a newly hatched chick, nudging him into activity whenever he showed signs of slowing, and out of harm's way whenever Albert showed signs of roaring.

' 'E turns my insides ter jelly,' the boy said as he and Nat trudged back up Church Lane late one night. 'I never 'eard no one roar quite like that. Never in me life.'

'Never you mind, young 'un,' Nat reassured him. ' 'E don't mean it, you know. It's all show. Got a heart a' gold really, old Ploochy.'

'Heart a' gold, my eye!' Frank protested. ' 'E said 'e'd kick me backside ter pulp!'

' 'E might *say*,' Nat explained. 'That's just 'is way, innit. Never you mind what 'e sez. That's all a load a' wind. It's what 'e *does* you got ter watch our for. Actions speak louder'n words wiv old Ploochy. Foreign, yer see!'

Frank saw but couldn't entirely believe. The reverberations of that roar were too much for him. He knew that Ploochy's words could have a terrible effect on you.

Later that summer they were to have a very bad effect on Alice, although, of course, neither of them said a word about it afterwards to anybody. It was private and painful and very personal. Something to be kept strictly between the four walls of their bedroom where it belonged.

Alice was pregnant again, and one of the difficulties about being pregnant was that it removed a useful and unanswerable reason for excusing herself from sex. In the early days of their marriage she had discovered, to her relief, that she only had to suggest modestly that it was 'that time of the month' and he would desist at once and leave her in peace for a week. Now that she was carrying he seemed to think she was available at any time, and this upset her and worried her. She wasn't sure whether pregnant women ought to do things like that or not. She had suspicion that it couldn't really be good for the baby, but it was far too delicate a subject to be talked about, and in any case she didn't have words for any of the things she wanted to say, or any of the questions she wanted to ask. So she simply had to accept whatever her husband suggested, put up with it and hope he'd get it over with quickly. That is, until one embarrassing night in early June, when not content with doing disgusting things, he'd actually started to talk about them afterwards. To her! In a bedroom lit by enough moonlight for him to see her face!

He'd just finished, had given his customary sigh, and was clambering back onto his side of the feather mattress. She was rearranging her nightgown, settling herself to sleep, hoping that this time her back wouldn't ache so much. There was nothing remarkable about the occasion. It had all happened as usual. There was certainly no reason for his sudden and unseemly outburst.

Instead of lying down beside her, he propped himself up on one elbow to look at her. That was disconcerting, for a start. But what followed was worse.

'Why you not move?' he asked awkwardly.

'Because I'm going to sleep,' she said, wondering at the question.

'No,' he persisted, 'when I love you, why you lie still? Why you not move?'

She was suffused with embarrassment, burning with it. She felt sure he must see her blushes. How indelicate! How disgusting! She couldn't trust herself to answer him, she was so upset.

'I love you,' he tried to explain, 'and you don't do nothing.' Then trying to correct his English, 'Anything. Why is this? You don't kiss me. You don't speak to me. You don't move. Why is this? You don't love me maybe?'

'Of course I love you,' she said, finding her tongue and annoyed to hear how sharp it was. 'I clean your house, I cook your meals, I look after your son. Everything I do shows I love you. I'm a good wife, aren't I? What more do you want?'

It was a silly question and she'd only asked it because she'd been so upset by the implication of what he was saying.

'I want you should move,' he said. 'Enjoy it. Kiss me back. Be with me.'

Shock filled her throat. For a long minute she couldn't speak she was so full of revulsion. Usually she tried to forget the shameful things he'd been doing to her, to put them out of her mind and get to sleep as soon as she possibly could. Now they returned to her memory in all their bestiality, all that jumping and jerking, all that grunting and puffing, all those horrible sub-human noises. Surely he wasn't suggesting that she ought to behave like that too?

But he was. And he went on suggesting it, in words she couldn't avoid. 'Why you don't move Alice?' he said. His voice was gentle, almost plaintive. 'Don't you like me to love you?'

What could she say? It was bad enough having to do things like that. Talking about them afterwards was like enduring them all over again. She had no intention of being dragged down into such squalid, lustful conversation. 'Albert,' she said sternly, 'this is not something ladies and gentlemen ever talk about. Not in England.' She sounded like Aunt Phoebe and this comforted her and gave her strength to continue. 'It isn't decent,' she explained.

'We are married!' he said, continuing stubbornly. 'We talk about everything.'

'No,' she said, feeling calmer now and more confident, 'not everything. There are plenty of things you do and say, because you're a man, that's quite understood. You'd never dream of telling me about them. Isn't that so?'

Of course, she was right. He would certainly never dare to tell her about the whores, and his dreams were a private necessity. 'I want you should enjoy,' he said, tailing off into a mutter because he had no words, English or Italian, to make his meaning clear.

'I do,' she lied. 'Now please don't worry about it any more. It's time we got some sleep. We shall never get up in the morning.'

And that was that. She'd been so controlled, so definite, so final, there was no way he could re-open the conversation, and yet it was more important to him to try and make her understand than it had ever been. He'd only spoken because he wanted her to feel pleasure too. He felt pretty sure that she didn't feel anything and he wanted to give as well as take. Now she'd wrong-footed him and made him feel more of a pariah than ever. It was all wrong. All wrong. Loving should be shared, talked about, enjoyed. She had turned it into a penance, a duty, a destruction. Where was the joy in that? Where was the love? What was the good of words when they couldn't say what you meant?

He slept badly that night and rose next morning bleary-eyed and bad-tempered. Whatever else he'd imagined about her, he'd never thought that his lovely Alice would end up sounding like fierce Aunt Phoebe.

When Alice's pregnancy became obvious Mrs Kelly was booked and made her first visit to reassure her that everything was 'coming along lovely' and that the second birth was always easier than the first. 'We'll manage by ourselves this time,' she said. 'We don't want that old Dr Fermanagh, do we?'

Alice wasn't sure. At least Dr Fermanagh had chloroformed her out of her pain and for that she would always be grateful, but on the other hand, he'd seen her like that, he'd actually dragged little Georgie out of her body. The very thought of it made her hot with shame. It *would* be much better if they could manage without a doctor. Mrs Kelly was right. Perhaps this time it wouldn't be so bad.

It was certainly different. For a start it began a week earlier than she'd expected and on a day when Albert was away visiting his wine merchants in the City. It was quite a relief to her that she wouldn't have to contend with his anxiety on top of everything else, and as she glanced at the kitchen clock that morning, she sent up a silent prayer to be allowed to get the whole thing over and done with before he came back. She felt very cool as she dispatched young Frank for the midwife and set about cooking a good midday meal.

Georgie behaved like a model child all through the day, sitting between them by the kitchen fire to drink his mug of cocoa, submitting to Mrs Kelly's rough ablutions and when the afternoon began to darken, agreeing to lie down on his little bed for 'forty winks'. To Alice's surprise he fell into a deep sleep within five minutes of his obedient departure.

'Doing very nicely,' Mrs Kelly said, resting her rough hand on Alice's tightening belly, and this time Alice agreed with her. They washed the tea things and made up the kitchen fire and put Albert's supper in the stove. Then, and only then, they climbed the narrow stairs to the bedroom, moving slowly and carefully because the pains were coming thick and fast. Mrs Kelly made up the bedroom fire, while Alice climbed bulkily into her oldest nightgown and made herself as comfortable as she could in the high bed.

It was peaceful in the bedroom, with the gas popping and the fire crackling and voices murmuring up from the shop below them. Lying propped against her mound of pillows, Alice started to labour, glad that she and Mrs Kelly were on their own and uninterrupted. She pushed and struggled and groaned but this time she didn't scream. She couldn't scream because that would wake Georgie and he'd be so frightened. She'd hold on for just one more. And just one more. The sweat ran into her eyes, and the next pain gripped her in its vice, but still she didn't call out. Then Mrs Kelly was at her elbow, mopping her forehead with a damp towel and smiling. 'One more push, my lovely,' she said. 'Just one more and we'll have this baby's head.'

'Born?' Alice asked huskily, before the next pain could overwhelm her. She felt drunk and bewildered and sure that she couldn't have got that far.

'Born!' Mrs Kelly said. And sure enough, after the next struggling effort, the child's head slithered out into the world and gave a lusty cry. Alice was weak with the combination of surprise, relief and effort.

It was a girl, a strong, compact baby girl with a mop of thick black hair and huge dark blue eyes, born twenty minutes before her father returned to the shop and woke Georgie by bounding up the stairs two at a time. He was delighted with her. 'She look just like me!' he said holding the small bundle with pride. 'She a lovely baby! A beauty! You clever, clever Alice!' The baby sang back at him 'A-la, a-la, a-la!' making her presence known, and he put back his head and roared with approval of her pink gums and the busy tongue lifting in that small red throat. 'Just like me!' he said. 'Feed her, Alice. We get no peace till you feed her.' She was exactly the sort of baby he could understand.

Poor little Georgie stood beside the bed, blinking away his sleep, his fair hair standing up on end and his mouth circular with amazement. Albert lifted him up into the mounds of pillows and Alice cuddled him with one arm while she supported the sucking infant with the other. They made a very pretty picture, Albert thought, admiring them from the doorway, his daughter's dark head dramatic among the white linens, fair hair and pale skin around her. I will buy my lovely Alice a splendid present, he decided, something spectacular to show how proud I am and how much I love her. And he did love her, so much it was making his chest ache.

For several days he considered the possibilities, but none of them even approached the magnificence he wanted. In the end the present simply arrived, without any effort on his behalf at all, and it arrived in the unlikely shape of a filthy pawn ticket crumpled in the hand of a small, evil-smelling, unshaven man with a squint.

'Worf a bottle a' gin that is,' the squinter urged, proferring the ticket. 'Straight up, guvnor! I ain't 'aving you on. A bottle!'

Albert had earned quite a reputation in Tooting for his readiness to exchange beer or spirits for one of Solly Isaac's pawn tickets. Drink was cheap and occasionally he made a good bargain. His hunter watch had come that way and so had a new set of flat irons for Minnie Holdsworthy. He felt he was beginning to develop a flair for spotting a fair exchange.

'I will give you half a bottle,' he said. 'No more. Half a bottle, and I'm a fool to myself!' It was a saying he enjoyed, particularly when he knew it wasn't true.

'You won't regret it, guvnor,' the squinter said. 'You got a choice piece, I promise yer.' He clutched his precious half bottle to his greasy bosom and was gone before Albert could change his mind.

It *was* a choice piece, a gold ring set with five fat diamonds that cost him a tenner to redeem.

'Come in the nick of time,' Solly said. 'I was losing it termorrer.'

'Hot is it?' Albert asked.

Solly tapped the side of his nose with a blunt forefinger. 'We ain't 'ad this conversation!' he said. ' 'Old on a tick. I'll find a box.'

It was a present for a princess, but the princess seemed unmoved by it. She thanked him prettily and put the costly jewel on her finger to please him, but as soon as he was out of the bedroom, she returned it to the box. He never saw her wear it again and he was too disappointed at the failure of his extravagant gesture to risk the ignominy of asking her about it. He redressed the balance in the only way available

236

to him, by giving his new daughter two old Italian names. She was christened Anna Maria, and the ring and the occasion were buried together in the top drawer of the linen press.

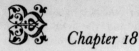

Chapter 18

Christmas was approaching and this year the season of goodwill saw an outbreak of active hostility in the London music halls. Urged on by the redoubtable Marie Lloyd, music-hall artists all over the town were organizing themselves for a strike. Queenie Dawson, as Albert had grown to expect, was happily and hotly in the thick of it.

'Them ol' managers 'ave took us fer a ride jest once too often,' she told him. 'The number a' times I been caught on the ol' matinee lark! It don't bear thinking about. Change yer bookings as soon as look at yer, and then swear blind they 'adn't. Rotten beggars! Well they'll laugh the other side of their faces when all their precious 'alls are empty!'

'You really think the Federation will strike?' Albert asked, intrigued.

'Don't I jest?' Queenie said, her eyes glinting.

The impending action caused another row in Dickie's fire-cracker household. For the first time in her life Tilley had got a pantomine booking, so she was appalled by the idea of a strike, just at the very moment when her career was developing so satisfactorily. Dickie did his best to persuade his incipient revolutionaries to back down, but no matter what he said Queenie had an answer for him. He emerged from every argument deflated and defeated, to confess to Albert and Harry that he was beginning to wish he'd stayed a brickie.

Queenie was very rarely in the house and that should have made life easier, but it didn't. Her absence was as alarming as her presence, for as Dickie explained, you never knew what she was up to, always off to some meeting or other. And then suddenly, the strike was spectacularly and successfully under way.

'Come up the 'Olborn Empire, New Year's Day, first house,' Queenie said to Albert hurriedly as she and Martha bundled into the cab that would take them off to their next performance late one Wednesday night. Their faces were still filmed with sweat from their last performance, so the excitement they were generating should have been unremarkable and usual. But this time there was a hard edge to both of them, a breathlessness about their excitement that alerted him as though the situation they were in was somehow dangerous. Their eyes and teeth glinted in the lamplight like knives, and their painted cheek-bones were taut and hard. They looked like warriors, he thought, and the image roused him and alarmed him.

'What is it?' he asked.

'It's the revolution!' Queenie said triumphantly. 'Come an' see,' and the cab rocked them both away.

Despite the mockery of the popular press and his own misgivings, Albert's curiosity was engaged. The fact that there was a sniff of danger about the enterprise would have made it attractive even if Queenie hadn't been involved in it. Life at home these days was boringly domestic and predictable. The flat above the shop was always full of wet napkins and baby's long clothes dripping from the airer or blocking the fire on an overcrowded clothes-horse. Since Anna's birth, Alice was entirely given over to motherhood. He never saw her these days without a baby on her lap or held against her shoulder. In fact she was so totally and exclusively absorbed in them he was beginning to think she no longer noticed him at all. No, there was nothing worth staying at home for. He might as well go and watch the revolution.

Dickie was of two minds whether to throw a party that month or not. There was very little money coming into the house because of the strike and Tilley's temper was extremely uncertain. 'Whatcha think?' he asked Harry and Albert.

'Do yer good,' Harry said. 'Buck you up. Jest what yer need.'

'I don't know,' Dickie said. His forehead was puckered with anxiety and even his moustache looked sorry for itself.

'Have a party!' Albert advised. 'Cheer yourself up.'

'Women!' Dickie said heavily. But he threw the party anyway and this one was rather unusual.

For a start it was a celebration because the strike was having an effect. The hated matinee clause had already been written out of several new contracts and bookings weren't being altered quite so frequently or so readily either. Queenie and Martha were jubilant. Despite her lack of earnings, Queenie had bought a length of copper coloured silk and made herself a fashionable frock specially for the occasion. She looked outstanding, because the colour matched her hair and the new simple style set off her slim figure to advantage. Watching her deftly manoeuvring through the crowded drawing room with a trayful of glasses, Albert found he was admiring her now as well as desiring her. The frock was a temptation. All those little buttons right down the back. He looked at them with longing, thinking how pleasant it would be to undo them one by one and reveal her long slender back. In his imagination he was running his fingers down her spine, and kissing her shoulders, and that bristling hair. In the middle of his daydream, the real Queenie Dawson served her last drink and began to edge back through the room. As she passed him, she looked straight into his eyes and winked. It was almost as if she knew what was in his mind. If only . . . If only . . .

Then Dickie was urged towards the piano and the sing-song began, so the moment, delicious though it was, had to be deferred. He didn't even get a chance to sit beside her until the party was nearly over, even though he'd spent most of the evening scheming and dodging towards that desired proximity. Tilley had served the mince pies and Dickie had heated the punch, and they were all sprawling around the room, well fed and relaxed and fatigued, some still more or less on chairs and settees, but most lying among the cushions on the floor. Boots were unlaced, high collars askew and waistcoats unbuttoned. The gas lights had long since been turned down to a flicker, the fire was more ash than coal, and their excitement was spent. Tilley lay with her head in Dickie's lap, and at long last Albert was sitting beside a drowsy Queenie, close enough to have put an arm around her shoulders if only he'd dared.

' 'Nother month!' Martha said, slumped in a comfortable heap in the old tub chair with a plate of mince pies balanced on her belly. ' 'Nother month an' we'll 'ave won.'

'Been a good fight,' Mr Perry said, yawning. 'I will say that. We've 'ad some good times.' His recollection and his speech were hazed with drink. He seemed to be under the impression that the strike had been a picnic.

The company were too contented to contradict him, although Dickie raised his eyebrows, which was about the only form of protest he had the energy for.

'Unity's strength!' Martha said with difficulty, trying to locate the edge of a mince pie so that she could lift it to her mouth.

'Oh Gaw, Martha!' Queenie said, grinning at her. 'You in 'alf sozzled!'

'Speak a' yerself!' Martha said pleasantly. 'Unisy . . . unasy is strength. I told yer.'

'We got right on our side,' Queenie said.

'You got Marie Lloyd and Gus Elan on your side,' Dickie said. 'That's why yer winning. It ain't nothink ter do with strength or right or unity.'

'No,' Queenie persisted, sitting up to hug her knees. 'We got right. We wouldn't a' got all this support if we 'adn't been right. You can't keep people down fer ever. You treat 'em bad, sooner or later they'll turn on yer.'

' 'Ark at our Queenie,' Mr Perry said. 'She's a Red, that's what!'

'You can't change the system, Queenie,' his wife, Maudie, said, picking crumps from her bodice. 'Stands ter reason. Been there too long, innit.'

'So 'as St Paul's,' Martha said, inconsequentially, and fell to giggling again.

Dickie was still giving the topic serious consideration. 'It ain't treating people bad,' he said, thinking as he spoke. 'It ain't meant *that* way.'

'What is it then?' Queenie asked, challenging him. 'If it ain't treating people bad, what is it?'

'It's making the best a' the system,' he said seriously. 'Making the best a' the system.'

'The best a' the system fer one man's the worst a' the system fer the next,' Queenie urged. 'Can't yer see? It's a rotten system. So why not chuck it out an' start a new one?'

'From scratch?' the juggler asked.

'Why not?' Queenie said and the upward tilt of her chin showed Albert she meant it, even though she spoke with bravado.

'All of it?' Tilley asked, suddenly opening her eyes and taking an interest.

'Why not?' Queenie said again.

'Even marriage?'

'If it's wrong. Why not?'

241

'It's wrong,' Tilley said with conviction. 'Don't I know it! I could tell you a thing or two about marriage.' Dickie soothed her hair to hush her, but she wouldn't be hushed. 'You marry fer love,' she said, 'an' 'e's Prince Charming and everyone says how suitable, and what a nice pair, and all on and on, and there you are, stuck, an' 'e turns out a drunk an' gives you a broken rib an' boozes all the money away. What sort a' system's that? Rotten!'

'Be all right, you could get a dirrorce . . . a drivor . . . a dri . . . get un-married, easy you can get married,' Martha said, finding her tongue rather inaccurately.

'Queenie'ud abolish marriage an' all,' the juggler's wife said, eating her crumbs. 'Wouldn'tcher, Queen?'

Queenie thought about it for a while. Then she turned to Maudie, and looked at her seriously. 'Why not?' she said again. 'Pr'aps we oughter do away wiv any sort a' contract. It's only slavery, when all's said an' done. No matter what yer call it.'

'Qui' right!' Martha agreed. 'Promise ter love an' honour an' obey an' all on and on, and then what? You end up 'is skivvy. Non-stop 'ousework all yer life.'

That provoked delighted laughter. 'Since when you even done any 'ousework, Martha?' they asked. 'That'll be the day!'

'No contracts,' Queenie said pursuing the thought. 'No promises. Total freedom ter come an' go as yer please. No strings. No honour and obey. Just love. While it lasts.'

'An' what 'appens when love flies out the winder?' the youngest singer wanted to know.

'You walk out the door,' Queenie said easily, smiling at her.

'Quite right!' Tilley said. 'No more dirty tricks. Freedom ter come an' go. I always said marriage was a silly idea. Didn't I, Dickie?'

Albert had been listening with such concentration he'd hardly dared to take time to draw breath in case he missed something. He was dizzy with pleasure at the thoughts she was putting into his mind. 'If you did away with marriage,' he said, leaning towards her determined spine, 'people would . . . um . . . would, um . . . like together whenever they felt like it, wouldn't they?'

'Why not?' Queenie said, turning to look straight at him, green eyes glimmering in the soft light. 'At least it'ud be fun.'

He could hardly believe his ears. Did she really mean it, he wondered. Or was it just the drink talking? If only . . . If only . . .

He was on tenterhooks until her next performance at the Duchess, and afterwards he waited for her at the stage door as breathless with anticipation as any sixteen-year-old in love for the first time. But she was cold and distant and took care to sit at the other end of the table when they all went on to Luigi's. It *had* been the drink, he decided sadly, although she'd been right about one thing. The strike was nearly over and to all intents and purposes the Federation had got them what they wanted.

Spring had come in a rush of new leaf and provocative scents. Verbena and lilac coloured all the established gardens in Tooting, blackbirds played their wistful flutes from every may tree and the hedges were quarrelsome with sparrows. The season always intensified the urgency of Albert's fantasies and this year they were sharper and more painful than ever. Queenie Dawson's pearl white skin and peridot eyes bejewelled his every dream and he was haunted by the power of the erotic images he conjured in his sleep. It made matters worse to see her on stage and eat in her company and yet say nothing. He was doing the very thing the priests of his adolescence had warned him against. He was lusting after her in his heart and now that he understood how painful it was, he could see the necessity for their warnings. But it was all too late. The more he saw her, the more he wanted her and loved her. The more he loved her, the more he understood how impossible the whole thing was.

Trade was slack, which was usual enough between the party season and the summer, and Alice was still besotted with babies. Spring didn't seem to rouse her at all, no matter how potent it was. She welcomed the fine weather, but only because it provided some good drying days for the washing. She didn't seem to hear the blackbirds nor feel the pang of all that burgeoning new life around her.

But Albert was bored and wished something exciting would happen. He got his action suddenly and dramatically and at a moment when he was least expecting it.

*

He'd been to the Duchess one Wednesday evening, and what with being irritated by the poor quality of the opening turns and frustrated by the sight of Queenie, spotlit and unapproachable, by the first interval he'd had enough of the place. It was close and sticky in the stalls and the heat was making him thirsty. He left the theatre and strolled up the hill towards Clapham and Young's good ale at the Windmill.

It was a wise decision because the pub turned out to be a far livelier place than the theatre. There was a noisy party going on in the ballroom and the guests were still arriving, most of them in a high old state of intoxication and excitement, tipping like lords, laughing at their own jokes and ready to greet even the most casual acquaintances as lifelong friends. Albert was seized upon immediately by a young man with a red nose and a white buttonhole, who insisted that he joined the party 'Pronto!' 'Come along Ploochy, there's a sport!' he said, and made a stumbling entrance into the ballroom, leaning heavily on Albert's shoulder, and calling for the best whisky in the house because 'only the best s'good 'nough fer my ol' friend, Ploochy!'

Albert only had the vaguest idea who he was, but the party looked as though it might be fun, so he took the proffered drink and joined in. It was just the sort of evening he enjoyed, so it was a shame to miss even a second of it, but he was so full of drink that eventually he had to go for a pee. On his way back, the landlord gave him a nod and a piece of unexpected information.

'Friend of yours in the Public,' he said.

'Is there?' Albert asked, without every much interest.

'Young lady,' the landlord said. 'One a' them theatricals. I seen 'er in 'ere before with you and Mr Chanter. Can't get her to go. Bit the worse fer wear, ter tell yer the truth. Wouldn't like to 'ave a word, would yer?'

It was Queenie Dawson and the sight of her sobered him immediately. She was sitting by the window, her red hair silhouetted against the love birds etched on the glass, and she was obviously and disagreeably drunk.

'Clear off!' she said, as he sat down beside her. 'I ain't leavin' till I'm good an' ready.'

'Quite right,' he agreed in the gentle reasonable voice he

always used for inebriates. 'Have another drink.' She was so far gone another wouldn't make any difference.

'Ta,' she said. 'Double gin.' He was surprised and showed it before he could control his face. She rounded on him at once. 'And you can take that look off yer face, an' all. I can 'old my drink same as the next. You needn't worry. I don't puke up no more.' She drank the gin as though it were water. ' 'Er and 'er bleedin' frills,' she grumbled. 'This is all on account a' "Sail Away" you know. She ain't never forgot. Like a bleedin' elephant. A bleedin' scraggy elephant.'

'I call a cab and take you home,' he said. 'It will all be different in the morning.'

'No, it bloody won't,' she said, more fiercely than ever. 'I ain't going home anyway. Home! That's a laugh! I never been at 'ome in that rotten place. It ain't jest 'er rotten frocks neither. She treats me like dirt. Rotten old 'asbeen!'

'I call a cab,' he offered again. He felt the situation was beginning to get out of hand. It had been a mistake to buy her that gin. The sooner he got her home the better.

'I ain't goin' in no cab,' she said. 'You got cloth ears or sommink? I ain't going 'ome. They won't 'ave me. Not after the strike. She says I'm a Red.'

'You can't stay here,' he said, still quite reasonably. 'They close in half an hour. Then what will you do?'

'They can close when they like,' she said truculently. 'You ain't listened to a word I've said, 'ave yer? I ain't going back. And fer why? Because I been chucked out. Chucked out! On the streets. That's the sort of old bag your Tilley is.'

'What, tonight?' he said. He could scarcely believe it. Surely Dickie wouldn't be so hard-hearted. She was only a girl after all, even if her tongue was sharp.

'Tonight!' she said. 'Out on the streets. I got nowhere ter go. Nobody loves me, Ploochy!'

I do, he thought, but it wasn't the time to tell her. 'I've got a good friend. She live round the corner,' he said, lifting her gradually to her feet. 'She put you up for tonight. Tomorrow I find a flat for you.'

'Oh my Gawd!' she said. 'I don't 'alf feel bad. This table's going round and round.'

'Come on,' he said. 'You be better in the air. It too hot in here.'

She allowed herself to be led out of the bar. The night air made her gasp and shocked her into silence. They walked slowly across the familiar common towards the High Street, she concentrating furiously on the almost impossible business of putting one foot in front of the other, he supporting her weight and praying that Mrs Molloy would have a bed to spare, or at least know somebody else who had.

The little house in Prescott Place looked smaller than he remembered. It was dark and silent and sleeping. Albert knocked and knocked and knocked, and finally the front bedroom window was raised and Mrs Molloy stuck her nightcap over the sill and demanded to know what was going on, in the name of all the saints. The curl papers protruding from her cap looked like a pantomime wig and even in anger her Irish lilt was charming. The minute she knew who it was, she lit a candle and came down to let them in. The hall was exactly the same boot polish brown and Molly Molloy, now fully awake, was her usual warm, loquacious self, drifting back towards the stairs like a plump white moth in the yellow corona of her gnarled candle.

'Well now, if this isn't the work of Providence,' she said, 'I'd like to know what is. With young Ned off to his cousins this very morning so he was. Bring the young lady up. It's the second back, you remember, the one young Mr Williams had when you were here, poor soul. Will you be after watching out for the rail. It's a wee bit loose away over on the corner there.'

They followed the flicker of candle and conversation into the second back, and Queenie, deprived of the support of Albert's arm, dropped across the bed, groaning, and fell asleep.

'Poorly, is she?' Mrs Molloy asked sympathetically, holding the candle to Queenie's face to investigate.

'Too much drink,' Albert explained, because there didn't seem to be any point in trying to hide it from Mrs Molloy's experienced eyes.

'Ah, to be sure,' she said, nodding her curl papers. 'I'll put a chamber by the bed, so I will, and a nice big towel. Save a power of cleaning up. Be extra for the washing, that's understood, isn't it, Mr Ploochy dear?'

Albert removed Queenie's boots and undid as many buttons on her frock as he considered decent. Then he pulled a blanket across her legs and left her, promising Mrs Molloy that he'd be back the next day to settle up.

He'd forgotten the shop windows. It wasn't until young Nat arrived the next morning with his shirt sleeves already rolled above his elbows, ready for action, that he realized what day it was. And groaned. Time to dress the windows.

By the time he could escape, it was late afternoon and Queenie's matinee was nearly over. The doorman let him in back stage to wait for her, and he sat by the window of her pokey dressing room and watched the flies crawling over the ceiling and felt disgruntled. When she came off stage he was too hot and tired to do more than nod, and she was too exhausted and hungover to even turn her head towards him. She sat wearily before the fly-blown mirror and creamed off her make-up as though every movement was a pain. Without greasepaint she was pale and subdued, her skin sallow and the shadows under her eyes the colour of storm clouds. 'Sorry about last night,' she said.

He brushed her apology aside and moved on to more important matters. 'Have you got somewhere for tonight?' he asked.

'I got a flat,' she said. 'Manor Road. Your old Mrs Molloy knows the landlord. Says it's reasonable. Bet you anythink it'll be too pricey fer me. Still there you are. Tilley's brought me things.'

There were two badly packed wicker-work baskets in the corner of the dressing room, their handles tied together by the torn remainder of her old grey shawl. It was a depressing sight so he didn't waste any time looking at it. 'Come on,' he said. 'First we see Mrs Molloy, then we arrange the flat.'

Although Mrs Molloy assured Queenie that her prospective landlord was a 'real nice gentleman', he turned out to be a wizened little creature with a profile like Mr Punch and a sharp eye for a bargain. He also held very strong opinions about the value of his property, which was one of the plain Georgian cottages Alice and Albert had deplored on their first exploration of Manor Road.

He showed them the front parlour that could be used as a bedroom and the back kitchen and the scullery with its stove and its boiler and its nice earthenware sink, and he even took them outside to demonstrate the new w.c., which was obviously his pride and joy. They admired it to please him, and stood outside the door while he clanked the handle importantly, down and up, down and up until, at last, the reluctant white torrent gushed and roared around the blue patterns on the bowl. 'There!' he said, with tremendous satisfaction. 'Whatcha think a' that?'

His foolish enthusiasm made Queenie smile and although it was a very pale version of her usual grin, Albert was glad to see it, because a Queenie subdued was a strange being for him to contend with.

'Course you got the added advantage,' Mr Punch said. 'Me being in the flat above ter keep an eye on everything.' He gave them the full benefit of his gimlet stare. 'You'll want to talk it over,' he said and withdrew to the other end of his little cabbage patch.

Queenie and Albert went back into the kitchen. 'Do you like it?' he asked her.

She didn't have the energy to like or dislike. 'It'll do,' she said. 'If it ain't too much. I can't go above seven bob. Not reg'lar.'

'Stay there,' he said and went back to the outhouses to discuss terms with Mr Punch. It took a little while because the gentleman was stubborn as well as shrewd. But after some argument he finally agreed that an assured income of ten shillings a week paid at least three months in advance made better economic sense than twelve and elevenpence for a week or two and the chance that the young lady might find something cheaper and leave. 'Was you thinking a' payin' now?' he asked.

Albert agreed that he was and Mr Punch gave him the hint of a smile, that was more insinuatingly knowledgeable than any number of words could have been. 'I see!' he said.

'She will need curtains at the scullery window,' Albert said stung into attack by the implied assumption of that smile, 'and a new chair. That one's only got three good legs. And a proper wash set in the bedroom. That one's chipped.'

So it was agreed.

'Seven shillings a week,' he lied to Queenie. 'I have paid him three months in advance. You pay me back, eh? Like the dress. Will that do?'

She smiled at him bleakly. 'You're an old love,' she said.

'Ta.' The two battered hampers stood beside the bed still tied together. 'I s'ppose I'd better unpack,' she said, but she didn't sound as if she meant it. Her face looked thin and pinched.

'What have you eaten today?' he asked abruptly. 'Have you eaten anything?'

'Not a lot,' she admitted. 'I didn't feel like it. I 'ad a cuppa wiv your Mrs Molloy.'

Now he could take action again. 'We will have a good meal,' he said, 'at Luigi's. Come along.'

She didn't protest or argue, which was most unlike her. But she followed him to the restaurant and Luigi's cooking finally tempted her out of her misery. He produced a roast duck, running with succulent juices, and enough vegetables to feed three people, new potatoes shiny with butter, fleshy runner beans, carrots as sweet as sugar and even broccoli in white sauce. Eventually, after a slow start, Queenie melted too. She didn't lick the plate but by the end of the meal she was at least licking her lips and grinning at Luigi and looking more like herself than she'd done for twenty-four hours.

Albert escorted her home to Manor Road feeling he'd won a victory. The kitchen stove had been lit and the offending chair replaced. 'There you are!' he said triumphantly. 'That's a lot better.'

She admitted it was. 'I could make a pot a' tea, if I 'ad a pot an' some tea,' she said. And that made them both laugh. But there was an awkwardness between them, a constraint, alone together in a strange house with the darkness gradually shutting them off from the road and their neighbours.

'Make up the stove,' he said. 'We will go shopping,' and although she grumbled that she was running up debts like nobody's business, they went.

The High Street was a cheerful place, full of shoppers and already brightly lit. There wasn't any bread to be had anywhere, but they bought eggs and two rashers of bacon, matches and candles, a twist of tea, a little blue bag of sugar and even a tin of condensed milk to colour the tea. They returned with their arms full of purchases to a flat now in complete darkness. Neither of them could remember where the gas jet was and they spent three or four matches searching along the walls in the kitchen before they found it. As the yellow light glowed beside the yellow wall the room looked a little more familiar, a little less strange. She found a kettle in the scullery and a chipped tea pot in the dresser and set about making tea.

Albert sat by the little square deal table and watched her. There was no doubt about it now. She was very, very nervous, flexing her fingers before she touched anything and darting about the kitchen with quick, jerky movements, off-balance and awkward and taking care not to look at him. They sat on either side of the table and tried to drink their tea. Constraint lay between them like a fog.

'I must go home,' he said when his mug was finally empty.

'Yes,' she agreed, but neither of them moved.

'You will be all right?' he asked and the anxiety on his face was clear to read.

'Yes,' she said again, tonelessly and not looking at him.

'Oh dear!' he said, more concerned than ever, and this time she did look up, straight at him and afraid.

'No,' she said. 'I ain't all right. Not really. I ain't never been on me own before yer see. At home there was always more kids than happence and at Dickie's . . . well you know what it's like at Dickie's.'

'Yes,' he said, still holding her gaze. There was an unspoken question between them now and his heart was roaring with the implication of it.

'I wish . . .' she said and stopped, biting her lip. 'You couldn't . . .'

'You would like for me to stay here till the morning,' he said, amazed at his daring but surprised at how easy it was to make the offer. He would have to think up a plausible excuse for Alice. That he stayed at Dickie's perhaps. That might do. But he'd sort that out in the morning.

'Could yer?' she said breathlessly and the expression on her face was an invitation too open to be avoided any longer. He leaned across the table and took her face in his hands. 'I love you,' he said.

'I know,' she said, and, leaning towards him, kissed him full on the mouth. He was so happy and so overwhelmed by pleasurable sensation his mind refused to move on to the next moment. It stayed where it was, suspended without thought, while he prolonged the kiss for a very long time. When they finally drew apart they were both breathless.

'If I stay, I will love you,' he said. 'More than just this. You understand?' He felt he had to make everything clear.

'Yes,' she said, looking at him steadily, rosy in the soft light. 'You ain't bought me though. You understand that dontcha?' Her voice was gentle but her chin was determined.

'Yes,' he said, almost as thought he were making her a promise.

She kissed him again, pushing her fingers through the thick curls above the nape of his neck.

'I will stay?' he asked. 'I will love you?' Although he couldn't have explained why, he felt he needed her permission.

She grinned at him suddenly, the old grin, full of life and daring. 'If I feel like it,' she said, 'I might let yer. Why not?'

The reason became obvious to both of them when she'd unpacked her nightgown and a pair of sheets. They made up the truckle bed in the front parlour with frequent stops for kisses which steadily became more and more passionate and more and more pleasurable. The little bed was barely big enough for one and impossible for two. Nevertheless they lay down side by side on its narrow inadequacy and returned to kissing. The moon flooded in through the filter of the may tree outside their half-open window and cast magical patterns on the bare walls above their heads. There wasn't a sound in the house or the street. It was as if the whole place had been cast under a spell for their benefit, peaceful and moon washed and heady with the scent of honeysuckle.

Presently she noticed that his collar was choking him and they stopped to remove it and hang up his tie. Then their shoes were a nuisance. Then shirt and blouse got in the way and had to be unbuttoned. Finally she propped herself up on one elbow and declared that she couldn't stand her stays a minute longer. A few delightful seconds later, she had stripped to her chemise and was standing before him scratching her belly and sides to celebrate the luxury of their release from that imprisoning whalebone. Watching her, he was almost afraid of his desire, it was so strong. How dreadful it would be to fail with this girl, too. Whatever else, he vowed, it must be good for both of us. It could be. He knew it could be. As he gathered her warm salty flesh back against his body, he was offering up a prayer for success. 'Please God, make it all right for both of us!'

It wasn't. He came too soon for her, and knew it. Disappointment and remorse drowned him instantly in their bitter waves. He couldn't bear to look at her.

There was a long silence between them. After a while he wondered whether she'd just gone to sleep and ventured to look sideways at her to see. She was wide awake, scowling with thought, and when she felt his look, she turned her head abruptly so that they were eye to eye, too straight and too close to be avoided.

'Is that it?' she said and, to his relief, her voice didn't sound cross, merely curious.

'Yes,' he confessed, his face crumpled with the shame of it.

She thought again, stroking his moustache with her fingertips. 'Um,' she said. 'Don't think much a that. You'll have ter start again, wontcha?'

Emotions and sensations roared through him one after the other as though they were being blown by a great gale. Shock and delight at her audacity, fear that he wouldn't respond, followed immediately by amazement and rejoicing that his flesh could and did rise to her suggestion. Perhaps it would be all right after all.

'Not so fast this time,' she said. 'Take it nice and easy. Um! I like that. Do that again.'

This time he allowed himself to be led. This time they talked. This time they were both rewarded. They slept, legs still entwined, arms round each other, almost mouth to mouth. Albert had never felt so happy in his life.

Chapter 19

There were times when Albert found his new life-style
extremely rewarding, with Alice happily running a smooth
household in Tooting, and Queenie warm and passionate and
welcoming in Clapham. But then there were the other times
when he wondered why he'd ever taken on such complicated
existence, when Alice threw out hints that she would like to
move house, and Queenie suggested that he really ought to
marry her and make an honest woman of her. Back in Italy, as
he remembered rather enviously, rich men had kept wives and
mistresses with apparent equanimity. But in Tooting, things
were different.

Fortunately there wasn't a lot of time to think about it, for
Tooting was a very busy place, and getting busier. The
tramline had been extended from Totterdown Street to the
Broadway, and now red-brick terraces were going up in all the
remaining plots of Pennyman's land between the old village
square and the fever hospital at the Grove, ready to accommodate all the new arrivals that cheap transport would bring
flocking out into the pleasant air of the countryside. Alarmed
by the impending influx, the Lords had sold out and gone to
an estate in Guildford. Now the Manor stood blank eyed in an
overgrown garden, deserted and ignored.

'Jolly good job an' all,' the practical Em declared. 'Fair
broke yer back keeping that lot clean. They can pull it down
any time they like.'

Soon the old Vestry had been pulled down and a new public
Bath House built in its place. The cypress and the great holm
oak were felled and cut to pieces and carted ignominiously
away in a dirty old wagon. There wasn't a trace of greenery
between the Broadway and St Nicholas' church. The Mitre
had been rebuilt and was now set diagonally across its corner
site so as to face the onrush of traffic from the Broadway. Its
rambling gardens had been bricked over to make a stable yard,
and the field where visiting horses used to graze and wander
was now a terrace of new shops. One of them was a bakery, a
fact which rather pleased Albert, but did nothing to placate

his wife, who felt that the convenience of having new bread baked so near to her front door was little compensation for the mess and muddle of the past twelve months, while all this new building had been going on.

There was nothing for it, she sighed to herself. She would just have to start spring cleaning earlier this year and make a very thorough job of it. She put on her brown jacket and her everyday hat, and set off to the Broadway to get in supplies of starch and Reckitt's blue scouring powder and soft soap.

Although the sun was bright for early March, and several of the better shopkeepers had responded to it at once by putting out their blinds, the air was chilly. Alice moved quickly through the crowds, made her purchases as fast as a slow-witted shop boy would allow, and began the homeward journey.

In front of her a tram had stopped at the newly built terminal rail, and the crowds waiting for its return journey were climbing aboard. The pointsman stood beside his lever ready to change the points. It was something she'd never seen done before, so she stayed where she was, just for a second, to watch. It was a great mistake.

As the driver whirled his brass handle with a flourish of important gloves, and the tram jolted forward grinding the rails, a terrible, high-pitched, anguished scream suddenly cut her thoughts to shreds. It stopped the tram, and froze the driver, conductor, passengers and passers-by with horror and an unendurable sympathy. It went on and on, higher and higher, an agony of tearing screams.

People ran from all directions towards the tram and Alice followed, full of instinctive pity. The screamer was being rent by a pain so excruciating that something had to be done to stop it, and done at once. The sound turned her insides. Somebody make it stop, she prayed. Please God, don't let it suffer any longer.

She was on the edge of the crowd. The screams continued even more terribly. 'What is it?' she asked, putting a hand on the shoulder in front of her. Others beside and before her were asking the same question.

'It's a cat,' a man in front informed them all. 'Caught under the wheels, poor little beggar.'

'Can't you get 'im out?' a white face asked.

'They're trying,' the man said, and turned to see what was going on.

A cat, Alice thought. What if it was Jude? Jude! Dear, soft, loving Jude, dying in agony and she couldn't do anything to help him. She couldn't bear it. 'What sort of cat is it?' she asked. 'Is it a tabby?' But they were all making too much noise to hear her. 'Somebody please tell me!' she begged. 'Is it a tabby cat?'

The screams stopped with a suddenness almost as terrible as the sound had been. For a few seconds nobody said anything at all. Then a child at the front of the crowd began to cry.

Alice picked up her skirts and ran. The tears were streaming down her cheeks but she didn't care. She wanted to get home, to cry in peace, to put a distance between herself and those terrible, terrible screams. Her belly was shaking with the horror of it. It was Jude. She knew it. Her own dear little Jude. She couldn't bear it. By the time she got into the shop she was beside herself, whey-faced, tear-stained and too out of breath to speak.

Albert took one look at her and hustled her upstairs to the privacy of the kitchen, away from the astonished curiosity of their customers.

'What is it?' he said. 'Alice! Alice! What is the matter?'

'Jude!' she panted. 'Jude!' She couldn't get her breath. 'Run over. A tram.' She was weeping so much it was difficult to shape the words.

He didn't know how to cope with her. Queenie's tears were easy to handle. They flowed so fast and for so little cause, they could be stilled with a smile or a cuddle. But Alice, usually so calm and controlled, Alice only cried when her tears were beyond his power. Now she stood in front of him looking wild and completely unlike herself, her hair straggling out of its pins, her nose running and her swimming eyes red and frantic like a hunted animal. She clung to the bars of the kitchen chair as though they were the bars of a cage and she were imprisoned behind it.

He tried to put an arm round her shoulders, but she shook it away, flinching at his touch. He didn't know what else to try so he went to the sink to get a glass of water. As he passed the window he caught sight of Jude sunning himself on the roof of the shed. 'He not dead!' he said. 'He out there!'

Alice fled to the window, still weeping. 'Oh he is!' she said. 'He is!' Then she rounded on her husband. 'But he might have been,' she wept. 'Can't you see that? He might have been. Or it could have been Georgie or Anna. We must find somewhere else to live, Albert. Now! This very minute! This is a terrible place. We shall all be killed if we stay here!'

The expression on her face and the hysterical urgency of her speech reminded him too painfully of their honeymoon. 'Nobody is killed,' he said, too severely for her present tender sensibilities. 'The cat is alive.'

'It was squashed to death!' she shrieked. 'Squashed to death by a tram. It screamed and screamed!' The memory of that scream was still tearing her nerve ends raw. 'It died in agony. Is that what you want? You heartless man! Do you want Georgie squashed by a tram? Is that it?'

Her hysteria frightened him, but he made one last attempt to reason with her. 'It is only a cat,' he said. 'Why you make so much fuss for an animal?' When old Dog died he'd got Harry to bury the corpse and bought himself a replacement the next day. It was quite unnecessary to have hysterics over a cat.

'It's not a cat!' she shrieked. 'That's not it!'

'You said it was a cat.'

'Leave me alone,' she yelled, wilder than ever. 'Don't keep on at me! I can't bear it!'

Albert filled the glass at the tap and set it firmly on the table before her. 'Drink the water!' he commanded, coldly. 'Calm yourself! I have work to do.' Then he left her to sort herself out, pausing at the kitchen door just long enough to remind her of her duties. 'It is delivery day tomorrow,' he said. 'I suggest you think of that.'

Left alone, Alice gradually recovered and began to feel ashamed of herself. She was behaving so badly. Whatever would Aunt Phoebe say if she could see her? She went to the bathroom to bathe her red eyes. Once she was safely beside the white porcelain bowl on the washstand, she was very, very sick.

Delivery day was always an event in the Pelucci household and it always began early. This one was no different from all the others except that the dray was late arriving.

'Cast a shoe, guvnor,' the drayman explained. 'Plumb in the middle a' Wandsworth High Street. Hardly got out the Ram afore we was back.' His four great shire horses stood patiently before their laden cart, occasionally giving their great heads a little nodding shake to rid themselves of flies, occasionally shifting their weight a little, clip, clop, from one iron hoof to the other.

Anna loved them and stood beside their shaggy feet, diminutive in her little white pinafore, patting whatever expanse of warm damp skin was nearest to her hand. Once her mother had been alarmed for her safety, but the drayman had reassured her that shires were the gentlest creatures on four legs. And so they seemed to be, standing so still and patient. So nowadays, once she'd checked that the blocks were under the wheels, she relaxed and turned her attention to the serious business of unloading. But she was glad Georgie kept out of the way and didn't run risks like his daring sister. From time to time she would smile approvingly at him, sitting quietly among the crates. A good obedient boy.

The child's meekness still aggravated his father and he knew it, but his mother approved of him and that was what really mattered to Georgie. From the moment the dray arrived, creaking and lumbering around the corner to grate to a halt beside the yard, the boy began to feel threatened, and when his father swung the double wooden doors open and the yard was suddenly exposed to the world outside, Georgie wanted to run away. He couldn't do that, of course, so he did the next best thing, which was to sit on the crates on the other side of the yard, as far away from the noise and bustle as he could get without being accused of cowardice.

Mitcham Lane was exceptionally busy. Every gig, dog cart and pony chaise in the district seemed to be on the road, rattling over the tramlines and kicking up a dust. Alice and Albert toiled on, sticky in the warm spring sun, growing steadily more and more thirsty. 'Four more barrels to go,' Albert was saying, when there was a crash in the road beyond the dray. It was followed immediately by the simultaneous screams of a horse and a child. For a second he was numb. His mind didn't seem to be functioning. But Alice had flung her crate aside and was running out of the yard, her face set, her

257

skirts swishing and crackling. Her movement galvanized him into action. He ran with her towards the screams.

On the other side of the road, a carter was struggling to control his horse, which had reared up between the shafts and was flailing wildly. The road was strewn with boxes and baskets, and sitting among them, stiff as a doll, was little Anna, her face red and distorted by her screams, clawing the air as she yelled. Alice scooped her daughter onto her hip and ran back into the yard. The child went on screaming, but the force of her mother's movement chopped the scream up into a series of short, staccato wails. Albert followed them, distraught, biting his lips with anxiety.

Back in the safety of the yard they examined the child limb by limb. 'Does it hurt?' they asked anxiously. 'Anna, you must tell us if it hurts anywhere.' But she sobbed on, quite unable to tell them anything. It *did* hurt, but she certainly couldn't tell her father where, for she knew that wouldn't do at all. It wouldn't be modest. Later she would confide in her mother, when they were quite alone and there wasn't anyone else to hear. It was her bottom that hurt. Only her bottom. But you couldn't say that. Not to a man.

By the time they'd finished they were all exhausted. But at least they were sure she wasn't injured, so they could begin to feel relief. It was very short lived. From the other side of the yard, Georgie had been watching in fascinated horror, his eyes like balloons. Now he gave the sudden cluck of stopped breath that both his parents knew too well, groaned and fell into a fit.

This was a familiar emergency, one they could cope with almost without thought. Anna was set firmly and immediately on the ground, as her mother turned her attention to the child most in need of it. 'Spoon!' she said, holding out her hand to her husband.

As they worked, Frank left the shop to see what all the commotion was about. 'Everything all right, guvnor?' he asked, putting his head round the door to the yard.

His appearance unleashed all the anger that Albert had been carefully containing. 'No! Everything is *not* all right! Fool! Imbecile!' he yelled at his luckless employee. 'Who told you to leave the shop? You out a' your mind? Get back at once! I don't pay you to idle in the yard!' He was shaking with bad temper.

Alice, turning Georgie's head deftly to one side and unbuttoning his collar, glanced up briefly at the black rage beside her. 'Don't take it out on young Frank,' she said sharply. 'It's not his fault.'

'Fault?' Albert roared. 'Fault? Who said anything about fault? He should be in the shop. Well, he got a choice. He don't do what I tell 'im, he can go . . . leave! The sack! He got a choice!'

'More than we have,' Alice said, so bitterly that it checked his rage. 'Fat lot of choice we've got. Stuck here in this death trap, working all hours. Next time one of them'll be killed. I've warned you and warned you. You can't say I haven't. A year ago I told you we ought to get out. But you wouldn't listen. Oh no!'

'This is our living,' Albert said, caught off-balance and feeling he ought to placate her bitterness in some way.

'Living!' Alice mocked. 'It'll be the death of us, if you ask me. But you don't, do you?' and she picked Georgie up in her arms, and carried him, still limp and ashen, into the house, with Anna trotting behind her.

'Mind the shop!' Albert roared at Frank. 'I got things ter do!' And he flung his apron on the ground, grabbed his bowler from its hook behind the door and stormed out.

It was a beautiful day, warm and balmy, the sort that makes you ache to be out of doors. The pot boys were slumped on the benches outside the Mitre, half asleep in the unaccustomed warmth, their boots undone and their caps over their eyes. The baker had started on his second batch of the day and the yeasty aroma filled the road, obliterating the acrid smells of beer and barrels and horses and sweat. As Albert followed his fury into Charlmont Road, he couldn't help noticing it, but he walked quickly past, still too cross even to think where he was going.

Halfway down Charlmont Road, he reached Harry's house, and there was Harry, happily dishevelled, in his gardening trousers, with his braces dangling, standing at the front gate.

'Off ter see the 'ouse, are yer?' he asked.

'The 'ouse?' Albert queried. What was he talking about?

'That 'ouse you're fer ever mooning about,' Harry explained. 'It's on the market.'

Despite the accident and the row, Albert was filled with

sudden elation. He'd buy the house. That's what he'd do. He said goodbye to Harry and walked on, trying to appear as though he was just taking a constitutional. But his legs betrayed him. Within ten paces, he was pounding along, vibrant with excitement, quick and jerky as a clockwork toy. By the time he reached the gate of the house he was almost running, the inside of his bowler slippery with sweat.

A black brougham stood by the kerb, new paint gleaming. The liveried driver was careful not to notice Albert, but continued to scratch his forehead with the tip of his whip. The door was open. He strode up the path over the graceful patterns of the tiles he'd admired all those years ago and he was on the step.

The hall was brown and shadowed, softened by a thick Persian carpet and heavy flocked wallpaper. It was just as he'd imagined it would be, lush, comfortable, rich. A rich man's house. And the languid young gentleman standing in the hall, admiring his reflection in the oval mirror of the hall stand, suited the house to perfection. When he sensed Albert hesitating on the step, he turned his head slightly away from his reflection and raised his eyebrows a fraction of an inch, in the manner of a man not born to exert himself, a man who expected to be served. 'Ye-es?' he said languidly. The inflection of that word managed to convey that Albert had no business to be there and that he should run along quickly and not make a further nuisance of himself. A lesser man might well have been deterred by such splendid superiority but it strengthened Albert's resolve.

'I 'ave come to view the 'ouse,' he said firmly, and walked into the hall.

'Only jest on the market, dontcha know,' the young man said. 'Rather a corker!' He took one last admiring peep at his reflection and began work. 'Follow me,' he said, and proceeded at once on his guided tour.

Albert walked from room to room in a besotted dream. It was all as he'd always known it would be, when he'd stood at the gate and envied and nursed his ambitions. There was the dining room with its heavy velvet curtains, enormous table and massive oak dresser as high as the ceiling. There was the drawing room, long and cool and elegant. There were the stairs, stained and dappled by the bright scarlet, blue and gold flooding through the coloured glass window on the little landing at the top of the first flight, a bathroom with a geyser for hot water, more bedrooms and dressing rooms than he could count in his present state of stupefaction, and above them, on the second floor, a suite of rooms 'for the servants' and even a billiard room with a fine green baize table. But it was the garden that would have sold it to him, if any selling had been needed.

It was the biggest plot of surviving land to have gladdened his eyes since the acres of Tooting disappeared under the weight of London brick. Syringa grew beside the kitchen window, a wide lawn stretched from one fence to the other and beyond it was a vegetable plot and an orchard of apple trees, pears and plums. By the left-hand fence a young cherry tree swelled with white blossom and beyond that a white lilac swooshed and swayed. Albert stood in middle of the lawn in a stave of such happiness and excitement that he couldn't trust himself to speak, the smell of grass and blossom and warm earth was such an acute pleasure.

The languid young man was drooping at his elbow examining the polish of his elegant shoes, which had not been improved by a contact with grass and mud that was much closer than he would have wished. 'Is there anything else that you would like to see?' he asked, looking hopefully back at the house.

'No,' Albert said, tearing himself back to the present. Now to business. 'What is the asking price?'

'Well high, naturally, for a corker like this,' the languid young man said, steering Albert back onto the path. 'It *is* rather a special property.'

'How much?' Albert said bluntly, his mouth set with determination.

'Five hundred pounds,' the young man said, smiling his superior smile and thinking, where would the likes of you get money like that?

'I will take it,' Albert said, his face expanding with satisfaction. 'I pay you fifty pounds deposit here and now. That will be acceptable I think?'

'Oh yes, yes, perfectly acceptable, sir,' the young man said, speaking very politely because Albert had taken him by surprise. The man was nothing but a vulgar tradesman. And foreign too. He couldn't afford a place like this. A vulgar tradesman standing there as bold as brass, smelling of sweat and horses, with his fist full of greasy bank notes. He watched with displeasure while Albert counted off fifty pound notes from the wad he'd taken so casually from the back pocket of his trousers. What was the world coming to? He'd be saying he had a bank account next.

'Now I see my bank manager,' Albert said grandly.

It was late afternoon by the time he finally got home. Albert remembered young Frank, still minding the shop, and wondered whether the poor little beggar had had anything to eat since their snatched sandwiches among the barrels that morning. It was all right for Nat, now happily married. He'd have gone home to his nice warm wife and his nice warm dinner. But he tended to forget about his brother these days and with no one around to take over, the boy could have been left holding the fort and unfed. The thought made him feel a twinge of guilt.

Frank was still serving cheerfully and didn't complain. The gas was lit, the beer handles polished and the shop looked clean and welcoming.

'Everythink hunky-dory, Mr P,' he said as his customer left the shop. 'Been a tip-top afternoon.'

'You better cut along for your dinner,' Albert told him.

' 'Ad me dinner, Guvnor,' Frank said happily. ' 'Ad it an' forgot it. Mrs P come down an kep' shop.'

Dear Alice, Albert thought, always so practical and responsible. The quarrel of the morning was long since forgotten. He couldn't wait to tell her his good news.

She was kneeling in front of the kitchen fire toasting bread, with a child cuddled against her on either side. All three of them turned together when they heard his foot on the stairs. He stood in the doorway, looking down at the three faces below him, and thinking what a pretty picture they made, their eyes gleaming and their cheeks flushed by the fire. He was flushed too, and breathless with the impact of his love for them and the enormity of what he'd just done.

'I have bought you a 'ouse,' he said.

Chapter 20

They moved on a warm day early in June and although Alice
had been dreading the move, it turned out to be remarkably
simple and easy. She packed clean sheets and a change of
clothing in the laundry basket and a nourishing cold meal in
a hamper and Albert put them in Harry's wheelbarrow and
pushed them round to the house. Anna enjoyed it immensely,
especially as she was allowed a ride after she'd walked halfway,
and even Georgie was smiling, because he'd been given a day
off school and the grown-up responsibility of carrying Jude in
the cat basket they'd hired from Mr Gulliver. Em and Minnie
were waiting on the doorstep, capped and aproned and ready
for action when the wheelbarrow arrived, and for the rest of
the day they were all pleasantly busy together.

Jude had his feet buttered and retired to the garden to clean
them, looking pained and puzzled by such incomprehensible
behaviour. The three children were packed off to the garden
too, with strict instructions that they weren't to pick flowers or
dig holes or climb trees, but were to play properly and keep
out of mischief. They spent the morning picking one of the
knotholes out of the fence so that they could see through into
next door, while the three women set about taming Alice's
unfamiliar kitchen.

Albert returned in the middle of the afternoon with the
bedroom furniture and the glass and the china and the
hundred and one bits and pieces they'd been packing away
since Sunday. He'd hired one of the new horseless carriages for
this removal. It was as big as a bus and made a terrible noise,
so his arrival caused quite a stir and impressed the neighbours.

Em and Minnie made up the beds, removed their dirty
aprons and went home to attend to their families. Alice, left
behind in her vast house, cooked a leg of lamb in her new
stove and was relieved when it turned out quite creditably.
Then the Pelucci family dined together for the very first time
in their impressive dining room. Albert was rapturous with
satisfaction.

That afternoon he took his children on a tour of their new

home. They explored the house from attic to cellar and were very taken with the attic rooms, lovely, empty, echoing spaces where the ceiling sloped down almost as far as the skirting boards and the dormer windows rose from the floorboards set in a little walled box like a doll's house.

Anna like the billiard room almost as much as her father had done and stood fingering the green baize while Albert raised the great green shaded lights and then lowered them again towards their upturned faces. And Georgie to his amazement and delight found that the bedroom next to his own wasn't a bedroom at all. It was a little library. Bookshelves lined all three walls from linoleum to ceiling, surrounding the window like an erudite curtain.

Georgie's face lit slowly, with the unexpected pleasure of it. 'All those books, Papa,' he said with awe. 'Are they all ours too?'

'Everything is ours,' Albert replied.

Later that evening when the children were in bed, Alice finally managed to ask her husband the question she'd been brewing all day. She had agreed that it was a splendid home, and had been lavish in her praise of the kitchen and the bathroom and the modern convenience of it all. 'But it's very big,' she said carefully, because she didn't want to upset him with criticism. 'It will be a lot of work for one person. Were you thinking of hiring a servant?'

Albert hadn't thought about it at all.

'We had a maid to help out at Crescent Road,' Alice persisted. 'A big house makes a lot of work.'

'I think about it later,' Albert said grudgingly. At the moment he was planning something else, and it irritated him that all she wanted to talk about was servants. 'We will have a big party,' he said, 'to warm the 'ouse. A big party. In the garden. A garden party.' He'd invite Dickie's crowd and introduce Alice and Queenie to one another. 'How would that be, eh?'

Privately Alice thought it would be a lot of hard work, but she didn't say so. She could see from his face that he was determined and it would be pointless trying to talk about anything else now. She would bide her time and ask again when he was more receptive.

It made a pleasant change for Albert to be happy in the middle of the summer. With Queenie away at a seaside concert party again, the season stretched before him long and boring and loveless. The garden party would be a spectacular way to welcome her home again.

But before he could begin to plan it, he had a letter from Georgie's schoolmaster, Mr Barden, that sent him spinning off into a fury.

There was no cause for concern, the master wrote. Georgie was a bright lad and doing well. But it did just occur to him that the child might not be able to see properly. He seemed to have some difficulty reading words from the blackboard. Did Mr Pelucci think he might need spectacles?

Mr Pelucci did not. 'What nonsense!' he roared. 'The man is a fool. There is nothing the matter with Georgie's eyes. Anyone can see that. No son of mine would need spectacles. *I* can see all right. *You* can see all right. We have good eyes. That man is an idiot!'

'It wouldn't hurt just to take him to the optician's, Alice said. 'Just to make sure. I don't suggest for a minute that there's anything the matter with him at all, but it would be nice to know, wouldn't it? It would show Mr Barden who was right.' Unlike her husband, she'd been watching their son as he read of an evening and knew that he'd acquired a new habit recently of screwing up his eyes to peer at the print. She was pretty certain Mr Barden knew what he was talking about.

Albert grumbled for several days, but in the end he capitulated and allowed her to make the appointment. The optician gave his opinion at once. 'A very good job you brought him when you did,' he said to Alice. 'Short sight gets worse if you don't treat it. We've seen him in the nick of time.' So Georgie was fitted with an expensive pair of spectacles and Albert had to swallow his pride.

For several weeks he ignored the spectacles and the child. It made him feel humiliated every time he saw those wretched frames across his meek son's nose. Nothing about this child was turning out as he intended it. Fits! Weak eyes! What next?

The only way he could cope with his disappointment was to work hard and look away.

Georgie himself didn't seem at all put out by any of this. He went about the house exactly as before, wearing the hated frames as naturally as if they were part of his body. Albert couldn't understand it, and eventually he was compelled to talk about it.

'Do you like your new spectacles, Georgie?' he asked his son, one morning after breakfast.

'Oh yes, Papa,' the boy said, with obvious truth. 'I do. Very much.'

Albert was taken aback. He had to rearrange his moustache before he would venture the next question. 'Why?' he said.

'You can see ever so well through them,' Georgie explained earnestly. 'I can see the blackboard clear as clear. And the trees outside. All the branches have neat edges.'

'Do they?' Albert asked, still surprised. 'Didn't they have neat edges before you had your spectacles?'

'Not always,' Georgie confessed. 'Sometimes they were a bit, sort of furry. It's very nice now.' He smiled Alice's slow smile at his father to show his appreciation.

Albert looked at his son with a new understanding. What a straight-laced, old-fashioned little thing he was becoming. But at least he told the truth.

'You look very handsome,' Alice told the boy. 'Don't you think so, Papa? Quite the scholar.'

Personally Albert thought he looked like a baffled, blond owl, but this time he kept his opinions to himself.

The second disappointment over Georgie made the garden party an absolute necessity. His success must be seen and admired and talked about. Poor Alice tried every excuse she could think of in a vain effort to avoid it, but he had an answer for every objection. If it rained they would simply transfer the whole affair into the drawing room; if it cost a lot of money, so much the better; if she thought the neighbours would be offended, then the neighbours would be invited; it wouldn't make a lot of work for her, because he would hand everything over to a catering firm, and hire maids and even a butler if

266

that was what she wanted. He threw himself into the preparations with abandon.

Alice dreaded it. Even the expensive beaded tea gown he would insist on buying for her did little to cheer her. It was a gorgeous gown with thick frills above the elbow and a centre panel so full it billowed with every step she took, the sort of gown a duchess could have made an entrance in, but she knew she would feel self-conscious wearing it and ill at ease as a hostess. It simply wasn't her style.

Nevertheless, despite worry, work and weather, the garden party went ahead and was adjudged a great success by everybody who attended it and especially by Albert. Alice, welcoming and watching, directing the maids and checking supplies of food and drink, had little time for more than an occasional glance at the scene to see that Anna and Georgie were still clean and behaving themselves. Only two events impinged themselves on her preoccupation. One was the arrival of Dickie Chanter's artists. The other was the appearance of Jesse Holdsworthy.

She and Minnie had spent so many hours discussing his terrifying behaviour, his bouts of swearing drunkenness, his black silences, his searing need to pick a quarrel, that she'd formed a very clear picture of the man. He would be huge and shambling, unshaven and dirty, with bloodshot eyes and a mat of uncombed hair, a man of rough hands, big boots and brutal muscles. It came as quite a shock to see that he looked so ordinary, a small, neat, quiet man, with regular even features, small well-kept hands and mouse-coloured hair as soft and fine as a girl's. He seemed so controlled, so contained, so sure of himself. She had to look at him again and again to convince herself that what she saw was true, and every time she looked he was smiling and talking easily and happily to one or other of the guests. He spent a long time talking to Albert, who obviously liked him, because he was nodding, and spreading his mouth in that wide grin of approval he gave so often to Anna and so rarely to poor little Georgie. How extraordinary!

Dickie and company were no surprise to her, because she'd seen many of them before, but there was no denying that their arrival had impact. They made one of their entrances, dressed to kill and all chattering and shrieking with laughter. As she confided to Em and Minnie afterwards, it made her head spin. There were supposed to be eight of them, but it felt more like eighty, they were so full of themselves and so loud. Among the well-mannered creams and whites and pastels already gathered on the lawn, they were garish and discordant, the men in check suits or the sort of blazers you'd only expect to see on the seaside promenade, and the women in the most violent assembly of colours she'd ever seen, emerald, cerise, electric blue and purple. Why there was even one dreadful girl with red hair who was wearing scarlet. How low! And what appalling lack of taste! She looked cheap and common and Alice determined to keep a very close eye on her in case she was light fingered too. You never knew with girls like that. Some of them had no respect for other people's property at all.

Albert, surveying the party from under the green masses of the syringa, thought that both his women looked particularly beautiful, Alice, so cool and calm in her new cream gown and Queenie so stunning in red.

It made him feel proud that he had brought so many different people together to share the hospitality of his new home, particularly as they all seemed to be enjoying themselves. Minnie and Em were giggling, that was a good sign, and the Reverend Simpson had button-holed Dickie and was well into a ferocious homily. The aunts were sitting under the cherry tree with their own jug of lemonade on a little table beside them. They were deep in conversation with Solly Isaacs who was concentrating hard, watching their faces and patting his beard, which had been specially combed for the occasion. Leah looked smaller than usual. She was sitting very still, like a cat taking the sun. The Major from next door was in full tropical kit, topee and all, and was strutting around the lawn as though it was his empire, with his wife anxiously hanging on to one arm to anchor him. Harry and Mr Gulliver were making short work of a pile of sandwiches, saying little, but munching with satisfaction, and Martha Goodyear had found the trifle and was now seraphically consuming a very large helping.

To have provided such a spread in such a setting was the realization of Albert's dream. He'd come a long way since the squalor of Saffron Hill and the slums of Old Clapham. Now he moved in an elegant society, where white muslins floated beside the lupins, and striped zephyrs swished and shimmered through the rose arbour, and pretty faces were framed in high frills of pin-tucked lawn, or white lace, or elaborate broderie anglaise. Yes, he thought, it was an elegant society, sophisticated and tolerant, where a man could be free to love two women and still be accepted. Ever since they'd moved in, he'd been toying with the enticing idea that one day it might be possible to install Queenie Dawson in the house as a tenant of the top floor flat. Now, watching the two of them together in the same garden, he was even beginning to hope that he would soon be able to tell Alice all about it. Just imagine if she took it well and allowed it, like the rich women did. After all she and Queenie were both so very different from one another, there was no need for them to feel that they were rivals. What a marvellous life they could all lead, together in a place like this.

The first raindrop that splashed hotly onto his forehead barely interrupted his reverie. But it was followed by a flurry of others, blown straight into his face by the wind that was whipping the tablecloths into the air, dislodging hats and scooping long skirts into fluttering confusion. Within seconds the garden party was running for cover, clutching hats and jugs and plates of half-eaten food. The two maids struggled into the conservatory with their two trestle tables, scattering vol-au-vents and sausage rolls as they went, while the men ran into the house with as many chairs as they could carry. In the confusion a pile of sandwiches was trampled into the lawn, Martha's hat was blown into the cherry tree and the Reverend Simpson got trifle all down his trousers and had to retire, blushingly, to the bathroom for what he called 'running repairs'. By the time they were all reassembled in the drawing room, they were confused and out of breath and dishevelled. Alice was sure that the party had been ruined.

But Tilley made a bee-line for the piano. 'You never told us you 'ad a joanna,' she said happily to Albert. 'Who's fer a ding-dong?' It was just what they all needed. Hats were removed, clothes set to rights and the entertainment began. Even Albert did a turn, singing loudly and off-key, so that his guests groaned and protested and enjoyed his every mistake. It was a sudden and unexpected success and rounded off the party in the best possible way.

*

The aftermath was nowhere near so pleasant.

Alice and Albert were late getting to bed that night, there were so many dishes to wash and so many visitors to discuss. It was midnight before they were finally settled and Alice had managed to steer the conversation around to the one guest she most wanted to criticize.

'That dreadful red head!' she said. 'Did you ever see such a sight, Albert? Somebody ought to tell her you can't wear scarlet with hair that colour. Wasn't she common!'

Albert didn't know what to say to this, so he grunted and hoped that would do.

'Tilley was telling me all about her,' Alice went on happily. 'She's a really dreadful girl by all accounts. A vicious tongue on her, so Tilley says. She made a lot of mischief when she was living at Longbeach Road. The things she said about poor Tilley you'd never believe. I'm not surprised they got rid of her. She's a mischief-maker, of course. Anybody can see that with half an eye.' She was enjoying the topic very much, knowing from what Tilley had said that the girl was fair game. You could complain about her as much as you liked and everybody would agree with you. 'I knew she was no good the minute I set eyes on her,' she said. 'Flaunting herself in that red frock. So common! Don't you think so, Albert?'

Albert was feeling most uncomfortable. He grunted again and closed his eyes in the hope that she would think he was falling asleep.

'What on earth made you invite her?' she persisted. 'There wasn't any need to, was there? Not now they've thrown her out.'

'I didn't want to hurt her feelings,' he said lamely, wishing he could think of some way to bring the conversation to an end.

'Girls like that don't have feelings,' Alice said with conviction. 'You're too kind-hearted, Albert. That's your trouble.'

He couldn't stand any more. 'My stomach is upset!' he proclaimed, rising angrily from the bed. 'I go and take a powder.' And he went downstairs, glad for once that Alice always insisted on keeping medicines in the scullery.

*

Perhaps he would get a better reaction from Queenie. After all, she enjoyed parties. But he was disappointed in her too.

'Not bad,' she said coolly, when he asked her what she'd thought of it. 'Good grub. I'll say that. Who was that funny old geyser in the pith 'elmet? Was 'e batty?'

He explained that the Major was a bit eccentric, but she wasn't really interested.

'Pity it 'ad ter rain,' she said. 'Still, we 'ad a good old sing-song, didn't we. Gaw, my feet are killin' me tonight. That last 'ouse was sticky an' no mistake. D'you see that old blighter in the front row? Eatin' 'is supper e' was, cheeky beggar!'

Later that night when they lay cuddled and contented in their big feather bed, he tried to reopen the subject. It was important for him to know what she thought, and she'd told him so little.

'How you like my children?' he asked, trying not to sound too proud.

'Um,' she said sleepily. 'You got a nice little lad. I like *'im*. An old tender-'eart. Like 'is old man.'

That wasn't what he wanted to hear at all. Georgie wasn't a bit like him. He was exactly like his mother. 'What about Alice?' he asked.

'She's yer wife,' she said tartly. 'Wish I was!'

He changed the subject quickly, sensing that he was treading on dangerous ground. 'What about Anna?' he asked. 'What you think of my Anna?'

She opened her eyes and looked at him, blunt and direct. 'You don't want ter know what I think,' she said. 'They ain't *my* kids.'

'I do want to know,' he insisted. 'It important.' Which it certainly was, at this stage in the conversation. There was something about the way she was looking at him that alerted him to caution and yet at the same time made him want to continue.

'All right,' she said, 'only don't blame me if you don't like it.' She gave him that level disquieting look again. 'You're spoiling that kid,' she said. 'You give 'er every mortal thing she wants. That's a daft thing ter do.'

He was outraged. 'I am not!' he said. 'I don't do that!'

'Told yer you wouldn't like it,' she said.

'Anna is a dear litle girl,' he cried, defending his favoured young. 'A good little girl. If I give her things, it because she deserve them.'

'She ain't a dear little girl,' Queenie said and the expression on her face looked like disgust. 'If you think that, you ain't seeing straight. She twists you round 'er little finger. She's a knowing little madam, you ask me, an' she'll get worse, you go on the way you're going. You should try saying' "No" to 'er, once in a while. Make 'er share things wiv 'er brother, poor little beggar. She'll grow up selfish otherwise. Well, you can't say you ain't been warned.' And she turned on her side and prepared to sleep.

He was furious. How dare she criticize the way he was bringing up his children. He couldn't stay in bed with her a minute longer, she'd upset him so much. He got up and dressed with a great deal of noise and energy. If he kept her awake, so much the better. She didn't deserve consideration, after talking like that. He'd catch the last tram back to Tooting, that's what he'd do, and leave her on her own. To his disappointment she seemed to be sleeping peacefully and didn't pay the slightest attention to him, not even when he went out banging the door behind him. As he knew, because he came back immediately afterwards just to see.

By the time he got back to the Plough, the last tram had gone. The place was dark and deserted, every window curtained and black, the street lights dull in a halo of smoky air. The night was colder than he expected and it smelled of soot. There was no way he could go back to Queenie now, so he turned up his coat collar against the chill, and set out across the common on the long walk home, kicking every kerb he crossed, partly because it was too dark to see properly and partly because he was still in such a temper.

How ridiculous his women were being. First Alice, saying all those unnecessary things about Queenie, and now Queenie being so hurtful about Anna. There was no sense in either of them. Well, he'd just put them both right out of his mind. He had plenty of other things to occupy him. Christmas would soon be here and this year he ought to do something really special to pull in the trade.

It took him nearly an hour to get home, but he felt he'd made good use of the time. With one level of his mind, he had planned an entirely new Christmas display; with another, and deeper level, he'd decided that his two women would have to be kept apart after all. His dream of a *ménage à trois* was like all other dreams, idle, misleading and a waste of time.

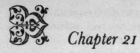

Chapter 21

Albert's ill-temper lasted for nearly five days, because although his initial storm of fury subsided quickly, it was replaced by a growing sense of injury that was hard for him to contend with because it was so foreign to his nature. He could have managed it if only he'd been able to apologize as soon as he woke up next morning. But next morning he woke in Alice's bed, and there he couldn't even acknowledge his feelings, let alone talk about them.

For two days he hoped that Queenie would send him one of her scrawled untidy postcards. A message could be answered and the answer could be the first step to a reconciliation. But the postman delivered only bills and a card from Dickie inviting him to a party on Saturday, and what was the good of that when he never invited Queenie. He couldn't think of an acceptable way to see her again. He didn't know where she was playing and he couldn't just turn up at the flat, not after the way he'd stormed out.

The days passed miserably, but the nights were worse. He couldn't sleep for thinking, and in the silence of his huge house he lay tossing and turning and racked with guilt. What if he never saw her again? What if he'd lost her with his silly blazing temper? After three days he couldn't even remember what it was they'd quarrelled about. He decided to go to Dickie's party after all and see if Martha Goodyear knew where she would be playing next week. Surely Martha kept in touch.

At breakfast, he told Alice about the party and on a sudden impulse asked her if she'd like to go with him.

She was pleased to be included, but of course refused, as she refused all his invitations. 'No, I don't think so,' she said. 'There's such a lot to do here. But you go. It'll do you good. A party always bucks you up, doesn't it.' It was extraordinary how she could imply criticism of him even when she was apparently giving her blessing to his activities.

*

The singsong had begun by the time Albert arrived at Dickie's crowded flat. Tilley was leading the chorus while Martha conducted, with a full and splashing beer mug. Standing beside Martha, spattered and singing with the rest, was Queenie Dawson. She looked across at him as he arrived, grinned and gave him a wink.

He wanted to roar and jump up and down, to dance and shout. It was all right! He hadn't ruined everything. She'd forgiven him.

At the end of the chorus she walked across to him and slipped a warm hand into the crook of his arm. 'Missed me?' she asked.

He was so overjoyed to be beside her again he could only nod.

'Good,' she said. 'Still love me, do yer?'

'So much!' he said, demonstrating the truth of the words by the movement of a mouth grown suddenly vulnerable to tears.

She squeezed his arm. 'We'll leave early, shall we?' she said.

Later that night he told her how miserable he'd been.

'Serves yer right!' she said. 'I been miserable an' all.' And probably more miserable than you, she thought, wondering just how much she ought to tell him. 'You ain't stopped ter think how I must a' felt coming into that great 'ouse a' yours.'

He was amazed. Surely she'd enjoyed it. She hadn't said . . .

'I don't always say everything that comes inter me head,' she rebuked him. 'I ain't like you.'

'You not enjoy the party?' he asked and now he felt quite anxious for her reply.

She'd hated the party, she thought to herself. She'd felt totally out of place in such a big rich house, with that awful Alice lording it over all the other women in her expensive dress. She'd been made to feel like a kept women, and it wasn't an experience she enjoyed. But how much of that could she tell him, without hurting his feelings? 'It was *your* house,' she tried, '*your* food, *your* wife, *your* children. Wasn't a corner anywhere for me. An' you say you love me!'

'I do!' he urged. 'Haven' I just showed you?'

She dismissed their love-making with a shrug. He always thought that was enough to prove anything, to make amends, to end a quarrel. And of course it often was. But not now. Not tonight. 'If you love someone really an' truly,' she told him seriously, 'you want to share everything wiv 'em. Meals, an' kids, an' loving, an' opinions, an' politics, an' everything. Half the time you don't know where I am, leave alone what I'm doin'. I got a whole life goin' on, Ploo, an' you ain't part of it.'

'I be part of it,' he promised, his smile so confident and his eyes snapping affection at her. 'You tell me what I do.'

That was Ploochy all over, she thought. He gave his promises so easily and with such charm. When they weren't about marriage. She decided to test him. 'There's a meeting of the Strike Committee up the Star, Sunday, an' a sort a concert. I'm singing. How about that?'

She was daring him, her green eyes bold. He gathered her warm body toward his to kiss her tenderly. 'I be there,' he promised.

The music hall was a squat, soot-stained building, and despite its unprepossessing appearance it was easy enough to find, as it was decorated with a huge scarlet sign, that was written inside an appropriate border of unlikely planets and surrounded by the most tempting advertisements of the fare on offer, from 'Flora Goldberg, your very own song bird', to Charlie Gallagher who, it was claimed, was 'The funniest man to tread shoe leather'. It looked what it was, a little local music hall, proud of its home-grown talent.

But once inside the door it was plain that this was not simply a place of entertainment. The room was crowded with men, as you would expect, but most of them were dockers still wearing their working clothes, which was extraordinary enough in itself, and even more unusual was the fact that so many of them were engaged in earnest and passionate conversation. The heat and vigour of their argument combined with the crush of many bodies in a small place drew out such a piquant melody of acrid smells that it made Albert's eyes water.

Up on the little square stage a pianist in full old-fashioned evening dress, cravat and all, was playing the latest songs on his tinny upright. There was no sign of Queenie, nor of any other entertainer and Albert was just beginning to wonder whether he'd chosen the wrong evening when a tall, skinny man in clerical grey walked out onto the stage and signalled to the pianist to stop playing. He had the full attention of the audience immediately, without shouting, or pounding the gavel, or even coughing, simply by standing there, bony wrists protruding from his tight sleeves, patient face pale in the strong stage light.

'Um – comrades,' he said, and his voice was as hesitant as his manner. 'Um – before your strike committee present their – um – report to you, I have some – um – um – um – news. I saw Jimmy Townsend in Guy's yesterday.'

Battered faces turned expectantly in his direction, and Albert, watching them, noticed how many of these men were scarred or deformed by their trade. With a rush of unbidden emotion, his mind was suddenly filled with the most vivid memory of his first sight of the London docks all those years ago.

The young clergyman was still speaking, earnestly and quietly. 'The bone will knit,' he promised, and the dockers growled their approval. 'However,' the young man said, and his tone was a warning that more serious matters were to follow. 'However, Jimmy's – um – wife and his – um – young children are in difficulties. I need say no more of that. And there is still – um – Mrs Millyard and Bill's widow and – um – others we all – um – know about.' The dockers watched him soberly. He gave a little gulp and plunged into his appeal. 'It is our proud boast,' he said, 'that we always look after our own; that those who have little are always the ones who give to those who have nothing at all.'

The sentiment was warmly applauded by every man in the audience and instantly acted upon. While the strike committee set their chairs and cleared their throats and got themselves into the right position to take command, two cloth caps went clinking from hand to hand. Even the most shabby pocket produced a copper or two, offered between blunt cracked fingers with a rueful comment, 'Better'n nothin', eh?' Albert was moved by the unselfish generosity all around him and decided that his donation had to be a sovereign. Nothing less would do. Unfortunately the boy guarding the cap passed him by, considering him too rich and foreign to be worth a touch, so he had to stand up and push his way through the crowd, with the result that his offering was given more boldly and publicly than he'd intended. It caused a stir, and attracted the attention of the platform party.

'Take a dekko at ol' moneybags, will yer,' the chairman asked his mate. 'Could be a rozzer!'

'Never on yer life!' the docker said. 'Nark more like. You ever see a rozzer flashin' the readies?' But he grumbled off through the crowd to make inquiries and returned with the calming and surprising news that ol' Moneybags was wiv Jackdaw's gel.

'Stone the crows!' the chairman said, impressed. 'She done all right fer 'erself then. Whatcher know about that!'

'Kep' it very quiet,' his mate observed, his eyes noting the gleam of Albert's watch chain.

'Got some sense,' the chairman approved. 'I wouldn't let on neither, if I was 'er. Jackdaw'll drink the poor bugger skint the minute 'e finds out.'

Despite the discretion of the strike committee there were plenty of others in the hall ready and eager to pass on the news to Jack Dawson that his young Queenie had struck it rich and got herself a toff for a fancy man. The chairman had only just begun a rousing call for action and solidarity when Albert was joined by a formidable-looking gentleman in a coal porter's long-skirted cap and a black donkey jacket more grease than cloth. Even before he introduced himself, it was obvious who he was, for he had the same sharp nose and the same unruly red hair as his daughter. Only where she was all skin and bone, he was all flesh and muscle. He had a neck as thick as his forehead, heavy unshaven jowls and a lumpy chin. The addition of so much superfluous flesh made his eyes appear small and cunning. He waited until he was able to speak under the cover of applause, and then came straight to the point, without preamble.

'Come wiv our Queenie, I 'ear,' he said. 'I'm 'er farver.'

'Pleased to meet you,' Albert mumbled, embarrassed to be talking during a speech, and feeling suddenly lost in a situation he hadn't foreseen. The man glowering before him was a challenge and looked it, the muscles in that thick neck flexed and intimidating. He's not a great deal older than I am, Albert thought, and was ashamed. Another flurry of applause gave

278

him the chance to talk again. 'Would you like a drink, Mr Dawson?' he offered.

'Not just at present,' Dawson said, still glowering. 'She never said nothing to us you know. Not a dicky bird! You know'd 'er fer long, 'ave yer?'

It was a disconcerting catechism, Albert thought. What was he supposed to say? Fortunately the speech continued for some time, unbroken by applause or comment, and that gave him a chance to gather his thoughts.

'She work for a friend of mine,' he tried at the next opportunity. 'Mr Dickie Chanter. You hear of him perhaps?'

'Ah!' Dawson said, relaxing a little. 'Dickie Chanter. Yes. We 'eard all about 'im. I will 'ave a beer, ta.'

So they drank together and pretended to listen to the speeches, and Albert was beginning to congratulate himself that he'd handled the situation rather well, when Dawson suddenly pushed his aggressive jaw to within an inch of Albert's nose and asked another alarming question.

'When you tyin' the knot then?' he asked. 'Eh?'

Albert took the only refuge available. He pretended he couldn't understand. 'Pardon?' he said, and managed not to sound surprised, merely curious. It bought him a little time but that was all, for there was no stopping Jack Dawson now.

'Getting spliced,' he explained. 'Married. Was yer thinking a' marryin' our Queenie?'

This time Albert said the first thing that came into his head. 'I never think of nothing else!' he said, truthfully. It was the wrong sentiment but the right answer. Dawson was delighted with it and ordered another beer. Then, and in the nick of time, the entertainment began and Queenie was on the cramped stage, bright as a poppy in her scarlet dress, singing a cheerfully saucy song called, 'They're shiftin' farver's grave ter build a sewer'. Albert watched her and admired; Dawson watched him and calculated.

At the end of the song, she came down to join them and to Albert's relief took her father immediately and thoroughly under her control. Soon they were surrounded by dockers and Queenie was introducing them one after the other, 'Our Ned, our Cal, Miffy, Spud, Tranter, Snuff,' so many men with scarred faces and explosive nicknames that Albert couldn't distinguish one from another. He plied them all with drinks, listened to their tales of dockyard injustice, avoided Jackdaw and grinned at Queenie. So the evening ended in high good humour.

'They mean to go on with this strike, don't they?' he said to Queenie as they undressed later that night.

' 'Course!' Queenie said. 'So would you an' all, if you 'ad ter live the way they do. Bread an' scrape. Two pennorth a' cagmag. Ain't fit fer pigs!' She had peeled off one stocking and tossed it into the corner of the room, and now she sat slumped in the wicker chair, with her legs astride and her heels jammed against the floor as she unpinned the tangle of her hair. Watching her, Albert was struck yet again by how peculiarly and unexpectedly attractive her careless inelegance could be. But desire must wait tonight. He wasn't sure how she would receive him, and in any case, his mind was still seething with the muddled impressions of their extraordinary evening.

'Jesse says they will call out the army,' he said.

' 'Course!' Queenie said again, dropping her hairpins into the tray with a clatter. 'An' shoot us in cold blood, I shouldn't wonder. They got an encampment up at the 'Ackney Marshes all a-ready. Can't 'ave the poor up on their 'ind legs demanding fair pay, now can yer?' She grinned.

'It will be like a war,' Albert said, concerned. 'People hurt.'

'We know all that,' Queenie said seriously. 'It *is* a war. You don't think ol' Devenport'll give in without a fight, do yer? If we win, 'e'll 'ave ter cut back his big fat profits ter pay us. 'E won't take kindly ter that, now will 'e?'

'It not your fight though, is it?' he tried to reason.

'Oh yes it is,' she said with determination. 'I like a good scrap. Bucks you up a treat.'

'But this is serious,' he said.

'Yes,' she agreed. 'It is. Bloody serious. You gotta fight if you want ter get anywhere in this world. That's a fact a life, innit. An' if you fight, you get 'urt. Bound to. Stands ter reason. But there you are. We just gotta beat the buggers, that's all.' She looked like a warrior again, her jawline hard and defiant and her eyes ablaze in the shadowy bedroom. The sight of her was irresistible.

'I love you so much,' he said.

It wasn't until the next day, when he got back to the shop, that he gave serious thought to the consequences of the strike. Then he realized that it was necessary for him to protect his family against the worst of it. In Tooting, especially among the wealthier families he served, the opinion was frequently and comfortably given that there was nothing to worry about because the dockers were only bluffing and would never actually see this strike through, being either too poor or too cowardly, or both. Well, he thought, Tooting was wrong.

Alice must go to market and stock up on all the foodstuffs that might be affected: flour, rice, sugar, syrup, tea, cornflour, coffee, pepper. He checked the list in his head, surprised and a bit annoyed to realize how heavily they had all come to rely on imported goods. He would fill the cellar with coal now, while stocks were high. And that reminded him. Old Challoner the wine merchant had been complaining about stocks only the other day. Very low, he'd said, and had urged Albert to buy more than he needed. Well, so he would. He'd fill the cellar and the bottling shed, and where else? The flat! Of course! He had an empty flat above the shop. The thought lifted his spirits. If this strike held, he could make a really healthy profit out of it. What good fortune!

Queenie couldn't see anything good about it at all.

'I got a sort a feelin',' she said. 'All them troops up the 'Ackney Marshes and Specials every which way yer look. You can't get near the nick fer rozzers. An' they're all rarin' ter go. Sweatin' like pigs. Red in the face. You can see the sort a state they're in. Thump you one as soon as look at yer. There'll be a punch-up sure as fate.'

'Have some more potatoes,' Albert suggested. They were dining at Luigi's, and the meal was far too good to waste a moment on politics.

'Um,' she said, helping herself to another portion of everything left on the table. But it didn't stop the direction of

281

her thoughts. 'Trouble is, I've booked up now. It's a real classy booking, the Gaiety. If I rat out I shall never get another one.'

'Why you would rat out, eh?' Albert asked mildly, watching with affection as a trickle of butter from the potatoes ran down her chin.

'I shall be away twelve weeks,' she said, collecting the butter with her forefinger, and then licking it clean. 'That's a long time wiv a strike on. An' Cal an' Ned in the thick of it an' all.'

'Then don't go,' he said. 'Stay here with me.' That seemed a much better idea. But it annoyed Queenie.

'You ain't 'eard a word I've said, 'ave yer?' she demanded, looking quite fierce. 'I can't pass up a bookin' like this one. What am I gonna do?' Despite the roast chicken she had an anguished expression on her face.

Albert decided he would have to take command of this situation. Really it was ridiculous for a girl like her to be worrying her head about strikes. Alice never paid the slightest attention to politics of any kind. 'If the booking important,' he said, 'keep it. You can write 'ome every day like you do to me. If anything 'appen you come straight 'ome on the next train. One, two hours, you are back. How about that?'

'One, two hours you could be down there wiv *me*,' she said, looking straight at him and daring him suddenly. 'How about *that*? You ain't never thought a' that, I'll be bound.'

Oh, he had. Many, many times during those lonely summer months. But he couldn't just pack up and leave the shop and Alice and the children and everything, just like that. Could he?

'Why not?' she said, sharp and direct, her green eyes hard. 'You could 'ave a summer 'oliday like all the other nobs. Spend it all wiv me. Why not?'

The idea took root. It seemed possible. Dammit, it *was* possible. Suddenly he couldn't think of any impediment to it, not even Alice. She was so set in her ways, he could barely persuade her to leave the house to go shopping. A fortnight with Queenie, just the two of them, as if they were married. 'I will do it,' he said.

*

He dined at home the next evening, and at a convenient break in the meal he told his family that he was thinking of taking a holiday. Alice took the news with so little concern that he knew he could ask her to accompany him with the perfect confidence of receiving a negative reply.

So Queenie accepted her booking at Hastings and at the end of May she and Albert parted. But this time it was only for a fortnight.

As the appointed day approached, his excitement ran higher and higher. He felt he ought to make an effort to appear calm, in case Alice began to suspect that this holiday was more important to him than it should have been. But his exhilaration was difficult to ride and it certainly couldn't be hidden. That and the combination of guilt and pity he felt far too frequently for his poor Alice made bad bedfellows. He woke at night, heart racing and damp with sweat, as though he'd just run a strenuous race, but with the uncomfortable residual sense that he hadn't won it.

Chapter 22

As Albert stepped out of Hasting's station into the clear sunlight of the cobbled station yard, a low flying sea-gull crapped on his head. The noxious white fluid plopped onto his holiday boater, fell across his face, smearing his nose and chin on the way, and finally ran down the lapel of his brand new blazer. He was very annoyed. What a way to start a holiday!

Queenie, skipping across the cobbles to meet him, thought it was very funny and laughed at him, uproariously and for far too long. She would! 'Your face!' she said. 'You oughter see your face, Ploochy! Cheer up cocker! Supposed ter be lucky, that is. A good omen, so they say.'

He wasn't persuaded.

'Come on, Ploochy, you poor old thing,' Queenie commiserated slipping her hand through the crook of his arm. 'Ain't the end a' the world. It'll come out in the wash! D'yer like me 'at?'

It was a most theatrical piece of head gear and it matched a most theatrical gown, a green and yellow creation in the very latest style, all soft gathers and flowing materials that clung to her figure and sheathed her legs. He realized with a shock of pleasure that she wasn't wearing any corsets, and that the women they passed, still tightly encased in the rigid whalebone of the old style, were looking at her with envy and disapproval. They were causing a sensation! What fun!

They strolled downhill towards the sea. The promenade was crowded, and the predominant colour of the crowd was white. Little girls in white pinafores, big ones in white blouses, white lace shawls and white embroidered parasols, white kid shoes and little white slippers, white shirts, white trousers, white bonnets, white petticoats; a summer snowstorm of impressive clean linen, a parade of white peacocks. Albert felt completely at home at once in such flamboyant company.

They walked arm in arm towards the old town, past a row of newly painted guest houses and a canopied arcade of expensive shops, a-flutter with bunting. At the end of the promenade, a little unexpected bay was suddenly scalloped out of the coastline and there, curved around the centre of it, was a crescent of terraced hotels. They were faced with pale grey stone, and set with three tiers of perfectly graded windows, each one framed with bold blue-green curtains, exactly the colour of the sea that day. It was an eye-catching place, shining grey and white, and gold and green, between the ginger pebbles of the beach that spread like a doormat at its feet, and the ginger strata of the sandstone cliffs that rose protectively above it.

'That,' Albert said, extending an imperious arm towards the vision, 'is where we stay.'

The room into which they were ushered by an important bellboy was wide and elegant and full of sunshine. It was decorated, predictably, in sea blue, white and gold, and the colours made a perfect foil for Queenie's translucent pallor and the wild mane of her red hair. Sunshine and sea air had made her skin glow and suffused her usually pallid cheeks with subtle colour. She looked like a ripening peach, and just the sight of her brought the remembered taste of her kisses vividly into Albert's mind and mouth. But there was a curious constraint between them now that they were finally alone together. The splendour of the building seemed to induce decorum, and neither of them was prepared even to risk an intimate conversation. They unpacked, and they explored the room, avoiding each other's eyes, almost like newly-weds.

Double French doors led to their curved balcony overlooking the sea; comfortable armchairs, plumply upholstered, held out fat arms in the most welcoming way; and in the middle of the room stood an opulent four poster bed, swathed in sea blue velvet. Queenie couldn't look at it. She stood by the opened window, one hand resting on the bustle of the velvet curtain, and gazed absent-mindedly out to sea. Albert wanted to clear his throat, but under this new constraint he didn't dare. There was a long silence, while the gulls mewed outside the window.

'Let's go swimming,' she said abruptly.

Albert cleared his throat at last. 'Now?' he asked.

'Why not?' she said, tossing her mane at him.

'I can't swim,' he protested, but weakly, for at least it would be something to do.

'I'll teach yer,' she promised and gave him a grin to reward him.

So he treated himself to one of the new swimming costumes that were all the rage that year, and presently emerged from his bathing machine feeling chilled and vulnerable and rather foolish, being striped black and yellow like a wasp with a moustache. The sea was shockingly cold, but he waded into it rapidly and was up to his waist in icy water before he could change his mind. Then he stood, while the sea slapped a chill hand into the small of his back, and looked back up the beach for the first glimpse of Queenie, who was changing, according to the rules of holiday propriety, in her own machine and on the ladies' beach.

The sight of her took his breath away. She looked even more enticing in this outlandish outfit than she did in her underwear, and he was quite glad that his reaction to her was decently subdued by the chill of the water. Her costume was pillar-box red, with a white-edged ruff at her neck like a pierrot, and triple frills from her waist to her thighs. She took her time to wade out towards him, hopping and squealing away from the impact of each small slapping wave, trailing her white fingers in the green sea, aware and glad that she was attracting him. When she was about a hundred yards away, she flopped into the water with a thwacking splash and actually began to swim, paddling frantically, like a dog, her bonneted head bobbing up and down, up and down, in syncopated rhythm. He watched her, touched and amused by her efforts. It was a talent he hadn't expected.

They spent the next hour chilled but happy, while Albert endured his holiday baptism with patience and curiosity, absorbing one unfamiliar experience after another. He had his chin held and did his best to 'let his legs go'. After considerable effort, he managed to open his eyes under water and was rewarded by a stinging glimpse of Queenie's trailing legs, pale green marble in the sea-filtered light. He was encouraged by rubbery kisses, cold and salty. They were still playing when the town band struck up, and Queenie said they'd better get back sharpish or they'd never have time for tea before the first house.

The chill of the sea had broken the ice. They chattered and babbled together all through their expensive tea. Then Albert sat in their expensive bathroom, on the edge of their expensive bath tub, while his salty darling luxuriated in warm water that made her arms and legs gleam as pink as a rose and etched her white breasts with sea blue veins. The old Queenie might be smiling lazily up at him through the steam, but she had certainly been enriched by the sea change.

Later that evening, watching from the plush stalls of the Gaiety Theatre, he noticed other changes in her, and was surprised again, and impressed. The theatre was a spectacular arena, baroque and very rich, and the audience matched the auditorium. They were all in full evening dress, they were well fed, they were perfectly groomed and they spoke in the loud arrogant bay peculiar to the established in England. Watching them, Albert couldn't help wondering what they would make of his vulgar, raucous Queenie. As the show progressed, he began to be afraid that she would be out of place in such a classy setting.

He needn't have worried. The young woman who strolled so confidently downstage towards the footlights knew exactly how to handle her affluent audience. She was dressed in white, in a full-skirted, old-fashioned gown, tightly laced at the waist, like a conventional shepherdess, and she looked young and pretty, and although it made Albert blush to have such an idea even enter his head, virginal. She sang a slow ballad in a gentle voice, her accent softened by languorous long notes, her demeanour the epitome of maidenly decorum. He hardly recognized her, and had to glance down at his programme to reassure himself that he wasn't imagining things.

It was a long evening. He couldn't wait to get back to that high bed. He was sustaining himself, all through the show, with the knowledge that once they were under the covers away from the world and really alone together, love would make them happy. But he was wrong. When he finally moved tentatively towards her, under those covers in their palatial bed, she intercepted his hands with a chilly determination. 'Nothing doing, Ploochy!' she said. 'I ain't in the mood.'

He was furious. 'I journey all this way to be with you,' he said angrily. 'I leave my work. I lose money. I have bad journey. I wait all day . . .' How could she be so heartless?

'You ain't bought me,' she said flatly, and turned her back

on him. She'd been working all evening. How insensitive he was.

It demoralized Albert. She made him feel unwanted, gauche and, even worse, aware of his age. He remembered the seagull and was more convinced than ever that if it was an omen, it was certainly a bad one.

She was asleep in minutes, breathing softly into the pillow, and now he felt she had deserted him. How could she treat him so badly? Anger boiled in his stomach, made worse by the fact that there was nothing he could do about it. No trains ran from Hastings after midnight and he could hardly walk back to Tooting. Not this time. So he lay beside her, uncomfortable and discontented, listening to the sea crashing against the pebbles. From time to time he dropped into a fitful doze, but only to be racked by guilty dreams. It was a long, miserable night.

At five o'clock, the fishing fleet returned to the old town and the gulls fell upon it with such a cacophony of screams and cackles and high pitched squeals that any further sleep for Albert was out of the question. Sunlight streamed into the room in a smoky column, and the sky was lilac with the promise of heat. He got up, dressed, left his unaccommodating partner still asleep and went down to the beach.

There was nobody about and without the crowds the promenade looked smaller.

The gulls were still screaming and circling above the old town, so he walked eastwards towards the racket, needing talk and companionship and the unequivocal company of men. The fishermen didn't disappoint him. They were friendly, correct and approachable.

'Good catch?' he asked the skipper of the first boat he reached.

'Fair, sir,' the skipper told him. 'Plenty uv plaice. Dovers a bit on the tiddley side. Was you after somming pertickler, sir?'

Albert bought two of the larger plaice, still slimy and frothing as they died, and was applauded for the quality of his choice.

'Thas good sweet flesh you got there, sir,' the skipper said, wiping his hands on his jersey. 'Wrap 'em up nicely fer the gent-man, Freddie. Holidayin' are yer, sir?'

Albert told him where he was staying and the skipper

grinned. 'That's Mrs Millbank's,' he said. 'You tell 'er you bin buying from Josh an' she'll 'ave them little beauties cooked a treat for you. Josh! You tell 'er. Don' forget!'

The exchange cheered Albert up. It felt normal and acceptable. It restored the balance. As he returned to the hotel clutching his damp newspaper parcel, he began to whistle. The sky was a cloudless blue above a sea as calm as a mirror, and the beach, swept tidy by the night tide, was clear and clean. It was as if it had all been newly created especially for him. However difficult the night might have been, the day had begun with a promise.

Queenie was sitting in the middle of the big bed darning the toe of a pink ballet slipper. Her brows were puckered with concentration and she had the tip of her tongue between her teeth. She was perfectly cheerful and seemed to have forgotten all about last night's temper. 'I'm dyin' a thirst,' she said.

So he rang for breakfast and went to wash his fishy hands. When he returned she was brushing the tangles out of her hair, holding her face up to the sunshine. He sat before her on the edge of the bed, and told her all about the fishing fleet, just for the pleasure of watching her. Then their breakfast arrived and they sat by the little round table in the window to eat bacon and eggs for all the world as if they were an old married couple.

Then, and at last, assuaged by tea and sticky with marmalade, she allowed him to take her back to bed.

As Albert had hoped, happily gratified desire spread its contentment over the rest of the day. The sun shone on them as they set off to explore the narrow alleys of the old town, where the cobbles were as uneven as pebbles and almost as hard on the feet, and the dusty shops sold netting and hooks, tarpaulins and tanned rope and twine. Just off the hilly High Street they found a little crowded pub where the beer was marvellously cold. Queenie had no sooner settled herself on the upholstered bench under the window when Josh and his cronies arrived and greeted Albert like an old friend. Soon they were all drinking happily together and swopping impossible stories.

'Can't take you nowhere,' Queenie complained happily as

they emerged more than an hour later, to the dazzle of the noonday sun. 'Always end up in a crowd, dontcha?'

He had to admit that he usually did and that it was just what he enjoyed.

'Mrs Ploochy!' Queenie said. 'Nice that. Bein' called Mrs Ploochy.' If only he'd take the hint and talk about getting married.

'It's what you are,' he said lovingly. 'To all intents and purposes.'

'But whose purposes, eh?' she asked, teasing and realizing that this wasn't the right moment. He took the question as a compliment.

When the tide was right and the machines had been carefully wheeled into position, they took their second swim together. This time Albert managed to dog paddle for several breathless seconds and was very pleased with himself for the second time that day. Despite the seagull it was beginning to feel like an excellent holiday.

Monday was equally warm and enjoyable. But on Tuesday the wind changed and so did Queenie's mood. The sea, beaten to a froth by a strong east wind was grey and choppy and fast moving. Ships keeled over, their taut sails close to the water, their hulls spitting white spray, and the few intrepid strollers who had dared to brave the promenade held on to their hats and shouted at one another against the noise in the air while the wind blew them along at an undignified trot or tried to push them back the way they'd come. But Queenie was touchy and irritable and didn't like it at all.

She'd made a very bad start to the day, dropping her toast on the pillow, buttered side down, and then snapping her comb in two the minute she began to do battle with her hair. The sight of her face in the mirror infuriated her.

Decisions were impossible and she couldn't settle to anything. A walk on the pier was soon abandoned because of 'that damned wind', and a stroll in the old town didn't suit either because the place 'stunk a' fish'; even the fine stores along the promenade were 'a load a' rubbish'. Albert didn't know what to do to please her.

Finally, in mid-afternoon, he took her back to the Gaiety

Theatre and ordered tea in the blue and gold restaurant where they usually dined after the show. It was quiet among the potted palms, out of the wind, and the little orchestra were fortunately working through their most soothing repertoire.

The tea was very hot, so she drew it into her mouth noisily, slurp, slurp, holding the cup in both hands, her elbows on the table. Even now, at her most irritating and her most irritable, he found her charming. 'What the matter, my darling?' he asked, and his voice and his eyes were tender with concern.

'Only Cal gettin' 'is fool 'ead kicked in on that damned march,' she said crossly, scowling at the tea, 'That's all. An' Ned 'an all. I shouldn't wonder. I never ought've come down 'ere, Ploochy. You should a' stopped me.'

He ignored the ingratitude of her last remark because now he understood. The march! Of course! Today was the day of the march from Rotherhithe to Tooley Street. And he'd forgotten all about it, he'd been so happy. Poor Queenie.

No wonder she was in a state. 'Perhaps,' he tried 'it is a great success. No trouble. No troops.'

'No it ain't,' she said. 'Told yer. I got a feeling about it. There's bound ter be trouble. All them rozzers! They been brewing fer this fer months. Bli! This tea's 'ot!'

The next morning the news was on the front page. 'Riot,' the headlines shrieked. 'Riot at Mill Pond Bridge.'

'Oh my good God!' she said. 'What did I tell yer? What's it say?'

He sat on the edge of the bed to read the paper aloud, while she knelt behind him among the pillows, her chin resting on his shoulder. 'The large crowd of dockers that gathered at Mill Pond Bridge yesterday were in an ugly mood. Volunteer workers were booed . . .' 'Blacklegs!' Queenie growled. '. . . as they arrived to unload perishable goods said by the Port Authority to be in a dangerous state and in need of instant attention. Police were called out to restore order . . .' 'What a laugh!' Queenie said bitterly. '. . . strike leaders being unable to control their membership. Police restored order with some difficulty. Several rioters were injured in the mêlée, some seriously.'

She was up and dressed before he could finish the account.

There was no washing for either of them and no waiting for breakfast. He followed the storm of her anxiety out of the hotel, through the blue air of the early morning up to the sleeping frontage of the Gaiety Theatre.

The doorman was in the foyer, polishing his boots. 'Yes,' he said slowly, 'I do have a card for you, Miss Dawson, I do believe. In the first post it was.' He took a long fraught minute to find it, while she grew steadily more and more pale, her green eyes hard with anxiety under her tangled hair.

It was from her mother. 'Thought you shd know,' it said 'Cal is hurt. Not bad. Ten stitches. Will right again tonite. Love.'

'I knew it! I knew it!' she yelled, her mouth square with anguish, like a baby's. 'Didn't I say they'd get 'urt. Bleedin' coppers!' She put the card in her bag and took out a handkerchief to blow her nose loudly and with determination. 'Well that's it!' she said. 'I'm off! When's the next train?'

There was no stopping her, he could see that. She was already on her way home to Bermondsey. The theatre didn't exist. Nor did her booking. Nor, he feared, did he.

The guard was poised ready to flag the London train out of the station as she hurtled through the barrier towards the nearest carriage.

'What shall I tell the theatre?' he puffed behind her, feeling lost and inadequate in the face of her driving emotion.

'I'll be back in time fer first 'ouse,' she promised, scrambling into the carriage. 'Just meet the train.'

The door slammed behind her. 'You haven't had anything to eat,' he worried as she dropped the window open.

'I'll grab a bite on the train,' she said. 'Don't fret!' She gave him an absent-minded kiss and was gone.

It had been such a rapid departure it hadn't given him time to think. Back in the cobbled yard, he still had the strongest impression that she was beside him. Yet he knew that the rest of the day, stretching its sunny hours enticingly before him, would be empty and anxious and, unless he did something about it, difficult.

So he went shopping and bought a ridiculously expensive doll for Anna and a mechanical crocodile for Georgie. It had square false teeth that clattered like castanets and was painted a violent green. He wasn't entirely sure that Georgie would like it, because he really knew very little about his reticent son, but the shop girl assured him it was all the rage that year. Finally, feeling distinctly guilty, he chose a sealskin muff for poor Alice.

Then he went to the pub.

She wasn't on the first train he met, nor on the second. He paced the platform, watching the station clock, fretting. If she hadn't caught the next train, she'd miss her entry. But third time was lucky. There she was, stepping wearily down from the end carriage. He rushed to greet her.

All the lovely seaside colour had gone from her face. She looked sallow and drawn and miserable, and there were lilac shadows under her eyes that hadn't been there when she'd left him that morning.

'How long 'ave I got?' she said, unsmiling.

'Twenty minutes,' he said. 'I got a cab waiting.'

Despite everything, she gave a beautiful performance at the Gaiety that night. He'd never seen her timing so good nor her control so apparently effortless. But after the show, in their favourite spot in the restaurant below, she was too tired to do more than pick at her food and her skin was translucent with fatigue. She sat quietly opposite him, making an effort to eat, saying nothing. He didn't dare ask questions. All he could do was yearn with sympathy for her, his mouth on the move, his eyes anxious in the candlelight.

She didn't cry until they were safe inside their four poster. Then she sobbed like a child with rage and impotence and scalding pity. 'Oh it ain't fair!' she cried. 'It ain't right. Good 'ardworking men like that beaten silly. Layin' into 'em, Ploochy. It ain't right. Nobody got the right ter do that. Nobody in the world. Didn't I say them rozzers was out fer trouble? Rotten bastards! I knew it. Didn't I, Ploochy? I said all along. Oh it ain't fair! It ain't fair!' She sat in the bed, hugging her knees, and rocking with distress. Tears streamed from her eyes and ran down her nose and into her mouth, but she was too upset to notice. Albert mopped her chin with his handkerchief and made soothing noises, but she didn't notice him either. He was a comforting presence, a listening ear, no more. 'Our Cal's got sixteen stitches in 'is 'ead,' she sobbed. 'An' 'is poor face beat black and blue. I tell yer, there's injured men all over Bermondsey. More'n twenty up our street, fer a start. They knocked Lily's ol' man senseless. An' Abby White was kicked in the kidneys. God knows 'ow they'll make out with a new baby an' all. It was a massacre! A bleedin' massacre!'

Albert didn't know what a massacre was, but he could guess. Her anger and grief were terrible for him to see because they made him feel so helpless. 'My poor Queenie,' he said stroking her hair tenderly. 'My poor girl!' He'd been sitting around in the sun all day, doing nothing, and she'd been living through all this.

'There weren't no call fer it neither,' she wailed. 'The march was going off lovely by all accounts, Cal said. And then they go and do a thing like that. It ain't civilized, Ploochy. Our Ned says they come down Paradise Street like a load a' loonies. Lammin' into anybody! Bleedin' coppers. They chucked some poor bugger through a shop winder. Nothink ter do with it, he was. Just walking along, mindin' 'is own business. Ravin' loonies! Oh, our poor Cal! 'Is poor face! All them stitches. It ain't fair, Ploochy!'

Albert held her until she'd cried and babbled and raged the worst of her grief away, doing what little he could, providing a fresh handkerchief when the first one was too wet to use, persuading her to put her cold feet under the covers. It was past three in the morning before she could answer questions or give a coherent account of what happened.

'They'd come all along Rotherhithe,' she said, 'and down by way of Union Street and Cherry Orchard, you know them little alleys, and they was in Mill Pond Bridge, where Southwark Park Road, an' West Street an' Union Street and all them, come out. And then along came a bus with a gang of blacklegs aboard, and they give 'em what-for, booin' an' all. Patterson's lot 'ad balls a' sawdust ter chuck at 'em. Serve the buggers right! What they expect? Anyway, there was rozzers all round the bus, perteckin' 'em. Bloody ridiculous! Pertecking blacklegs. They should a' got out the way an' let 'em take what was comin' to 'em. But they never. Anyway, then the crowd started all up singin', "We don't care fer the boys in

294

blue" an' all on. And the cops got narked. And then the other mob came down from Paradise Street an' just laid into everybody regardless. Truncheons, boots! They 'ad a field day! Ned says they was enjoyin' theirselves, you could tell from their faces.'

'Is Ned all right?' Albert asked.

'Yes,' she said. ' 'E kep' out of it. Bit a' luck!'

'And your father?'

'In the boozer!' she said succinctly. 'Where d'yer think? Not a mark on 'im. Missed everythink.' He was surprised by the bitterness in her voice. It was the first time he'd heard her speak badly of any of her relations.

'I can't get over the coppers going on like that,' she said. 'After all's said an' done, they ain't exactly rich theirselves. You'd think they'd be more on our side. Workers like us!'

'Jesse Holdsworthy says they are lackeys,' Albert observed. 'Rich man's lackeys. Paid to do their dirty work.'

' 'E's dead right an' all!' Queenie said. 'All this, just ter make sure the rich don't 'ave ter part with a penny a' their profits. D'you know how much that bleedin' Lord Devenport made last year? 'Undred an' forty thousand pounds! 'Undred and forty bleedin' thousand! An' 'e begrudges 'is workers a livin' wage. We gotta eat rotten meat an' stinkin' ol' fish 'eads, an' see our kids go barefoot, so's 'e can live on rumpsteak an' champagne and tart 'is wife an' kids up with fancy furs. It's bleedin' ridiculous. We don't want the earth, after all's said an' done. Just enough money not ter be 'ungry.'

'You will get it in the end,' he promised her, but more to comfort her than because he really believed it. 'You'll see! Dry your eyes!'

The handkerchief she held crumpled in one hand was absolutely sodden. He removed it from her gently and padded across to the wardrobe to get a fresh one. At the bottom of the cupboard next to the doll and the mechanical crocodile, the sealskin muff lay in its quilted box, no longer soft and enticing and desirable, but as prickly as a bad conscience.

He shut the door on it quickly, but it returned to haunt his dreams.

Chapter 23

Despite this unexpected jolt to both their sensibilities, Albert and Queenie continued their holiday. Even after a bad night's sleep, they were gradually revived by the comforting routines of a vacation, breakfast beside the balcony, an early morning stroll, a dip in the sea, music at the bandstand, drinks with Josh and his mates, late night supper after the show. By the end of the day they were enjoying themselves again, by the end of three it was as if they'd never been parted. But Queenie had come back more determined than ever to talk about marriage and it wasn't long before she got her chance.

They were on top of East Hill, sitting on the cropped turf, watching the sandy-green sea and the long succession of waves rolling white tipped towards the shore below them.

Albert was remembering the *Belinda May*.

'I was eighteen,' he said, 'I thought I'd make a fortune in England.'

'Well you ain't done bad fer yerself,' she said. 'You got a darn sight more money then most, ain'cha?'

He had to admit that she was right but added that he'd worked hard for it, looking down at his broken nails and the lines now deeply etched on the palms of his hands.

'So you 'ave cocker,' she said and gave him one of her rewarding smiles. 'No question about that. I bet yer never thought you'd meet no one like me, did yer?'

'No,' he agreed. 'I didn't. You beggar imagination.'

She took it for the compliment it was. 'I wasn't part a' yer plan then?' she said, and the inflection of her voice alerted him to the seriousness of the subject they were now skirting. He thought for a few minutes before answering.

'I wanted a beautiful English lady to love me,' he said.

'Well, you got that!' she said still smiling, still open, still encouraging him.

'If only I could a' met you when I arrived,' he said, sighing. She was too great a temptation for him to ignore and say nothing.

'Fat lot a good that would a' done,' she said. 'I was two.'

'Two?' he echoed, dismayed, although of course he knew it, he must have known it.

'That's right,' she said. 'Born on the old Queen's Jubilee, I told yer. So I was two years old be then.'

The knowledge upset him. He put a hand up to cover his mouth and his distress. She is so terribly young, he thought. Young enough to be my daughter. The thought made him cringe with shame. It was all wrong. I should never have started this affair in the first place, he thought. I've no right to love her at all. Not with a wife and children. He looked up at her miserably. 'I am too old for you,' he said.

She kissed him at once, and remarkably passionately considering they were out in the open air. 'It don't make no difference ter me how old you are,' she said. 'I'd love you if you was a hundred and ninety.'

It was an instant, faultless response, and it was his undoing. His desire for her was so sudden and so strong, and he loved her so much, that he said the first thing that came into his head without pausing to consider the consequences. 'If only I had met you first,' he said, 'we could a' married and settled down and been together all the time.'

The words hung in the air between them and resounded in both their minds. He regretted them at once. She gave him a long calculating look.

'Well, why dontcha do it now.' she said.

'Do what?' he asked, fearfully, because he already knew.

'Marry me,' she said. She was perfectly cool, steely, daring him.

'How can I do that, my dear darling?' he asked. 'I am married to Alice!'

'Then you get a divorce,' she said.

He didn't want a divorce. He didn't want to think about it. He didn't want to continue the conversation. But he'd trapped himself, letting his silly feelings run away with him. It was the old, old reason for all his stupid behaviour. He made an effort to extricate himself. 'What you say we go for a dip before tea?' he suggested.

'Tide's out,' she said, more steely than ever. 'You ain't wriggling out of it, Ploochy. Not now we've started.'

'I can't divorce Alice,' he said, trying to regroup the thoughts that were spinning in panic inside his head.

'Why not?' she said.

'Divorce is difficult,' he pleaded miserably, knowing what an inadequate answer it was and how much he was refusing to admit.

'Blin' me, Ploochy, what sort of a damn fool answer d'yer call that?' she said. How hard her eyes were. ' 'Course it's difficult. Life's difficult. It ain't exactly a picnic fer me livin' the way we do. You ain't thought a' that, 'ave yer?'

'Yes,' he said, now totally downcast. 'Yes I have. Often and often. Because it is all my fault. I should never have started this.'

'Oh that's nice, innit!' she mocked furiously. 'That's lovely! I don't think! Muck me about. Bit a' fun when yer fancy it. And now you say you wish you'd never started it.'

'I didn't mean . . .' he said, confused and distressed. 'It wasn't . . . I didn't mean . . .'

'No. That's your trouble, ain't it,' she said. 'You never mean nothink. Well I do. Whatcha gonna do about it?'

'I don't know,' he mumbled. His face was wrinkled with distress but she was too far gone in her anger now to pity him.

'I ain't kiddin', Ploochy,' she said. 'We can't go on fer ever like this, neither one thing nor the other.' She paused, waiting for him to make the statement she wanted, but he sat locked mutely in his misery, so she tried another tack. 'Dontcha love me no more?' she said.

'Queenie,' he implored, 'please, please don't say things like that. I love you so much. I can't tell you how much.'

'Then marry me,' she said flatly. 'Divorce Alice and marry me.'

'I can't,' he said.

'Can't! Can't! Whatcha talkin' about?' she shouted. 'You ain't even tried to. I bet you never told her nothink about me, ever!'

Of course he hadn't. What sort of man did she think he was? Didn't she value discretion anymore? Her anger and passion were now completely beyond his control, and the sight of her blazing eyes and her stiff furious face alarmed him so much that he couldn't think of any words. He didn't know what to say to her. Worse than that, he recognized with his instincts and his deeper emotions that they were in the middle of a serious row, and if he didn't handle it with the utmost affection and caution, he could lose her. He must think carefully this time before he said a word. He mustn't rush or speak too soon.

'I have Georgie and Anna to consider,' he said after a long pause and was pleased that he sounded calm.

'Oh yes!' she said and her voice was a snarl. 'Them bloomin' kids a' yours. It ain't never occurred to you I might want kids an' all.'

It hadn't and it surprised him. 'Do you?' he said.

'I'm twenty-five,' she said. 'Quarter of a century, that is. Gettin' on. Yes, 'course I want kids. Husband, home a' me own, kids. Like me ma. Shan't never get none of them off a' you though shall I? You're just a fancy man!'

If only he could take that bitter note out of her voice. He put out a hand towards her, but she flung her body aside out of his reach. 'Don't start that!' she said fiercely. 'That ain't the answer.'

'What answer do you want?' he said, staying controlled and patient with an effort.

'Oh blin' Ol' Reilly!' she said, exasperated. 'You got cloth ears or sommink? 'Ow many times I got ter tell yer?' And she got up and marched furiously off towards the cable car. Her movement dragged him out of his misery and energized him.

'Queenie!' he called, sprinting after her. 'Queenie, please! Don't run off!'

She stopped and turned to face him, a face hard and cold and challenging. 'Well?' she said.

He couldn't avoid committing himself. The moment was too fraught, the likelihood of losing her too immediate. 'I can't promise to divorce Alice,' he said reasonably. 'Not now. Not straight away. I talk to her first, get her used to the idea. Arrange to look after her. Do things for the children.' His entire face was an entreaty. He bit his top lip anxiously and his moustache was pulled askew. She glanced at it and then gave him a ghost of a grin, partly because she could sense victory, partly because she felt the first stirrings of a re-awakening pity for him.

'All right,' she said, but her voice was still firm. 'But you ain't letting things slide. I won't 'ave that.'

'I will tell her on Saturday,' he promised.

'Tell 'er what?' she said sternly, still making demands.

He gathered his strength so that he wouldn't be pushed too far by her determination. 'I will tell her about us,' he said.

'Just that?'

'It a lot,' he protested. Couldn't she see what a lot it was? 'It the first step.'

'All right,' she said again, and this time the word was an acceptance. 'Come on, let's go an' 'ave tea. I'm starvin' 'ungry!'

She held him to his promise, and although they didn't quarrel over it she teased him about it and reminded him of it on every possible occasion and several impossible ones; from behind the candles in the Gaiety restaurant, her face glowing; through the bead curtain of tumbling water-drops she'd just kicked out of the sea towards him; even between kisses, like a sudden thorn among roses; 'You promised, didn'tcha, Ploochy? Tell me you promised!' It had almost become a game, and although he pretended to be as sanguine about it as she was, beneath the badinage he was heavy-hearted.

Yet there were still so many pleasures in this holiday, despite everything. To wake up each morning cuddled against her welcoming flesh, breathing the scent of her skin, was an experience that spread contentment over the rest of the day, no matter what else it might contain; and to love and be loved whenever they both felt the urge for it was nothing less than luxury. Saturday came all too soon, and their fortnight had shrunk to the last snatched five minutes on a crowded station.

'Don't forget yer promise will yer, Ploochy?' she said smiling at him lovingly.

He deliberately misunderstood her, because he couldn't have borne even the hint of a row 'We will have another 'oliday in August,' he said. 'I promise!'

She was firm in her purpose and wouldn't be deflected. 'That's two promises,' she said. 'I'll keep yer ter that one an' all.' The guard blew his whistle. 'Ta-ta, Ploochy,' she said. 'Don't forget yer *real* promise, will yer?'

He thought about it all the way back to Clapham Junction. It was all very well for her to say 'remember your promises', she didn't have to find the words. How did you suddenly tell your wife you loved somebody else? He couldn't even think how to start such a conversation. He tried out some possible opening sentences, speaking them in his mind, listening to them, and they all sounded silly. 'My dear Alice, I have something to tell you.' No, that was dreadful. It sounded like a speech from some old melodrama, false and theatrical. She wouldn't take it seriously for a moment. 'I have been thinking about our marriage.' No, that wasn't any good either. It sounded foolish and it wasn't true. He hadn't been thinking about his marriage at all. He'd been too busy living. 'I have found another woman.' Like a piece of lost property, he thought. Oh dear! The idea made him giggle. He couldn't possibly say that. 'Something happened while I was on holiday.' That was better. But it might alarm her. She'd think he'd had an accident. He knew how easily her anxiety could be roused. 'Have you ever thought we could be happier if we didn't live together?' No, of course she hadn't. He'd taken particular care that such thoughts would never enter her head. He returned at last to 'I have something to tell you.' It still sounded ridiculous.

I'll take the children to Mitcham Fair first, he decided, and then I'll talk to her. Hedgerows flicked past the carriage windows, the rails tut-tutted, the train rattled and the engine hooted like an owl. It was all unreal.

Anna didn't want her father to come home from his holiday at all. She'd had a very pleasant fortnight without him, and she knew that all the enjoyable things she'd been doing would have to stop the minute he came back. Mamma had said so. And so had Aunt Min, only yesterday. 'I can't think what your Papa would say if he could see us now! We shall have to mind our Ps and Qs tomorrow. There'll be no larking about then!'

Anna liked larking about, especially in the sunshine out in the enormous back garden. It was like having a common all to herself. Aunt Min and Renee had come round nearly every afternoon and they'd made up such games together out there. Once they'd played Indians with feathers in their hair. They'd tied Aunt Min to the plum tree and pretended they were going to sacrifice her to the chicken god. Georgie wasn't sure there was such a thing as a chicken god, but Aunt Min said she didn't mind, any old god would do. Then they built a little platform up among the leaves of the sturdiest apple tree and Aunt Min said it was a pirate ship, so they played pirates for two whole days and walked the plank along the widest bough, which was very, very dangerous, and found a treasure island all pegged out ready for croquet and Georgie said that showed what desperadoes the natives were. So the next afternoon they played desperadoes and carried croquet mallets about to show how desperate they were and wore Mamma's hats for crowns and tablecloths for cloaks. And Georgie wrote a secret message in code and left it under the cherry tree in the secret hideaway that they all knew about, and when they found it, nobody could read it, not even Georgie, and Renee said the fairies must have changed it. The sun shone every day from breakfast to bedtime and nobody got cross. When it was too hot for larking around, Mamma and Aunt Min made jugs of lemonade and they had picnics under the shade of the cherry tree, instead of meals, which was much nicer, because you could leave things at picnics, and spill lemonade, and it didn't matter.

And now he'd come home to spoil everything and they were all inside the house, in their Sunday best, which was very unfair, seeing it was Saturday, sitting round the dining room table taking tea in the most terribly polite way, and Aunt Min and Renee weren't there, and Mamma was being careful and guarded, and Georgie hadn't said a word all day. It was too bad. Not for the first time she wondered whether fathers really were as necessary as grown ups seemed to assume.

'Was Hastings a nice place for a holiday?' Alice asked, re-filling the proferred cup.

'Very nice,' he said, wondering if he would ever be able to tell her exactly how nice. 'It has all sorts of places to go, a good theatre, a pier, very good pubs, a bandstand.'

'You found plenty to amuse you then?' she said, but her tone was so matter-of-fact there was no telling whether she was pleased or annoyed by what he was saying. 'Anna, I hope you're going to eat those crusts.'

'Did you see the sea, Papa?' Anna asked sweetly, so as to take her mother's mind off the crusts.

'I did,' her father said, smiling at her.

'What is it like?' she asked.

My poor children, Albert thought, they've never seen the sea. How dreadful. He must make amends at once. 'If you are good children,' he promised, 'I will take you to the seaside, too. Next year perhaps. What do you think Alice?'

Alice looked at him, unsmiling. 'We'll see,' she said, giving her usual evasive half-promise.

'People swim in the sea at the seaside,' Georgie observed solemnly.

'Yes,' his father agreed, remembering Queenie in her red swimming suit.

He glanced across at his daughter, and the sight of her dark curls suddenly rescued him. They reminded him of the doll.

'I buy you presents,' he said, 'and I forget them. Lovely presents!' He was warmed by his generosity. 'Come along Anna, we get them.'

'Won't they wait till after tea?' Alice said.

'No,' he answered, looking at his children. 'You'd like them now wouldn't you?' Georgie agreed politely, sitting still beside his mother, but Anna took her cue from the excitement in her father's voice and jumped up at once to squeal. 'Yes! Yes, Papa! Now! Now!' in just the way she knew he wanted. How typical of him, Alice thought. He can't wait five minutes for anything.

So the presents were snatched from the case he'd left beside the hall-stand, and were distributed with the first real sense of pleasure he'd had since his return.

They weren't the success he'd expected. Alice thanked him politely for the muff and ran her fingers over its softness and said it was lovely, but he noticed that she wrapped it up again almost immediately and then took Jude's living fur onto her lap to stroke and caress just a little too markedly. Georgie was baffled by the crocodile, but he too said 'Thank you!' politely and took his gift out of its wrapping paper and looked at it. His meekness annoyed Albert, and initiated him into action. He seized the toy roughly and wound it up, click, click, click. The crocodile, set down with a crash on the table cloth, creaked off obediently towards the tea pot, its emerald green tail clanking from side to side, its false teeth chattering. Privately, Georgie thought it was hideous, but when it had finally rattled to a halt beside the milk jug, he dutifully wound it up and set it off on its ugly jerking way again. He was relieved when his father patted him on the head and told him he was a good boy.

Only Anna, dear little Anna, responded in the way he wanted. It wasn't difficult for her to do because she liked the doll and had only to enlarge her pleasure just a little to be able to clap her hands and squeal and cry 'Oh Papa!' in the theatrical way she knew would please him. So for a few minutes he was able to bask in the warmth of her almost unfeigned delight, and she was able to slip those horrid crusts off her plate and into her apron pocket under cover of all the noise she was making, and in the confusion of all that rustling tissue paper that was now heaped beside her plate.

Then it was time for her father to rush off to see how the shop was doing, and Alice and Georgie could be left to dispose of their new possessions in the way they thought fit, Georgie to the furthest corner of his bedroom, and Alice to the bottom drawer of the linen press, where that vulgar diamond ring still lay decently hidden in its box. She was put out by such an unsuitable present, as she complained to Minnie afterwards. 'He hasn't got the sense he was born with,' she said. 'An expensive thing like that! Where could I wear it, Minnie, I ask you? The sort of life I lead! A new broom would have been more to the point!'

Chapter 24

Alice was always tired these days. She woke in the morning aching with fatigue and daunted by the chores that accumulated for her day by relentless day. There was never enough time to get through them all, and she was beginning to feel guilty because there were some rooms in her vast house that hadn't seen a broom for more than a fortnight. The trouble was that the more drained she became, the less energy she had to open up a discussion with Albert over the possibility of hiring a servant. He was so distant with her nowadays.

But at least he'd taken the children off her hands today so that she could get on with the washing. She only had to get that dreadful boiler lit and she could begin.

The boiler had been a terror to her ever since they'd moved. It was heated by gas which she had to light with a long wax taper, kneeling on the stone flags of the scullery floor and peering through the black porthole into the bowels of the machine. The gas jets caught fire with a bang like an explosion, and then roared at her in an inferno of blue and yellow flames. It frightened her every time she had to do it, and she was more nervous of it this morning than ever. As she filled the boiler with water she was scolding herself for her cowardice. There was nothing to be gained by making a fuss, for there was no one in the house to sympathize.

She put the dirty sheets in a pile on the scullery floor so that she could kneel on them while she set a match to the taper and turned the gas tap as gradually and gently as she could. Then, gingerly peering into the abyss, she inched the taper forward. There was an explosion so loud that the scullery seemed to rock all around her. The force of it punched her back against the sink, where she sat for a few seconds too stunned to move or think. Her mind seemed to be working completely independently of the rest of her. She could smell something burning, and looking down, she saw that the sheets and the hem of her skirt were smouldering. Little orange flames leapt sideways from the cloth. It looked most unnatural. I must turn off the gas, she told herself, still

305

perfectly calm. I must turn off the gas before it explodes again. The mouth of the boiler was mercifully black and empty, even though there was a really terrible smell of gas. She juggled with the gas tap, with fingers inexplicably clumsy, easing it back until she was sure it was off.

The sheets were still burning and so was her skirt. She unbuttoned the skirt, slowly and painstakingly, and stepped out of it. Then she put the whole smouldering bundle into the boiler. As she straightened her back she saw that the tea towels she'd hung above the boiler to dry were all on fire, blazing and disintegrating. The paintwork all around them was blistering and the window frames seemed to be melting. She threw the remains of line and burning cloth into the water at once and, taking a saucepan from the cupboard under the sink, sprayed pan loads of water at the wall and the window until all traces of red flame had gone. She was still calm. She seemed to be working in slow motion, entirely without panic, but with plenty of time to plan and observe.

When she dropped the sheets into the water, she'd been aware that she could see them splashing down and the water leaping in a silver column on either side of them, but she couldn't hear a thing. I must have gone deaf, she thought without surprise. Now, standing in the puddles she'd made, her petticoats soaking wet, she looked at the reflection of her own face, looming towards her in the dark mirror of the water, patched by lumps of the scorched linen. Her cheeks and forehead were red and blotchy and her fair hair had gone. In its place was a black frizzy wig, like a golliwog. I've burnt my face, she thought, I'd better put that in the water too. She leaned over the edge of the boiler and dunked her head. The water was cool on her skin and soothing. I must look very silly, she thought. Then she realized that her hands were very uncomfortable too. She didn't want to look at them. Not just yet. Just in case they were bad. She slipped them into the water on either side of her shrivelled hair and kept them there.

As she crouched, bent double over the boiler, the silence that had smothered her since the explosion began to throb. It was several seconds before she recognized that it was her heart she could hear and that it was beating painfully, in a laboured, frightening way. The realization made her feel suddenly very ill indeed. I must lie down, she thought. I must go to bed and lie down.

It was a very long way to the bedroom. She groped along the kitchen passage, her heart pounding and her legs moving only occasionally and very awkwardly. Halfway up the first flight of stairs she began to shake and was afraid she would fall. She stopped at the turn of the stairs where the stained glass window cast lozenges of jelly red and ice blue onto the carpet and a breeze from the opened upper frame touched her hot face softly. Here at last, she plucked up courage to look at her hands. They were red-raw, swelling and blistered. The sight of them made her feel much worse. She *must* lie down. If she didn't get to her bed at once she would faint where she was. She struggled to her feet again and toiled up the second flight, one painful step after the other. Then there was only the landing to cross. She staggered over it like a drunkard, and fell across her bed, at last, shaking and weeping violently.

Albert was enjoying himself at Mitcham fair. It was always the sort of occasion he revelled in, loud, vulgar and full of people. He liked the oily smell of the place, and the clamour of those tinny organ pipes jerkily playing the latest songs in thumping syncopation, but above all he enjoyed the crowds, wandering aimlessly from stall to stall, their faces empty and relaxed, their jaws busy with unaccustomed delicacies, a holiday crowd, friendly, cheerful, bawdy, quarrelsome, alive. It increased his sense of worth to be part of such a gathering, greeted by so many people he knew and liked.

This year was even better than last, because Harry's two boys had come along with them, and that gave him four excuses to play silly games and have fun.

They'd all been on the swings at least three times, and crossed a gypsy's palm with silver and won a coconut on the fourth attempt and a hideous china rabbit when they weren't even trying, and seen the performing dogs pushing prams and walking on barrels, and ridden the biggest round-about in the world, and now they were examining the freaks.

The Jones boys weren't impressed. 'I reckon it's a sell,' Johnnie said and Billy agreed with him. 'It ain't much ter write 'ome about.' Which was true enough. The only living mermaid was fast asleep with her mouth wide open and her wig slipping over one eye, the biggest rat in the world was humped in the corner of his cage like a grey stone, the dwarf with six fingers was smoking a pipe and smelt as though he was decomposing, and the two-headed baby turned out to be the pickled remains of a new born calf, grey and rubbery, and floating in oily water under a glass dome. Now there was only the talking head left, lurking somewhere inside its inner tent, and they didn't think that would be at all promising even though it was lavishly advertised as 'The Wonder of the Age'. 'Human Head Without A Body,' the poster proclaimed. 'Natures Miricle. Will Talk, Sing or Eat before your very eyes. Don't miss this amazing Marvel. Be the Envy of your Friends. Only 1d.'

The showman came swooping down on their hesitation. 'Five is it, Guvnor?' he asked hopefully.

'I don't want to see it if it's dead,' Georgie said. He'd found the little rubbery calf rather upsetting.

'Lord love yer,' the showman said. 'This ain't dead. Liveliest 'ead you'll see in a month a Sundays!'

So they paid their pennies and stepped gingerly through the flap into the musty interior of the inner tent. It was very dark and smelled of joss sticks, which burned like narrow pencils in their triangular brass holders, trailing grey smoke in all four shadowy corners. In the middle of the tent, on the centre of a square table that was swathed in heavy folds of maroon chenille, the head lay on a silver platter with a thick paper doily round its neck. It was lit by two silver candelabra which stood one on each side of the doily. Its hair was dark brown and bushy and its mouth and cheeks were very red, but its eyes were shut and it didn't move an inch. They boys were all disappointed.

'There!' Johnnie said. 'It's another sell! Watcha bet it's made a' wax!'

The head turned on its doily, opened blue eyes and grinned at him. 'No I ain't, young shaver!' it said.

The frisson of delighted shock this produced in all four youngsters was worth every penny they'd spent that day. Johnnie put his hand to his mouth as though he wanted to cram his words down his throat, and Anna's eyes were bolting out of her head.

'You should jest see your faces!' the head said triumphantly. And then it looked up at Albert. 'Why darn me!' it said. 'Ploochy, as I'm a Christian soul! How are ye, cock?'

This was even better. All four pairs of juvenile eyes swung from the head to Albert, stupefied and delighted. Fancy actually knowing a talking head!

'Hello, Maisie,' Albert said. 'Thought you was at Eastbourne with the others.'

'' 'Ad ter come back,' the head explained. 'Fred's got the asthma that bad you'd never believe. You can't leave 'em when they're ill can yer? Them nippers yourn?'

Albert acknowledged his own and explained Harry's.

'Pleased ter meetcha,' the head said politely, nodding to each of them in turn.

'D'you like being a talking head?' Billy asked, fingering the table cloth.

'Makes a change,' the head said. 'Change as good as a rest, so they say. 'Ere, yer wouldn't like ter scratch me nose, would yer? It's been itching sommink chronic this morning.' Billy put out a hesitant hand and rubbed the offending nose, which the head much enjoyed. 'Ah!' it said. 'Lovely! Ta! Can't very well scratch mesself, can I? Give the game away good and proper that would.'

It was a very cheerful head. Georgie decided to question it further, while Billy took a surreptitious look at his hand to see whether any of the wax had rubbed off. 'Is it difficult being a head?' Georgie asked.

'Gets a bit lonely,' the head confessed, 'when there ain't a lot a' trade. And then, a' course, there's the cramp. Catches you out sommink cruel cramp does.'

'You don't get cramp in the 'ead,' Johnnie protested. This was pushing the illusion too far.

'Don't you believe it, cock,' the head said. 'You can get cramp in all sorts of strange places. Ain't I right, Ploochy?'

Albert said he didn't doubt it and gave her a wink because he was finding it hard not to laugh and he had to do something with his face.

'Why've they nailed this table cloth ter the floor?' Billy

asked, accusingly. He'd walked all round the table cloth and examined every fold.

'Get nicked else,' the head said easily. 'They're a right lot a' tea leaves round 'ere. You wanna watch out they don't get their greasy fingers in *your* pocket.' It swivelled on the doily so that they were suddenly eye to eye. 'You bin on the shootin' range, 'ave yer?' it asked. 'All the go this year, them rifles.'

Shooting range? That would be fun. Billy and Johnnie were eager to be off at once and their faces showed it, but they remembered their manners and waited politely for Albert to say goodbye.

'Tat-a, then,' the head said. 'Be a love and shift them candles, afore yer go, will yer, Ploochy. Last lot in 'ere 'ad some sport with them. I thought they was gonna set light ter me 'air. Kept all on, chyiking, they did. "Boil yer 'ead! Boil yer 'ead!" Very funny, I don't think!'

Albert moved the candelabra as far away from the head as they would go. 'How's that?' he asked.

'Much better,' the head said, smiling. 'Don't like the idea a' being burnt.'

Alice was woken from a most uncomfortable sleep by the cry of the cat's meat man. 'Walla, walla ca-at's meat! Walla, walla, walla, ca-at's meat!' For a moment she couldn't think why she should be lying in her bed in the middle of the afternoon, but then she moved her hands and the pain reminded her. I must have been lying here for hours, she thought. If the cat's meat man was in the road it would be nearly four o'clock. She felt heavy and tired and her mind was functioning very slowly. What day was it, she wondered? The cat's meat man didn't come every day. Surely there was something special about today. A holiday perhaps? Then she remembered that, too. Bank Holiday, and it was already four o'clock. Albert would be back with the children in less than an hour. They mustn't see her like this. It would frighten poor Georgie out of his wits. She must get up at once and do something.

She sat up quickly. Her head spun with weakness and sudden movement, and she raised it slowly and found she was facing her terrible reflection in the dressing table mirror. She was unrecognizable. Her hair was black and spiky and broken and there were two angry red blisters where her eyebrows had been. The rest of her face was red and blistered and so swollen that her eyes seemed to have disappeared inside all that awful flesh. The sight was so upsetting she had to look away. She glanced down at her blouse and petticoat instead, but they were almost as bad, smeared and stained and as crumpled as used rags. How would she ever get them clean? Then she remembered that she hadn't even started the weekly wash, and the vision of her burnt and flooded kitchen filled her mind. She pushed the thought away from her. Time enough for that tomorrow. Now she must get into clean clothes at once and bandage her face and hands so that the children wouldn't be frightened.

It took her a long time to do because her hands were so sore, but she persevered grimly. First she took a pair of scissors and cut off all her burnt hair, hiding the pieces away in her hair tidy. Then she crept down to the bathroom for the oldest and softest sheet she could find and cut it into strips for bandages to cover her face and hands and hide the ugliness. By the time she'd finished, it was ten to five and she was exhausted. She made her way wearily downstairs and there, in the cool hall, she waited for her family, sitting at the foot of the stairs where she couldn't see the hall-stand mirror. She felt ill again but she stayed where she was, knowing how important it was not to upset people.

When she heard their feet on the path and Anna's shrill voice approaching, she got up and opened the door clumsily with her mittened hands. Despite all her efforts, they were shocked. She looked like an Egyptian mummy.

'Alice! Alice!' Albert said, brows drawn in extreme anxiety, mouth working.

She stopped him before he could alarm the children any further. 'It's all right,' she said, pleased that her voice sounded calm. 'I've had a little accident, that's all.' She turned to Anna and even managed to laugh. 'Isn't your Mamma an old silly,' she said. 'Don't I look funny all wrapped up like this?'

Albert recovered quickly, warned by the terror gathering on Georgie's face. 'What a joke to play on us!' he said jovially to Alice, taking her by the elbow and steering her into the front parlour. 'Anna, get the rug from the hall. We will tuck Mamma up in this chair and I will buy her a little plaster to put on her face and she will look like Mamma again.'

'What is it?' Georgie asked, pale but determined to find out.

'It's a little scratch,' Alice explained, taking her cue from Albert. 'Nothing at all really. I had to wrap it all up to keep the bandages on. Don't I look funny?'

Georgie wasn't sure. There was something odd about her eyes, but with Papa tucking that great rug round her knees and Anna dodging about in the way, he couldn't get close enough to see what it was. 'Come along!' Papa said briskly, and he and Anna were whisked off out of the house again.

'We have salmon and cucumber for tea today,' Anna reminded him. She'd been looking forward to the treat all afternoon and didn't intend to be done out of it.

'Not today,' Albert said. 'Didden I tell you? Today you have tea with Johnnie and Billy.'

Em took their unexpected arrival with unruffled calm, recognizing the urgency of Albert's casual greeting.

'Here they are, Aunt Em. All ready for their tea,' he said, signalling with his eyes, and pushing his children ahead of him so that they couldn't see what he was doing. Em had two plates set for them before even Georgie could notice. Billy had just begun the story of the talking head and soon all four of them were giggling together.

'I will be back in one hour,' Albert promised.

'Take as long as yer need,' Em said.

Albert worked with the speed and urgency of guilty alarm. From the puffy flesh he'd glimpsed around Alice's sunken pleading eyes among the bandages, he knew with a heart-crushing certainty that she was badly hurt. While he was tucking the rug about her, she'd managed to whisper that the boiler had blown up and she was 'a bit burnt'. Her courage shamed him, and the fact that she'd bandaged herself, and was behaving in such a calm, controlled way, made him feel even worse. She'd been alone and in pain all day long, and he'd been gadding about the Mitcham Fair, enjoying himself and planning how to tell her that he'd started an affair with another woman. All the silly phrases he'd been rehearsing were again revealed as insincere and cruel. He rushed about Tooting trying to make amends, driven to frantic speed by his guilt.

Dr Fermanagh arrived at the house forty minutes after Albert left it, and was quickly followed by Mrs Kelly, plump in her nursing linen. They put their patient to bed and dressed her burns and ordered rest and plenty of fluids. Dr Fermanagh was avuncular and kindly, telling Alice it wouldn't do at all, and soothing, and clucking his tongue whenever he thought he might be hurting her, although he was as gentle as he could possibly be; and Mrs Kelly was her usual cheerful self, looking straight at the gargoyle of Alice's face without curiosity or revulsion or even pity, but simply as though there was nothing the matter with it. It was most encouraging and calming. Under their professional influence, Alice relaxed at last and her pains began to recede. It was almost as though she was beginning to recover already.

'There now, Mrs P.,' Molly Kelly said, when Alice was comfortably settled with a mound of pillows to support her head and shoulders and bolsters under the painful bundles of her arms. 'That's a lot better I know. Could you fancy a cup of tea?'

The tea, in a white feeding cup with a spout like a watering can, was brought to her a few minutes later, not by Mrs Kelly as she'd expected, but by Minnie Holdsworthy, her round face puckered with anxiety. She put the cup on the dressing table and came straight to the bed to take her poor burnt cousin in her arms. Then, in that quiet room, sitting on a bed drenched in inappropriate golden sunlight, the two women wept, and Alice sucked her tea and was refreshed and the story of the accident was told and talked out and began to be digested. When Albert came home with the children, they were still so deep in tearful conversation, he merely looked in, smiled with relief and a little hope and went away again.

Nobody was surprised, except Alice, that after all this she should fall asleep. When she woke, for the third time that day, Minnie was at her elbow.

'Shouldn't you go home?' she worried. 'Who's getting Jesse's tea?'

'Had it and forgot it, me dear,' Minnie reassured. 'Don't you go fretting yourself about that.'

But Alice was a born worrier. 'It isn't right to keep you here like this, Minnie dear,' she said. 'What about the children?'

So Minnie told her, even though Mr P. had given strict instructions that the news was to be kept until the morning. 'We've come here to live, me dear,' she said. 'All the lot uv us. Your Albert's got it all fixed and Jesse's quite agreeable. We're to pay a little rent, peppercorn or some such, your Albert called it, and I'm to help you with the house. And we're to have a general maid an' a daily woman. You're not to be left alone ever again so he says. Now what do you think uv that?'

A week passed and Alice gradually began to get better. But Albert was further away than ever from any sort of solution to his most pressing problem.

It took him more than a week to pluck up sufficient courage to write to Queenie and explain what had happened, and even though he composed his letter with the most meticulous, lip-chewing care, it still felt like a betrayal. He waited for her reply in a state of hyperactive anxiety and for two days he was so bad tempered that poor Frank was reduced to jumping out of his skin at every passing shadow.

The reply, when it finally came, was a reprieve. 'Poor Alice,' Queenie wrote. 'How orfull! A' course you can't say nothink. She must be feeling sore poor thing. I never did like them new-fangled boilers myself.' And that was all. It was almost too easy. I'll make it up to her when she comes home, he thought. Everything will be all right once we're together again.

Their reunion was pleasant rather than rapturous, and the flat seemed cheap and stale and uncomfortable after their sensuous accommodation in Hastings.

On their first night together he slept fitfully, in a bed grown unfamiliar since the spring, his mind full of troubling thoughts. By the morning he'd decided that the very least he could do for his Queenie would be to provide her with a better quality flat. After all, she and her family had so little, and he and Alice had so much.

'Tomorrow we will find a better flat,' he promised, as he got dressed the next morning.

She didn't open her eyes. 'Shouldn't bovver,' she said. 'We ain't 'ere long enough.'

'Wouldn't you like something better?' he asked surprised.

'Don't make no difference ter me,' she said, eyes still closed. 'Suit yerself.'

For the rest of the week he turned the matter over in his mind. In the event and uncharacteristically he decided not to do anything, at least for the time being. He felt he ought to talk it over with Queenie. But Queenie, warm and loving and welcoming as she was, had a new air of detachment about her that made lengthy conversations almost impossible. She always seemed to be thinking of something else, her latest song and dance or her brothers' attempts to find work, and although they were all predictable and proper subjects for her attention, he wished they weren't so constantly in the way between them.

'You still livin' with that Ploochy bloke?' Ethel said when Queenie came to visit her at the end of the season.

'Yes,' Queenie said and she sounded weary. 'Want me head examining!' She'd used a lot of energy and emotion in her attempt to bring him to a decision and now it was all wasted.

'Poor old Quee!' her sister commiserated, understanding her expression.

'I don't think he'll ever marry me, Eth,' Queenie said. She'd been facing the possibility ever since Albert's letter arrived, and it was almost a relief to be admitting it.

'No more do I,' Ethel said, 'or 'e'd a' done it be now.'

'I tried real hard this time,' Queenie said, sipping her tea. 'I really thought I'd got 'im to agree. I can't go on like this for ever.'

'Find someone else,' Ethel advised, eating her bread and marg. 'There's many more fish in the sea.'

'I can't,' Queenie admitted. 'I love 'im too much. That's the trouble. 'E's such a nice man.'

'Only 'e won't marry you.'

'No,' Queenie said. 'I don't think 'e ever will. Take an earthquake to get 'im away from that wife of 'is.'

'An' we don't run to earthquakes in this part a' the world,' Ethel said.

'No,' Queenie said, beginning to perk up and grin again, 'No more we do!'

Had they known it, what was ahead of them was a great deal worse.

Chapter 25

Nobody was a bit surprised when war was declared. There'd been such a lot of talk about it and for such a long time, it was no more than they expected. But it was marvellously exciting just the same.

The Joneses and Peluccis and Holdsworthys all went up to Parliament Square on that first afternoon, to wave Union Jacks and watch the politicians driving into the House of Commons to make history. And that evening Albert and Alice held an impromptu party. After all, as Alice so rightly pointed out, they could hardly sit at home and do nothing on the very day the British lion had finally bestirred itself and was all set to give the Hun a trouncing.

The boys took their wheelbarrows down to the shop, to return with enough beer and spirits to float a battleship. Percy was sent scuttling next door to invite the Morrises, and presently Dickie and his patriotic company arrived in full theatrical regalia to provide the entertainment.

It was a marvellous party. Excitement seemed to have speeded up the pace of their lives. They talked nineteen to the dozen, running from group to group, and from room to room, eyes, tongues, hands and feet continually on the move. Within twenty minutes they'd consumed all the food, drunk a vast quantity of beer and lemonade, and begun to make inroads on the spirits. Within forty, the entertainment had begun, and Tilley had astounded them all by the number of patriotic songs she could remember, and Martha had sung 'Land of Hope and Glory' with tears in her eyes and a beer mug in each hand. They drank so many toasts they ran out of the subjects, and young Billy Jones stood on the table and made an incoherent speech about the honour of Old England which was applauded with such gusto that the lustres on the mantelpiece were rattling with emotion for a good five minutes afterwards.

Then Dickie had one of his ideas. 'Let's 'ave a knees-up,' he suggested, polishing his bald patch with his pocket handkerchief. 'I'll play the joanna.'

The men set about rearranging the furniture immediately, and Percy got his toes trodden on, and Harry got the giggles, and Major Morris was in his element, barking unnecessary orders at anything that moved. He got in the way of the *chaise longue*, was thumped in the back by the what-not and finally managed to get himself wedged into a corner behind a pallisade of chairs, where he stood, red-faced with delight, shouting 'Steady the Buffs!' until the memsahib came to his rescue. Alice and Minnie set candles in the gilt candlesticks beside all four wall mirrors and soon their fine gold and white room was gentled by a soft diffusion of honey coloured light. Then Dickie settled himself at the piano and started them all off at a gallop with his own adaptation of 'All the nice girls, love a sailor.'

They danced, and refreshed themselves with lemonade, and danced again, polkas and waltzes, marches and gallops. They even tried a military two-step, and Harry walked in the wrong direction every single time and never knew when to salute, and Em laughed at him so much that she had a coughing fit, and Albert had to mix a bowl of fruit punch to help her recover.

At eleven o'clock little Renee fell into a rosy sleep across her mother's knees and was carried gently to bed. By midnight the three elder children were finally exhausted and retired while they could still keep their eyes open. But the adults danced on. It was well past two before Dickie and his riotous company decided they really ought to leave, and the party finally erupted onto the front doorstep, still giggling.

'Well it's been a rare ol' day, an' no mistake,' Em said with enormous approval, as she kissed Alice goodbye.

'Least we can lie in termorrer,' Harry said, combing his hair with his fingers so that he could settle his cap somewhere on top of the thatch. 'Two Bank 'Olidays, eh? Can't be bad!'

Alice and Albert stood together on the step and watched their happy guests depart. The stars were sharp and white in the dark blue sky above the rooftops, and an old moon lay among them, on its back like an empty cradle. It looked bleak and cold and deserted, a decidedly alien presence. Alice shivered as the night air struck chill on her overheated flesh, and when Albert put an arm about her shoulders to warm her she allowed the movement and even swayed willingly towards him. Em was right, he thought, it had been a rare old day.

*

The next morning, while military gentlemen all over Europe were watching the gratifying realization of their long-nurtured aggressive fantasies, Alice and Minnie held a war council of their own as they cleared up after the party.

'Food'll be short as sure as fate,' Alice predicted, removing the beer mugs from the piano. She was remembering the dock strike and the way she'd crammed the larder. 'There's three more down beside the cabinet, Minnie.'

Minnie retrieved the three glasses and set them on the dinner wagon among the rest. 'What shall we do, me dear?' she asked.

'We'll start with sugar!' she said. Which they did.

By the end of the week, and after more furious and ferocious shopping expeditions than either of them could bear to think about, the larder was ready for whatever siege the war might bring, heaped with sackloads of dry goods, hung with onions and salt bacon, stacked with tins, salmon and sardines and pilchards, milk condensed and evaporated, even bully beef, despite the fact that until then Alice had always sworn there was no nourishment in it. 'Better safe than sorry,' she said darkly to Minnie. 'If there's no fresh meat in the shops, we've got to have something.'

Albert, watching all their activity with admiration, provided Alice with all the extra money she needed and was impressed by her good sense and energy. The newspapers took a different view, castigating the hoarders for alarmist behaviour, and deploring the fact that they'd emptied the stores and caused shortages in all the major commodities. But whichever way you looked at it, war was certainly good for trade, and it had given Alice a purpose.

It changed Queenie's life style too. In the middle of August she left the concert party and came home to Clapham. The staid approval of her comfortable holiday audiences had always dampened her spirits and now Martha Goodyear had found her a spot in a new show designed to aid recruitment.

'Waste a' time stayin' in Bournemouth,' she said. 'Dead an' alive that is. Specially now. Old Marth' says they're pulling 'em in down 'Oxton way.' She found recruiting drives far more to her taste, especially when she realized how easy it was to inspire the ardent young men who flocked to see her every night.

'We're at the Duchess, Friday,' she told Albert. 'Buy a ticket. It's worth seeing. I'm on number six, end a' the first 'alf.'

So he went and was thrilled by her performance.

She was a dazzling Britannia, a swirling blue cloak gathered about her and an unlikely blue helmet perched on her red curls. She stood as still as marble as the red curtains looped up on either side of her and the orchestra thumped the opening bars of her song. Then with a luxurious shrug, she dropped the cloak and stood swathed in blood-red silk, her bare arms and shoulders very white in the strong stage light. The impact of the moment was unmistakable, and when she began to move, swaying down towards the footlights, there were gasps and groans from men on every side of the house. She was deliberately provoking them, Albert realized, using her body the way she did at home, when she wallowed in the tub, or strutted about their bedroom, delighting in the power of her sexuality, aware that he was admiring and desiring. No wonder the men all around him were in such a lather.

'We don't want to lose you,' she sang, 'but we think you ought to go!' smiling down directly at all the unseen eyes gleaming towards her in the heated darkness of the auditorium. At the end of the first verse she swept to the left of the stage as the silver curtains were slowly raised to reveal a crude map of the British Isles and beside it a descending staircase crowded with chorus girls in clinging white robes, tall under helmets painted like Union Jacks. When they too began to strut downstage, singing, smiling and provoking until their toes were almost touching the footlights, the audience exploded into cheers and catcalls. As the song ended and all those delectable ladies were promising to 'Kiss you – when you come home again,' most of the men in the audience were up, and a lot of them were on their feet too, a few short steps away from the recruiting sergeant who appeared beside the proscenium arch, as the lights were suddenly raised. How the women and the old men cheered as their young heroes blushed their way into the army, to be rewarded by hugs and kisses, right there, in public, in the middle of the stage.

Queenie was still flushed with the triumph and glory of it

when she and Albert finally got home to Manor Road that night. 'I reckon I could get that ol' Kitchener 'is million all by mesself,' she bragged, snuggled up to Albert in their wide moonlit bed. 'All I got ter do is smile at 'em, an' they're standin' in line. I got a real talent for it.'

Albert began to kiss her. 'You – are – mag – nificent,' he said, tasting the greasepaint on her mouth. 'How can they resist you? I can't resist you.'

'Good!' she said pulling him closer.

What good fortune, Albert thought, that he was the one to receive the full force of her new, confident ardour. Now he was loved more often and more passionately than ever before. Trade was lively. Alice was happily busy. He couldn't think why he'd ever been alarmed by the prospect of this war. It was turning out to be a very good thing after all. And all those fine brave boys enlisting. It did your heart good to see them. Nat had joined in the very first week and so had Billy Jones, Harry's eldest boy.

By September, although the roses still bloomed in shaggy abundance in Albert's peaceful garden, and the evenings were languorous with honeysuckle, there was a chill in the morning air. Albert, immersed in the re-doubled delights of his love affair, didn't notice it, and neither did Alice. She was too busy. Housework, as she and Minnie told one another with puritan-ical satisfaction, had to be done whether the country was at war or peace. But Georgie felt it keenly because his life was changing too, and this time Mamma seemed to think he was old enough to cope with it all on his own. When he crept from the house, pale with apprehension, early one September morning, to start his new career as a grammar school boy, the road was as quiet as a tomb and the hedges were draped in a white shroud of dew.

The first rains of autumn brought down a ceiling of scowling cloud to obscure the sunlight, and when dusk fell it did so with an abruptness and a totality that only the very old in Tooting could remember. All through the summer gangs of workmen had been busy masking the tops and sides of all the street lamps with black paint, and now the little illumination they provided was no better than a candle. On the first dark evening, Albert walked into a pillar-box on his way home, and stubbed his toe and was very disagreeable in consequence. War was one thing, not being able to see your way home in your own town was another.

Then on the very day the first snow fell on those shivering trenches, Billy Jones came home on leave to announce with soldierly calm that his battalion, the Territorial Battalion of Fusiliers, was being sent to France. Em and Harry were at once proud and tearful and confused, torn between patriotism and anxiety and not at all sure which of them it was proper to express.

Albert didn't stop to consider the proprieties at all, but set off to organize the most elaborate and expensive send-off he could contrive. All Billy's workmates were invited and all his relations from Tooting and Norfolk. Em's little front parlour was packed from wall to wall, her guests sitting so close to one another at the narrow trestle tables that they could only eat if they all lifted their forks in unison. It was very rowdy and jolly and Billy presided over it all as the hero of the hour.

Em and Minnie got the giggles, and Harry was soon flushed with an excess of beer and high spirits, his carefully combed hair tousled and comfortable again, and old man Jones, who had grown extremely deaf since his move to Norfolk, punctuated every speech with a cheerful 'What's 'at? What's 'e say?' and was vigorously applauded for his every interruption.

Then it was Billy's farewell speech and the tables were gradually hushed to receive it. He looked so splendid in his new uniform, standing before the fire, ruddy with heat and good food and attention, and he said all the right things in his rough soldier's voice. Em, he said, was the best Ma in the whole wide world, and Harry the best Dad a feller could wish for and Ploochy was a man in a million, and best a' friends fer the entire family. Em and Harry ducked their heads in delighted embarrassment, and Harry said 'Go on with yer!' to cover his emotion, and Albert beamed so widely that the waxed ends of his moustaches stood to attention like guardsmen.

Then Johnnie Jones sprang to his feet and climbed up on the bench he'd been sitting on. Whether he intended to cheer or was going to make a speech of his own, nobody ever found out, for the bench gave way under his weight, and he and his friends fell into a sprawling shrieking heap among the crush of boots and bottles under the table, and had to be retrieved from the wreckage by being dragged along the floor by their legs. In the ribald confusion that followed, the banquet and the speeches both came to an end.

In any case, as Harry pointed out, it was time for Billy to catch his train. So he was kissed, shaken by the hand and thumped on the back until he and his well wishers were quite red in the face with the exertion of it all. Then, hung about with so much equipment that Dickie vowed it weighed a darn sight more than he did, he shouldered his kitbag, kissed his mother and marched off down Charlmont Road without looking back.

Em stood at the gate and waved until even the peak of his cap had disappeared from her sight and by then her feelings were too strong for her to contain. Her guests, glancing at her tear-stained face, took themselves off quietly and delicately, so that she could weep undisturbed. 'Tears of pride,' they said.

They were stirring times.

Chapter 26

Contrary to popular expectation, the war wasn't over by Christmas. December came and went and the battles dragged on. Soon the Peluccis had consumed all Alice's careful stores and were beginning to learn to cope with shortages. Spring brought no hope, the summer was miserable and autumn depressing. 'I'm sure I don't know what the world is coming to,' Alice said as she read the daily casualty lists.

Queenie would have agreed with her. Faced by the steady arrival of wounded men into the capital, she changed her mind about the glorious purpose of the recruiting company, and joined another that was dedicated to cheering the wounded. But by November the sight of so many shattered young bodies was beginning to wear her down.

'Poor beggars,' she said to Albert, who had come to Clapham Junction to welcome her home after a particularly lengthy tour. 'You should 'ear some a' the things they tell us, Ploo. They been livin' in hell out there in them trenches.'

Albert wasn't terribly interested in wounded soldiers. He hadn't seen her for nearly a fortnight and he was anxious to get home to their flat and a warm fire and a welcoming bed. They would have the best meal Luigi could provide and then they would go home together.

The flat was icy cold, and the bed wasn't made. 'It's no way ter live,' she said, shaking her head at the mess she'd returned to. 'I tell yer, Ploo, I'd chuck it in tomorrow if I 'ad the chance.'

'We make the bed together,' he said, hoping activity would deflect her from a topic he didn't want to discuss.

'I've 'alf a mind ter chuck it all in regardless,' she said, furiously tucking in the blankets on her side of the bed. 'Bli! It's nippy ternight. Ain't standin' around in me shimmy in this cold.' She kicked off her shoes and wriggled out of her dress. 'Jump in quick!' she said.

Albert had been undressing carefully, and was just unbuttoning his shirt. She pulled him under the covers into the mound of stays and petticoats and stockings she was removing under the blankets. 'Quick, quick, cuddle me up warm. I'm freezing!' she said.

He obeyed at once and hopefully, but was disappointed to find that she meant what she said and wasn't the least bit amorous. 'What *is* all this stuff in here?' he complained as his legs became entangled in linen.

'It's me clothes,' she said. 'Don't fuss so. Just kick 'em out. Only don't let the air in.' She put her cold feet between his calves and her cold hands in his armpits. 'You gotta admit,' she said, 'It's no sort a life, ter come 'ome to a cold 'ouse this time a' night. You just think 'ow much nicer it'd be if we 'ad a fire in ere.'

'Never mind,' he said, hoping her cold extremities would warm up quickly because they were draining all the heat out of his body. 'We soon get warm. You can't light fires if you're away entertaining the troops, now can you?'

'Could if I wasn't though, couldn't I?' she said.

'Yes,' he admitted, 'but you like bein' on the stage. You'd be bored if you left the company.' It was the wrong thing to say and he realized it as soon as the words were out of his mouth.

She looked straight up at him, dark eyed among the pillows. 'I wouldn't be bored,' she said. 'We could get married. Like you promised. Or 'ave you forgotten?'

'No,' he said, his heart sinking at the strength of her attack. 'I haven't forgotten.'

'Well then,' she said. 'What about it?'

They were back on dangerously familiar ground. 'We can't do nothing now,' he said. 'Not with a war on. I can't leave the children in the middle of a war.'

She drew her body away from him. 'It's always the same,' she said angrily. 'Any excuse is better than none. I reckon I'm wasting my time with you. D'you know that? I don't think you'll ever marry me.'

'I will!' he said, aggrieved. 'I will! Only not now. Not with a war on.'

She flung the covers aside and jumped out of the bed. 'Now where you going?' he said, alarmed.

'Turn the gas out,' she said. 'I'm going to sleep. It's a waste a' time talkin' ter you.' She was standing under the gaslight, her hair like bronze, and the cold was making her shiver.

'I couldn't bear to live without you,' he said, moved by the picture she made. 'I will marry you. I promise. Just wait till the war's over, that all.'

She looked at him steadily but said nothing. It was more disturbing than he cared to admit. 'Just wait till the war's over,' he urged. 'After all, it can't last for ever.'

'You're right there,' she said, turning away from him. 'Nothink lasts fer ever, Ploochy!' And she turned out the gas abruptly, plunging the room into total darkness.

Albert slept badly that night and woke with a headache. Groaning, he wandered through in to the kitchen to see what they could cook for breakfast. There was no food in the cupboard at all. He slammed the kitchen door in fury and stormed back to the bedroom. 'Get up,' he ordered. 'We don't stay in this house a minute longer.'

She rubbed the sleep out of her eyes and blinked at him. 'What we need,' he said, his mouth square with determination, 'is a 'oliday. I will take you to the seaside.'

'In November?' she queried, tucking the covers under her chin. 'Don't be daft!'

'Get up,' he insisted. 'We are going. It just what we need.' And he seized all the bedclothes and threw them on the floor.

'You're bein' ridiculous,' she grumbled, shivering and searching frantically for her clothes.

'We got nothing for breakfast,' he said. 'Nothing to do. Nothing to stay 'ere for. We will go to 'Astings an' have a good time. Do us a power a' good.' He was packing already, his mind quite made up.

'Nobody goes on 'oliday in November,' she said, trying to reason with him.

'We do!' he said, cheerfully. 'We will catch the nine eighteen.'

He was so horribly determined and she was so tired and so cold she couldn't oppose him for long. So he wrote a hasty postcard to Alice, pleading a sudden business meeting, and they went. And were disappointed.

Hastings in November was a very different place from the packed, friendly town where they'd spent their summer holiday. It was bitterly cold, the sky was a dirty grey, and the streets were empty except for a white sea mist swirling uphill towards the station, darkening pavements and dropping a film of dank dew on all the paintwork as it passed.

The flower-beds were bare and the potted plants had all disappeared, along with the bunting, the striped awnings, the deckchairs, the donkey carts, the ice cream vans and all the bright cheerful paraphernalia of holiday. Without them the town looked dusty and disreputable and eerie, like a stage-set partly dismantled. There were very few people about. One or two shoppers walked briskly through the damp streets, looking neither left nor right, entirely wrapped up in their overcoats and themselves. It was most unwelcoming.

And if the town was bleak, the beach was worse. The sea was a sullen grey under the mist and it hissed along a beach strewn with rubbish, spars of rotting wood, trailing weed, old boots and bottles, fish bones, frayed rope and blobs of tar. It looked like a rubbish tip and the air they breathed smelled of decay and damp, of filth accumulated and fish long dead. The promenade was heaped with pebbles, the pier was shut, the bandstand deserted and the hotels they'd come to visit were nothing but empty skulls, peering, black eyed through the mist towards that disagreeable sea. The hoteliers seemed to have left the country *en masse*. There wasn't a welcome mat the length of the promenade.

'Well, it's all right, innit!' Queenie said very crossly. 'Traipsing all the way down 'ere an' then everythink shut. We shouldn't a' come, Ploochy.' Her nose was red and pinched and the cold was making her eyes water.

'We will look in the Old Town,' Albert said, feeling guilty at her discomfort, and he set off at a brisk pace towards the valley between the two cliffs. 'Least the gulls are still here. Look!'

And so they were, sitting plumply on the breakwater posts, a bird to each post, and every single one facing east, like cavalry waiting for the order to advance.

'What they all lookin' at?' Queenie said, intrigued, and as if in answer to her question, the birds rose suddenly and heavily into the mist, calling and squawking, to swing and soar on their curved wings, white breasted against the grey sky. They were moving gradually and noisily towards the fishing fleet.

'Come on,' Albert said, remembering, 'let's see if old Josh is anywhere about.'

He was. Busily unravelling his nets, grizzled, blue jerseyed, fish scaled and friendly as ever. It made them feel warmer just to see his familiar face. 'Vell!' he said. 'Vould you believe that! Mr and Mrs Ploochy or I'm a Dutchman. You en't never a holidayin' in November!'

They explained their presence.

'You got lodgin's then, 'ave you?' he asked, giving his nets a sharp tug to dislodge a knot of weed.

'No,' Albert admitted. 'Not yet.'

'There en't much open this time uv year,' Josh said. 'You could try me sister's, if you like. On'y bed and breakfast, mind. Lizzie Maybury, Sinnock Square. Second twitten to the left.'

It was better than nothing, especially as the mist had thickened and was becoming as pervasive as rain. They trudged damply up the uneven cobbles of the High Street, Queenie sniffing and coughing, Albert scowling.

The twitten was approached by a steep flight of stone steps, which rose suddenly and sharply between the wet stone and blackened timbers of two ancient houses in the High Street. It was a small, paved yard, surrounded by a huddle of weather-boarded cottages, grey and lopsided and hung about with elderly ropes and swathes of old net, stained in every possible shade of green and brown and purple. There was an old tarpaulin in one corner full of decaying fish heads, and the door of the nearest shack was propped shut by two broken oars. It wasn't a bit promising but by now Albert was too cross to be deterred. He rapped loudly on the front door of the second cottage.

For a few seconds there was a sodden silence in the little square, then they could hear scuffling noises from somewhere on the top floor, and the window just above their heads was opened cautiously to reveal a small red nose and one dark suspicious eye.

'Oo's there?' a sharp voice inquired. 'Fish is all sold. All sold. Every bit. All sold.'

Albert explained what they wanted and the dark eye regarded him seriously. 'Josh!' it said. 'Ah yes! Josh! To be sure! Josh!' Then the window was shut again and silence dropped damply back upon them.

'Let's go 'ome,' Queenie said. 'I told yer we shouldn't a' come.' She was already moving out of the yard.

But the front door was being grudgingly opened and the owner of the small red nose and the one dark eye was inviting them in. They were glad to be out of the mist, even though the room they entered smelled of boiled fish, and was so hung about with nets that the ceiling was completely hidden. But at least it had a fire and beside it a wooden settle heaped with patchwork cushions. Josh's sister invited them to 'sit be the hearth,' and Albert watched with relief as Queenie settled herself among the cushions and put her cold feet on the fender. Now perhaps something could be settled. He turned his attention to Lizzie Maybury.

She was an odd-looking woman, stumpy and misshapen, like a little wooden bird. Her neck was so thick and rigid there was no division between her skull and her spine. She held her elbows away from her sides like slightly flexed wooden wings and she seemed quite incapable of simply turning her head. When she wanted to look to left or to right she had to pivot her shoulders. The stance and the action made her look like a mechanical toy.

'Yes,' she agreed. 'I *do* 'ave a room. Vell yes, I do. Vould be a bit dampish this time uv year. A bit dampish. Vould expect that sir, now vouldn't you. Expect it. Uv course! Bein' dampish. I could get that all aired for you be bedtime. Yes. Vould that suit you sir?'

'We will see it,' Albert said, and the wooden bird flexed its wings and opened a cupboard door in the corner of the room to reveal a steep spiral staircase, which they all climbed carefully. It was an extraordinary room, built under the eaves with a low dormer window letting in the merest blink of light and a floor that sloped so suddenly and unexpectedly that crossing the room was a climb. The bed was wedged against the sloping ceiling and there was just enough room for a washstand beside it. The air was damp and the bed felt cold to the touch. Albert's heart sank again, but he couldn't go back now.

'We will take it,' he told Lizzie Maybury. 'If you air the mattress very thoroughly. Come along, Queenie. Time for a quick one. We will go to the First In, and then we will see

329

what on at the Gaiety.' And he whisked her out of the house quickly before she could complain.

Fortunately the First In Last Out was as welcoming as ever and very warm. The publican kept a very big fire in his very small room. His veal and ham pie was passable and his beer, if anything, marginally better than it had been in the summer. Refreshed, warmed, and somewhat cheered, they set off for the Saturday matinee at the Gaiety Theatre.

Minnie Holdsworthy was standing very quietly just inside the dining room door, hidden by the folds of the draught curtain, watching with all her senses, like a cat stalking a bird. And the person she was watching was Anna, who was sitting absolutely still between the enveloping sides of the leather armchair, reading a book. It was so unlike the child to be reading at all that just the sight of her stopped Minnie in her tracks. And then there was something peculiar about the way she was reading. She was concentrating so hard it was making her breathe heavily. Minnie could hear her right across the room. It wasn't like her and it wasn't natural.

Anna turned a page with a rasp and a flick and Minnie pounced. She had the child by the shoulder and the book under her palm before the page had settled. 'What's this?' she said fiercely.

'Nothing, Aunt Min,' Anna said, assuming an innocent expression as quickly as she could. She was very frightened, for she knew the things she'd been trying to read about were taboo and dangerous.

'It don't look like nothing to me,' Minnie said. 'Where d'you get it from? You tell me that.'

'Georgie gave it to me,' Anna said. 'Georgie told me to read it.'

'Hum!' Minnie snorted. 'You come with me. We'll just see what your mother has to say about it. Think yourself lucky your father's away, that's all!'

Anna didn't share her aunt's opinion. If Papa had found her instead of Aunt Min, she could have charmed her way out of it. Now she had Mamma to contend with and you couldn't charm Mamma. Her heart thudded with fear as she followed her aunt to the kitchen.

Alice was shocked and angered.

'It's no fit way for a properly brought up child to behave,' Alice said sternly to her quaking daughter. 'I can't think what possessed you.'

Anna, who knew very well that she had been possessed by an overpowering curiosity, kept very quiet and tried to look innocent again.

'Whatever made you read such a dreadful book?' her mother insisted.

'I didn't read it Mamma,' Anna tried. 'I was only looking at it.'

'Don't lie to me, miss,' Alice said crossly. 'Your aunt caught you reading it.'

'I couldn't read much, Mamma,' Anna pleaded. 'It was all long words.' That was true enough. She'd had quite a job to tease the information she wanted from all those complicated phrases.

Alice and Minnie exchanged significant glances. Perhaps her ignorance had protected her after all. There was a long pause while Anna stared at the floor and Minnie twiddled her thumbs and Alice regarded her son. He was very pale but quite composed and he didn't flinch under her gaze. There was no sound in the kitchen except for the flicker of the fire and the faint rasp of Minnie's thumbs. When the clock struck the half hour and the cuckoo clattered through its wooden door with a metallic whirr of springs, both children jumped visibly.

'And you admit you showed this . . . ,' Alice hesitated, unable to find a word bad enough to convey the shame of the book she was holding.

'Yes, Mamma,' Georgie said miserably. She already knew. Why was she asking him everything twice over?

'I can't understand you,' Alice said. 'Whatever made you do such a thing?'

'I don't know, Mamma,' Georgie mumbled. What else could he say? If he told the truth he would be a tell-tale-tit, and that would be absolutely shameful. Besides, Anna was glaring at him as if she wanted to kill him. He was in an impossible situation, and a very unfair one, for he really had done everything he could to try to avoid it. The trouble was that Anna had simply been too strong for him. From the first unguarded moment when he'd admitted to her that he knew where babies came from, she'd been badgering and coaxing, and cajoling on every possible occasion. 'Tell me! Go on, tell me! If you know. If you're such an old clever dick! Please Georgie! For me! I won't tell anyone! I promise!'

He had become more and more deeply embarrassed as the days passed and Anna persisted. It wasn't a subject you could talk about to a girl. It was far too delicate for that. Why he couldn't even mention it to his best friend, or at least not in the daylight. But as she was a girl, he supposed she wouldn't even know *that*. It worried him very much. Finally he plucked up courage and asked his very, very best friend, Ashby Minor, what he thought he ought to do, and Ashby Minor recommended the encyclopedia. 'Only keep it hidden, young Ploochy,' he warned. 'Specially from the mater. Women are the very devil when it comes to babies!'

Even from the depths of his present misery, Georgie felt an upsurge of admiration for Ashby Minor. He certainly knew what he was talking about. But it was upsetting to think that Mamma was reacting just like all the other women, because he'd always assumed that she would be able to understand everything. And now he'd upset her, as he could see from the way she was pulling her mouth into that hard, straight line, and he hadn't meant to. He wouldn't have deliberately upset her for the world.

'I don't know what I'm to do about it,' Alice said. She put the encyclopedia on the dresser and covered it decently with a white table napkin. 'Your father will have to deal with it when he gets home. And in the meantime I don't want to hear so much as a peep out of either of you. Is that understood? Not one peep. You've both been thoroughly wicked children.'

Anna began to weep, squeezing her eyelids so that the tears would roll dramatically down her cheeks. But Georgie gritted his teeth to stop his mouth from trembling, and even though his eyes were stinging with distress he valiantly managed to hold on to his self control.

It was a cold, uncomfortable night, wakeful with guilt and fear in Tooting, thwarted by an uncomfortable mattress in Hastings. Mrs Maybury had done as she was told and aired the bed and even provided them with a hot water bottle, but the mattress had obviously been designed by the same man who produced the bedroom floor. It was full of lumps and slopes and unexpected hollows, so that Albert's attempt to make love to his delicious Queenie very quickly became ridiculous. Within minutes Queenie was in fits of helpless laughter and Albert had to resign himself to his frustration. It was very annoying.

They slept fitfully and whenever Queenie woke she complained because they weren't in their own nice comfortable bed. She was still crabby the next morning, and objected to her breakfast and spilled her tea and told the mirror she looked 'a right old frump'. Albert agreed with her. 'Serve you right for bein' so bad-tempered,' he said, and was scowled at for his honesty. By the time they'd left Mrs Maybury's higgledy-piggledy cottage and were negotiating the broken steps down to the High Street, clutching their luggage, they were both in a foul mood.

'I told yer we shouldn't a' come,' she said, stomping alongside him over the damp cobbles. 'Place full a' gargoyles! God awful bed! Freezin' cold!'

'You don't 'ave sun in November,' Albert said furiously. 'Stupid woman!' The mist was still swirling uphill from the beach and she was rushing straight into it.

'You should a' thought a' that before we come,' she said, glaring at him. Tendrils of curly hair were already damp and dark against her forehead and her nose was red. 'You never think, do yer?' she said.

The ingratitude of it! 'You agree to come here!' he roared at her. 'You want a 'oliday. I do all this for you. Ungrateful woman!'

'I didn't want ter come in the first place,' she said, growling off ahead of him. '*You* were the one. I should a' stuck ter me guns and stayed where I was. I shall 'ave more sense next time.'

'You make me sick,' he roared, enjoying his anger now that he'd released it. 'I do all this for you. How dare you shout at me! You don't know when you're well off. What more d'you want? A luxury cruise?'

'I'm off 'ome!' she yelled, and disappeared into the mist.

'All right!' he yelled back. But there was no sound of her.

Furiously he pounded up the hill to the station. He would go home anyway, no matter what she decided to do.

To his surprise he found a train was actually standing by the platform, with a good head of steam on, ready to depart. Queenie was in the second coach, cross and silent in the corner seat. She didn't look at him or speak when he climbed aboard, but they had the coach to themselves and fortunately the train started the minute the door was closed behind him. It was a good train, too. Soon they were clear of the mist and clattering through the sodden fields of Sussex, and although Queenie was still too obviously angry, Albert was restored by the speed and purpose of their journey.

'Be home in no time,' he said with approval as they rushed through stations without stopping. 'No dawdling for us.'

Their quarrel was receding with the miles. They were almost at ease with one another again. Until the train carried them on through Clapham Junction.

'You idiot!' Queenie said, watching with exasperation as the high tower of Arding and Hobbs department store shot past the window. 'It's an express.'

'Why didden' they tell us at 'Astings?' Albert said crossly, forgetting that they'd rushed into the train without giving anybody time to tell them anything.

'Now we shall 'ave ter come all the way back from Victoria,' Queenie said, frowning as the bare trees of Wandsworth common flicked across their vision. 'I tell you straight, Ploochy, I wish we'd never come on this silly weekend.'

She was getting irritable again, Albert thought, so he swallowed his own annoyance and tried to reassure her. 'The speed this train is going,' he said, 'we shall be there and back in no time.'

But he was wrong. Just as they were crossing the Thames, and almost within sight of Victoria, the train slowed down and ground to a halt, brakes squealing.

'*Now* what happening?' Albert said, his eyebrows descending in a scowl. A gust of sleety rain pattered against their unmoving window and below them the Thames was the oily brown of dirty washing-up water.

Ten minutes passed. Albert began to prowl, up and down their empty carriage, from one window to the other, fretting with impatience. 'Oh come on! Come on!' he urged their moribund transport. 'What the matter with you? We shall be here all day.'

They could hear voices murmuring in the next compartment and presently a window was lowered with a thud. Albert buttoned up his coat and let down their window too. 'What's up?' he said to the man in the next compartment. But nobody seemed to know. Up and down the train they were all asking the same question.

'Broken down, I'll betcha,' Queenie said, joining him at the window. The rain driving against their cheeks was unpleasantly hard and the air was icy. 'We shall get the new-monia,' she said. 'Close the winder, Ploochy!'

'Not yet,' Albert said. 'There's another train coming. Let see what that does.'

So they stood at the window and watched. The second train was travelling slowly and remarkably gently. It didn't whistle as it approached and even from a distance they could see that there was something extraordinary about it. It was drawn by a huge sage green engine. A thoroughbred, Albert thought admiring it. And as it drew nearer they could see that the coaches were all different colours. Some bore the insignia of other companies, but some were painted khaki and marked by large red crosses. It was a hospital train.

Complaint and speculation were silenced at once. Albert and his fellow passengers watched with respect as the great train gradually passed beside them, its wheels rocking like a cradle, every blind drawn, hushed and dignified and private, like grief.

After that it seemed proper that they should wait their turn. But the express was buzzing with excited interest, and by the time it finally sighed to a halt against the buffers, most of the passengers had decided that they really ought to go and see how the wounded were. Albert and Queenie were as eager for this new experience as the rest, although afterwards they both admitted that if they'd known what they were going to see, they'd have gone straight home to Clapham. For this was not the sanitized image of war they'd grown accustomed to from the cheerful pictures in the daily papers. This was a horrible reality.

Despite the size of the terminus, it was obvious where the hospital train had come in, for an odd convoy of vehicles was being driven straight through the crowd towards it, buses and charabancs, a variety of ambulances, even taxis. Inside the barrier, a mobile canteen had been set up, and teams of Red Cross nurses and grey-coated orderlies were already hard at work among the wounded. They were dealing with the stretcher cases first, and the stretcher cases were mostly amputees, their stumps horrifyingly obvious in bulky padded bandages. The walking wounded were helping one another out of the train, and then waiting patiently in the stinging rain. There seemed to be hundreds of them, resting awkwardly on crutches, leaning against crates and trolleys, sitting in a companionable huddle of battle-stained khaki and tattered bandages. So many men, so many injuries, so much pain. So many young faces discoloured or disfigured, burnt black, or torn like raw meat, ridged with scars or sweaty pale like white wax. Albert and Queenie watched and were appalled.

'Poor buggers,' Queenie said softly. 'What did they ever do ter deserve this?'

Albert was chewing his upper lip with impotent sympathy. 'Too young to be cripples,' he said. 'It dreadful! I can't bear to look.'

'Then don't,' she said, practical but gentle again. 'I'm off home. You coming?' In the face of this mass suffering, their quarrel seemed petty and shameful. He was grateful for her kindness. She was thankful for his health and strength.

It was late afternoon by the time he got back to Tooting and the streets were already growing dark. The weekend had exhausted him. Too many strong emotions, he thought, and was glad that he was going back to the peace and order of his fine house.

Alice met him in the hall, wearing her most disapproving expression. 'Did the meeting go well?' she said, and her politeness was just a shade too obvious.

'Oh yes. Yes,' he answered vaguely. He'd forgotten what excuse he'd given in that postcard, and he was too weary to make the effort to remember. He hung up his hat and coat and examined his travel-strained reflection in the hall mirror.

'I'm glad to hear it,' she said, and led him into the dining room where the children couldn't hear what they were saying.

'Something unpleasant happened in this house yesterday,' she said. 'Now you are home, you will have to deal with it.'

His heart gave a lurch of anxiety. 'What is it?' he said.

So she told him.

This was not what he'd come home for. Fatigue and the turmoil of his emotions made him sharp-tempered. 'Hell's teeth!' he roared. 'Is there no peace in the world?' He flung himself into the sofa to demonstrate his exhaustion and his displeasure.

'I had a dreadful weekend,' he said. 'Dreadful! I need peace and quiet. Not this.'

Alice was contained and steely. 'They are your children,' she said.

He made a last attempt to avoid the issue. 'Can't it wait till morning?' he said and was annoyed to hear that he was almost pleading.

'No,' she said firmly. 'In the morning there will be no time.' Her determination was impossible for him to oppose. 'Very well,' he said, miserably resigned to it. 'I will have a wash and a meal and then I will talk to them. One at a time. Anna first.'

He hadn't the faintest idea how he would broach such a subject at all, especially to his daughter. After all, it wasn't something you ever talked about and certainly not to children, who ought to be entirely innocent of any knowledge of it. Why, he'd never discussed it with anyone in his whole life. Except Queenie, of course, and she was different. He was horribly embarrassed, and annoyed with Alice for shirking her responsibilities in the matter. And close to the heat of his annoyance came a spurt of furious anger against his stupid foreign son. Why couldn't he find out about it like everybody else did? What was the matter with him? Reading a book about it! The very idea was effeminate. A book!

Fortunately little Anna was a sensible girl and made no fuss. In fact it was almost as though she was trying to make things easy for him. She told him at once that she'd only read the book because Georgie gave it to her, and when he pressed her, it was obvious that she hadn't read much of it because it was too difficult.

'No harm done,' he said to Alice, when the child had been sent up to bed with the unnecessary admonition not to repeat her error. 'She doesn't even know what it was about.'

But Georgie was different and difficult. He stood quietly in front of his father, the firelight glinting on those wretched spectacles, pale and withdrawn and looking far too like Alice for comfort. His pallor and his appearance roused Albert to immediate anger.

'And what is the meaning of this?' he roared and was pleased when he saw that the boy had to swallow nervously.

'The meaning of what, Papa?' Georgie said, and his voice wasn't entirely under control.

Was the child half-witted? Albert wondered. 'You know very well,' he said. 'This filth you bring into my house the minute my back is turned. How dare you make trouble for your mother when I'm away. Have you no sense of decency at all?'

'I don't know,' Georgie said miserably.

'Don't know!' Albert roared. 'Don't know!' What sort of damn fool answer was that? 'Of course you know. Why you do it? Eh? You tell me that.'

Georgie stood his ground, although he was very frightened and breathing fast. He was debating whether he ought to risk telling his father the truth. The firelight was making patterns like little clouds on the red tiles of the hearth and as the silence continued he could hear a damp coal spurting and hissing as it dried.

'I'm waiting for you, Georgie,' his father said, and the words were a threat.

Georgie took a deep breath and decided to tell the truth.

'Anna asked me to get it for her,' he said. The effort it had required made the words sound too bold. Albert was instantly flushed with rage and disbelief.

'Don't lie to me, you hateful child,' he said. 'Your sister is a good girl. She wouldn't do such a thing. She isn't interest in filth. No little girl is interest in filth.'

Georgie stared back at him, owlish and dismayed, and the sight of him made Albert more angry than ever. He strode across to the child and stood above him, threatening with his body as well as his voice. 'You will not blame your sister for your disgusting behaviour,' he said. 'You hear me? You will tell the truth.'

Georgie stood still, although it was difficult because he was trembling. 'It is the truth, Papa,' he said.

338

Albert's anger boiled over. He struck his son hard across the side of the face. 'Don't lie!' he roared. 'You tell me the truth, you understand?'

Georgie was shocked and hurt, but he didn't say anything and he still didn't move. He simply stood quietly in front of his father, looking at the fire, as the red handprint deepened on his cheek. The truth had failed, so what could he say?

Albert's fury was rushing him along. There was no turning back for either of them now. 'We will stay here all night,' he said. 'I warn you. I want another answer, do you understand. A proper answer. Why did you do it?'

Georgie's mind was spinning in terror. What did Papa want him to say? He couldn't think. 'I don't know,' he whispered.

Albert's face was dark with anger, his mouth triangular, his hair bristling. He unbuckled his belt and laid it on the table beside his son. 'You have ten seconds to give me the answer I want,' he warned. 'And if you don't, I beat you.'

There was a thundering in Georgie's ears, but no words that could rescue either of them. The truth was no good and now he was too far gone in fear to think of anything else. He stayed absolutely still and absolutely quiet, watching the belt and feeling the force of it on his back already.

'Five seconds,' Albert said. 'I will not be defied. I warn you. You'd better tell me!'

Silence, as the coal hissed and spat.

'Answer me!' Albert roared. 'Do you hear? Answer me! I will not be defied!' He had one end of the belt wrapped round his knuckles. It was almost too late. Georgie looked away from the belt and concentrated on the hearth again. His face was as pale as wax in the firelight. Albert waited for two more seconds, trembling with the passion of his anger, overflowing with it, unable to contain it any longer. Then he brought down the end of the strap onto that unyielding spine in an explosion of all the anger and frustration he'd accumulated over the weekend. He knew he was out of control and he knew he was screaming abuse with every stroke, 'Vile! Hateful! Beastly boy!' but he didn't care.

As the belt descended for the sixth or seventh time, Georgie gave a groan and flailed backwards onto the carpet in a fit. He knocked over a chair as he fell, his back curved horribly, his legs jerking. Alice was in the room and on her knees beside him immediately, loosening his tie, wedging a spoon in his foaming mouth. Albert stood beside them, his belt still in his hand, feeling spent and ashamed and curiously detached.

The paroxysms continued for a long time, but at last they were over and the boy lay still. Albert put his belt on and Alice regained her breath, sitting on the carpet with Georgie's groaning head on her lap, stroking his hair and crooning to him the way she always did. She glanced up briefly at her husband and her glance was venomous. 'I hope you're satisfied!' she said.

Albert was stunned by the injustice of it. 'You wanted me to deal with him,' he said.

'Not this way,' she answered, looking back at Georgie. 'My poor lamb!'

Confusion and fatigue brought a sudden craving for the comfort of brandy. Albert left the room and the house without another word. He would go to Jack Beard's and have a drink with Harry and Joe Summers and put all this unpleasantness out of his mind.

It wasn't until he was halfway down the Broadway that the full realization of what he had done flooded him so violently that it stopped him walking. He remembered his father's terrible belt and his own fear and anger and impotence as the leather thudded onto his back. And now he'd done exactly the same thing to his own son. In exactly the same way. I'm no better than he was, he thought, and his shame was a physical pain. The image of that fit filled his mind, and now he felt responsible for it.

He had to force himself to continue walking. I'll make it up to him, he thought, as his feet padded over the wet pavement. I'll put it right somehow. After all, Christmas was coming, and Christmas was a grand opportunity to make peace. I'll buy him the best present he's ever had, he thought. We'll have the best Christmas ever, to make up for it.

But he was afraid of the damage he might have done.

Chapter 27

Albert spent a lot of time and energy to ensure that this Christmas was a success. There was no shortage of turkeys and a ham could always be found for a fellow shopkeeper who sold good whisky, so the dinner had been splendid. He'd spent a small fortune on presents, new clothes for everybody, a toy theatre for Anna, and for Georgie, every single book on the reading list the English master at Rutlish School had eventually provided for him. There were twenty altogether, but he bought them all, being convinced that such an expensive gift must surely heal the rift.

Now they lay in seven bulky parcels beside Georgie's plate. He watched hopefully as the boy unwrapped them one by one, folding the paper neatly and putting it to one side. Anna was looking decidedly jealous, but that couldn't be helped. The gift was too important to be marred by her childish emotions. 'Well?' he asked, as the last book was set quietly on the pile with the others.

'Thank you very much, Pater,' Georgie said politely. Then to his father's surprise, instead of picking up the first book and beginning to read it, which was what everybody expected, the boy solemnly divided his collection into two neat piles. His family continued to drink their tea as they watched him, puzzled. When he'd finished his task, he pushed the second and smaller pile towards his father's plate. 'These are all in our library already, Pater,' he said. 'Did you know?'

His tone was carefully neutral, but Albert wasn't fooled. He knew that he'd been thoroughly and expertly snubbed. Of course he didn't know what books were in his library. He never read any of them and Georgie knew it. It was a public humiliation, even if nobody else around the table that morning appeared to notice it. And the worst of it was that he had to endure it without comment.

It was a bad way to start Christmas, so he was glad when his guests began to arrive and gave him the excuse to rush about and release his uncomfortable emotions in action. As soon as Harry and Em and young Johnny were through the

341

front door, he rushed them off into the drawing room at once for the unveiling of his other spectacular purchase. It was one of the new gramophones and he was very proud of it. This would certainly be a success.

It was. Anna was allowed the privilege of choosing the first dance and decided on a gallop. The black plate was removed from its wrapper, and laid upon the turntable with a flourish. Then they all watched with bated breath as Albert wound the handle, the disc began to rotate and the needle was dropped down upon it. After a series of rasping, scratching sounds, the gallop actually began, and brassy music rose out of the trumpet as if by magic.

The children were so intrigued they spent the whole of the first dance standing in a circle round the machine, watching the black disc as it spun, their eyes almost as round as the record itself.

Then the Morrises arrived and the Major flung himself into the party with tremendous enthusiasm, taking all the children with him. Dust rose from the carpet as they jumped and capered, and soon they were all hot and sticky and Alice was wondering whether she ought to damp down the fire before she went back to the kitchen to see how the turkey was getting along.

Dinner was a very jolly meal after all their exertions. So Albert was able to preside over a happy table with immense satisfaction. This was better. This was how Christmas ought to be.

'You like my gramophone eh, Minnie?' he said, eyes sparkling at the sight of her flushed face and untidy hair.

'What will they think of next, Mr P?' Minnie said. 'That's what I should like to know.'

'No end to the marvels a' modern science,' Em said happily. She was even more dishevelled than Minnie, her curls plastered to her forehead with sweat. 'Motor cars and airy-planes!'

'And dirigibles,' Aunt Phoebe said.

'And telephones and electric light,' Georgie offered.

'Carpet sweepers,' Alice suggested, joining the game and hoping Albert would notice what she was saying. What a blessing it would be not to have to sweep the carpet on your hands and knees.

342

'Telegrams,' Albert said. 'Sendin' a message through the air. That pretty marvellous when you come ter think about it.'

'And bombs,' Jesse put in sourly. 'Don't forget bombs. And machine guns. They're modern inventions, too.'

All the women round the table shot warning glances at him at once. 'We don't want to talk about war, Jesse,' Minnie rebuked. 'Not at Christmas.'

He ignored them. 'We should talk about it more often,' he said, far too seriously, 'then maybe we'd take the papers with a pinch a' salt.'

'Oh, get on with yer,' Em said, trying to jolly him out of it. 'You mean ter say the papers ain't tellin' us the truth?'

'They bend it, Em,' he said. 'You look on the front page and what d'yer see? Banner headlines. "Splendid victory. Glorious attack." It's a load a codswallop. It's a different story inside the rag. Two, three, four pages full a' casualties there. That don't look much like a vict'ry ter me.'

'You can't 'ave a war without casualties,' Albert said. 'That unpleasant but it a fact.'

'Some casualties, I grant you,' Jesse said. 'Only not on this scale. Thousands they're killing off. Every day. And they call it a vict'ry.'

'Well whatcha want 'em ter do?' Harry said. 'You jest imagine. You open the papers every morning an' they say, "Defeat! We're losing the war!" How'd yer feel then?'

Young Johnnie Jones had been contentedly drinking his beer until this conversation began. Now he set his glass aside and joined in. He'd drunk rather a lot over dinner and he wasn't entirely sure what they were talking about, but he felt he ought to defend whatever it was he sensed was being attacked. 'Our boys are very brave,' he said carefully. 'They'll win the war. Look at our Billy.'

'No one's denying that, son,' Jesse said. 'All I'm sayin' is, people oughter be told the truth. I reckon if they really understood what was goin' on out there, they'd 'ave this war stopped inside a month.'

'I never heard such defeatist talk!' Harry complained, growing quite flushed. 'We should be thinking how to *win* this war, not how ter stop it. You're a bloody defeatist, Jesse!'

Alice looked quickly round the table to see if she could find someone who would turn this conversation in a different direction. She'd had quite enough of Jesse Holdsworthy. And she saw Major Morris. He was sitting at the other end of the table, trying to pick all the nuts out of his portion of trifle, so that they wouldn't get stuck in his false teeth. The memsahib had been watching him with disapproving anxiety for the last five minutes. 'Jesse here has been telling us we ought to stop the war,' she said to him. 'What do you think, Major?'

'What! What!' the Major barked. 'Never stop a war, dear lady. Deuce take it! If we'd gone round stoppin' wars, we'd never have had an Empire. What!'

Watching his earnest old face, Albert was struck by the fact that the major was the only man in the room who had actually seen active service. This man knew what it was like to see his comrades being killed. And yet he never spoke of it. They'd talked about India so many times, and yet he'd never once mentioned a battle. Now, it suddenly seemed important to find out what he really thought about it. 'Tell me, Major,' he said, ' 'ave you ever been in a battle and thought, "I wish this would stop?" '

'Oh yes, me dear chap,' the Major admitted freely. 'You all think that, one time or another. But you can't stop, dontcha see. That ain't the soldier's business.'

'What *is* the soldier's business?' Johnny Jones asked, genuinely interested and ready for a reply that he could treasure.

Major Morris considered this for a few minutes, his spoon raised like a baton. 'Hold the line!' he said and his faded eyes gleamed beneath his untidy eyebrows. 'Take the fire! Win the day!'

Later in the holiday, Albert took Alice and Minnie and the aunts and the four children as far away from all talk of war as he could, to Wimbledon Theatre and the happy fantasy of *Babes in the Wood*. Christmas wouldn't have been Christmas without a visit to a pantomime, and this year he had chosen their entertainment very particularly and was more than usually concerned to hear what they thought of it.

Now they were in Fullers tea rooms, with three pots of tea and more fancy cakes than they could possibly have hoped for in war time, and he was waiting for their opinion.

Anna liked the good fairy. 'She was the best,' she said. The good fairy had worn a long white dress and had flown down onto the stage like an angel, and everybody liked her. Besides, she had dark curly hair and the sort of face that Anna herself tried to see in her mirror every morning. 'When I grow up,' she said, 'I'm going to be just like her.'

'Good fairies go to bed the minute they're told,' Aunt Phoebe said. 'So we shall see, shan't we.'

Georgie had been quietly eating a slice of battenburg while they talked. He'd unravelled it carefully so that he could leave the marzipan till last. Now he offered his opinion. 'I liked the bad fairy best,' he said. 'The one with the red hair. She was pretty. When she jumped out of that swing and the huntsman caught her! That was very good.' He was looking inward at the memory, so he didn't see the pleasure on his father's face. But Alice did and wasn't surprised. It confirmed her suspicions.

'Wasn't she one of Dickie's singers once upon a time?' she asked. 'You invited her to one of your parties, didn't you?'

'Oh yes, yes,' Albert said, far too casually. 'Yes, I believe I did.'

So she's the one, Alice thought, with an uncomfortable mixture of annoyance and satisfaction. A nasty, vulgar-looking thing! He really ought to know better than to mix with such common creatures. When Dickie had let drop that he'd seen Albert in Luigi's and had made all those ridiculous jokes to avoid telling her who he was with, she knew there was more in it than met the eye. He might be a good business man, she thought, and he was certainly very generous, but he had no taste at all.

Albert's friends at the Chamber of Commerce were toying with the idea of cutting him in on an unusual and possibly hazardous business venture. They had always been impressed by his astuteness and his extraordinary generosity was invariably good for trade. This Christmas he had excelled himself, taking over the organization of the orphans' party and decorating the church hall with an extravagance that quite took their breath away.

'Foreign, of course,' the chairman explained to his immediate circle, 'but there's no denying he's got a flair for business. And a heart of gold. He might be our man. Is he financially sound, Mr Chalmers?'

'As the Bank of England,' Mr Chalmers assured them. 'We only need two more substantial backers, as you know. Would you like me to mention it to him? See what he says.'

'Would he be prepared to take this sort of risk?' the chairman asked.

Mr Chalmers knew his man. 'Like a shot!' he said.

Which, of course, was exactly how Albert accepted the offer. To be a major shareholder in a brand new picture palace looked like a profitable business venture in any circumstances. The fact that the site chosen for it was almost immediately opposite his own shop made it very attractive indeed.

'Whatcha think a' that?' he asked Dickie and Harry, the next time they all met in Jack Beard's saloon.

'We never know what you'll get up to next. Do we, Dickie?' Harry said, scratching his untidy head. 'I give up tryin' ter keep pace with you years ago. Tell yer what though, I shall expect free seats fer me an' Em once in a while.'

'That goes without saying,' Albert promised.

But Dickie was miserable. 'It's all very well fer you,' he grumbled. 'Don't seem ter matter what state the world's in, you make a profit out've it. This war's killin' the 'alls. I tell you straight, if it hadn't been fer the pantomine an' a good summer season, we'd a' been in Queer Street last year. An' God alone knows 'ow we shall make out this summer.'

It was a familiar complaint. Albert and Harry, who had heard it all several times since Christmas, signalled their exasperated sympathy to one another. But Dickie continued. 'I used ter think I was on to a good thing once. Ain't so sure now. D'you remember that music-'all strike, Ploochy? 'Ad a company a' twelve then. Now there's four of us, Tilley an' me, an' old Martha, an' Jacko an' those god-awful dogs.' He looked into his beer morosely. Harry looked into his tactfully. And Albert had another idea.

'Why don't you buy shares in the picture palace?' he asked. 'Cut your losses while the going's good. We could find work fer Tilley and Martha. In the box office perhaps. Entertainment in the interval. An' you could be resident pianist.'

'You're barmy!' Dickie said, but he was giving the matter thought, as Albert could tell from the distant expression on his face. 'I'd 'ave to ask the others,' he said slowly, still thinking. 'It ain't a thing you can rush.'

But in the event it was something they decided they could do. Jacko took his god-awful dogs off to Scarborough, Martha said she wouldn't mind helping in the box office and Tilley, rather to Dickie's surprise, said she'd had more than enough of singing and the time was ripe for a change. So it was settled.

Alice took the news with perfunctory interest. It would be nice for him to move among a better class of people, she said. And that was all. It irritated Albert that she paid so little attention to what he was doing. Was it any wonder he couldn't wait to see Queenie again? For the one thing you could depend on with Queenie was her interest. But she'd gone back to that wretched touring company after the pantomime and now she was off in Surrey somewhere entertaining the troops again, and he wouldn't see her for more than a week. He wasn't at all sure that all that rushing about the country was either necessary or helpful. But there was nothing he could do about it, so he had to wait.

She came home to Clapham Junction with half the company. Albert could hear them all laughing and joking before she jumped from the carriage giggling goodbyes like a child leaving a party. As always when she'd been away for more than a week, he saw her again with a rush of pleasure. He'd grown accustomed to the sober browns and greys and navy blues favoured by the women in his house, and had forgotten how brightly coloured she was. Now she was wearing one of the new triple-tiered skirts, each tier a darker shade of green than the one above it, and her red hair bloomed on either side of a little round hat.

He watched as her volatile companions passed all her luggage out to her and piled it at her feet. There was a ridiculous amount of it, three travelling bags, a variety of striped parcels, at least five hat boxes and a bouquet so huge that when it had been heaped in her arms there was nothing to be seen between her waist and her chin but a mass of flowers, yellow, pink, purple, white and even a carroty red like her hair. She had to lean across the top of it all to give him a kiss.

'Missed me?' she asked.

'Now and then,' he lied happily, but his face was shining at her with quite another answer.

'Look at all these flowers,' she said, and she sounded proud

of the armful she carried. 'One a' them poor soldier fellers give
'em ter me. Must a' cost 'im the earth. Week's pay, I shouldn't
wonder. Wasn't it kind? 'E said I was the best thing that 'ad
'appened to 'im since 'e joined the army. Ever such a nice
bloke, Ploo.'

Albert wasn't interested in wounded soldiers, however nice
they might be. 'I've 'ad a . . .' he began, but she wasn't
listening.

'We shall need a porter fer this lot,' she said. 'You got a
cab?'

It took two porters and a considerable effort to get her and
her luggage into the cab, but at last they were settled and on
their way to Clapham. 'I never 'ad so many flowers in all me
life,' she said. ' 'E was a nice chap. Come from round our way.
Used ter work with Cal and Spud once. Part a' Cal's team,
afore the war. Just fancy that. Said it done 'im a power a' good
just talking about the old place. 'Spect it did, too. The doctors
are very good, very kind and everything, but they speak
terribly la-di-da all the time. An' so do the nurses an' all. Puts
'em off, poor beggars. Ned said it was a real treat to 'ave me
to talk to.' She paused, looking down at the flowers in her lap.
She was extraordinarily beautiful, Albert thought, like a
madonna looking down at her child. 'He didn't 'ave ter go an'
buy me all these, though, did 'e?'

'I am so glad you're back,' he said.

'It's been a long tour,' she said. But she didn't look at him,
and her preoccupation put a constraint between them that
lasted for the rest of the journey. He decided to wait until they
were in the flat before he told her his good news.

But when they got home, she declared she was starving to
death, so they had to rush off to Luigi's before she collapsed
with hunger. She talked about the soldiers all through the
meal. It wasn't until she'd consumed a huge steak and two
helpings of apple pie, and licked the plate and dropped pastry
all down the front of her new blouse that Albert finally got the
chance to tell her about his new venture.

'Clever old thing, aintcha,' she said, her eyes applauding
him. 'Be a millionaire one a' these days I shouldn't wonder.
Whatcha gonna call it?' He hadn't thought. 'Call it the Regal,'
she said, picking another crumb of pastry out of her blouse,

'after me. An' I'll come to the grand opening in me tiara, an' cause a stir. Whatcha think?'

He thought it was wonderful to have her home again.

'If we got married, an' 'ad kids, I could be at 'ome all the time,' she said, and now her eyes were calculating, not laughing.

Albert decided to ignore such provocation and took her off to the Windmill before she could say any more.

But the subject lay between them, nevertheless, and even after a cheerful party at the pub and a sensuous reunion in their moon-dappled bed, it returned to upset them again.

They were talking idly about the war, and the way it was beginning to affect people's lives. She had told him about the patient way the wounded endured the awful things that were happening to them, and he had told her how people crowded to see the newsreels from the Front. Then he was unwise enough to claim that he thought he was adapting to the war situation extremely well.

'Adapt, my eye,' she said, lovingly. 'You don't know the meaning a' the word. I never known you adapt ter nothink.'

'How can you say such a thing?' he asked, propping himself up on one elbow so that he could see her face. He was hurt by her frankness, especially as he hadn't expected it.

' 'Cause it's true,' she said, unabashed. 'You don't adapt. You act. Well, I tell you, I reckon if I could just think up the right sort a' situation, I could even get you ter chuck Alice an' marry me. All on the spur a' the moment. That's what it wants. Chop-chop! No time ter think! An' we could be mister and missus.'

He was most upset, partly because he recognized the truth of what she was saying, but more because it hadn't occurred to him that she would ever try to manipulate him, and now she was actually describing how it could be done. Besides it was a most unsuitable moment to be talking like this. After all that love-making they should have been happy and gentle with one another. 'We should get some sleep,' he said, and was annoyed with himself because the words sounded formal and ridiculous.

'All right!' she said, but the word wasn't an agreement, it was a challenge. She sat up and turned towards him, her face angry, her skin gleaming like pearl in the moonlight. 'If you're so good at adapting, see 'ow you adapt ter this. I signed on with the Boodles fer the duration.'

'The duration?' he echoed. What was she talking about now? The duration of what?

'The war,' she explained. 'I signed on till the end a' the war.'

'You can't do that!' he said, appalled. 'What about our 'olidays?' They took two holidays every summer nowadays. Whatever was she thinking of?

'Can't be done,' she said, brusquely. 'We'll 'ave ter give 'em a miss, that's all.'

'Don't be ridiculous!' he said, crossly. 'We need our 'olidays. You can't do this.'

'It's done,' she said. 'They're in a dreadful state some a' them poor fellers, Ploo. One a' them 'ad no arms nor legs. You just think a' that, instead a carryin' on about your 'oliday. An' they get the shakes an' sit an' cry fer hours on end. The nurses was tellin' us. We're the best tonic they've ever 'ad. They need us.'

'I need you,' he said stubbornly, biting his moustache, and aggrieved because she'd put him in the wrong with all this talk of wounded men.

'No you never,' she said. 'You'd marry me else.'

Their conversation had gone round in a circle. 'When the war is over,' he tried. 'I marry you then. You know that. It won't be long, I promise.'

'This war could go on fer years an' years,' she said.

'No,' he argued. 'Things are bound ter pick up. You see.'

But he couldn't change her mind or her plans. And the news from the Front got worse and worse.

That summer, the Regal opened its doors to the Tooting public for the first time, and Dickie tried his hand at a new skill, accompanying those flickering, unpredictable pictures. He found he was rather good at it and soon learned a whole new repertoire of useful tunes. In the interval Martha sold sweets from a little padded tray and he and Tilley entertained the audience with patriotic songs. Martha enjoyed selling tickets too, although the little box office was really too small for her bulk and she filled it like a cushion in a cabinet. They all missed the tension and squabbles of backstage life, but this new world had its excitements too, and, what was more important, it paid a regular wage.

When the six major shareholders met for the first time at the end of their first month, they found they'd made a considerable profit, even after paying exorbitant wages to the projectionist, a surly character called Claude, who ruled them all with the mysteries of his trade, and spoke an incomprehensible jargon that none of them were bold enough to question.

They decided that Ploochy should continue to select the films, because he seemed to have an instinctive understanding of public taste. It pleased Albert well enough, for the job was a sinecure. All he had to do was to choose the films he enjoyed himself, slapstick comedy, touching love stories, impossible adventures. If he then added as many newsreels about the Great War as he could possibly get, the mixture was about perfect.

After a few weeks he'd seen so many films about soldiers and soldiering he felt he was immune to the war and the wounded.

Until the morning Frank was late to work.

It was most unlike him, and Albert was just beginning to think that he'd have to set to and light the office fire himself, when the boy arrived, his cap askew, his face pale with shock and anxiety and the terrible importance of the news he carried. 'Our Nat's been gassed,' he gasped. 'His Ruthie got the card this morning. Ma can't get her ter stop crying.'

'No!' Albert roared. Not Nat! It couldn't be true. Other people got wounded. People you didn't know. Not Nat. Nat couldn't be wounded. It wasn't right. He was too full of life and cheek and much too smart to be gassed.

Then he saw that Frank was nearly in tears, so he controlled himself and took him off into the office and made him sit down and got him a glass of brandy.

'He got good strong lungs,' he said, trying to encourage them both. 'He will get over it in no time. You see. It could a' been worse. He could a' been blown up.'

'Yes,' Frank said, looking at the ashes of the dead fire. He wasn't encouraged.

'Where is he?' Albert asked.

'Base hospital somewhere. Amens or sommink,' Frank said

and he added sadly, 'I suppose I'll 'ave ter join up now, won't I, Mr P? Can't let them Jerries get away with this.'

Albert had to agree with him, although neither of them wanted him to. The war had come too close to both their lives and there was no glory or excitement in enlisting these days.

'Talk it over with Johnnie Jones,' he suggested.

Johnnie wasn't certain about it either. But in the event Lord Derby's scheme made their decision for them. Since all eligible young men had to sign on, they really had no choice. Later that month the two of them went quietly off to Wandsworth to attest their willingness to serve in the army as soon as the authorities decided to call them. There were no parties this time and no celebrations.

In the same week Nat was pronounced fit enough to travel and was shipped home to Bournemouth. His mother and father took the first train down to see him, taking Ruthie with them. They returned in tears, shocked beyond words by the state he was in.

'Couldn't even lie down properly,' Ruthie told Albert later. ' 'E's the most terrible colour, Mr Ploochy, an' wheezin' all the time. It's terrible! My poor Nat!'

Albert made comforting noises, and as soon as she'd left the shop, he sent Frank down to Davey Greig's for a huge hamper of nourishing food for her to take down to Bournemouth on her next visit. But no amount of nourishment would ever restore Nat to health now and they all knew it.

'What did I tell yer, Ploo,' Queenie said compassionately, when she heard about it. 'It's different when it's one a' yer own.'

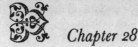 *Chapter 28*

It was the third autumn of the war and London was alert with horrific rumours. The battle of the Somme had produced more casualties than the capital had ever seen, even from Ypres, and now there was no way that the authorities could pretend that this was a victory or that the British losses were small. Hospital trains had been arriving one after the other ever since the Wednesday after the attack, and the wounded told a very different tale to the daily papers. The news soon spread that the great battle of the Somme had been a bloody fiasco, that twenty thousand men had died on the first day alone, and not a yard of ground gained. And to confirm the bad news, if confirmation were needed, attested men began to be called up in larger numbers than ever before.

Frank Hawthorne and Johnnie Jones left Tooting within a fortnight of one another, Frank to Newmarket to join the Hertfordshire Regiment, Johnnie to Salisbury Plain with a brand new London regiment. Nat was still in hospital in Bournemouth, but he came home on leave in time to say goodbye to his brother. Then he laboured round to the shop to see Albert, and get to know the latest Dog.

Albert was horrified by his appearance. He looked like a little old man, bent and shrivelled. His skin was an alarming yellowish grey, which seemed worse above the crude blue of his uniform, and his eyes were horribly bloodshot. He walked with a stoop, and very slowly, stopping every now and then to cough or catch his breath. For breathing was no longer easy for him. The air rasped into his throat and rattled in his lungs, and when he coughed, phlegm bubbled and knocked inside him, like water boiling in an old tin kettle. He was a very sick man and looked it.

They remembered old customers, and wondered how Charlie Chamberlain was getting on in France and said what a pity it was that Mrs Kelly's nephew was killed. And at last Nat turned from the door just as he was leaving, to ask the question he'd been afraid of ever since he got back to England.

'I was wonderin',' he said, in his thickened voice, 'I don't suppose you'd 'ave any sort a' room fer me now, would yer, Mr P. seein' as I'm . . .' His voice and his hopes trailed away together, and Albert was torn by an instant and protective pity for him.

'There is always a job for you in this shop, Nat,' he said. 'After all you've done, it the least you deserve.'

'Ta,' Nat said, and they were both embarrassed to realize that his eyes were brimming with tears.

'You just concentrate on gettin' better,' Albert advised. 'The job will wait for you.'

Which was all very well, but it didn't fill Frank's vacant space behind the counter. 'I shall advertise for a boy,' he told Alice later that evening.

She was sitting beside the kitchen fire, repairing shirts. 'Percy leaves school in two week's time,' she said, biting off the thread. 'Would he do?'

Albert had almost forgotten Percy Holdsworthy's existence. He'd grown into a fine strong boy, a good head taller than his father, but he was rarely in the house. When he wasn't at school, he was out roaming the streets with his gang. But he was Minnie's son, so he might be worth a fortnight's trial.

So Percy was made presentable and given a pep-talk by his mother and Aunt Alice, and sent to work in the shop. At the end of the fortnight, Albert pronounced judgement. He wasn't marvellous, but he'd do. Percy and his mother accepted this as the praise it was, and the matter was settled.

As the months went by, attested men continued to be called to the colours, and soon it was plain that even that wasn't going to be enough to replace the terrible losses of this war of attrition.

One morning Jesse came home in a furious temper just as Albert was leaving for work. He flung his customary bundle of papers down on the hall stand. 'Military Bloody Service Act now we're having!' he said.

Albert glanced at the headlines, as Jesse ranted on. 'The poor old man in the street ain't so easy ter fool these days,' he said. 'Too many people know what a cock-up this bloody war's turning out. Not so keen to go rushing into it, now. So recruitment figures fall. Nat'rally. And that won't do fer our beloved leaders. Oh dear no! They got to have their cannon fodder. If we all said "No" to their stinking war, they might 'ave to go an' fight it themselves. So they've made it law now, we've all got to go and join up. Never mind conscription. We all have ter serve whether we like it or not. So much fer Liberty and Freedom I *don't* think. Military Bloody Service fer everybody between nineteen and forty. That's what they done!'

'I thought Lord Derby did that last year,' Albert said, 'when young Frank and Johnnie Jones had to volunteer. They didn't get a lot a' choice.'

'Bastards!' Jesse said. 'That's what they are. Well they won't get me, I tell you straight. I'm not fighting their bloody war for 'em. Not if I can help it,' and he went off grumbling to his breakfast.

'If they want 'im, they'll get 'im,' Harry said sagely later that morning. 'They got my two when all's said and done. Why should 'e be any different?' Harry had another and more worrying problem to contend with.

All six of Pennyman's attested labourers had been called into the army and now he'd made up his mind to sell off the remaining acres he owned in Tooting and concentrate his efforts in Epsom, where land was cheaper. After the harvest was gathered, Harry would be out of a job.

He was very depressed about it. 'I shall soon be follerin' the old man ter Norfolk,' he said miserably. 'End up diggin' graves, I shouldn't wonder.'

Albert offered him a job at the Regal, at once, but he turned it down, saying he'd suffocate if he worked indoors. 'I been out in the open all me life, don't ferget,' he pointed out reasonably. 'Too old to change now.'

But Albert had no intention of allowing his old friend to go to Norfolk or to remain depressed. He asked around, and after a week discovered that Mrs Adams of Waterfall House needed a gardener to keep her grounds in order. Harry protested that he wasn't a gardener, and she certainly wouldn't want him, and it was all a waste of time, but Albert and Em ignored his gloom and nagged him into his best suit and sent him off to ask for the job.

He returned considerably cheered, and employed. 'Start on Monday,' he said. 'Ta, Ploochy! You're a pal!'

Little successes like these were more necessary to Albert than ever in such depressing times. Especially as Queenie was busier than she'd ever been with that wretched concert party of hers, and Alice was always preoccupied with food. In fact, there were days when he felt that the war was taking both his women away from him.

Still the casualties arrived in London. Soon the hospitals were so overcrowded that special measures had to be taken to accommodate the new arrivals.

The Pelucci family were just finishing their supper one evening when they had a visit from an army officer. He was obviously a gentleman, beautifully dressed in a tailormade uniform and self-assured under neatly groomed grey hair. He wanted to know if Albert would be willing to billet two or three of 'our wounded lads' until they were well enough to return to base. They would need a room of their own where they could sleep at night and rest during the day when necessary. Major Morris had agreed to take five.

Albert signed for two soldiers at once. It was the proper thing to do.

Afterwards, when the officer had thanked him courteously, and entered the allocation in his little notebook and left, Albert remembered Alice, and wondered whether he ought to have consulted her before he made his decision. But he needn't have worried. Alice was reasonable and sensible about it. 'We have to do our bit,' she said. 'It's only right when you think what these poor boys are doing for us.' But it would make a lot of extra work, as she and Minnie admitted to one another privately, and just at the wrong time too, when food was getting short and a great deal more expensive, and the cold weather was beginning.

Their first two soldiers arrived three days later, a short, dark-haired, voluble Welshman called Taffy, and a quiet lad called Bob, who said he came from the country. Alice put them into the spare bedroom, next to the bathroom, where they would be quiet and out of the way, and warned the children that their new guests were not to be pestered. 'Just imagine they're not there,' she advised.

It was a wasted warning, for all three children were far too excited by these heroic young men to be able to ignore their presence, and the soldiers were quite happy to sit in the garden in the autumn sunlight and would talk to anybody. Bob, as Anna very quickly discovered, didn't have a great deal to say for himself, and in any case, he was always falling asleep, sometimes even in the middle of a sentence, and once in the middle of a meal, to Anna's delight and her mother's embarrassment. But Taffy was a prodigious talker and a source of quite extraordinary information.

He told them about whizz-bangs and how they went so fast you couldn't hear them coming; and about a rat called Fritz who lived in an empty bully-beef can and was the company pet; and about machine guns and what marvellous machines they were. They learned how to shield the barrel of the gun so that the enemy wouldn't see the sparks unless they were right in front of you, and how to keep the firing chamber cool, and how to run off the steam into a bucket of cold water so that it wouldn't give your position away. Best of all, he told them about lice, and how they bit, and how they gathered in the seams of your clothes and how a lighted match would make them go 'Pop!' 'Jerusalem cattle we call them,' he said. 'Little beggars! When me and Boyo Jones got crackin' we could kill two dozen in thirty seconds. All the blood comes spurtin' out all over your face when you pop 'em.'

It wasn't long before the intriguing habits of the human body louse suddenly became the topic of conversation at the family breakfast table. It was Sunday morning and they were having bacon for breakfast. It was a weekly treat these days and therefore special.

'Do pigs have lice?' Renee asked, looking at her slice with interest.

'Bound to,' Georgie said, 'if we have them.'

'Poor pigs!' Anna said sympathetically. 'How do they squash them when they haven't got thumbs?'

Alice and Minnie could hardly believe their ears.

'I beg your pardon,' Alice said and the chill in her tone should have warned her children to desist. It took the grin off

357

Albert's face, but they were still happily involved in their new knowledge and didn't hear the danger signals.

'You can kill a louse quite easily, Mamma,' Anna explained. 'You squash it between your thumbnails. Like this,' and she picked up a crumb from the tablecloth and gave a demonstration too vivid for her mother's gently nurtured sensibilities.

'Leave the table at once!' Alice said, and when the child had gone, in chastened surprise, she rounded on the other two. 'I will not have disgusting conversation at meal times,' she said. 'Is that clear?' She was very upset.

The rest of the meal was eaten in almost monastic silence, and when the dishes had been cleared, and hats and coats obediently donned, and the family were on their way down Longley Road to church, she allowed the children to walk on out of earshot so that she could have a few serious words with Albert.

'It's that dreadful Welshman,' she said buttoning her gloves tightly against the chill autumn air. 'Filling their minds with his dirty talk. You'll have to get him transferred to some other house. He just isn't fit company for us. We can't have the children upset like this.'

Albert looked at the tight mouth of her distress and heard the cheerful voices of his two children as they walked happily together ahead of him and agreed that something would have to be done. He didn't have the faintest idea what, but at least his promise placated her into a more Christian frame of mind.

However, the very next Saturday evening she reversed her opinion of the little Welshman. For that was the night of the first Zeppelin raid on Tooting and by Sunday morning they were all seeing one another in the altered light of a new experience.

When the maroons sounded late that evening, thomp, thomp, thomp like heavy lead weights dropping one after the other, nobody was particularly alarmed. Jesse was upstairs finishing his supper in his own kitchen on the second floor; the children were in bed and asleep; so was Bob, of course; Albert and Percy hadn't come home from the shop. Taffy was polishing his boots in the scullery; and Minnie and Alice were quietly setting the table for breakfast. They were all accustomed to air raids now and had accepted that the Zeppelins were merely passing somewhere to the north of them, following the bright ribbon of the Thames straight to the docks. Distant explosions were still upsetting but no longer frightening and the sound of gunfire was comforting and sustaining, providing they were all safely indoors out of the path of falling shrapnel.

So the children were woken gently, and bundled into warm clothes, and ambled downstairs to sleep out the rest of the raid on sofas and armchairs in the drawing room. There was no urgency about their activity and little alarm.

When Albert and Percy came home from the shop, they rushed straight upstairs as usual to watch the raid.

'Come on, Georgie,' Albert said. 'It a big one tonight!'

Jesse put his blunt head over the banister. 'Come on up,' he called. 'There's a grand view from our kitchen. Done some damage up the docks ternight an' no mistake.'

He had put out the light and opened the kitchen window to the night air. They stood together beside the open space and looked out over their city. Below them in the bright moonlight the grey roofs of Tooting gleamed as if they were wet, and the silence was so intense they could hear it hissing. There was a tension in the air above all those unlit, vulnerable homes, listening and waiting and impotent under the implacable stare of a full, bold moon. The night sky was the colour of blue ink, studded with stars and, towards the City, criss-crossed with searchlights, like elegant white pencils panning slowly over the vast expanse before them. But they revealed nothing, although the fires the Germans had started were visible even at this distance. There was a dusty, brick-red glow on the north-eastern horizon, and from time to time red and white sparks spurted up into it like miniature fireworks.

'Warehouses,' Jesse said knowledgeably. 'Wood or paper most likely, to burn like that. Wouldn't like ter be them.'

As he spoke the pom-poms started up again, ferdum-ferdum-ferdum, and two more bombs exploded among the fires, each with a thud and a reverberating roar. Georgie shivered.

'Are you cold?' Albert asked, mindful of Alice's concern.

'No, Pater,' the boy said. 'It's just . . . there are people being blown up.' He was feeling helpless, just watching like this and didn't like the sensation. 'I wish I could be there,' he said, and he spoke with sadness and the need to translate his pity into action.

'We couldn't do nothink if we *was* there,' Percy said practically. He was quite enjoying himself, watching the raid from a safe distance.

His father grunted agreement. 'Too late to do anything now,' he said. 'Once bombs are falling. Much too late.'

Albert put a hand on Georgie's shoulder. 'We are watching history, Georgie,' he said. 'Think of that!' The prickling sense of danger and vulnerability all around them simply sharpened his senses and made him more full of himself than ever. His heart might be racing with excitement, but he was certain of his indestructibility.

'There's a cloud coming up,' Percy said with satisfaction, looking east towards Streatham. 'That'll fox the beggars.' Like the others he felt exposed by the strength of the moonlight in such a clear sky. Cloud cover was just what they all needed.

They watched the cloud as it drifted towards them in the indigo sky, a vague grey mass, gauzy thin and only just discernible. It seemed to be changing direction, Albert thought, and he just had time to wonder whether a stronger wind had sprung up when the clear light of the moon suddenly brought the shifting cloud into focus. Silvery grey. Sausage shaped. Straight edges sharply defined.

'Christ Almighty!' Jesse said, leaping back from the window. 'It's a bloody Zeppelin!' Before anyone else could move or think they heard a high pitched screaming whistle descending upon them, followed almost immediately by a second even more terrifying and then two violent explosions, so loud and so close that they could have been at the end of the road. Albert and the two boys flung themselves to the ground, where they lay panting among the floor level smells of coal dust, boot leather and wax polish. Their ears were ringing and their hearts pounding alarmingly. From what seemed a very long way away they could hear the girls crying and Alice and Minnie calling 'Georgie! Percy! Are you all right?' but for the moment none of them had the urge or the energy to reply. Then there was another high pitched whistle and a third explosion, even louder and more alarming.

'Downstairs,' Albert said, struggling to speak normally. 'Quick as you can! Tell your mothers we are all right. I will be down directly.' He needed time to get his breath back, and if, as he feared, he was going to start shaking, then he had to have a bit of privacy. It wouldn't do to let Alice see him in a state. He got to his feet cautiously. 'Run!' he urged, as the boys remained where they were, and the command released them from shock and spurred them into activity.

They hurtled down the stairs, moving more quickly than they'd ever done in their lives, panting and bolt-eyed, their hearts pounding painfully. Taffy was waiting for them on the landing, his uniform buttoned correctly, his boots newly polished, cool and controlled as though an air raid was no more unusual than breakfast. 'Good lads!' he said. 'Come along.' His calm was infectious. By the time they all got down to the hall, where Alice and Minnie were waiting, white faced in the low gaslight, the boys had control of themselves again.

'All safe, missus,' Taffy said to Alice.

'Where's Albert?' she said anxiously.

'Keeping watch,' Taffy lied.

The two girls trailed out of the drawing room and stood in the hall, huddled together and wearing an eiderdown swathed about their shoulders like an ungainly shawl. They had both stopped crying but were still sniffling and giving the occasional sob when they couldn't help it. 'Are we going to be killed, Mamma?' Anna asked.

'Not if we're quick,' Taffy assured them. 'We got to get in a safe place. That's all. A dugout, like. That's what we want. In yere, ma-am.' He was shepherding them all into the dining room away from the glass of the conservatory. His authority was unquestioned and comforting.

Another bomb whistled down as they groped into the dark room. The girls flinched, but Taffy didn't give them time to cry. 'Under the table, quick as you can,' he said. 'That's the ticket! You got any cushions ma-am?' He was extraordinarily gentle, as Alice noticed with her instincts even though her mind was quite unable to respond to it in the turmoil of protective fear that the bomb had set juddering.

Within seconds the girls were settled under the table in a nest of cushions and eiderdowns, and Taffy and the two boys had wedged the sofa and the armchairs all around their makeshift shelter. 'Safe as 'ouses, ma-am!' the little Welshman

361

said proudly. 'Nip inside, boys. An' if you two ladies will come by yere in these chairs, we'll have you comfy in a jiffy.'

The raid was still going on. They could hear the pom-poms beating like drums somewhere to the north of them. But somehow, perhaps because they'd been working together so quickly and efficiently, they'd reduced their fear to a mere tickling unease that they could easily hide from one another. Minnie and Alice settled themselves into their chairs at the head of the table, tucking their skirts neatly around their legs to keep in the warmth. Then they remembered their husbands.

'It's about time Albert came downstairs,' Alice said, almost as though she was aggrieved by his absence.

'He's with Jesse, don't forget,' Minnie said, as if that explained it all.

'No 'e ain't!' Percy said, from the cave beneath the table. 'I ain't seen Dad since the first bomb.'

'What d'you mean?' Minnie said quite fiercely, leaning forward to peer at him. 'Where is he then?'

'Don't ask me,' Percy said. 'Off like a shot, first sign a trouble. Could be anywhere.'

Minnie hesitated, torn between a conventional desire to scold her child for maligning her husband, and the realization that as a working man he was probably entitled to say what he liked, particularly if it was true. In the pause that followed they could hear somebody walking slowly down the stairs. The two women looked their question at one another.

But it wasn't Jesse and it wasn't Albert. The footsteps crept to the dining room door. Then there was a silence. Then an apologetic tap. Taffy got up to answer it. As he opened the door a terrible smell pervaded the room. 'Taff!' they heard Bob's voice, speaking low, as though he was ashamed. 'I've shit mesself.'

All four children gasped, the girls shocked, the boys delighted, but even as they breathed out they began to giggle. 'I've shit mesself!' How terrible! How terribly funny! What a scream! Taffy went out into the hall and closed the door behind him.

'Hush!' Alice said trying to be severe. But her mouth was spreading with the urge to laugh. 'I've shit mesself!' Oh dear, oh dear! 'We shouldn't laugh,' she said to Minnie, beginning to giggle.

'I know! I know!' Minnie said, cackling aloud. 'Oh poor man! How dreadful!' It was no good. They couldn't control themselves. The more they tried to be serious, the louder and more hysterical their laughter became. Soon they were rocking in their chairs, the tears streaming down their cheeks, choking and gurgling. 'I've shit mesself!' How terribly funny!

They didn't solve the mystery of Jesse's disappearance until the next morning when Minnie went down to the cellar to refill the coal scuttle. She came giggling back to the kitchen almost immediately, her face alert with malicious delight.

'Just come and see what I've found,' she said. 'Don't make a noise!'

They followed her down to the cellar, and creaked down the wooden steps, making a great deal of noise in their attempts to be quiet. Jesse was sitting in a deckchair beside the smallest heap of coal. He was fast asleep, wrapped in an old brown blanket, with a copy of the *Evening Standard* spread across his knees and a collection of empty beer bottles surrounding his feet. Their over-cautious approach woke him up at once.

'All right! What time is it?' he said aggressively. And as they continued to stare at him, he increased his attack. 'Ain't yer got nothink better ter do than stand around gawping?' he said, and he got up, gathered his blankets around him and pushed past them up the stairs. 'Damn silly fools!' he said.

Afterwards, when they were talking over the night's events, Minnie and Alice felt very ashamed of their dreadful laughter. It really wasn't the right sort of behaviour for either of them. 'Never mind,' Minnie comforted. 'Perhaps it's just as well to see the funny side. This war 'ud get you down something dreadful otherwise.'

But there was nothing funny about any of the events that followed.

On one particularly blustery morning that autumn, Albert was totting up figures with his back to the fire when he heard a commotion of boots in the shop and a strange voice calling his name. It was old Mr Jung's apprentice, flour stained, breathless and bareheaded. His hair was so wet it was stuck to his skull like strips of black leather and under the flour Albert could see that he was shocked pale. 'Mr Jung sez could yer come, please Mr Ploochy,' he said. 'They're smashing 'is shop ter smithereens.'

Albert grabbed his coat and hat and ran from the shop, triggered into immediate activity by the boy's expression. 'Who is it?' he asked as they pounded through the wet streets together. But the boy couldn't tell him.

They reached the bend in the road beside the new Methodist Central Hall, and Albert could see a dark crowd heaving before Jung's shop window. They were making a lot of noise. Even over the rattle of traffic he could hear guttural roars and screams and the clatter of glass breaking. Dark arms rose above the bobbing heads to hurl bricks and brandish sticks. Yobs, Albert thought, and a sizeable gang of them, smashing poor old Jung's window. But what was worse, as he discovered when he reached the Broadway, an even larger crowd of Tooting shoppers had gathered to watch them do it, and it didn't seem to have entered any of their heads to try and stop it. He was furiously angry. 'Out the way!' he roared, shoving a passage through the onlookers, using his shoulders as a wedge to push the more reluctant aside.

It took a few seconds to reach the attackers, and his anger grew all the time, which was just as well because they were an ugly looking mob and they'd whipped themselves into a frenzy of patriotic hatred. 'Hun bastards!' they shrieked. 'Smash the lot of 'em!' as they hacked at the broken window with their bars and kicked loaves and broken glass out onto the pavement. 'Fucking Hun!' To Albert, glaring at them through the haze of rain and fury they looked like bluebottles blowing good meat.

'Stop that!' he yelled. 'Stop it, d'you hear?'

But they jeered. ' 'Ere's another one!' 'Shut yer face!' ' 'Op it or we'll do you an' all.'

Their leader appeared to be a short, evil smelling man in a ripped donkey jacket and a pair of dilapidated moleskins. He was yelling obscene encouragement to his demented followers, and carried the longest iron bar of them all, held horizontally before him like a barrier. 'Come on boys,' he urged. 'What say we sling the old bleeder up? Give 'im a taste of 'is own med'cine.'

'No you bloody won't!' Albert said, leaping up into the window so that his body was between the mob and any further attack. He seized the bar in both hands and wrestled it away from its owner, swinging it into the man's ribs, as hard as he could, so that he fell with a crack of bones and a look of baffled incomprehension. 'What's a matter wiv *you*?' he asked thickly, and Albert realized, with relief, that he was very drunk. He kicked out viciously at the sprawling moleskins. 'Get off out of it!' he said. The man half rose, shook his shaggy head and then shuffled away, still stooping and touching the ground with one hand for support. His gang didn't notice him go. They were still too frenzied with the pleasure and release of destruction.

Albert took up his stand in front of the wreckage of the shop holding the bar before him. 'Who's next?' he roared, jabbing it towards the mob. 'Come on then! Who's next?'

It was a mistake. Three of them came at him at once, and others were moving in behind their hunched shoulders. He caught the first one round the ear with the end of the bar, but the second had him by the throat and then he was engulfed in a flailing mass of clenched fists and steel-tipped boots. He caught a glimpse of the watching crowd, open mouthed and unhelpful, and then Dickie's face swung across his line of vision, scowling furiously, and bodies were heaved away from him. He could hear the thud of punches somewhere and Harry's voice growling 'Clear off. We don't want you round 'ere,' and then the distorted face swearing an inch away from his eyes suddenly changed its expression from hatred to pain, drew back and turned away. Then, suddenly, the fight was over and dark figures were running precipitately down the High Street, because someone was blowing a police whistle.

It was Constable Tullett, grey whiskers bristling and already puffing with the exertion of his approach. 'You all right sir?' he asked Albert.

'Of course,' Albert said. He knew he'd been bruised and he could taste blood running down the back of his throat, but he was still borne up by his anger and the most satisfactory sense of victory.

Constable Tullett took over. 'Get them shutters up directly,' he said to the apprentice, 'and then we'll 'ave a broom ter that lot.' The pavement was littered with ice spears of broken glass and the trampled remains of bread and buns, smeared grey and brown by the slush underfoot.

'Where's Mr Jung?' Albert asked the apprentice.

'Went out the back,' the boy said, swinging the shutters across in front of the shattered window. 'Got through next door. Amy took 'im down ter Solly Isaacs.'

Harry was cheerfully dusting down his trousers, and seemed none the worse for his fight. 'I'm back off ter work then,' he said, as if breaking up a mob were nothing unusual. Dickie had lost his hat and was now dabbing a cut on his bald head. Blood had streaked into his hair and was dripping onto his collar. 'Good job we was follerin',' he said to Albert. 'I knew you was up ter something.'

'Ta,' Albert said, grinning his gratitude. 'Let go an' see how old Jung is.'

He was sitting in Leah's kitchen, wrapped in her knitted shawl and sipping a glass of her lemon tea. He looked stunned and was talking in a disjointed, bewildered way that was upsetting Solly, as Albert could see from the way the pawn-broker was plucking his mottled beard and clearing his throat with that recurrent, growling cough.

'Ai!' Leah said, looking at the bloodstained faces of her two visitors. 'Albert, my dear boy, what you done?'

'Seen 'em all off, Mrs Isaacs,' Albert said proudly. 'It all clear now, Mr Jung.'

But the baker didn't seem to hear. 'I been here thirty years,' he said. 'Thirty years! I can't understand it. I never done a bad thing to no one. Never in thirty years!' He shook his head and a long tear dropped off the end of his nose into his tea.

'Sit down, Albert my dear,' Leah said. 'you too, Mr Chanter. I get you fixed.'

So they sat patiently and sipped tea as she cleaned them up and bandaged them, tut-tutting her disapproval but careful not to hurt them if she could help it. And as she worked, they tried to persuade Mr Jung that his shop was safely shuttered, that no one would attack him again, that Constable Tullett had everything under control, that he could go back home. But he didn't seem able to understand them.

'Why they hate me?' he mourned. 'What have I ever done? All my life I bake them bread. They say we are friends. We talk. We belong to Tooting. Now they say, "Foreigners! Huns!" Other things.' He winced away from the memory of those dreadful obscenities. 'Why they hate me?'

'It the war,' Albert tried to explain, but the old man wasn't listening.

'Man is born for trouble,' Leah said. 'Don't I always tell you. Us they hate because we are Jews. You they hate because you are German. It's the way of the world. Full of hate. Always they got to hate. Don't I know it!'

But it didn't comfort Mr Jung. 'Why they hate me?' he wailed. 'It don't make sense!'

'You. Me. It don't matter,' Leah said, pinning Dickie's bandage into position. 'You get in the way of hate, you get hurt. Sense you want, sense you don't get.'

The children were impressed by Albert's injuries, when he got home, and Alice made him sit by the fire and showed a proper wifely concern, but she listened to his tale with a calm that was so detached it was almost insulting.

'Poor old Jung,' he said, trying to rouse her sympathy. 'He just can't understand it. To be set on like that. For no reason at all.'

'He *is* a German,' she said coolly. 'Don't forget that.'

'He is Mr Jung,' he said, angered by her response. Good God, she was behaving just like those heartless people watching in the crowd. 'We 'ave known 'im for years. 'E is good man.'

'If your son had been killed by the Germans,' Alice said, 'you would understand. Em and Harry will understand. Now, they'll understand. Poor things! They're the ones I'm sorry for.'

Em and Harry? What was she talking about?

'Em had the telegram this afternoon,' she said flatly. 'Johnnie died last Tuesday.'

For a second, after all the emotion and action of the afternoon, he couldn't take it in. It must be a mistake. She must have got it wrong. But she was clearing the tea things and the heaviness of her movements betrayed her sorrow.

'Oh my God!' he said. 'Poor Harry. 'E was with me at the fight. When did 'e know?'

'She was waiting for him to come home from work,' Alice said. 'Her sister's with her. I've sent a letter. Georgie ran round with it.'

Even after three years of carnage and more war dead from

Tooting than anybody wanted to count, this death had the power to stun them all. Why Johnnie? Gentle, hardworking Johnnie, who'd never done a bad thing in his short life. Albert found he was echoing Mr Jung. It didn't make sense.

It made even less sense when the letter arrived from his commanding officer. For Johnnie had died of the cold and the rain and the appalling conditions in the trenches. He had caught bronchitis, the officer wrote, which had rapidly become double pneumonia. In his weakened state he had not been able to survive the crisis of the disease. They were all very sorry to lose such a good soldier. He had died on active service, defending his country. They offered their deepest sympathy to his parents.

The neighbours offered their sympathy in practical ways, by doing the shopping or making little nourishing soups and stews, for they knew only too well that in grief you need gentleness and care. But Em was inconsolable and wept until there were no tears left to shed. Harry went out to work as usual, quietly and saying nothing, stooped and dispirited and grey.

And the drawn blinds of their house were like the eyes of the dead. Albert couldn't bear to look at them.

Chapter 29

'I don't reckon this war's ever gonna end,' Queenie said sadly
as she and Albert strolled back to their flat late one afternoon.
It was early August but it already felt like autumn, the grass
coated with grey dust, the chestnuts casting yellow leaves, the
roses small and tattered, their petals burnt brown by an
unseasonable wind. 'Three years it's been going on now, d'you
realize that? Next month we'll be in ter the fourth year.'

It was a depressing thought in a depressing month. The war
was affecting everybody now. More and more families were in
mourning and food was in parlous short supply. Sugar was
rarely seen, tea was more dust than leaf and flour was so
adulterated that the National loaf, far from living up to its
grandiose title, was grey, gritty and unappetizing. In fact,
there'd only been one moment since the start of the year that
had been even mildly entertaining, and that was when the
War Office finally caught up with Jesse Holdsworthy and sent
him off to France. It had amused them all to see how wickedly
delighted Minnie had been.

'Victory next year perhaps,' Albert said, trying to cheer
them both up.

But she was very low. ' 'Bout as much chance a' that,' she
said, 'as you and me getting ter the altar. And don't start all
on about how you'll marry me after the war. I don't believe a
word of it. An' anyway we shall both be a hundred an' ninety
be then. A bit past it!'

This subdued, miserable mood was very hard for Albert to
contend with. And of course, she was right. He ought to marry
her. 'We go home, an' change, an' go to Luigi's and 'ave the
best meal in the place. Whatcha say?'

'It'll be cagmag,' she said. 'Not worth the effort.'

They went anyway. And she was right. Nevertheless, despite
a poor meal and fatigue that was etching mauve shadows
under her green eyes, she loved him most tenderly that night.
Then, as they lay together in the darkness, she told him, as she
so often did these days, about all the painful treatments her
poor wounded soldiers were having to endure. 'Ned's 'ad a

rotten setback, poor devil,' she said. 'Just when 'e thought 'e was coming along so well an' all. One of 'is lungs collapsed, so they said. 'E was in chronic pain, poor beggar. You could see. Never said a word though. I never seen a man as brave as 'im. Never in all me life.'

I must get her away from all this, Albert thought, as her sad voice rambled on beside him. It isn't doing her any good. And he made up his mind that he would make another attempt to speak to Alice. The very next morning.

But speaking to Alice was easier intended than achieved. She always seemed to have so many other things demanding her attention.

On this particular morning, Georgie was going out for the day with two of his friends, so she was packing sandwiches for them all and giving him careful instructions about the route they were to take. Anna and Renee had brought their dolls to the table and were in the middle of an involved game which apparently required them to speak to one another in high pitched voices. The noise and the distraction of it all soon drove Albert to roaring, which was a bad way to start. But at last they were all dispersed and he and Alice had the kitchen to themselves. He took a deep breath and plunged in to what he had to say. 'We 'ave something serious to consider, Alice,' he said.

The peculiar tone of his voice alerted Alice's instincts at once. She decided to deflect him. 'And not before time,' she agreed, clearing the dirty dishes. 'I've got all the prospectuses. They're in the first drawer.'

Prospectuses? 'Sit down!' he said, more brusquely than he intended, because she'd thrown him. 'We can't discuss this standing up.'

She went on clearing the table. 'I favour the Streatham school myself,' she said. 'It's near enough for her to come home in the dinner hour, and Em says they're very well behaved. It's the second book in the bundle, you'll find.'

Anna's new school, he thought irritably. She'd been nagging him to make a decision about it for weeks. He'd better attend to it, now he'd started. He could move on to the other topic afterwards.

So the Streatham school was decided upon, and the table cloth brushed, and Alice went off into the scullery to wash up. He trailed after her, feeling foolish to be making a second attempt. 'We 'ave another matter . . .' he said, glowering in the doorway of the little green room.

She misunderstood that opening too. 'You should let them have the flat,' she told him firmly. 'I've said that all along. Tilley would love it, so near to all the shops, and just across the road from the cinema. Nice and handy for Dickie. It's only going to waste, lying empty like that.'

Dickie and Tilley had been hunting for a flat in Tooting for more than two months now. He'd forgotten all about it. Must he deal with this too, before he was to be allowed to speak?

'Dickie's coming in to see you today,' Alice said, reaching for a drying-up cloth. 'Tilley was telling me only yesterday. I should offer it to them, if I were you.'

Albert didn't want to let the flat to anyone. He'd kept it empty for a very long time, just in case Queenie ever decided she would like to live in Tooting. Now the very idea seemed ludicrous. He might as well let it go. 'I will arrange it,' he promised, and took his third preparatory breath of the morning.

It was too late. Before he could say a word, the door bell was ringing as though the house were on fire, and the daily had arrived. 'It like living in Piccadilly Circus!' he grumbled. 'Never a minute's peace!' And he went to work, banging the door behind him.

During the next week he made several attempts to find the right moment to open his serious conversation with Alice again, but none presented themselves, and in the end he relinquished the effort, with a mixture of shame and relief. If it wasn't possible, he couldn't do it. He comforted himself that at least he'd settled the matter of Anna's schooling and Dickie's accommodation. He would find an opportunity when Anna was settled, and they hadn't got quite so much to attend to.

Dickie was delighted to be offered the flat, just as Alice had predicted. The huge establishment he'd been running in Longbeach Road was far too expensive, and he was glad to be coming back to Tooting.

'Be like old times,' Harry said. 'The three of us tergether again. When yer moving?'

They arrived six days later, on a fine day and in total disorder. Tilley had wanted to hire Carter Paterson's, but the three friends were determined to handle the move themselves. It was a bit of unlooked-for excitement, and Albert enjoyed it very much.

Harry was detailed to hire the van. 'Don't 'ave ter be a big 'un,' Dickie said. 'We only got a few bits and bobs.' Unfortunately Harry took him at his word and arrived with a little cart, drawn by a skewbald pony and driven by an undersized boy who had so many teeth protruding from his upper jaw that he couldn't close his mouth, and was consequently forced to face the world with a perpetual and hideously jagged grin. Dickie christened him the Croc, immediately, but Tilley said he looked like an imbecile, and was furious when she saw the size of his cart.

' 'Oo's the comedian ordered that?' she said. 'You surely don't imagine we can get all our stuff on a thing like that?'

'Two trips,' Dickie suggested hopefully, but his remark merely triggered the first row of the day.

'Two trips, my eye!' she said. 'You ain't got the sense you was born with, you lot. We shall be at it all day!'

Which they were.

Their arrival at the shop quickly attracted a crowd, which was just as well because the dresser had to be manhandled across the counter and it required the efforts of at least six men to manoeuvre it up the narrow staircase and round the tight bend at the top of the flight. They all enjoyed it very much, even though Dog got trodden on and had to retire squealing, and when they all finally trooped downstairs again they found they'd removed several strips of wallpaper and a considerable quantity of plaster. Nevertheless congratulatory drinks were ordered and consumed, and then the three removal men set off for the second phrase of their adventure.

They returned with the bed, several chairs and Tilley, sitting bolt upright beside the Croc, stony faced with disapproval and fatigue. The crowd greeted the bed with rapture, for if the dresser had been difficult, the bed was impossible. It was passed over the counter with comparative ease, but there was no way that any of them could squeeze it through the door and into the well of the stairs without demolishing part of the wall of the shop. Dickie suggested that they should put it up for auction, and Tilley lost her temper with him for the second time that day. The Croc was alarmed by the passion of the ensuing row, and begged to be allowed across the road to the Mitre to quench his thirst. Then the impossible bed was eased back into the street again, and the crowd gathered happily around it, discussing ways and means with a great deal of noise and enthusiasm but to little purpose. Harry scratched his head so thoroughly that every hair upon it was soon standing on end, and Dickie giggled, and Dog sat at Albert's feet with his head cocked to one side and his great pink tongue lolling out of his mouth, listening to every word.

They were no nearer a solution when Em, Minnie and Alice arrived bearing brooms and baskets.

'Great boobies!' Em said at once. 'If it won't go up the stairs, it'll 'ave ter go through the winder. Got any rope?'

The crowd redoubled almost immediately and a passing tram paused at the points a great deal longer than was necessary so that all the passengers could get a good view of what was going on. As the bed was slowly hoisted up the front of the building, a fat pigeon landed on it with a great clatter of wings and to the delight of the crowd. Tilley did her best to dislodge it by whacking the underside of the bed with a broom as it passed the living room window, but the bird was unperturbed and rode all movement with rolling unconcern, like a sailor keeping his balance in a difficult sea. The crowd was on the pigeon's side, to a man. 'Leave 'im alone, ma!' they shouted to Tilley. 'Poor little beggar! What's 'e ever done ter you?' and when the bed and its passenger finally arrived alongside the bedroom window, they broke into a cheer. The pigeon rose heavily into the air and flew off to the Mitre, crapping on its supporters as it went.

Then the fun really started, for having expended all that effort to get the bed to the window, the three removal men discovered that it was too big to go through. There was nothing for it but to remove both windows, which gave the crowd immense pleasure, especially when Dickie snapped one of the sash-cords in two and Harry got an arm caught underneath the rapidly descending frame. But at last the windows were out, and standing incongruously in the fireplace, and the bed could be eased diagonally through the gap, and the crowd, after one final cheer, could disperse to their more mundane affairs.

When Harry and Albert got down to the pavement again, they had a nasty shock. The horse and cart were gone.

'Oh my Gawd!' Harry said, glancing up at the bedroom. 'That'll tear it! She'll go barmy! What we gonna do now?'

'Find that damned boy, for a start,' Albert said firmly.

They dodged through the traffic to the Mitre to look for the Croc, and found him almost at once, dipping his fangs into his fourth pint of milk stout. He was slurred and affable with drink, and wasn't the least bit concerned at the loss of his horse and cart. 'How should I know, guv?' he said cheerily, when Albert asked him where they were. ' 'Avin' a rest, I 'spect. Don't wanna kill the 'orse.'

Albert lifted him from his seat by the ear, and shook him to his feet. 'I don't wanna kill the 'orse,' he said furiously, 'but I just might kill you. Go and find it! Double quick! You understand?'

'Ow!' the urchin howled. 'Give over. I ain't done nothink. You're tearing me lug off!'

Fortunately he was saved from further injury by the timely arrival of two bare-foot boys, eager for reward, with the news that the horse and cart were 'in the loony bin.'

'Which is where we'll all be, if this goes on,' Dickie grumbled as they trailed up Church Lane to retrieve their wandering transport. 'I never known such a day.'

The skewbald was greedily cropping the lawn in front of the asylum and had no intention of abandoning such a feast without a struggle. As soon as he saw the Croc staggering towards him, he kicked up his heels and galloped off to the rose garden, with the cart rocking and tipping behind him, and the three friends in heated pursuit. Astonished faces watched from every window, and presently two male nurses came running down the front steps to join in the chase. By the time the pony was under control again he was in a muck sweat and flecked with foam, two rose bushes had been knocked sideways, and the three friends were exhausted. The Croc was nowhere to be seen. He'd settled himself comfortably against the trunk of the nearest tree and was now deep in a drunken slumber, his mouth wide open and his fangs yellow in the afternoon sun. It took one bucket of water to rouse him and two more to satisfy the wrath of all three of his employers.

It was supper time when they finally returned to the shop with their very last load, and paid off the repentant Croc, after suitable reductions. The kitchen had been scrubbed clean, and the stove lit, but the flat was deserted.

Alice had left a note on the kitchen table. 'We have gone home to supper,' it said. 'Tilley will be all the better for a meal and some time away.' 'Very true,' Dickie agreed. 'You might like to have something here,' the note went on, tactfully. 'There are three portions of pie and mash in the stove. The beer is in a bucket under the sink.'

'You got a pearl in your Alice,' Dickie said appreciatively, as he removed the three hot plates from the stove. 'She knows how ter treat a man proper, an' no mistake. A pearl.'

Chapter 30

September arrived, and Anna was prised into her school uniform and walked across the damp fields of Furzedown to the school she was determined not to like. On her second morning she came down to breakfast pale and miserable, to explain that she had a terrible headache and felt far too ill to go to school. Her father was heartless. 'You will feel better once you are there,' he said firmly. 'Get her hat, Alice.' On the third morning she felt sick, and on the fourth she had a nose bleed, but he remained implacable no matter how much she was suffering. By Friday she went to school without a word. Albert, watching her go, congratulated himself on the way he'd handled his difficult daughter.

'There you are,' he said to Alice. 'All she need is a firm hand.' Soon he would be able to tell them all about his decision.

At midday Anna came home flushed with a fever and obviously ill. Alice put her to bed at once and called the doctor. Then she and Minnie fretted away the afternoon in an anxiety of impatience, while the child tossed and slept and burned red. It was late in the afternoon before Dr Fermanagh reached them and by then they both knew that she was seriously ill. He took her temperature, examined her throat and pushed up the sleeves of her nightgown to look at her wrists, 'Scarlet fever,' he said calmly. 'She must go to the Fever Hospital as soon as possible. I'll see if I can arrange it tonight. Keep her in bed until the ambulance arrives.'

Anna began to cry as soon as the doctor's grey back disappeared behind her bedroom door. She wept with complete abandon and in an extremity of fever and terror. 'Please don't send me to hospital,' she begged her mother. 'Please! Please! I shall die in hospital! I know I shall! Please! Please! Please!'

'Hush, my lamb,' Alice said, torn with distress. 'Don't cry like that. You'll make yourself worse. If the doctor says you've got to go to hospital, I'm sure it's for the best.'

But that only made the child cry louder. 'I shall die!' she

wailed. 'Please don't send me! Please! Please!' Her entreaty was so shrill it sounded like a scream.

'She's getting hysterical,' Alice said to Minnie. 'We can't let her go on like this.'

'Send for Albert,' Minnie advised in a whisper. 'He'll know what to do.'

Albert was annoyed when Georgie came puffing into the shop with the news. He'd intended to go straight to the Duchess that evening and have supper with Queenie. And now this! He wrote a quick note to Queenie explaining, and rushed home.

The ambulance had already arrived and was standing darkly at the kerb, as foreboding as a hearse. The sight of it made Albert shudder as he struggled to fit a slippery key into the damp lock. Anna was still screaming, the noise of her distress echoing down the stairwell. He leapt up the stairs, two at a time, to put a stop to it.

The bedroom was very hot and the air in it was already sickly with the cloying smell of fever. Alice and Dr Fermanagh stood beside the bed in pale and earnest conversation, and Anna, her face brick red and blotchy, was flinging herself from side to side on a pillow streaked with tears and sweat. She'd cried for such a long time that now her sobs were painful to her, each one pattering through her throat in a series of juddering gulps.

This was dreadful, Albert thought. He must stop it at once. Despite the doctor's attempt at intervention, he strode to the bed and took the child's damp head between his hands. 'You are not going to hospital,' he said. 'You are staying here. Can you hear me, Anna? You are staying here.'

Anna opened bloodshot eyes and looked at him briefly before closing them again. Then she said, 'Oh!' on a long-drawn-out sigh of relief, and although her sobs took a considerable time to diminish, from that moment on she was calm.

Dr Fermanagh looked annoyed for a second, but then, catching the force of the determination on Albert's face, he became brisk and businesslike. 'Very well,' he said. 'Mrs Ploochy, she must be kept isolated in this room for the next six weeks, you understand. If you nurse her, you must remain with her at all times and have no contact with any other

377

members of the household. That is most important. The door must be hung at all times with a sheet steeped in disinfectant. And you, Mr Ploochy, should stay out of the room until your daughter is fully recovered. Now I would advise an immediate bath and a complete change of clothing. You must all do everything you can to avoid spreading the infection. There are other children in the house. We are dealing with a very dangerous illness, you understand. No more wounded of course. They must go elsewhere.'

Alice listened carefully and patiently to all his instructions. Now that the decision had been made she looked haggard with exhaustion. Anna was asleep.

By the time he finally went to work the next morning, Albert's house had been transformed into a hospital and smelt quite foully of disinfectant and washing on the boil. Percy had been sent to St Benedict's to explain that no more wounded soldiers could be accommodated for the time being. And Mrs Kelly had made her first reassuring visit.

A letter from Queenie arrived at the shop in the mid-afternoon post. He'd almost forgotten writing to her, so much had happened since. He couldn't even remember what he'd written. That Anna was ill, wasn't it? That was all he'd known then. Her answer was curt and cross. 'She would be,' she wrote. 'I am at the Duchess Tuesday. If you care.'

Her bad temper crushed him, and then angered him. She wrote as though it was all his fault that the child was ill. There were times, he thought angrily, when she was positively unfeeling. He crumpled the letter and flung it on the fire, making up his mind that he'd keep her waiting for once, it wasn't good for her to think she had him at her beck and call.

So he delayed his next visit, even though his house was a tense and miserable place to stay in. But after nine days of oppressive gloom and uncomfortable celibacy he gave in and went to Clapham bearing two pounds of granulated sugar as a peace offering.

He met his beautiful Queenie at the stage door of the Duchess, and just the sight of her made him feel happy and normal again. Her eyes shone him loving welcome, before she could remember to dim them, but she made him pay for his absence just the same.

'Well look 'oo's turned up!' she said sarcastically. 'Thought you'd gone fer a soldier.'

He ignored the barb, because he was so happy to be near her again. 'Hello, my lovely darling,' he said, kissing her.

'Never mind kissin',' she said, kissing him back. 'You ain't been near me fer nine whole days, I hope you realize.'

He ignored that too. 'If I could tell you where to find a packet of sugar,' he said, 'would you make me a cup of tea to put it in?'

'You never 'ave, 'ave yer?' she said, grinning.

'Left hand pocket,' he told her happily, pleased to think how sensible and acceptable his choice of gift had been.

Luigi did them proud that night. They returned to the flat arm in arm and well fed. The stove was lit and tea made almost ceremonially. Then the precious packet of sugar was opened and enjoyed.

'Sweet tea!' Queenie said, with languorous appreciation. 'Nothing like sweet tea. How d'yer get it, Ploo?'

'Swapped it fer a bottle a gin,' Albert said, enjoying the sight of her pleasure.

'Ain't 'alf missed yer,' she said, smiling at him over the sweetened teacup. 'You might a' sent a letter.'

'Anna's been very ill,' he said, but now he felt ashamed at the petty way he'd treated her.

'It's always somethink with that family a' yours,' she said, and to his alarm she began to scowl again. He leant across their narrow kitchen table and kissed her just as he'd done on their very first night together 'My lovely . . . lovely . . . Queenie,' he said between kisses. 'I love you so much.'

'Daft old 'apporth,' she said, affectionately, kissing him back. Then desire rose in them both strongly and simultaneously and any remaining awkwardness was rushed away by their easy familiar pleasure.

Their lovemaking that night was so prolonged and so delightful that it exhausted them beyond speech. As sleep warmed her away Queenie managed to say 'I got sommink ter tell yer,' but she didn't have the energy to continue.

'In the morning,' he murmured dreamily, breathing in the

scent of her lovely satisfied flesh. Then he slipped into his first untroubled sleep for more than a fortnight.

When he woke next morning she was still sleeping peacefully beside him, her red hair bold against the white pillows and one bare arm pale as pearl among the massed colours of the patchwork quilt. He loved her too much to disturb her. It was happiness enough just to stroke that hair, and brush a gentle kiss across her cheek. He wrote her a note, 'see you tonight my darling,' surrounded it with a border of loving crosses, and left it for her propped against the clock in the kitchen.

Dr Fermanagh was pleased with Anna's progress. She was obviously better. He prescribed a light diet and said he wouldn't call again for a day or two unless they sent for him. At last, Albert thought, their lives were beginning to improve.

That night, after work, he washed with special care, determined to remove all the smells of the shop and the stink of that over-powering disinfectant. Then newly shaved and dressed in his best he went downstairs for his hat and coat.

Minnie was waiting for him in the hall, her little round face so squashed with worry that her eyes looked unnaturally small and her lips didn't seem to be contained within their contours.

'What's the matter?' he said, catching her anxiety at once.

'Oh dear, Mr P.,' Minnie said. 'I'm sure I don't mean to be a nuisance but I'm at me wit's end.'

He led her into the dining room where the fire was still giving off a pleasant heat and sat her at the table. 'You're not a nuisance,' he said. 'Never think that. Now just tell me what it's all about.'

'It's my little Renee,' she said. 'It's not the scarlet. I do know that. I've been watching for the rash. Every day. But she's not at all well.' The corners of her mouth were trembling and her eyes filling with tears.

'What did the doctor say?'

'He didn't see her,' she said, apologetically.

'Good God!' Albert said, surprised and angered. 'Why ever not? He was in the 'ouse this afternoon.'

'I didn't like to . . .' she faltered. 'I mean . . . With Jesse away an' all. It's not . . .'

She couldn't afford it, Albert thought, and she didn't like to ask him for help. 'He shall see her tomorrow,' he promised. 'I will leave him a note on my way out. And don't you go worrying about the bill. I'll deal with that.'

'It's ever so good of you,' she said, tears spilling over. But she didn't seem relieved, and she remained where she was, dithering as though there was something else she wanted to say.

He was beginning to feel impatient, because she was keeping him from Queenie, but he couldn't ignore her distress. 'What is it?' he asked, being gentle with effort.

'Could you jest come an' look at her, Mr P.,' she begged. 'I'd be easier in me mind if you could just come an' look at her. You'd know if she was really bad, wouldn't you?'

Resigned to delay, he followed her up the stairs to the back bedroom that had now become 'the soldiers' room'. What he saw and heard there put all thought of Queenie right out of his mind and propelled him into the frantic activity of a panic he was only just able to control.

For Renee was obviously terribly ill, far, far worse than her recovering cousin had ever been. She lay in her little white bed, her back arched like Georgie's during a fit, her head thrown back, blue lips parted, eyes half open but unseeing. She was fighting for breath and the noise of air rattling and grinding in her throat was so terrifying that it froze them both where they stood.

Then Minnie managed speech, 'Oh my dear, good God,' and sound released Albert into activity. He lifted the child quickly and forced open her mouth with his thumb and two fingers. The air that rose from her throat was so putrid that it made him gag, but he pressed her mouth open as far as he could, despite her groans. If there was something blocking her windpipe, the sooner he got it out the better. It looked as though the back of her throat was covered in some sort of membrane, like thick grey cobwebs. He put his forefingers down into her mouth and tugged at it. It felt slimy under his fingers and was tougher than it looked. He had to pull quite violently before he could dislodge it, and pulling made the child choke and gurgle so alarmingly that he was frightened by the horror of what he'd started. Then suddenly the membrane tore and came away in his fingers, trailing out of her mouth in a long grey strand, as air hissed down through the gap he'd made and the child retched and panted. He threw the foul stuff into the fire, sick with relief and chill with fear.

Minnie was crouching beside the bed, easing a clean towel under her daughter's mouth before she was sick.

'We must get her to the hospital, Minnie,' he said. 'Straight away. You know that, don't you? Make a hot water bottle while I go and get a cab. I'll be back directly.'

He was as good as his word, finding a cab so quickly he even surprised himself. When he got back, Renee was awake and trying to talk, even though the air was still rattling in her throat. She made no fuss when they wrapped her in an eiderdown with the hot water bottle beside her and Albert picked her up to carry her down to the cab.

The cabbie, on the other hand, was far less meek. 'Nah look 'ere Mr Ploochy,' he protested. 'You never said nothink about no kid. That's infectious, that is. Not a proper fare. I'll 'ave to 'ave the cab fumigated after, like as not. I can't take 'er. You'll 'ave ter get someone else.'

'Twice the fare,' Albert said. 'Come on, Horrie, the kid's ill.'

'Can't be done,' Horrie said. 'What if I give it ter someone else?'

'She got something stuck in her throat,' Albert lied. 'That's all. Four time the fare. How about that?'

Four times the fare was too great a temptation. 'It ain't right,' Horrie said, 'but seein' as it's you.' He drove them to the hospital at such a speed that the car trembled and juddered as though it was going to fall apart.

From the moment he'd entered the sick room, Albert had acted so swiftly and events had crowded in upon him so urgently that he hadn't had time to doubt or even think. Now as the nurses took over smoothly and without panic it was easy to let himself feel with them that even a serious illness was nothing to be alarmed about. The two who arrived wheeling a little white bed were calm and smiling and smelled reassuringly of soap and starch. They tucked Renee neatly under a red blanket and wheeled her off to the ward, and then the receptionist took over, equally smoothly, to write what she call their 'particulars' into her register. 'Thank you, Mrs Holdsworthy,' she said when the job was done. 'Now if you and Mr Ploochy would like to wait for just a while, I'm sure there will be some news for you.'

They waited for nearly an hour, suspended in a limbo of non-activity. Now their terrible anxiety returned to churn their insides and interfere with their breathing. They were both very cold and waiting made them colder, but they were afraid to leave the room, even to find a toilet, just in case they were called for. Soon they knew every grain of every chair by heart. There was nothing more to see on the green walls or the blank windows and they didn't dare to look too closely at each other. From time to time Minnie said she hoped everything was all right and Albert reassured her that it was bound to be, but apart from that no conversation was possible under the increasing weight of their fear. They sat side by side on their awkward chairs listening to the clock woodenly beating their lives away. There was nothing else to do.

But at long, cold last, one of the nice starched nurses came swishing back to them with the hot water bottle and some news. Renee was in Ward seven and settled for the night. They'd made a little hole in her throat to help her to breathe and she was quite comfortable, all things considered.

Minnie was tearful with gratitude. 'Could I see her please, miss?' she asked humbly.

'Oh no!' the nurse said. She sounded shocked and rather surprised. 'We don't allow visitors in Ward seven. Because of the infection, you see. It's an isolation ward.'

'Oh!' Minnie said, disappointed but still meek. 'Oh I see.' She hesitated, looking at the nurse's kindly face. Then at last she asked the question she'd been dreading ever since the child first took ill, five long days ago. 'What's the matter with her, miss?'

'She has diphtheria,' the nurse said gently. 'Didn't you know?'

Diphtheria. The word sunk into their minds like a death knell.

The nurse patted Minnie on the shoulder. 'You can come

down for news of her first thing in the morning,' she said. 'She's in good hands.'

Although her face was strained by unshed tears, Minnie held on to her self control until they were safely home. Then she wept aloud with terror and despair. There was nothing Albert could do or say to comfort her, but fortunately her sobs woke Alice who opened the door of her isolation ward and called down to them. 'What's the matter, Minnie dear? Come up and tell me for pity's sake!' Minnie put her handkerchief in her pocket and fled upstairs.

Albert stayed tactfully out of the way while the two women talked to one another through the barrier of disinfectant. Their voices murmured on for a very long time, but he thought it better to let Minnie's anguish run its course and not interfere. Eventually he heard her climbing the stairs to her bedroom, and at last considered it safe to get to bed himself. Then and only then he remembered Queenie.

The days that followed were harrowed with anxiety and taut with necessary irritating chores. On Dr Fermanagh's advice, Georgie was moved from the threat of their second terrible infection, and sent to stay with the aunts. Nat had bronchitis, as he often had since he'd been back working in the shop, so there was more work for Albert. Coal was in short supply and the larder was more depleted than it had been for months. There was plenty to keep them occupied, but however much they busied themselves their minds returned obsessively to the ward they weren't allowed to visit and the uncomplaining child who was suffering there so undeservedly.

Albert wrote a long explanatory letter to Queenie, and this time she wrote back with sympathy. 'Poor little blighter,' she said. 'I wouldn't wish that on my worse enemy. 'Course you got to stay home for a while. See you Wednesday.'

Poor Minnie haunted the hospital, visiting night and morning. For the first few days the news was always the same, a non-committal 'as well as can be expected', but on Wednesday morning she returned breathless with hope. Renee was being moved to a side ward, and she was to be allowed to go and see her at six o'clock that evening. She was so happy that Albert didn't have the heart to disillusion her, even though he knew just a little too well that removal to a side ward was usually a very bad sign indeed. He wrote yet another excuse to Queenie and then escorted his poor encouraged cousin to the ward.

Renee was lying quietly in a white cot in a small room full of the flowers they'd sent her. She was very pale and there were black shadows under her eyes, but apart from that and the bandage round her neck, she looked remarkably normal. She was pathetically pleased to see her mother and the two of them were soon head to head in whispered talk, but Albert noticed that she lay very still, and although she patted her mother's face with her left hand, she didn't move the right one at all. He went back to the entrance of the ward to see if he could find someone who would tell him the truth about her condition.

The Sister brisked him into her office at once, and when she'd established that he was a close relation and could be trusted with the truth, she told him what he asked to know. 'The poison has entered her blood stream, I'm afraid,' she said. 'We gave her the serum, of course, but it was too late.'

She's going to die, Albert thought, absorbing the nightmare information with the appalled calm of shock. But he couldn't say the words. 'She won't get better will she?' he said. His face felt frozen.

'No,' the Sister said gently. 'She will get worse, I'm sorry to say.'

'What will happen?' he asked. 'Please tell me. I would rather know.'

'The poison will paralyse her,' the Sister said. 'Her legs are paralysed already. You probably noticed. It will spread, gradually of course, but it *will* spread. Until it reaches the heart and lungs. We can't stop it.' She looked at him with pity. 'I'm sorry, Mr Ploochy.'

'Poor little thing!' he mourned. 'Poor little thing!'

'It's a terrible disease,' the Sister agreed. 'Do you think her mother should be told?'

'Not yet,' Albert said. 'Let them be happy with one another for as long as they can. I will write to her father. He ought to know.'

They were happy for nearly a fortnight. But at last even Minnie couldn't ignore the fact that her gentle daughter was fading, no longer able to eat, visibly losing flesh and scarcely moving at all.

'How do you think she is?' she asked Albert, as they walked down to the hospital on one particularly cold evening.

It was such an abrupt question that for a moment he didn't know how to reply. 'About the same,' he tried, wondering whether he ought to comfort or admit.

'No,' she said quietly. 'She's worse. A lot worse.' She thought for a little, plodding along beside him through the deepening shadows. 'She's going, isn't she?' She seemed quite calm about it, even though she didn't look at him.

'Yes,' he said, aching with pity for her.

'Yes,' she echoed sadly. 'I've known it all along, really. Ever since that first night. When we brought her down in the cab.' They walked in silence until they reached the Trafalgar Arms and the corner of the Grove? Then she put her hand in the crook of his arm. 'You've been very good to me,' she said. 'Coming here night after night like this. You're a good man, Albert.'

Her courage was almost too painful to bear. And it embarrassed him to be considered 'good'. After all, what else could he have done? He could hardly have left her to cope with all this on her own. Nevertheless, as they walked quietly down towards the dark lodge gates and the harrowing death lingering beyond it, he was thinking of Queenie and wishing he could make her understand his lack of choice.

He wrote to her later that evening, very, very carefully, trying to explain. 'Jesse will be home on compassionate leave in a few days. Then I will come and see you. I promise. I do care what happens to you.'

But Jesse's return made everything worse. He came home with a kit bag full of dirty clothes, an insatiable appetite and no sympathy whatever for the prolonged dying of his daughter, or the anguish of his wife. He spent his first afternoon at home complaining about the war, in language worse than any they'd ever heard him use. He seemed to be getting some perverse pleasure out of shocking Minnie. Albert was quite glad that Alice was still in quarantine and out of earshot. But at least, he thought happily, now he would be able to see Queenie again.

When the Holdsworthys left for the hospital that evening

he watched them go with relief and satisfaction. They were short-lived emotions, for although they'd set off together, Minnie came back on her own. Jesse had stopped off at the Trafalgar Arms 'for a quick one' and as far as she knew he was still there. She was cold with anger against him.

'Nothing compassionate about this leave,' she told Alice sourly through the sheet-hung door. 'It's just an excuse for a good booze-up, that's all.'

'Never mind,' Alice comforted. 'I shall be out of here in a week's time and then I'll come with you. And in the meantime I know Albert won't mind.'

Albert did mind, of course, but he was caught in a situation he couldn't control, and so he had to agree. He wrote to Queenie again trying to explain but by now even he was weary of excuses, and none of his seemed feasible, let alone true.

She didn't answer his letter and he was glad of the respite, for he knew her answer would have been angry, and her anger was almost impossible to deal with at a distance.

So the long vigil continued, and he and Minnie went down to the hospital every evening to do what little they could. Gradually Renee was losing the use of all her muscles, and now even turning her to prevent bed sores caused her such distress that it was painful to witness. She followed her mother's every movement with eyes grown enormous in a face stripped of all the plump pretty flesh of her childhood. Minnie stayed beside her as long as she possibly could, talking, soothing and stroking her hair, as death advanced upon her by inches.

But at least the six weeks of Anna's illness were over, and Dr Fermanagh pronounced her cured and she and Alice were allowed out of their isolation. Albert was too weary to feel relieved, but he recognized that now, at last, he was free to go to Clapham and see Queenie and start putting everything right between them.

As he walked to the shop that morning through the October streets, the sun was warm on his forehead and the fallen leaves blew in a scurry of brown and gold at his feet. He felt almost happy again.

There was a telegram waiting for him on the counter. It was from Queenie, and even in his present state of exhaustion, it roused a most unpleasant alarm.

'Be at flat before noon today,' she commanded. 'Too late after.'

'Mind the shop,' he said to Percy, and rushed off at once to see what was the matter.

Chapter 31

Someone had left a horse and cart in the road immediately in front of the flat. A rag and bone man, Albert explained to himself, pushing a more uncomfortable thought aside. The cart was rough and scruffy. There wasn't a touch of paint on it anywhere and the wheels were coated with grime. As it was empty except for a cardboard box and a carpet bag, the horse had dragged it onto the pavement so that he could stretch his shaggy head over the low privet hedge and crop the grass in the front garden. Mr Punch won't like that, Albert thought, pleased that the animal's boldness would aggravate his peppery landlord.

Sure enough, even before he reached the front gate, he could hear Mr Punch whining, ' 'Oo left it unattended then, I should like ter know. I shall 'ave sommink ter say if it's ate my dahlias!'

The front door was open and the kitchen was empty and unnaturally clean and clear, the table bare and newly scrubbed, all the crockery out of sight, even the grate cleared and more or less washed. The place smelled damp and dusty, as if it had been uninhabited for quite a long time. The smell and the sense of desertion alerted Albert unpleasantly, but he tried to take comfort from the sound of voices in the bedroom. What was she doing? Surely she hadn't found another flat without telling him. Perhaps she'd had a row with Mr Punch. He rushed into the bedroom, heart pounding with anxiety.

At first sight it seemed to be full of men. Two of them were dismantling the bed, and a third was carefully rolling up the mattress. The bedding lay in a heap on the dressing table, roughly tied together with string and old rope. Queenie was on her knees at the fireplace. She had a bucket full of soapy water beside her and she was flicking a grey cloth over the bars of the grate. They shone blackly for a few seconds after their brief wash, but then they dried to a smeared film that actually made them look dirtier than they usually did when they were covered in ash. Even in the middle of all the confusion, Albert was warmed to affection by her inadequate attempt at housekeeping. He thought fleetingly of Alice and her determined and professional use of the black lead box, and Queenie's busy ineffectual hands seemed precious to him by comparison. Whatever was she doing, the dear silly girl?

The noise of his entry made her turn her head. She didn't smile, and what was worse, she didn't seem to want to look at him. What she gave him was deliberately no more than a glance, flicked towards him without expression and almost without recognition. 'You know my Cal, dontcha?' she said, giving her head a backward nod in the direction of the man rolling the mattress.

'Oh yes, yes,' Albert answered, off-balance and unsure of himself. Her brother, wasn't he? He tried to remember. 'Pleased to meet you,' he said. The words sounded stiff and insincere, but the docker didn't seem to notice.

'That'll 'ave ter do,' Queenie said, rising from her knees and dropping the grey rag back into the bucket with a splash. 'Never be out be twelve o'clock else. Shift yer feet, Ned.'

Out by twelve o'clock, Albert thought, stupid with shock. Then she *is* leaving. Something must have happened.

Ned, shifting his feet as ordered, smiled directly into Queenie's eyes. The intimacy of the look made Albert's stomach lurch with a distress he didn't want to understand. Then Queenie smiled too, her easy open, welcoming smile, but she was smiling at the wrong person. She was smiling at the stranger. At Ned. Not at him. Look at *me*, Queenie, he thought. Look at me, for God's sake. It was beginning to feel like a nightmare.

Ned took the bedhead in his left hand and propped it up against the wall. As he turned, Albert could see that his right arm was missing, the empty sleeve pinned neatly to his jacket, and that his neck and the right side of his face were puckered with a mass of ugly scar tissue, ridged and pitted and as red as raw meat. Another one of the wounded, Albert thought, and pity for the man rose instinctively, to battle against the resentment he'd already aroused by that smile. Under the impact of those two, strong, conflicting emotions, he felt trapped and checked. He could hardly get angry with a wounded soldier, simply because the poor wretch smiled at his girl. And yet he had to admit the smile rankled. What sort of terrible situation were they all in? It felt worse by the minute.

Queenie gave him her deliberately empty look again. 'This is Ned,' she said. 'Ned, this is Ploochy, one a Dickie Chanter's mob.' They shook hands, right with left, awkwardly. Albert was beginning to feel slightly sick.

'Now then,' Queenie went on, brisk and businesslike, and avoiding Albert's eye, 'we gotta decide about this bed. Belongs ter Ploochy, be rights,' she explained to Ned, smiling at him again. It was too bold, that smile, Albert thought. Too provocative. Almost as if she was trying to punish him with it. He put up a hand to stroke his moustache and cover the distress he knew his mouth was revealing. 'So what we want ter know is, do yer want it back?' Queenie said, matter-of-factly.

'Oh no,' Albert said, quickly so as to subdue his embarrassment. 'No, no! You have it!' It was humiliating to be discussing their bed like this, in a room full of strange men. Their bed, where they'd loved so often, and so passionately.

'That's all right then,' Queenie said with obvious relief. 'You can load it up, Cal.'

Albert stood in their way as they dismantled the room around him. He couldn't find the motive for moving and he was afraid his distress would show if he said anything. Queenie scuttled from room to room, tense and nervous and deliberately busy. She was flexing her fingers before she touched anything, he noticed, and was very careful never to look at him, no matter how close they might be when she passed. He watched as the bedstead was eased through the door and the bedding was bundled through the window into the waiting hands of the man with the horse. Soon there was only the rag rug left. Queenie lifted it from the floor, wrinkling her nose against the dust she was raising. There was a pile of dirt underneath it, almost as thick as the rug itself.

'Come on, Queenie!' Cal urged her. 'Roll it down the 'ill. Ain't worth shiftin'. Connie'll make another one.'

'Right!' Queenie said, as though she'd made an important decision. 'Ta-ta then, Ploochy.' She still didn't look at him, and he didn't know how to answer her. They couldn't just say goodbye. Not like this. Then suddenly she and her protective gang were gone. He was left on his own with the rag rug in a room full of swirling dust.

This can't be happening, he thought. This is some terrible

dream. Or a trick. She'll come back in a minute and say she was only teasing, and we'll laugh and make up. It can't end like this. Not after all this time. But he knew with his deeper sense that their affair was over. He couldn't understand why or how it had happened but he knew it was finished.

The rag and bone man put his head in the open window. 'That the lot?' he asked, glancing round the room, and when Albert nodded mechanically, he touched his cap. 'Righto!' he said. 'See you at the weddin' then.'

Wedding? What wedding? The word dropped straight through Albert's body like a stone into a well. He ran to the window and called, 'Queenie! Queenie!' It sounded like a cry of despair even to his shocked ears but he was too distressed to care. 'Queenie! Come back! Please!'

She was climbing into the back of the cart, but she paused and looked across at him and hesitated. 'Please!' he begged again. His voice echoed tremulously across the little front garden, as the horse snorted and scraped his hooves, and Queenie struggled to make up her mind. Then she jumped down from the cart and picked her way across the damp lawn to the window, where she stood just far enough away to prevent him from touching her but at least looking at him directly. Her eyes were strained and her mouth downturned as if she was on the verge of tears. Be quick, he told himself, or she'll run again.

'What wedding, Queenie my darling?' he asked, almost in a whisper, for now he was aware of the ears in the cart. 'You must tell me. Please!'

'Mine,' she said huskily. 'Sat-day. Me an' Ned.'

'No,' he said, in disbelief. 'No. No. No.'

'Don't start,' she begged. 'It's all fixed.'

'No,' he said again. His mind was roaring with outrage but he couldn't think of anything to say.

'We couldn't go on fer ever,' she said, and her face showed how difficult it was for her to be talking about it all. 'You know that, dontcha? An' Ned needs me. You can see.' She paused for a second and tried to control her expression and become businesslike again. 'The rent's all paid up,' she said. 'I've give 'im me key. Don't ferget ter shut the winder.' She gave him a lopsided grin and fled.

When she was back in the cart, and the rag and bone man

was clicking his horse into action, Albert knew what it was he wanted to say. But it was all too late.

He returned his key to Mr Punch. There was nothing else to do. The landlord was mightily interested in the move and wanted to know where 'the Ploochys' were setting up next. 'Tooting,' Albert told him, trying to restore his sense of conversation. But the ugly features beside him were leering at him far too knowledgeably. He put the key in the gnarled paw held out beneath his nose and left while he still had sufficient control to walk away with dignity.

He didn't know where he was going or what he was going to do next. He was numb with misery. Life and purpose seemed to have come to a halt together. He drifted northwards down Manor Road, away from the High Street and away from the flat, following his feet, without thought.

Presently he found himself approaching a church. It looked familiar, but he was too miserable to make the effort to recognize it. It wasn't until he'd wandered along a side path between yews and hollies, and come out onto the cold north side of the building that he realized where he was. Below him stretched a landscape he remembered, the blue slates and blackened brick of the Wandsworth Road, a glimpse of the distant river glimmering between the rooftops, a viaduct, graceful among all those crowded dwellings, a Chelsea milky white and misty on the far bank of the Thames, and above it all an autumn sky heaped with smoky cloud. He was standing behind the church of St Paul on the same cold north-facing terrace where he'd proposed to Alice all those years ago. The irony of the situation wasn't lost on him. He stood, clutching the chill railings, pretending to look at the view, feeling utterly miserable.

A green dusk was closing in upon him as he drove home to Tooting, and the shop windows all along the High Street glinted like tears in the sharp light. He went bleakly back to the shop, to the automatic familiarity of beer and banter, but he was still numb and incapable of logical thought. Nevertheless, he balanced the books before he left, and was careful to

393

lock up and close the shutters, even though it all seemed a ridiculous waste of time.

The street lamps, hooded under their blue paint, gave a very faint light indeed that evening and the house was completely dark. But as he walked up the path, Em's face appeared between the dining room curtains, gleaming like a white moon of anxiety. He recognized that her presence probably meant bad news but he was still too numb to feel alarm or even surprise.

'They're all down the Grove,' she said. 'I'm staying 'ere with your two, jest ter be on the safe side.'

He nodded but there was nothing he could say.

'Be ternight they reckon,' Em told him. 'Poor little soul.'

'I'd better go down,' he said, knowing in some remote part of his mind that this was the right thing to say and do.

The Grove was as dark as a churchyard, the yews creaking in the night breeze, and the smell of ancient dust and decaying leaves rising strongly from the earth path.

At the lodge gate the porter nodded him through as though he was expected, but the hospital seemed to be deserted. There was no one behind the counter in Admissions and the long open corridor leading to the isolation wards was an empty tunnel. He walked along it, still swaddled in his private nightmare, past dimly lit wards where the crowded sleepers groaned and muttered, and the smell of disinfectant and wax floor polish lingered in the enclosed air. He was noticing every detail with a quite unnecessary clarity, experiencing each moment keenly but as though he was distanced from it and no longer belonged to the world.

When he saw Alice and Minnie sitting beside the desk in the Sister's office, he felt that he had a foreknowledge that that was where he would find them, and yet there was an unreality about them, too. They looked like a painting or a *tableau vivant*, framed in the window of that small square cell and seen from the darkness of the corridor. They were listening to the Sister and all three women were still, their faces marble pale, their jaw-lines and nostrils and eye sockets blackened and distorted by the angle of the blue light on the desk below them. As he entered the three faces that turned towards him were stark and staring like tragic masks.

'Ah, Mr-um-Ploochy,' the Sister said. 'I'm afraid . . .'

'I know,' Albert told her.

Alice stood up. 'We'll go home, now you're here,' she said. 'You'll be able to . . .' Her eyes wavered towards the papers on the desk.

'Yes,' Albert agreed. 'Leave everything to me.' Their words sounded clumsy in that hushed cell. He felt impelled to say as little as possible.

Alice lifted her cousin wordlessly to her feet, and buttoned her coat, and eased her through the door. The Sister indicated that Albert should sit down and suggested a batch of papers towards him that he ought to sign. As he scrawled an unfamiliar signature at the bottom of the first unread document, Minnie began to weep, her terrible smothered wails resounding in the empty corridor like the cries of some unearthly bird.

Albert and the Sister didn't look at one another until the sounds had all died away. Then the necessary papers were completed and the desk tidied and the Sister stood up for her last harrowing question, 'You'd like to see her?'

He didn't want to at all, but it would have been improper to refuse, so he went where he was led. The child lay lovingly arranged under her white sheet, her hair combed into unnatural neatness and each frill at the neck of her nightgown smoothed into precise folds. But her face was already grey with death in the chill room. She looked unreal, like a wax doll long discarded. He couldn't feel anything for her or about her, at all.

Out in the dust of the Grove, he remembered Jesse and wondered what had become of him. The Trafalgar Arms was shut and there wasn't a soul in the street except for a drunk lying like a sack in the gutter outside the public bar. As he passed the reeking bundle, it rolled over to reveal a dark face and two white hands clutching a bottle. It was Jesse.

'Tha' you, Ploochy?' he said thickly, trying to focus his eyes.

'Renee is dead,' Albert told him, as cruelly and coldly as he could.

'Thought as much,' Jesse said and, to Albert's disgust, he began to giggle foolishly. 'Stopped off fer a quick one,' he explained, waving the bottle vaguely towards the Trafalgar Arms. 'Couldn't stand all that carry on.'

Albert could see his face quite clearly, grinning and giggling in the moonlight. 'Get up and go home,' he said coldly.

'Can't be done, squire,' Jesse said and lay back in the gutter again.

Now as he watched this disgusting man wallowing in the grime, emotion reasserted itself in Albert, pity for Minnie and Alice and that poor dead child, pity for himself, but above everything else an overwhelming, burning anger. He had to walk away quickly or he would have kicked out at the mess at his feet.

He was still shivering with emotion when he got home. What sort of world was this, that could part lovers, and kill Renee, and gas Nat, and drop bombs on women and children, and lie giggling in the gutter, and let this dreadful war drag on and on? There was no health or pattern in anything. Nothing made sense anymore.

When they woke next morning, Jesse had gone back to France, leaving a note on the kitchen table for all of them to see. 'Sorry,' it said. 'Couldn't face it.' Alice threw it on the fire, without a word and before Minnie could come downstairs and read it.

With all the blinds down, the house was shadowed with grief, a muted, miserable place. Minnie stayed in her room for the next three days, to cope with her grief alone, and Alice cooked light nourishing meals for anyone who felt able to eat them, and the children kept out of the way, too stunned by the news even to talk about it. And Albert was left to arrange the funeral.

The Reverend Simpson spoke tenderly at the graveside and did his best to comfort them as the white box was lowered into its muddy trench, but the women were too far gone in grief to hear him, and Albert was too numb to concentrate. He was distracted by the least movement, and there was riotous movement all round him. The wind had beaten the clouds into a creamy froth and was now scudding the great curdled masses across the sky with visible speed; the yews and hollies were rattling with life and energy, and rooks attempting flight in the wild air were lifted and flung back into the branches as though they were made of paper.

As he watched, a sudden squall lifted the dead leaves and sent them spinning before the black clothes of the mourners, like a flight of yellow butterflies, bright and inconsequential and inappropriate. Although they couldn't lift his spirits, they pleased his eye, and when they fell, to rustle down onto the path, and spiral into the open grave, he was almost sorry to see them go. Then his attention was caught by another patch of light colour and soft texture against the black of Alice's skirt, and he glanced up idly to see what it was. The sight jolted his memory and stirred his sense of loss. It was the sealskin muff, that expensive guilt-ridden present he'd brought back from Hastings after his first extraordinary holiday with Queenie. What on earth made her wear it? Now, after all these years? She couldn't have chosen a worse moment.

They were all glad to go home, to a warm dining room and a cup of nice strong tea. Minnie was seated by the fire with a rug round her knees, and although she was still quiet with shock, she drank her tea obediently, and gradually stopped shivering, to everyone's relief. Alice handed round the sandwiches and Aunt Phoebe started the conversation in the right direction by praising the wreaths and saying how kind it was of the neighbours to send so many. And the worst of the day was over. Or so it seemed, until the Reverend Simpson inadvertently said the wrong thing.

He was beginning to extricate himself from the group and was saying goodbye, gently and privately, to each member of the family in turn. 'Goodbye, Mrs Holdsworthy,' he said, bending towards her. 'This is a sad day for any mother, but at least you have the consolation of knowing that your little girl is with God, safe in His love. Nothing can ever hurt her again.'

Minnie hadn't said anything since her return, but now she took a juddering breath and spoke, spitting the words from a face distorted by rage and pain. 'God!' she said. 'Don't talk to me about God! I don't want to hear about him. He don't love us! Never did. He killed my little Renee, that's what He did. Where's the love in that? You tell me. If He 'ad to kill someone, why didn't He take Jesse? Foul-mouthed evil man! But no. Not him. He'll come through this war without a scratch on him. And for why? Because the Devil takes care of his own.

And your God kills the innocent. My little Renee. Never done a bad thing in her life. Don't you talk to me about God! I'd rather have Satan,' and she fell into such a paroxysm of weeping that they were all alarmed, and Alice rushed to lead her out of the room before she could damage herself or her guests any further.

They were all dreadfully embarrassed, and none more so than Albert, who escorted his reverend friend to the gate, struggling to think of something he could say to put matters right. He needn't have worried for the Reverend Simpson took it all philosophically. 'She doesn't mean it, Mr Ploochy,' he reassured. 'In the first transports of grief people say the most terrible things. If the war has taught me nothing else, it's taught me that. God will understand.'

When the guests had all soft-footed away, Albert sat on alone by the fire, watching the flames leap and spurt from the orange coals, too unhappy for thought and too tired for anything else. When the door opened with a swish of the curtain across the polished floor, he didn't even bother to look up.

'So there you are,' Alice said crossly. 'I thought you'd gone to the shop.'

'Nat can manage,' he said and closed his eyes against the day and his memories and the harsh tone of her voice.

'I'm glad to hear it,' she said, and she still sounded angry. 'It will give us a chance to talk.'

He opened his eyes in surprise. Talk? What had they got to talk about? The funeral was over. She was standing beside the fire, one foot on the fender, one arm black against the marble fireplace. He noticed that she was wearing corsets and that her spine was ramrod straight. She looked angry and she looked unyielding, and despite his fatigue that alarmed him. 'Won't it wait till morning?' he said.

'It's waited for ten whole years,' she told him. 'High time we spoke of it, I should say.'

The words gave him a shock. It sounded almost as though she knew about Queenie. What else had been going on for ten years? Surely she didn't know about Queenie.

She watched the expression on his face, and laughed at him.

'Oh yes!' she said. 'You know what I'm going to say right enough, don't you!'

'No,' he lied, hoping she would stop.

'Oh yes, you do,' she said, and she sounded as though she was gloating. 'You knew this afternoon when you saw my muff. Your peace offering! Did she choose it or did you? Not that it matters.' She paused to let her words sink in, and he realized to his dismay that his heart was pounding with an emotion that felt very much like fear. 'We are talking about your . . .' she paused because the next word was so distasteful to her '. . . your affair with that cheap little redhead.'

'She is not a cheap little redhead,' he said, wishing he didn't sound so feeble.

'Cheap or expensive, it makes no difference now,' she said. 'You had no business setting her up in a flat, keeping her, and letting us go short. How do you imagine I feel knowing that? You don't think about me ever, do you?'

Her accusations were coming too quickly for him to cope with. 'I didden' keep you short,' he said, picking the most unfair. 'Don't talk nonsense. You always had the best of everything. All of you.'

'But you don't deny you've been keeping this woman,' she persisted.

'Queenie gave me more love in a day that you've done in years,' he said. 'You don't know what you're talking about.'

She was flushed and hard eyed with anger. 'How dare you compare me with a woman like that!' she said. 'A street walker!'

'That's a filthy thing to say!'

'Very well then! A whore! Is that better?'

He was shocked. 'You are forgetting yourself,' he said coldly, rising to face her at last. 'I do not expect my wife to use such language.'

Her answer was flung back at him like a ricochet. 'I do not expect my husband to commit adultery.'

'Stop it!' he shouted at her. 'Do you hear me? Stop it!'

'No,' she answered, facing him with her hatred. 'You're the one who's got to stop it. I'm warning you, Albert. This affair has gone on long enough. Now I'm telling you, if you don't stop it at once, and promise me never to see that whore again,

I will leave you.' Behind her furious eyes, the lustres glinted like sharp red knives.

He was suddenly overcome with total weariness and lowered himself into the armchair like an old man. 'You don't know everything, Alice,' he said, 'or you wouldn't say these silly things.'

'They are not silly,' she stormed. 'I mean every word.'

'The affair is over,' he said, looking at the knife edge of the lustre. 'You've already got what you want. It's over.'

She was surprised, but she recovered quickly. He realized from the expression on her face, that there was more and worse to come. 'Oh no, it's not!' she said. 'Don't you think that for a minute.' She was shaking with passion, and her cheeks were burning with unnatural colour. 'You've been humiliating me for ten whole years. Treating me like dirt. Making a public exhibition of me. Don't imagine for one moment that you're going to get away with it.' He looked up to implore her to stop but she rushed on, breathless and out of control. 'You just listen to what I've got to say, for once in your life. If you think I'm going to sleep with you now, after you've been with that whore, you've got another think coming. I will cook for you, and run the house, and look after the children, but that's all. I will not sleep with you. Ever again. Do you understand? We will continue to live as man and wife for appearance's sake. But that is all. I will never forgive you! Never, never, never!'

He had closed his eyes so that he didn't have to see the terrible ugliness of her face, so he didn't see her leave the room. He felt completely and unnecessarily defeated. Why now? he thought, when everything is over.

Outside the house the wind was moaning in the May tree and rain was falling like shrapnel.

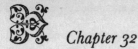 *Chapter 32*

Life went on. Miserably and automatically, without pleasure, or hope. For the women there was always housework, and for Albert there was a shop to run and customers to serve. He did his best to tease and joke as usual, but now the gaiety was forced. His mouth smiled long before his eyes, and people who had known him for years and been lifted by the speed and warmth of his ready grin, were depressed by its loss. 'Poor Ol' Ploochy,' they said. 'His little niece gone, they do say. Took it bad, poor man.'

Harry arrived in the spring, businesslike and quiet, to plant the allotment, as usual. The two men worked companionably together through what remained of the afternoon and well into the smoky dusk, their boots clogged with dark London clay, their hands busy and their minds almost given over to their labour.

From time to time, when the half light gave him cover for his emotions and the blackbirds were singing with infinite tenderness and melancholy, Harry would speak of his dead son, recalling his skill on the farm and his gentleness with the livestock. 'Proper ol' tender-'eart 'e was,' he said. 'Couldn't bear ter see the pigs go off to market. 'E give one a' the litters names one time, I remember. Even the runt. And now 'e's gone hisself. Don't make sense.'

'Nothing make sense,' Albert agreed sadly. 'Little Renee gone. Nat like an old man.' And Queenie, he thought, keeping his most acute loss to himself, Queenie married to someone else. Where was the sense in that?

'Sometimes,' Harry said, 'I think ter mesself, "I wonder what 'e's doing?" Or I think, "I'll get that room all ready fer when 'e comes 'ome." I find mesself looking at things an' thinking, "I'll tell 'im about that when 'e comes 'ome." Don't seem as if 'e's gone at all. I found 'is boots the other day . . .' He sighed and set about earthing up another row of seed potatoes. 'Don't make sense,' he said, keeping his eyes on the spade.

'I know,' Albert said, wishing that he could tell his old

friend how well he understood, and why. This was so exactly the way he felt about Queenie.

Above their heads the cherry was heavy with delicate white blossom and the blackbird sang again, clear and sad and full of pity.

Tooting was an unhappy, shabby place, its paintwork peeling, blinds faded, stucco chipped, streets unswept for weeks at a time. The few goods in the shop were dull and predictable and shoppers themselves wore clothes that had been patched and turned and dyed until there was nothing more to be done for them. There were too many women in mourning and too many men crippled, too much sorrow and too little hope.

When the German armies returned from the Eastern front and massed for their final spring offensive, the papers explained that this was their last chance to win the war. But few hopes were raised in England, for as Albert's customers were quick to point out, they'd heard it all before, over and over again. At the end of March, when the British army on the Somme was pushed back by the attack, they accepted the news wearily. It was only what they expected. And when June began and the much-vaunted American army repulsed a German attack at a place called Château Thierry, they were glad of it but couldn't see that it would make much difference. Too many tragedies had deadened their capacity to sympathize or even understand. As far as they could see, the war would simply go on and on, for ever and ever. Even Lord Rothermere said so.

Then early in November Harry arrived one Sunday morning to help tidy the garden. He had a ridiculous grin on his face and a well-thumbed copy of the *News of the World* in his pocket. 'Watcha think a' that?' he said to Albert, handing the paper across.

The headlines were enormous. 'The War is Won,' they yelled. 'Victory is Ours. German Army crushed to Ruins.' Neither of them knew whether to take it seriously or not.

The next morning, at eleven o'clock, the maroons sounded and went on sounding for a very long time. Albert and Percy ran out of the shop to see what it was. Like everybody else, Mitcham Road was soon full of excited people and it wasn't long before the good news was being passed from one to the other, with cheers and tears. The Great War was over. Germany had signed an armistice.

Even then, in the middle of so much emotion, such weeping relief, such flag-waving triumph, Albert was unmoved. He felt vaguely pleased that the fighting had stopped, and that was all. The armistice couldn't restore Renee or Johnnie to life, or cure Nat or make Queenie come back to him.

That night Dickie and Tilley put on their best clothes and went 'up west' to celebrate, but Harry stayed at home to comfort Em, so Albert was left on his own. He'd lost the taste for parties. After all, what was there for him to be happy about? So he and his family ate their dull supper, quietly, and the women returned to their chores, and Georgie to his books and Anna went to bed, just as though it was an ordinary day. Albert, at once restless and lonely, wandered out of the house to walk in the empty streets.

The blackout had been lifted immediately and dramatically by the simple expedient of turning on the gas and not drawing the blinds. To Albert, the brightly lit windows were like golden stage sets, each one revealing a happy scene, parties rejoicing, families at peace, lovers arm in arm. They made him feel more lonely and isolated than ever. He walked on aimlessly, following his feet and trying not to think, and his feet took him to the shop, shuttered and empty on its dark corner. He ignored the party in raucous progress inside the Mitre, and crossed the road to the churchyard.

The grey headstones were like rows of ghostly shadows in the darkness, and they all looked disconcertingly similar. It took him some time to find Renee's little grave under the chestnuts, but once he had, he felt satisfied, as though that was the only really appropriate place for him to be. He stood there for over an hour, listening to the distant sounds of muddled rejoicing and the close cries of the church owls, harsh and clear and brassy as trumpets. Soon his hair was damp with mist, his moustaches dripping water, and he couldn't feel his feet because they were so cold. But he stayed where he was, partly because he didn't know what else to do, and partly because, in his own fashion, he was mourning the dead.

Much to Minnie's annoyance, Jesse contrived to get himself

released from the army long before anybody else they knew. He had a job waiting for him, and a loud voice with which to demand his rights. 'Glad to get shot of him, I shouldn't wonder,' she said sourly, when she got a letter announcing his return. It aggravated her that he'd come through the war unscathed. His early demobilization was just another proof that the Devil took care of his own.

Frank was next to appear, limping from a wound in the thigh that had shattered a bone and ruptured an artery and would have killed him, so he said, if he'd been left in no-man's-land for a minute longer. Now there were four men to run one shop, and although trade was brisker than ever, with so many returning thirsts to satisfy, there wasn't enough work for four. But by now Albert was making such a steady profit, it was easy enough to find a solution. He simply bought two more shops, and installed Frank in one and Percy in the other. When Georgie was sixteen, as he explained to Alice, he would have a choice of three stores in which to learn the trade.

Alice wasn't sure she wanted her son 'in the trade' at all. 'His teachers think he ought to continue his studies,' she said. 'They've been talking about higher examinations after he matriculates.'

'Out of the question,' Albert said harshly, sensing her disapproval. 'He's had quite enough book learning. Time he did some work. When I was his age, I'd been working in the fields for more than three years.'

'Times have changed,' Alice tried, but she was overruled.

So Georgie left school and quietly started work in the Trinity Road shop with Frank, and although he found it almost impossible to laugh and joke with the customers, he kept the accounts neatly and accurately in his beautiful copperplate handwriting, and his father paid him well enough and seemed to be pleased with him.

Albert was making more money now than he'd ever done in his life. Everything he became involved in seemed profitable, now that profit no longer mattered. The consortium had bought another hall to convert into a cinema and was negotiating for a third, for the pictures were more popular than ever, their magical fantasies just the right antidote for the weary aftermath of war, and the immediate dread of illness. So he had plenty of spare cash and nothing else to do but spend it. He spent with abandon, never a man to do anything by halves.

When the electricity came to Tooting, he had electric light fitted in the house and all three shops. When a new telephone exchange was opened in Streatham, he was one of the first to become a subscriber. And he lavished money on Anna.

Alice and Georgie refused his gifts, but Anna was always quick to accept them whatever they might be. In fact, as she learned a new trick very early on in her father's spending spree, she often got twice as much as even he had intended to give her. In a rash mood, he'd promised her a ring for her birthday. She found two, both equally expensive and equally tempting, and had taken such a long time to make up her mind between them, that he'd lost his patience, and in a fit of reckless and dramatic generosity he bought them both. Alice was very cross indeed, grumbling to Minnie that the child was selfish enough without him making her worse, but the damage was done. Soon Anna had two winter coats, two complete outfits, more hats than she knew what to do with, and so many pairs of shoes that she couldn't get them all into the cupboard. It gave her a sense of power and superiority to be able to tease so many pretty things from her father, and anyway, he was rich enough, so why shouldn't she?

Soon he was on the look-out for a bigger and better house.

'How would you like to live in one of those nice big houses up on the common?' he asked Alice casually one evening.

'Whatever you like,' she said carefully, because she'd learned that her disapproval of any project invariably meant that he would press ahead with it. She certainly didn't want the upheaval of a move, especially after all that dreadful decorating, and with the Spanish flu still raging about them. She must think of some way to deflect him quickly.

In the event the flu solved her problem for her. She'd been watching over the children daily and anxiously ever since the epidemic came to London, but it was Albert who was the first to catch the infection. He began to feel feverish on the way home from work, and the disease took hold so rapidly that by the time he reached the house he was too ill to stand, and collapsed in the hall, panting and dizzy.

Although she'd been dreading the moment for months, Alice was calm once it happened. Her first thought was to protect the children, who were instantly sent to their rooms with strict instructions not to emerge until she gave them permission; her second was to protect herself with a face mask made out of the toughest linen she possessed. Then and only then she went to attend to her husband, who was crouched at the foot of the stairs with his head against the banisters, groaning and swimmy-eyed with fever. It took quite a while and a lot of energy to get him upstairs, and even longer to persuade him out of his clothes and into bed, so both of them were sweating and ill-tempered by the time he was under the sheets. She lit a fire, provided a chamber pot as a spittoon and hung a sheet at the door dipped into two bowls of strong disinfectant. Then she dragged her single bed into the corner of the room, as far away from his infection as she could get it, and settled down to nurse him.

When he'd been a young man trying to survive in the shop during that first awful winter in Tooting, Albert had resisted the flu, resenting its power to stop him working, and fighting against it with all his strength. Now he took it as a punishment, and accepted it with uncharacteristic resignation. He felt too ill to fight anyway, all he wanted to do was sleep.

He took aspirins obediently whenever Alice offered them and did his best to swallow spoonfuls of soup and beef broth, but his bones ached with a terrible weariness and for several days it was too much of an effort even to open his eyes. On the fourth or fifth day he recognized that it was Minnie who was spooning him broth and croaked a question at her through swollen lips.

'Now don't you go worrying your head about Alice,' she told him kindly. 'She's all right. Just a bit under the weather today, that's all.' She didn't admit that her cousin had caught the flu until several more days had passed and she judged him strong enough to accept it.

Three days later still, even Minnie didn't appear. He woke to a white sky and somebody knocking at the bedroom door, timidly but persistently. 'Who is it?' he said, annoyed that his voice sounded so hoarse and inadequate.

'It's me,' Anna said. 'There's some porridge on a tray outside the door. Could you come and get it? I'm not to bring it in.'

'Where's your Aunt Minnie?' he asked.

'Gone to Clapham,' Anna said. 'Aunt Amelia sent a letter this morning. They've got flu.'

'How is your mother?' he said. But Anna had gone.

He got up very slowly because his legs had no strength in them at all. The porridge was full of lumps but he made an effort to swallow the warm and watery parts. Then he decided it was about time to get better.

Alice was ill for a great deal longer than he was. She had bronchitis after the flu and just as she was beginning to recover, Minnie came home with the news that although Phoebe was getting better, Aunt Amelia was dead. Alice was distraught, and wept with grief for more than twenty-four hours.

'Oh, poor Aunt Phoebe,' she said over and over again, between tears and outbursts of coughing. 'Poor Aunt Phoebe. I must get up, Albert. I ought to be with her.'

'You will do nothing of the sort,' Albert told her sternly. 'You will stay where you are and get better yourself. I will attend to it.'

'Poor Aunt Phoebe,' she insisted. 'What will become of her? She'll be all on her own.'

'She will come here and live with us,' he said, finding the solution at once and obviously.

But Alice still wasn't comforted. 'I must go to the funeral,' she wept. 'Amelia brought me up! I must go to the funeral.'

'Stay where you are for now,' he said, speaking more gently than usual out of pity for her distress. 'We will see about the funeral when the time comes.'

But when the time came she was still too ill to get up and so was Aunt Phoebe who was recovering very slowly indeed. So Albert and Georgie were the only mourners and both of them were glad that the funeral was quick and quiet. It was one of rather too many, and the vicar was too ill himself to want to stand by a cold graveside for any longer than was strictly necessary.

As soon as Phoebe was well enough to travel, Minnie cocooned her in travelling rugs and brought her home to Longley Road in a cab. She looked very frail and seemed to have shrunk, but she was as determined as ever and insisted on bringing all the family portraits with her. They settled her into the soldiers' room where Alice had lit a good fire, and

Georgie hung the pictures for her, and Albert resigned himself to the fact that his house was more full of women than ever and that somehow or other life had got beyond his control again.

But the new decade was approaching and with it a feeling that once they were all in the twenties, things would improve. As Harry said, in his dry way, 'Couldn't get no worse, an' that's a fact!'

He and Dickie and Albert had slipped into the old easy routine of regular evenings at the pub, and for Albert at least the time they spent together was the best part of the week.

New Year's Eve at Jack Beard's was always a riotous celebration. In 1919, the serious drinking began early and the pianola was played non-stop, so by the time midnight arrived the singing was cheerfully vulgar and Dickie had become splendidly and amusingly drunk. 'Shober ash a judsh!' he declared, sitting with his legs astride to steady himself. 'Walk a straight line, any time yer like. Jush wash!'

So they drew a chalk line right across the bar room and cheered and stamped as he walked solemnly across it, scowling with effort. Nobody really noticed whether his feet actually touched the chalk, because they were all too far gone for such considerations, but he was acclaimed a champion and, being Dickie, immediately flung down a challenge. 'Outdrink the lot a' yer!' he boasted, 'shtill walk a straight line. Shober ash a judsh! 'Nother round, Jack.'

Harry fell over halfway along the line and sat on the floor for the rest of the competition, scratching his thatch and giggling. Albert did rather well and managed to sway in time to the music so that he could claim to be dancing rather than stumbling, a feat which brought him loud applause and gave rise to the next and even more drunken round of the contest.

'Thish line,' Dickie announced, squinting at the chalk mark to get it into focus. 'This line'sh no good. Mush too short. Needa longa one. Got an idea!' and he led them all, reeling and giggling out into the Mitcham Road.

'Walk a tramline!' he said. 'Thash a ticket!' The sudden rush of cold air made him very unsteady on his feet and the tramlines were slippery, but he started his balancing act along them. The party crowded the pavements urging him on. To their inebriated logic it seemed the natural extension of the contest and none of them saw any harm in it.

Afterwards Albert couldn't remember exactly what happened next. He was trying to clear the beer mist from his eyes, holding himself steady on Harry's unsteady shoulder when somebody yelled, 'Look out, Dick! Tram!' and above the shout he heard the whirr and rattle of a tram approaching from the Broadway. Then people were on the move all around him, waving their arms and yelling, and he saw Dickie stagger backwards away from the tramline, but then there were two trams, thundering and rocking towards each other, and Dickie had disappeared, caught somewhere between the two or under their wheels. Then the confusion of shock and charging activity, screams and drunken feet running heavily, fists pounding on the sides of the nearest vehicle, no sign of Dickie through the mass of moving bodies. He could hear Tilley shouting, 'Dickie! Dickie! Oh my dear good God! Don't you dare be dead!' and saw that the trams had both stopped and the drivers were walking back to see what had happened.

Dickie lay still between the tramlines, like a bundle of old clothes. Horribly still. Tilley, crouched over him, was struggling to undo his coat to feel for his heart. She was grumbling and sobbing, and the crowd, awed by her terrible combination of fear and fury had given her plenty of room. There didn't seem to be any blood, either on the clothes or the road, as far as Albert could see, although it was difficult to be sure in the darkness and crush of the crowd.

'Don't you dare be dead!' Tilley scolded. 'I'll never speak to you again if you're dead! How shall I manage? You never stop ter think. Oh, you're not ter be dead!'

Suddenly, and to everybody's relief, the body stirred and opened its eyes. 'There y'are,' it said. 'She loves me!' and it stood up and became Dickie again just as though nothing extraordinary had happened. Tilley instantly had hysterics, screaming and screaming from a mouth like a black tunnel.

'If you're going ter start that,' Dickie said reasonably. 'I'm off,' and he walked, surprisingly steadily, back into the pub.

Somebody had gone to fetch a doctor, but by the time he arrived there was hardly anything for him to do. Tilley had stopped screaming, both trams had departed, and Dickie was cheerfully declaring that he was 'right as ninepence'. The doctor was a young man and very frank. He examined his beer-sodden patient carefully. 'No bones broken,' he said. 'You'll have a fine crop of bruises by tomorrow but that's all. Lucky you're so drunk. If you'd been sober the blow could have killed you. I wouldn't want to go arguing with a tram. Ointment for the bruises, Mrs Chanter. Aspirin for the hangover. That'll be ten guineas.'

By the time Albert had settled his massive bill, Dickie was asleep.

The next morning, when the three friends were all nursing skulls made fragile by excruciating headaches, a reporter arrived from the *News and Mercury* eager for the story. He had a photographer with him, so when he'd taken copious notes from all three of them, he escorted Dickie tenderly out into the middle of the road and arranged him in a valiant pose in front of the next tram to come rattling by, to the great surprise of the driver.

Tilley didn't approve at all and said it was nothing to go showing off about 'acting the giddy goat and nearly getting yourself killed'. But when the paper was printed, she really quite enjoyed the article, and thought the picture was a good likeness and the headline excellent. 'Local celebrity has lucky escape.' 'Celebrity, eh?' she said with satisfaction, but then she saw Dickie was grinning, so she changed her tune, put the paper carefully away in the linen cupboard and told him she hoped that would be the end of it.

And so it was. At least for eighteen months. But then, one warm day in June the story suddenly had repercussions that Albert certainly hadn't expected.

Minnie and Alice were away at the seaside with their three children, and as Albert sorted through the first post that morning he was vaguely hoping that Anna had sent him a card. The letter, addressed in familiar scrawling handwriting gave him such a shock that his hands were shaking as he opened it.

It was short and to the point but it really was from Queenie. His heart was pounding so hard it was making the words leap up and down. 'Seen the cutting about Mr Chanter. What a thing to happen. Hope he is OK. Thought you would like to see the picture of me and my Mary Ann. Took her third birthday, May 1st. Love Q.'

And there she was, caught by the camera, smiling at him from that postcard. For a moment, bemused by shock and the sudden impact of pleasure, he couldn't understand why little Anna should be standing beside his Queenie. Then as his heart recovered a little, he realized that this was Queenie's child, and another even more extraordinary idea began to swell in his mind. He looked at the letter again. Three. On May 1st. Then in October when she married that awful soldier, she'd have been . . . My child! he thought and the idea roared with delight inside his head.

Then another realization set his heart ricocheting all over again. He examined the envelope. Posted yesterday afternoon in Hastings. They must still be there!

'Mind the shop!' he said to Nat.

Chapter 33

The heady pace of his sudden decision sustained him all the way down to Hastings, speeding the time from hours to minutes and skating his emotions on the quick bright ice of hope. His darling Queenie was in Hastings. Now. With his child. Minutes away, just along the line, waiting for him to answer her message. Everything was going to be all right after all.

The fact that she'd send no address didn't bother him until he was walking down the cobbles of the station approach, taking in his first breath of sea air, and even then it seemed a little problem, one he could solve with intelligence and a methodical search. The sun was shining, white gulls were barking overhead, and happiness was just around the corner.

Mrs Edwards said she didn't take theatricals no more on account of her son being wounded, but number thirty-two did, so why not try there. Number thirty-two had never let to a redhead in her life. It was one of her strictest rules, she said, regarding him sternly. She obviously thought it highly suspicious that he couldn't remember the name of the woman he claimed to be his sister. It was a nasty moment, and it made him realize that it was going to be difficult to find his Queenie after all.

Nevertheless he searched methodically, visiting every boarding house he could remember from the old days, and then checking the current accommodation in the local paper. But nobody remembered Queenie, or recognized his description of her.

So he tried the hotels. But he had no luck there either, even at the Embassy, which had changed owners since his last visit. Nobody remembered him or cared to understand what he was talking about. 'If I was you, sir,' one of the more superior receptionists advised, patting her shingled hair, 'I'd wait till your sister got home and then go and visit her. You'd know her home address, I'm sure.' The sneer was barely disguised.

By the end of the afternoon, he was tired out, and beginning to face the fact that he was on a wild goose chase. He walked sadly away from the promenade towards the old town and the harbour, where the tall huts of the fishermen still stood flimsily on the dirty pebbles. The fishing fleet was in, and the fishing fleet reminded him of Josh. Fancy forgetting Josh. Why, if there was one person in the whole town Queenie would certainly have seen during her holiday, that person would have been Josh. Hope renewed his energy. He found he was almost running to the beach and when he reached the first boat he was quite out of breath.

Its owner was a young man with a sandy beard, who was busily preparing his catch for sale. 'Josh?' he said, gutting a plaice with his thumb. 'Died uv the flu, two or three years back. Just arter the var t'vould be. A good ol' man, Josh!'

'Oh!' Albert said, shocked and disappointed by this sudden news.

'His sister's still 'ere,' the fisherman offered. 'Lives in Sinnock Square, don't she, Bob? Name uv Maybury. Lizzie Maybury.'

Back up the High Street, still out of breath, but hoping again. The twitten was just as he remembered it, heaped with sea-bleached ropes and broken lobster pots and discarded boxes still smeared with the blood and scales of the fish they'd recently contained. As he knocked at the door of Lizzie Maybury's topsy-turvy cottage, he was torn between hope and the certainty of disappointment. It didn't look like the sort of place that anyone would stay in for five minutes, let alone a holiday.

Lizzie Maybury hadn't changed at all. She opened the door stiffly, and stood stolidly before him, holding the wooden wings of her arms just away from her wooden sides. It encouraged him just to see her.

'Mrs Maybury,' he began politely. 'Do you remember me? I stayed at your house once, during the war, with my wife.'

'Stayed,' she echoed blankly. 'Yes. Stayed. In the war. Stayed.'

'I'm looking for my wife,' he explained. 'We missed one another in the crowd. She hasn't called here, by any chance, has she?'

'Stayed,' she said, still completely without expression. 'Yes. Yes. Uv course. In the war.' She pecked her wooden head in his direction, but her face was blank.

'Have you seen my wife?' Albert asked, harshly, because her slow speech was making him angry. 'Pretty woman. With red hair. Do you remember?'

'No,' she said. 'En't seen no one. In the war, you say. Stayed. No. En't seen no one.'

Dear God, Albert thought, what was the matter with her. She sounded half-witted. It was like trying to hold a conversation with a parrot. He had to get away from her quickly before he lost his temper with her idiocy.

He turned and stomped away, pounding down the stone steps from the twitten, charging along the High Street, full of the furious energy of bad temper. In front of him the familiar slopes of East Hill blocked his view. He didn't even have to think where he was going, it beckoned him so strongly.

The headland was the same peaceful expanse he remembered, and he had it almost to himself, for apart from a courting couple murmuring to one another beside the turreted entrance to the cliff railway, there was no one else about. He strode across the springy turf to the rough bench by the edge of the cliff, where he and Queenie had spent so many hours enjoying the sun on their conversation.

The courting couple watched him with some annoyance.

'What's that silly ol' man want ter come up 'ere for?' the boy said. 'You see 'im, Winnie?'

'Yes,' Winnie said, examining him closely. ' 'E en't a silly ol' man. 'E's got class. Thas a diamond in 'is tiepin.' She watched admiringly as the stone flashed red fire towards her. ' 'Ere, perhaps 'e's a talent scout. Lookin' fer a new star.'

'Nah,' her lover said. 'Give us a kiss, Win. 'E en't lookin' now.'

'You never know,' Winnie said, arranging her hair. Then she kissed him, professionally, holding her head back to reveal her profile and closing her eyes like the film star she wanted to be.

But the talent scout didn't notice her. He was deep in his own thoughts and more tired than he'd realized, battered by the fluctuations of hope and disappointment. Now that he'd stopped running from door to door, he felt depressed and self-critical, aware that he'd wasted a great deal of energy to no purpose, rushing off like that, without thinking. Everything he'd ever done, he thought, he'd done like that, on the spur of the moment, quickly, almost carelessly. He'd bought the shop that way, and the house. He'd met Alice that way, and started his affair with Queenie. Was it any wonder he got into situations he couldn't manage?

There was a slight, tickling sensation on the skin of his forearm, and glancing down, he saw that a fly had settled on him and was now busily cleaning itself, spinning its head so rapidly between spiky legs that it was nothing but a grey blur. Its thorax was as black as jet and carved like a gemstone, and its abdomen was striped, silver and green, like inlaid enamel. Despite himself he was charmed by it. It's like a little jewelled brooch, he thought, and wished idly that someone would make a brooch like it so that he could give it to Queenie when he found her. If he found her.

He turned his head to alter the direction of his thoughts, and looked at the courting couple, still self-consciously kissing beside their tower. The girl's silk-clad legs, swelling from those teetering shoes, looked quite a different shape from Queenie's, even if his memory wasn't accurate after all this time. Suddenly and vividly he recalled how she used to sit in her wickerwork chair in their flat in Manor Road, legs carelessly astride, heels jammed against the floor to steady herself, shaking the pins out of her hair. Herself, natural and beautiful and desirable, and without artifice, dropping bread and butter on the sheets, kicking her shoes into the corner, collapsing backwards onto the bed, cackling with laughter, talking and kissing and eating all at the same time. How could he have let her go?

Miserably, he let his eyes wander again, this time to the Channel below him. To the east, the sea was pale green under a low rain cloud as blue as wood smoke and tattered at the edges like the fringe of a shawl. The eastern horizon was as blue as the cloud and against it the sails of three distant ships glowed like pearl white shells. To the west, the sea became lighter and brighter until it was almost white and shone like a mirror, under layers of blue and white cloud, heaped like soft plumage, a feathery nest for the bright white disc of the sun. The western horizon was white as pearl, and above it, the sky was the palest shade of lavender, so that the fishing boats silhouetted there appeared so dark as to be almost black. There was a beautiful balance about the scene, as if Nature had deliberately contrived it to satisfy the senses.

Despite the turmoil of his emotions, the muddle of his thoughts and the demoralizing knowledge that he'd been making a fool of himself, Albert was calmed and restored. It was good to be alive in such a place, even though he hadn't found his Queenie yet, or seen his daughter. At least she'd written to him, and at least he had a picture of them both.

He took out his wallet and removed the little portrait. How very like Anna the little girl was. Anna when she was young and charming and he hadn't spoiled her. Mary Ann, he thought, Queenie and Mary Ann. The quiet, truthful image between his fingers made him yearn with the need to see them both.

I mustn't give up, he decided. I must go on searching. For this new child, this second daughter, was a second chance. With this child he could do things differently. She could be brought up Queenie's way and not spoilt. There were so many possibilities. And really all he had to do was find them. That was all.

He looked again at the two faces, caught with their smiles, forever, and given to him. His Queenie. His Mary Ann.

'Now!' Winnie said to her young man. 'Kiss me, now. Like Rudolph Valentino. 'E's lookin' this way!'

But although Albert had turned his head vaguely in their direction, he was looking straight through them. He had found another dream.